With good wishes that all ripples
in your life will be positive.

RIPPLES
in a
POND

IS THERE A JAMIE
IN YOUR NEIGHBOURHOOD?

SHEILA SHAW

Matador
9 Priory Business Park,
Wistow Road, Kibworth Beauchamp,
Leicestershire. LE8 0RX
Tel: 0116 279 2299
Email: books@troubador.co.uk
Web: www.troubador.co.uk/matador
Twitter: @matadorbooks

ISBN 978 1785890 499

British Library Cataloguing in Publication Data.
A catalogue record for this book is available from the British Library.

Printed and bound by CPI Group (UK) Ltd, Croydon, CR0 4YY
Typeset in 11pt Aldine401 BT by Troubador Publishing Ltd, Leicester, UK

Matador is an imprint of Troubador Publishing Ltd

To all the children, and adults of all ages whom I have known in my life and who have inspired some of the characterisations in this book, I extend my grateful thanks.

To my uncomplaining (well, mostly) husband who has supported me in creating this novel and the prodigious efforts to get it into print, I can confirm he is in no way the model for Matt.
Our daughter's helpful advice is greatly appreciated.

Whilst none of the events described are necessarily an accurate factual representation of any incident occurring during my extensive working life as a Headteacher and Educational Psychologist, for the most part each is based on actual experiences which either happened or were recounted to me. For the purpose of drawing attention to the problems encountered by individuals like Jamie and Max, some of these have been a little over-dramatised. Any likeness to any known person, apart from myself, is purely coincidental.

I am also grateful to Tim Baynes for his delightful illustrations and also to ARC Editorial Consultancy for editing the manuscript in its earlier draft forms.

SAS 2016

Chapter One

An excruciating scream, sufficient to shatter glass, reverberated through the balmy air of a late September afternoon. A hysterical child pushed past his startled mother, scrambling up the stairs as fast as his six-year-old legs would carry him. Carefully arranging his collection of stegosauruses and diplodocuses on the hall rug in front of her one minute, then charging dementedly across the make-believe African veldt which he had so painstakingly created earlier, it was a miracle her son avoided knocking her off her feet. A fluffy beige towel representing the parched grass, cut-up scouring pads deputising for the occasional bush, all skidded across the polished pinewood flooring, dinosaurs flying in all directions. A bewildered Sarah, in the middle of a phone conversation, became startlingly aware from the sudden dramatic change in Jamie's demeanour that he must have injured himself in some way.

'I must ring you back, Jane. I'm sorry to cut you off so abruptly but Jamie has unaccountably taken leave of his senses. I have to find out what has caused him to react so strongly.' Realising some sort of hypothesis was called for as Jane had muttered something about children's unexpected meltdowns, she lamely added the first excuse which came into her mind: 'It's possible he has been stung by a wasp: we think we may have a nest somewhere. Oh God, I do apologise for the quite extraordinary noise you must have heard.'

Renewed shrieks from the landing exacerbated Sarah's rising alarm. Upstairs a door slammed. Flinging her mobile onto the hall chair and disregarding the fact that it had fallen to the floor, Sarah raced upstairs two at a time to her son's bedroom, heart pounding more than she would have liked Jane to have heard. The entire neighbourhood knew that Jane's imagination was always fuelled by gossip she could elaborate upon to all and sundry.

'Jamie, Jamie, whatever is the matter?'

The urgency of her enquiry fell on deaf ears. The bedroom door was closed and something very solid was behind it. Even pushing as hard as she could, it would not budge an inch.

'What is blocking your door? Jamie, move it at once. You are behaving like a two-year-old.' As the shuddering moans from inside the room suggested Jamie's own body was the culprit, Sarah added sharply and with considerable irritation, 'How can I get in to help you if you are lying down in front of it? Move away.'

Groaning could be heard from the other side but no action.

'Get away from that door *at once*, do you hear?'

The moaning inside the room amplified and intensified into heart-rending screams, piercing Sarah's eardrums and making her wince, despite the muffling barrier of a fire door. Had a wasp, lurking amongst the yellowy-black hues of the diorama Jamie had been constructing, really been disturbed from its autumn sluggishness? She knew these insects were more troublesome at this time of the year because of their tendency to lurk in unexpected places and sleepy ones, moving sluggishly across the floor, could be lethal to those affected by their venom. It was years since she had been stung but, somehow, she felt, the sharpness of such pain released a more staccato noise in the victim than the prolonged, terrified shrieking she was being subjected to. There definitely seemed to be something much more sinister that was causing Jamie's perverse reaction. Had Jamie got hold of a Stanley knife again, despite this being a banned tool unless used under strict supervision? It had terrified her a few weeks ago when she found him trying to use one which had been left so carelessly by the sink when she had been helping Freya to make an exotic mask for her class's Mayan project. Would he have thought the mere presence of his mother, however otherwise distracted, constituted the required protection? But she hadn't noticed any trails of blood, so accidentally cutting himself was unlikely to be the cause of such an inexplicable reaction.

Nonetheless, to establish some kind of rapport with Jane under the circumstances, she had to respond to the immediacy of the situation and offer the more benign reason that an insect sting was the cause. Sarah had not wanted Dominic's mother to gain the impression that Jamie was an 'out of control' child and had offered this pathetic justification as a spontaneous excuse to put his seemingly unwarranted tantrum into better perspective. Without any other clues as to the origin of his distress, this had seemed to her as plausible an explanation as any other. If Jane perceived Jamie as a child whose behaviour was mercurial to say the least, or one whose parents were lax in controlling their offspring's dysfunctional behaviour, never setting boundaries for what they allowed him to do, the welcomed invitation might not be renewed. Their family had heard so much of Jamie's 'new bestest friend' since the start of the autumn term, to the point that Freya had churlishly announced that she would strangle this child if ever he set foot in their house: he sounded such a paragon of virtue. Little did Sarah know that Dominic's recession-hit parents had been forced to transfer their son from the independent to the state sector but guessed that he would have been only too pleased to find a child readily available to befriend him in his new school, knowing from her teaching days that it was never easy to break into established groups. Not all teachers were well experienced in the social engineering techniques sometimes necessary.

Jamie had never seemed to be able to sustain any really meaningful relationships, she mused, and close friendships such as this burgeoning association with Dominic should be nurtured at all costs, she felt. Sadly, Jamie's relationships seemed to be short-lived unless the children were misfits and unpopular. Sarah was unsure as to whether these boys or girls appealed to Jamie because he felt they had something in common with him, he felt sorry for their inadequacy, or whether any kind of playmate was better than none. Matt always maintained that the real reason was that Jamie had always been mollycoddled before he started school and had not acquired the rough and tumble skills that would attract other boys to want him to join their games. It was a relief to her that Dominic appeared to enjoy his company. Jane and Sarah had been acquaintances from the tennis club she had once belonged to and although she could no longer afford to pay the annual subscription, nonetheless they had previously enjoyed the occasional coffee on club nights and Sarah had met Dominic on a couple of occasions, finding him to be a very level-headed, well-mannered child, a little older than Jamie. She couldn't believe it when term got underway and 'Dominic does this' and 'Dominic said that' became their son's favourite topics of conversation, infuriating their daughter who would flounce out of the room in disdain.

As the unbelievably raucous sounds from inside the room intensified, Sarah put her reflections to the back of her mind and changed tack, her voice taking on a conciliatory tone, despite her exasperation. Her son was obviously terrified and she had to get to the bottom of his problem and make a decision as to whether NHS Direct should be called.

'Jamie, there's no way I can help you, darling, unless you let me in. Then you can show me where it hurts and I can rub some magic cream on to make it better.' The strangled response which met her appeasing words sent a chilling tingle down her spine, taking her concern into a completely different arena.

'I hate you, Mummy, I h-h-h-hate you, hate you, hate you! And I'm not your darling.'

'Now, Jamie, this is outrageous. What appalling things to say. And Dominic was asking you over to his house for supper and a sleepover. His mummy phoned to invite you and I had to cut her off in the middle of our conversation.'

Renewed raucous screams cut into Sarah's remonstrations, chilling her to the marrow. Any idea of conciliation went through the window as she banged on the door in extreme irritation with the futility of the situation and her own ineptitude in dealing with her son's reaction.

'Just stop it, Jamie, stop it and pull yourself together. I just can't imagine what Dominic's mummy will be thinking, having had to listen to that dreadful noise you made. And there's no way you can go in the state you're in.'

Shrieks rent the house, staccato shrieks of the like she had never heard before.

Again Sarah put her shoulder to the door, her hand on the handle releasing the catch and gradually creating a small aperture sufficient to put her foot inside. The resistance in Jamie's small-framed body was almost, but not quite, spent. Daylight streaked through, lightening the hallway on that unseasonably sunny mid-afternoon.

'Don't you come in, Mummy, don't, don't, don't you dare. You're a wicked, horrible lady and I'm going to tell the police what nasty things you're going to do to me. And … and … and what you said you'd do to Dominic's mummy.'

The door resisted Sarah's further pressure. Sarah's anxiety was turning to perplexity and her patience was vanishing fast. Her son's behaviour bore no relation to that of the recent past when he would willingly accept 'a kiss to make it better' in similar circumstances, not that he had ever created such a scene as he was doing now. A feeling of impotence and bewilderment engulfed her. If Jamie really had been stung, or had cut himself, why did he think *she* had inflicted pain on him … and why was Dominic's mother also perceived to be a potential victim of her alleged temper? Had his vivid imagination sparked some horror in his mind? A revived memory of an incident which had disturbed him in that dinosaur film they took him to? Had he ingested some poison which was causing hallucinations? Lead paint from the model dinosaurs, perhaps? No, there were laws against lead in children's toys – though these might not apply in Third World countries where the routine checking of export licences could be sparse to say the least. Where did the creatures come from – had they bought them from the Saturday market? Unscrupulous traders might turn a blind eye to the working practices of cheap suppliers. But the change in behaviour had been so inexplicably extreme and without warning that possibly an insect sting *was* the cause, after all. Perhaps his seemingly perverse reactions were justified: Sarah grimly recalled one of her own friends who was allergic to bee stings, so much so that she once went into anaphylactic shock when stung and now wore a special bracelet to alert any bystander that she was carrying a syringe containing an antidote around with her in her handbag at all times. Indeed, she was lucky that she was married to a doctor who knew how to revive her the first time she had lost consciousness and needed to use the EpiPen. Had Jamie overheard the conversation she, Sarah, had had with Matt shortly after her friend had told her of her distressing condition and, as a result, was fearful he was about to die? Now she came to think of it, Sarah recalled Jamie had enquired a day or so later if he could have 'a p-pen', explaining to his mystified parents that it would help him write his letter 'p's' properly, his teacher frequently making him practise these at breaktime.

Certainly it was eminently possible that Jamie, too, had a severe allergy to insect poison and was in a state of shock, therefore not responsible for his seemingly bizarre reactions at this moment. As far as she could remember, Freya was the only member of the family who had suffered an insect bite, and on her lip, too. Jamie was about four then and had mocked his big sister, calling her 'Fat chops' which had upset Freya immensely. It was the only time she had ever thumped her brother. Oh, Sarah fretted, if only her daughter was back home from her netball match and not spending the evening at her friend's house, she could have sent her downstairs to look for a frantic wasp, a hornet or the carcass of a dead bee. Even the presence of a discarded modelling knife would have gone some way towards solving this frustrating problem.

As she waited for Jamie to crumple, Sarah made the silent decision to speak to Dr. Allinson tomorrow and ask for her son to be tested for allergies. But why not tonight? Perhaps she should get an emergency appointment for this evening. Enduring the wrath of the secretaries would be a small price to pay: late surgery hours were for the convenience of commuters, not families with the whole day at their disposal. But what should she do right now? Should she dial 999 instead of NHS Direct?? Oh, for God's sake keep calm, Sarah chided herself, wishing she had Matt's presence of mind in critical situations such as this: he never became flustered at times of family crisis and could be relied upon to keep his cool. She tried to think what she would have done had such a commotion been caused by a child in her class. Colleagues admired the fact that she always made the right judgment on such occasions. Huh, so much easier when emotionally detached, she felt.

With a mighty effort of will, Sarah forced herself to think more rationally. After all, shock affects people in different ways and it certainly didn't seem Jamie was losing consciousness. Rather the contrary, in fact: he was behaving like a little demon. It was Friday so Matt would be home quite soon now, he always was in order to avoid the early starters to the West Country, and he would most certainly be able to knock some sense into the distraught boy. But then the recriminations would rain down upon her as they often seemed to do these days. The recession was responsible for so many hiccups in previously harmonious and loving relationships: bad day at work: come home and kick the proverbial cat … but for 'cat', read 'wife'. What was she doing, allowing Jamie to get himself into a state like this? Why couldn't she instil some discipline into the 'mummy's-baby' boy, Matt would say unkindly. But what if, what if … Sarah shuddered. Delayed anaphylactic shock didn't bear thinking about. At least with the outrageous noise Jamie was kicking up, there was no indication of a comatose state. Surely, for example, if he had been stung in the mouth his lips and throat would have swollen, precluding the emission of anything but strangulated sobs? Certainly, when she had a girl in her class with a peanut allergy, the dangers she had to be aware of happening were the closing of airways and associated choking when there was any contact whatsoever with substances which would cause an adverse reaction. Perhaps she should be relieved that there seemed to be no danger of such symptoms occurring in Jamie.

Coming out of her reverie, panic reasserted itself but, with it, a superhuman surge of power. Following an almighty heave of her shoulder, the door succumbed to the force exerted upon it. The little boy's shuddering body could no longer withstand the onslaught. Sarah forced herself through, just succeeding in stepping over her terrified child who was curled tightly up into a ball, hands protecting his ears as if he was expecting a barrage of blows. Yet Sarah had never, ever hit either of her children; why should Jamie be anticipating she would start now? In frustration that she felt so much out of her depth in managing this incident, Sarah ordered her mutinous child to get up from the floor.

'Stand up this minute, Jamie. Stand up. Stop that dreadful racket and tell me whether or not you have been stung. If so, I need to know if it was a wasp or a bee so that I can get the right medicine.'

Terrified screams again rent the air as Sarah bent down to lift her son's shaking body to a standing position. As a six-year-old's resistance is a force to be reckoned with, Sarah had to invest all her strength in order once more to gain the momentum she needed. Jamie's still-shod feet lashed out at her, crashing into her shin bone, drawing blood and causing her to cry out in sharp pain, relaxing her hold and providing Jamie with the advantage he sought. Seizing the moment and quick as a flash, Jamie dived under his bed like a demon possessed.

'Go away. Go aw-ay. You are a nasty, nasty cruel lady and I'm not going to have you as my mummy anymore. I shall tell the policeman who comes to our school to warn us of dangerous people like you.'

Still smarting from her wound, blood beginning to trickle down her leg, Sarah's consternation at her son's indescribable behaviour caused her to change tack once again. In a renewed feeling of inadequacy and growing desperation, she again attempted a consoling tone:

'Jamie darling, this just isn't you speaking, it really isn't. I can't understand what has got into you to make you say such strange things.'

The distressing noise started up again, splicing the air and Sarah's ears. A note of pure fear sounded in Jamie's wailing response.

'There is nothing, nothing, nothing in me, is there? Oh, what have you put in me? Tell me, Mummy, tell me. What is it, please, please, plea-ea-ease. Oh, I'm going to be sick.'

From under the bed came the hideous sound of retching.

'You're a murder-lady and the police will come and take you away,' spluttered out between the eruptions.

At that moment, to Sarah's ears came the more than welcome sound of tyre on gravel on the driveway. It had to be Matt. With immense relief that she was no longer the sole parent dealing with a possible medical emergency (she would withstand the later put-downs), Sarah flew to the window. Oh God, where's the window-lock key? What would happen if there was a fire? To hell with the risk of burglars: insurance companies drive me mad with their outrageous demands. I bet they don't have children who hide away the keys. Oh there it is: in the toy box. It had only taken milliseconds for these thoughts to flood into Sarah's distracted mind and Matt was only just emerging from his car when Sarah was able to fling the window wide open.

'Escaped just before the pile-up on the M25, thank God. Was on the news; did you hear it? Same old story: lorry overturning, cartons all over the road, causing gridlock,' the work-weary voice of her husband called up on seeing Sarah leaning out of the window. 'What's for supper – made it yet? If not, let's get a babysitter and we'll try the new restaurant down the road. I need a break: today's been hell.'

Nothing he said registered on Sarah.

'Matt, for God's sake, hurry up fast to Jamie's room. He's having hysterics and accusing me of all sorts of obnoxious and crazy things. He's beyond reason.'

Matt felt as if he had been deluged with a bucketful of Arctic water when all he thirsted for was an ice-cold gin and tonic. At times like these, increasingly prevalent during the credit-squeeze with its accompaniment of frozen salary rises and absence of bonuses, the sentiments expressed by his father, normally ridiculed by them both, sprang to mind: What had his wife to do all day except amuse the children and keep a clean house clean? Bloody hell: they're at school all day. Was he to have an evening of whining about the boredom of career-minded, entrapped housewives? He recalled Sarah's recent ironic comment when told she would be sitting next to the finance director at the Agency's annual dinner: 'I must mug up on some interesting topical conversation, otherwise when he asks about my leisure activities I might tell him that I usually spend my free time agonising over which washing powder to buy.' Her cutting response had been a body-blow to his pride.

But in some as yet unfathomable fashion, the note in Sarah's voice did not sound like an exhausted, 'I'd love you to take over now and give me some time to think for myself,' but far more urgency was being conveyed by her tone. Cursing Sarah for leaving her phone on the floor amongst a mess of scouring pads and Jamie's bloody dinosaurs (Christ Almighty, does she let Jamie pretend it, too, is a prehistoric monster?), he bounded up the stairs without throwing his jacket on the chair as he usually did, telling himself it was certainly unlike Sarah to get cross with their son or daughter. He wished she would do so more often: he couldn't stand undisciplined children. However, he could certainly detect she was in some distress. The resentment within him dissipated, diffusing into concern.

As he reached the landing, he could hear his wife talking to Jamie in a strangulated, 'I'm trying to be calm', voice from the bathroom where, unaccountably, she seemed to be swabbing her leg. Funny thing to do in a crisis; what was she doing? Painting her legs with self-tanning lotion? Irritation surged through him again as he strode across the hall and turned into his son's unaccustomedly untidy room. Feeling faint, with legs which scarcely held her up, Sarah limped across to join Matt in Jamie's bedroom. Jamie's screams, which had transmuted into juddering sobs now metamorphosed into frenetic howling once again as his mother re-appeared on the scene. Little fists clenched tightly under the bed, Jamie's blind panic intermingled with simmering fury, loosening the demented child's hold on reality. In his despair Jamie made up his mind to find the leaflets retained in the medicine cabinet which advised parents to 'Keep away from children'. He would use his new yellow hi-lighter to underline this critical sentence, put these on his mother's pillow and then perhaps he could feel safe once more.

'Leave us together, Sarah,' Matt tersely addressed her over his shoulder. 'I'll find out what is troubling him. What set him off?'

'I've got no idea, Matt; it's an absolute mystery. I can't get out of him what it is all about. Started just as I was accepting an invitation for him to go for supper and watch a film with Dominic, then stay over. It being Saturday tomorrow, the boys could have slept in to make up for a late night.'

Sarah did her best over the constant moaning of their son to relate the extraordinary sequence of events which had escalated so fast. Matt eventually managed to draw the conclusion that there had been no discernible provocation and the possibility of an insect sting was only surmise, associated with the prodigious number of lazy wasps troubling them in the past few days.

As Sarah left the room the full impact of her son's hurtful remarks began to hit home with meteoric force. What was causing him to make such horrifying accusations? Had he ever watched a horror film which could have preyed on his mind? She should not have allowed him to go to the unsuitable home of that boy in his class the other day. Hadn't his father been seen buying those despicable top-shelf films in the corner shop? You never know what children are going to watch when parents are lax and leave adult things lying around. What had he watched on TV that night she had come downstairs when she had seen the light on in the sitting room and found him asleep on the sofa with the television running? She had got Matt to carry him back upstairs to bed without waking him and they had agreed not to question him about the episode of sleepwalking in case it frightened him to think he had got up in the middle of the night without any knowledge of having done so. Whilst she had intended to check the previous evening's TV programmes the following day, sadly, as it happened she had forgotten to do so. What murky stuff had older boys in the school shown him? Mr. Holmes had assured parents that safety locks were on all of the computers in use in the school and it was a loosely monitored rule that no pupil was allowed to bring their phone or tablet onto the premises. But recalling the 'bike-shed culture' of her own teenage days, Sarah knew there were 'ways and means' of circumnavigating rules which were irritating and clearly there to be ignored. Indeed, Freya always gave her a meaningful 'Little does he know' look whenever a reminder was issued to parents. Furthermore, although she was aware Jamie had been bullied from time to time, seeming to be a ready victim of others' fun, his teacher was believed to be keeping a watchful eye on the situation and such incidents seemed to be under control in Year 2. Having a friend to occupy him and keep him out of harm's way was an essential part of his protection and Dominic was innocently fulfilling that role. It was unlikely that his hysterics were associated with events in school, in any case. If they were, she mused, what could have evoked the memories? A late-afternoon showing of a Jurassic period brawl?

Sarah's body began to shake uncontrollably in delayed emotional reaction to Jamie's perplexingly vicious remarks directed personally at her. Whilst as a teacher of nine-to eleven-year-olds the children in her care had been able to keep to themselves their strong feelings of animosity towards adults they disliked, she knew from staffroom talk that this was not necessarily the case for Early Years children. Some of the anecdotes related included one in which a teacher of the Reception class had remonstrated with a little girl for angrily calling her an old witch. The woman herself had found this uproariously funny, especially as the miscreant had later said her teacher could take home with her one of the pictures she had drawn that day. A colleague had winked knowingly and suggested that the girl's mother was probably called this by her husband: 'Out of the mouths of babes …' Perhaps Jamie had heard classmates giving vent to powerful feelings against adults and felt it OK to do the same. But why would he do this to his own mother?

However hard Sarah tried to rationalise her son's vitriolic and hateful accusations, she could not shake off the growing feeling that perhaps all was not well with her son's emotional development. Nonetheless, she consoled herself with her knowledge that ability to understand feelings and how to react in social situations did not keep up with intelligence necessarily. There was no doubt that Jamie's scholastic attainments were exceptional for his age but although his vocabulary was extensive for a just-six-year-old, not only his choice of words but also his manner of expression was sometimes misplaced. She fondly recalled Freya's rage at around the age of three when her mother had thwarted her desires for some perfectly justifiable reason, stuttering as she had fought for a suitable descriptor to express her apoplectic state, 'Mummy, Mummy, you are, you are, you are … you are dis-*gusting*'. Quite an acceptable statement for a child of that age, struggling to express feelings; amusing as well, otherwise why else should she remember this incident in Freya's life? Very strangely, Jamie seemed at the same stage at six.

Upstairs in the bedroom Matt wondered whether to employ the strict, commanding approach his father had used on him as a small boy to masterful effect. No; this was no ordinary tantrum: his son was clearly in the depths of despair. A man-to-man discussion might be the best technique.

'Jamie, whatever is the matter, old son? Mummy has been trying to help you and you seem to have got yourself into a real state. Come on, Jamie, come and cry on my shoulder and tell me what this is all about'.

Matt's hand slid under the bed. A small, moist hand gripped his.

'That's my boy. Hold on tight and I'll help you out. Silly old thing. Why did you think Mummy would hurt you?'

Jamie allowed himself to be pulled out. Matt lifted his son and set him down on the bed beside him, his body heaving with repressed sobs, his head burying itself in the jacket of Matt's business suit. Unable to suppress a frown of irritation, Matt silently wiped the wet snot from his collar, using the same handkerchief in a vain attempt to dry the tears from the sodden face in front of him. What the hell, he mused grimly, both are bodily secretions which probably emanate from the same source.

'Dommie had asked me to go round to his house this evening to watch a Harry Potter film and, and, and his mummy talked to my mummy on the phone about what Dommie wanted me to do and Mummy said ...' The stuttering boy's body shuddered with renewed convulsive sobs, rendering interpretation of his increasingly more incoherent explanation well-nigh impossible.

'Yes, Jamie, what did Mummy say?'

'She said, oh, it's so horrible. She said she was, she was, she was going to kill me.' His voice rose to a shriek as he added, 'And cut Dommie's mummy up.'

'Oh Jamie, that's ridiculous. You must have misheard.' Silently he wondered whether Sarah was going through an early 'change'; he was aware from Agency gossip that some women become irrational at that time.

'I didn't, Daddy, I didn't, I didn't. She said it as clear as a bell.'

'Look, Jamie, you are being a very, very silly boy,' Matt said firmly, mustering up as much authority as he could in mind of the lousy day he had had at work and his desperate need for a pick-me-up. 'This is absolute nonsense, do you hear? You've worked yourself into a frenzy for nothing. Neither Mummy nor I would ever do anything to harm you and you know that. Now, I just want you to put your head on the pillow and I'll cover you up with your duvet, clothes and all.' Dutifully, but with heaving shoulders and clinging on to his father as if his life depended on his protection, Jamie allowed him to slide his body into the bed but not before wiping his running nose against the sleeve of Matt's jacket which already looked as if a trip to the dry cleaners would not come amiss.

'And Mummy said just now there was something nasty that had crawled into me but I sicked it all out. It's under the bed, Daddy. Please take it away. It might be alive still.'

Uttering these words, Jamie sank back into his pillow, his slight frame wracked with exhaustion. Matt, as tired as he was, stroked his son's quivering body until, it seemed an eternity later to him, sleep overtook the emotionally drained child. Matt cautiously crept downstairs, gingerly dropping a screwed up handkerchief containing evil-smelling vomit into the waste basket by the hall table.

Sarah, anxious to maintain the rudimentary friendship between the two boys and taking the first mitigating opportunity to contact her friend, was speaking to Jane again as promised, determined to disguise her own shattered composure and attempting to appear light-hearted.

'Jane, I'm so sorry to put you out like this, giving back-word so late in the day. Anyway, it's lucky I didn't run him over because he's also been violently sick and this is the last thing you want when I believe you've got your parents staying with you at the moment. Dominic must come over here after school one day for a playdate instead. If Jamie is no better in the morning, I'll take him up to the surgery.' Agreement was reached that the date with Dominic was merely postponed until after half-term.

Matt, looking for the keys to the drinks cupboard, was unable to hear Jane's morbid response that she hoped the fuss wasn't over an insect sting as her daughter's friend had died, stung by a bee, her family not knowing that she was allergic to the poison it injected. Sarah was steadily learning that Jane's imagination was always triggered by disasters, hers or those of others.

'Oh God! How ghastly, Jane. Well, we're no nearer to a resolution of the problem but Matt was marvellous with him and calmed him down. Thanks for your forbearance. It's great of you to invite Jamie again sometime in the future. As before, I'll run him over after school. And I'll take my turn as well before Christmas. Must say "bye for now" – Matt has got Jamie to bed. I'll let you know what the doctor says.'

Behind her, drink in hand, Matt enquired in extraordinarily measured tones as Sara replaced the landline in its cradle,

'What did you say you would do to Jamie, my dearest – darling – thoughtless – apology for a wife?'

Collapsing into a chair, the blood draining from her face, Sarah replied weakly and in an equally fractured voice, 'I said... I'd... run... him... over. Oh my God, if ever I needed a very, very strong gin and tonic, I need it now.'

'That makes two of us, only make mine whisky,' Matt responded through gritted teeth as he returned to the cocktail cabinet and took an enormous swig directly from the bottle, his second that night but this time from a precious twenty-year-old Kentucky Bourbon, a Christmas gift from an American client and 45% alcohol.

At that point his mobile rang: it was Freya. 'Dad, could you collect me from Miranda's – you know where she lives.'

Matt certainly did. Miranda lived three or more miles away – next door to the village police station.

Chapter Two

'Would you mind teaching your little boy some manners?'

Having collected Jamie from school and given Freya permission to stay on for netball practice, Sarah was using the free time available to change Jamie's library book before she had to pick up her car from the garage where she had left it for its regular service and M.O.T. earlier that day. Now ready to leave, mother and son were standing in the check-out queue.

Startled by the sharp tone by which she was addressed, Sarah turned to face a rather frigid-looking woman who was glaring at her accusingly.

'I'm sorry,' Sarah replied equally tartly, 'my son has been taught to be polite at all times. Please explain the implication of your remark as I find it most offensive.'

'Your no doubt "dear" little boy was unbelievably and embarrassingly rude to me in public just now … and then compounded his rudeness with impertinence.'

Feeling distinctly uneasy, and with the all-too-familiar pinkness diffusing her cheeks and the irritating blotchiness mounting on her neck and chest which always occurred whenever she was upset or anxious and trying not to show it, Sarah did her best to probe the nature of the woman's displeasure, but to no avail: her pleas fell on a departing figure.

Uncertain whether to reprimand Jamie or sympathise, Sarah decided not to be collusive in case he really had overstepped the bounds of propriety. She turned her attention to her son who was standing on one leg and looking equally mystified.

'Why was that lady so angry, Jamie?'

Jamie, not at all sure why his kind remark (for that was his intention) was causing so much consternation, offered his explanation.

'I told her, Mummy, her nose needed blowing. It did, Mummy, it did. There was a big dewdrop at the end of it and it was going to fall on the counter. The next one went on her library book but I wasn't able to tell her in time 'cos she wiped it off the cover, so she knew about that one and there was no need to warn her.'

To his surprise, his mother's tone changed. He thought she sounded now rather like the lady had done when he had given her the helpful advice.

'Oh Jamie, Jamie,' Sarah said in mounting despair, quickly changing to displeasure as her neighbour behind her in the queue stepped backwards to leave a wider distance between Sarah herself and her son. 'You must never make personal remarks like that. Not to strangers or to any grown-ups. That was extremely rude of you. You will have upset the lady very much and that's not at all kind.'

'But you tell me, Mummy, when my nose needs blowing. You say, "what will people think?" and I didn't think that lady would like people to see her dripping nose. They might think bad things about her. Anyway, I told the counter-lady she ought to dry the book off. You always make me wash my hands if I touch my nose and people reading that book might catch her cold.'

With a sinking feeling in the pit of her stomach and feeling she was in need of her increasingly more customary stiff gin, Sarah feebly asked Jamie what he had said next to make the woman even angrier.

'She said I was a very rude little boy and I ought to be ashamed of myself.'

'And you replied?' asked Sarah, dreading the response her son could have given when an apology or an innocuous remark might have saved the day and forestalled this inquisition.

'I said I wasn't being a rude little boy as I'm six and not little any more. And it did need wiping so I was telling the truth.'

Jamie continued, in the plaintive hope he would placate his mother by letting her know he had explained how well she was teaching him. 'I informed her that my mummy says I should always tell the truth and that it's not rude to do so.'

Sarah felt a little weak at the knees. Odd incidents like this were happening ever more frequently. She told herself that she ought to be pleased Jamie was honest, truthful and had a growing sense of justice, not like some of his friends who seemed to get away with murder and could be right little tearaways. Weren't truth and honesty better qualities to nurture, even at the expense of giving offence from time to time? But the number of occasions when his behaviour belied his age was becoming increasingly embarrassing and could not be excused as that of a pre-school child. She recalled that he had explained to his amused teacher at the age of four that his refusal to be taken to see the head for disobedience was because it would be far too scary to have to look at a head without its body. Acceptable to make such errors as a young infant but by the age of six Jamie should have developed a realistic perspective of when and what to say and to whom.

But the 'here and now' had to be dealt with and the matter could not rest yet.

'Sometimes, Jamie, I just do not know what to do with you. I teach you the difference between right and wrong and you are beginning to learn that pretty well.' Nodding his head, Jamie affirmed that, indeed, he understood the lesson and always, always told the truth. 'But you have just got to know when it's not right or kind to be truthful. It is better to tell a white lie sometimes. Do you know what a "white lie" is?'

Jamie said incredulously he didn't know lies had colours in them. What sort of lies were red or black ones, he mused. Did that help you to know when someone was lying if you saw the colour it was? How did words get colour in them? Do liars carry paint pots round in their pockets and do they paint their lies before they say them? Colours come through the air on to your TV screen and rainbows are there one minute and gone the next, so it did seem they could fly from one place to another. God must send them. In a flash, Jamie understood: perhaps God needed a little help sometimes. Word-lies were only coloured when they were written down. You could use felt-tips then.

He came out of his reverie and turned his attention to his mother once more. Was she still cross with him?

Patiently, beginning to see the amusing side of the situation at long last (and heaven knows that unpleasant woman had had a serious sense of humour failure), Sarah enquired whether she now had her son's attention. A serious Jamie assured her she had.

Sarah explained that sometimes the truth made people very unhappy and upset. It was better not to be so honest in the faults we would like to point out, or the confidences which we would like to share but, on more careful consideration, should decide to keep to ourselves.

'You see, if Grandma Eleanor says she is getting very old it is not kind to agree with her. It's better to say something like, "We are all getting old, Grandma, and I love hearing about all the things you did as a little girl. Will you tell me some more?" And if Grandma tells you the same story all over again that you have heard many times before, say that you always love hearing that. You see, although that is not the truth, it is a white lie and quite OK because you are trying not to hurt her feelings. That helps Grandma to stop feeling sad and, maybe, she will tell you a different one next time. It is hurtful for her to hear that she forgets what she has told you.'

Privately Jamie imagined his grandma must be hurt a lot because she was always taking those different-coloured sweetie-things which she kept in her handbag and said they were not for little boys. Mummy told him then that they were to stop Grandma having a pain. He remembered she had eaten two orangey ones when he had a fist-fight with her and she had screamed, an awful sound, and said he'd nearly broken her arm. He never knew why he was sent up to his room after that. His daddy had asked him what on earth he thought he was doing, fighting an old lady? He'd thought that was a most unfair thing to say because you weren't supposed to fight people younger and smaller than yourself … and Grandma had agreed she would like to see how strong he was when he'd asked if she would like him to wrestle with her. Huh, why did grown-ups always change their minds? Of course he had to twist her arm as hard as he could: she was twice his size and about ten times his age. When he asked her she always said she was as old as her legs and older than her teeth. He could not decide whether this made sense or that was a white lie but when he mentioned this to his mother at this point, she just sighed and told him to work it out for himself. What sort of an answer was that? A blue one? Jamie's face puckered up in bewilderment.

'Mummy, you are muddling me up. I don't know what colour to use. Oh yes I do!' Jamie's eyes lit up with the delight of sudden insight. 'I'll write it down for her. I can spell "white" w.h.i.t., – you have to put an "h" in it. I keep on telling Alfie that, but he says that's silly and doesn't do what I say and gets told off. So I'll write her a lie in chalk on my blackboard, then she won't know why I am saying that I want to hear her stories, 'cos I don't. She uses silly baby-talk like bunny and doggie, even bow-wow the other day and it is not nice to have to sit on her knee as if I'm about two; it's all wobbly. She bumps me up and down and says, "This little piggy goes to market", and then squeaks in my ear when the last one runs home. It's horrible.' His shoulders shuddered at the memory.

Sarah felt it was time to move on from the nature of white lies. Surely what she was trying to explain was not too advanced for a bright six-year-old to absorb? Not having any brothers herself, being an Upper Primary teacher she had always enjoyed being on playground duty when she could observe the infants at play and took pleasure in listening to the arguments going to and fro when the rules of their self-initiated games were infringed. Often the points the antagonists made were impressive. It would be interesting to talk her concerns over with Matt tonight: his take on the matter could be insightful.

For the past few weeks, ever since the wasp-sting debacle, Matt had been more like his old self and a degree of welcome intimacy had filtered back into their marriage. Time had been found for each other; Matt had been calmer and some of the earlier romance had rekindled. There had been a glorious weekend when Matt had whisked her off to Paris, her parents holding the fort, and the clock had scrolled back to the carefree days of their early life together. Matt had been the instigator of their Agency obtaining a few lucrative new clients, accordingly for which he was to receive a modest recruitment fee. The Paris break was Matt's celebration of this, his return to being the provider of goodies as well as simply basic housekeeping. No longer, in his own mind, was his manhood being compromised. The loss of her salary when the joint decision had been made for her to become a full-time mother when her maternity leave for Jamie had expired had had serious financial consequences as, coincidentally and unforeseen, the recession hit home. Inevitably, reins had had to be tightened. Matt had been happy to enjoy the fruits of Sarah's labours as 'the icing on the cake', but when the cake had gone dry and the icing faded, responsibility for a lifestyle which could no longer be maintained rested firmly on his shoulders. It did not fit him well. How often when spirits are low do individuals revert back to instilled values, imparted by parental attitudes, Sarah pondered. Resentment festered, pride had to be appeased and the relationship began to show signs of neglect. Neglect of the signs and symbols of affection, neglect of pillow-talk, neglect of due respect and neglect of shared family responsibilities. Magazines seemed to be full of advice for couples beleaguered by the threat of down-sizing and the effect of such pressures on relationships: even strong partnerships wilted and became vulnerable. Not surprisingly, anger at situations at the agency Matt was hoping to gain a partnership in had metamorphosed into flare-ups at home: futile to blow up at work, so take out your frustrations on the metaphorical animal dozing by the fireside.

Now that frightening time seemed a mere blip in their marital happiness and was over, for ever, ever, ever. Sarah reminded herself of the promises they had whispered to each other in that dreamy little boutique hotel in Montmartre Matt had found for them. Holding each other tightly, they had vowed that their marriage was an inviolable bond and, whatever the future held for them, they would face it together as one. For richer, for poorer …

With firmness in her voice, Sarah brought the subject back to the issues of the present situation. She concluded their discussion by emphasising that to make personal remarks to strangers was bad enough but to compound the rudeness by trying to justify himself afterwards when taken to task was unforgivable.

'So let's get your book checked out and then collect our car from the garage. There's time for you to read a page or two to me before tea, if we go home now.'

Grown-ups are funny, Jamie thought, still puzzling over why it was acceptable for Mummy to tell him to blow his nose and not for him to let others know they should wipe theirs. Just as he did not always notice runny bits trickling down his nose to that funny bit of your face just above your mouth where there was a dent in it – not, at least, until it felt moist

– and a quick upward switch of his tongue got rid of it more quickly than if he had got his hankie out of his pocket. How did he know whether the lady was already aware she needed to get hers out and was just about to do the same thing with her tongue as he usually did? Would it have been alright to have told her not to do that 'cos he could see her, just like Miss Griffin had told him in class yesterday. The boys all laughed then; they thought it was very funny. Would the people in the library have laughed, as well? Oh, well, Mummy had stopped being cross. Yes, he would read her two pages before tea; she must like the story as she had chosen it, which was more than he thought he would have done if asked, but it was the least he could do to make her happy after what he had done. Not, he conjectured, that he had done anything other than try to be helpful. Should he ask her to tell him what the story was all about when he had finished, like she generally asked him? Would he be as strange as some adults were when he was grown up, he wondered?

'Just time to pick up my car before we have to be home for Freya.' Catching Jamie's hand, Sarah urged him onwards. 'Quick, there's a number 14 bus; that will take us to Dexter's Motors. If we run, we'll just catch it.'

As he puffed along beside her, Jamie reminded Sarah of the time when he was 'a very little boy' and he had asked his daddy how you caught buses. He had thrown his toy bus into the air, nearly hitting his father on the nose when it dropped, caught it before it hit the ground but had then questioned his parents how you could catch heavy things like real buses or trains. 'Wasn't that funny, Mummy?'

Ignoring Jamie's interruption which had naturally caused him to slow down, with a joint burst of energy they beat the bus to the bus stop. The driver looked down at Jamie. 'Hop on, little 'un,' he smiled. 'There's a seat at the back if your mum has enough money for the two of you.'

Jamie looked relieved when he saw Sarah counting out the fare, adding, 'one child fare, please'. Now they could stay in the bus and wouldn't have to walk.

'Careful, sonny, careful,' growled an old gentleman as Jamie hopped his way down the bus, staggering as the jolting of the bus gathered momentum as it moved away from the stop and accidentally kicking the old man's foot on the way.

'Mind where you're going,' scolded a smartly dressed lady whose carrier bag was almost knocked from her lap by Jamie's flailing arms as he tried manfully to keep his balance. With an accusing glare at Sarah, she added caustically,

'Your child should walk, not practise gymnastics down the aisle. Teach him some respect for people.'

Sarah apologised profusely to her fellow passengers who were still looking aggrieved, glowering at her as she passed them. Four stops later Jamie, puzzled at the furore he had unwittingly caused, felt equally put out when Sarah told him not to be so ridiculous when he said he was only doing what the driver had asked him to do. After all, they didn't go on buses very often so how was he to know 'hop on the bus' meant 'to get on'. Why didn't the driver-man say what he meant? He had wondered at the time why his mother hadn't obeyed his instruction and assumed it would have been awkward for her to do that whilst carrying her bag containing their books. Those people should be cross with the man in charge, not him. It was not at all kind to get him into trouble.

The bus stop was very close to the garage. Stepping off, Sarah and Jamie wound their way round the vehicles in the forecourt waiting for collection and walked into the showroom where 'the desk' was sited which dealt with repairs, customer queries, salesmen, etc.

'Your car is nearly ready, Mrs. Chilton; the mechanic is getting it down from the ramp now. You just need to settle the bill at the Accounts desk.'

Jamie lingered behind, eyes transfixed at the low neckline of the receptionist's blouse.

'Can I ask a question, please?' Jamie thought he was not going to have this lady saying he hadn't got any manners, like Mummy said the people on the bus had told her. Having received a smiling nod of encouragement, he continued,

'The question I want to ask you is, "Why do you keep your bottom in such a funny place?" Both men and ladies have theirs at the bottom of their backs – that's why they are called bottoms. Though,' he reflected, 'there is another one at the front so when Mummy tells me to wash my bottom in the bath I ask her whether she means my front bottom or my back bottom. Do you have two front bottoms and no back bottom?'

Sarah, a few paces ahead, froze in her tracks. Would there be no end to her son's faux pas? Concurrently, the expressions on the receptionist's face went through the full spectrum. At last she composed herself to walk the few paces to Mrs. Chilton and tell her that she had just been asked the funniest question that she'd ever been asked by a child, one in which she would have a great deal of enjoyment in repeating to her friends. She would certainly be able to dine out on this gem.

'Don't be cross with your little boy; it was such an innocent question. But I do think you need to explain anatomy to him a little better. Tell your mummy, darling, what you asked me.'

Sarah, who had heard every word, was dumbfounded that her son had not learned from the lessons of the day so far, and at a loss to know whether to show her appreciation of the humour of the situation or demand to know why Jamie had blithely overridden her previous remonstrations. But Jamie had other questions to ask and ignored the lady with the peculiarly placed bottom.

'Mummy, what does the car look like now it's got an emmotee? Dommie's daddy has a special silver jaguar on his car. Is it like that? Oh, and were you too late to pick up your car? I saw a man lower it down from a platform and drive it to the car-wash. It's in there now. If we'd been earlier, we could've turned that handle thing to pick your car up, instead of the man doing it, couldn't we?'

Jamie reflected on the strange mysteries of catching buses, picking up cars. He thought he would choose that moment, too, to mention another strange feature he had noted about the garage man:

'Why did the man who took our car to be washed have such a big forehead? It went on and on and on, right to the back of his head and that's where his hair started. It did look funny but I tried not to stare 'cos it might be a special illness he's got. Is it, do you think?'

Sarah's head was in a whirl. What goes on in Jamie's head? He has the strangest ideas going through his mind. She reflected on the determination of both Matt and herself to ensure they did not fall into the common trap of sex-stereotyping their children: neutral clothing, interchangeable toys, equivalent chores set for both yet, despite such equality, it was becoming blatantly obvious that the temperaments of their son and daughter were markedly different. Jamie seemed to be so much harder work to bring up than Freya who had been a most sensible companion with whom to share outings or shopping with when aged just six. Freya had been far more mature than her brother at the same age and now, at nine, was quite independent. Maybe, she mused, inventors, or scientists, show themselves to think in a different manner to the rest of civilisation when they are children: after all, even in 2008, there are a greater number of male graduates taking up scientific and engineering careers despite efforts to persuade girls into such career possibilities. Perhaps Jamie's fertile mind could be channelled into some unique occupation. It might be harmful and would destroy his creativity if she and Matt tried to divert him into more conventional ways of thinking. Yes, she reflected, innocence is a good description of the way he seems to see the world. It would be wrong to 'knock it out of him', as Matt had been telling her to do with monotonous and demeaning regularity before the trip to Paris had brought back the caring husband of pre-recession days. She had previously begun to wonder whether his earlier agreement that gender stereotypes were to be discouraged had pertained only to female children, recalling his mother's present of a pink shawl for her first granddaughter had been flatly refused by Matt as suitable for his firstborn, to her considerable chagrin. Furthermore, he had later, none-too-politely, prevented his parents from buying Freya a doll's pram together with other feminine accoutrements. Why, then, could he not appreciate his son's softer side, his charming innocence, instead wanting him to be more macho?

Having quietly corrected Jamie's misperceptions of female anatomy and male baldness, Sarah agreed with her puzzled son that neither she nor Dominic's mummy, nor Miss Griffin, had such big boobies as could be mistaken for bottoms. She reminded him of the time when, sitting next to Rachel on their friend's motor cruiser, Rachel had rebuked him for poking her bikini top and in answer to his question what she had got underneath, was told, 'Boobies; the same as all ladies have.'

'Do you remember, Jamie, you embarrassed me by stoutly announcing to everyone that she was wrong because *your* mummy hadn't got any. Didn't you learn from that experience that discussing boobies was a taboo subject?'

Jamie wondered silently what 'to boo' had got to do with boo-bies but kept silent. He knew the two words both had 'boo' in them but thought he would try to work that out later. It was mystifying why he was expected to cry like a booby when calling ladies' top bumpy-things 'boobies'. Weird. After all, Freya always mocked him when he cried, saying 'boo-hoo, boo-hoo; only babies cry.' This day really is not going at all well for me, he reflected as he decided not to make his mother even crosser than she was by putting the question to her. Thankfully she was taking up his query about emmotees and then his puzzlement about picking up cars.

'An M.O.T.,' (she spelt out the letters), 'is a test the government makes car owners have each year to ensure their vehicles are safe to drive.' She went on to explain that the word 'pick' could be used in different ways and mean different things. Sarah then hustled her son out of Dexter's and into the car, leaving behind an accounts clerk feeling she was fast losing the battle to keep a straight face. The two then drove home discussing various ways 'pick up' could be used. Jamie came up with 'pick-up' truck, 'Pick'n'Mix' at the sweet counter, while Sarah used 'pick up' in varied forms to press home the multiplicity of meanings, a little nonplussed as to how to explain 'pick up tarts', which apparently Alfie had told Jamie his dad looked for when driving his truck. Apparently Alfie had asked him to bring some home for tea one day and his dad had 'given him a clip round the ear' for his cheekiness.

'But Alfie told me one of those coloured lies, he did, 'cos he doesn't wear any jewellery round his ear: we're not allowed to at school and it would be only the girls who would, anyway. Alfie didn't like it when I told him so and hit me round the head. It wasn't very kind of him: it hurt a lot but I didn't cry.'

For the rest of the journey home Jamie was in reflective mood. Would he be as difficult for children to understand when he was a grown-up? Bottoms, bottoms, bottoms. Boobies, boobies, boobies. Pick-up truck, pick-up tart. He began to giggle. So much did he giggle that Sarah had to stop the car until he had regained his composure. Sarah was not amused.

★

Back at home, Jamie quickly got out his library book from Mummy's bag. He would much rather have picked one of his dinosaur books, the one about Tyrannasaurus rex, but Mummy had said he was always choosing those and he should have something different this time. 'But there is no point in reading anything I don't want to read about,' thought Jamie. 'Never mind, when I go to bed I'll get the dinosaur books out and read them with my torch under the clothes.'

In a soothing tone, feeling all incidents should be closed now, at least until she told Matt about the funny side of Jamie's indiscretions, Sarah asked him if he liked his new book. 'It's not new, Mummy, we got it from the library; we didn't buy it.' Jamie is a master of wordplay, reflected Sarah fondly, and he is such a good reader for a six-year-old, probably the best in his class.

'Charlie and the Chocolate Factory', Jamie began, thinking how nice it would be to have a house made out of chocolate. It was wasted on a factory: those are always grimy, at least the ones he had seen were when they went to visit Grandma Eleanor in Rotherham. 'I expect the workers in the factory have a little nibble when no one is watching them, don't you, Mummy? What happens when it is sunny: does it melt or is it a special sort of chocolate that doesn't?'

Sarah wondered whether this was a diversionary tactic to put off the chore of reading aloud and, rather distractedly, told him she wanted to hear what the story said, not about silly ideas which probably had nothing to do with the content, although she knew outlandish things which Roald Dahl introduces children to were often far-fetched. To her irritation, Matt had annoyed her by saying she shouldn't get Roald Dahl books for Jamie; Jamie had enough idiotic thoughts of his own without pandering to his too fertile imagination by handing stupid nonsense to him on a plate. Mind you, he explained to Sarah, he'd never enjoyed the books his mother made him read.

Swallows and Amazons he recalled loathing, and soon adopted the ruse of reading the helpful synopses on the blurb of birthday and Christmas books he'd received from his grandmother, spouting these during their Sunday lunches. He could never believe how gullible they all were, assuming he had read and enjoyed the beastly books themselves. Worth every penny of the 5p he would give his sister (now living in Australia) for not piping up with the truth. It was lucky his only brother was older and away at public school; he would have lost no time in spilling the beans and getting him into trouble. There was no way that Matt would have been able to afford the blackmailing fee George would have demanded in order not to blab.

'The last time we saw Charlie,' Jamie continued, curling up to Sarah on the sofa. He loved it when he was close to Mummy and snuggled up even closer until Sarah thought she would ease him ever so slightly away as he was pushing her uncomfortably into the solid arm of the chair making it difficult to breathe, only stopping when his head was resting in the crook of her arm. Relaxing for the first time that day, Sarah felt a sudden glow of pride in her son. His reading was so fluent and, even though he had not seen this story before, he was making the characters come alive in a most theatrical manner. Would he be chosen for a big part in the annual school play? Events of the afternoon faded into insignificance. What a ridiculous woman to make such a song and dance about a little boy's apparent eccentricities. She probably had never had any children of her own – and if she had, then they must have spent their childhood in terror of her. On the other hand, she was just a sad old lady and probably didn't get much fun out of life, so perhaps, Sarah reflected, she should feel sorry for her.

Turning these thoughts over in her mind, it seemed to Sarah that it would be wrong to tell Matt tonight when he asked what sort of a day she had had. Especially as they had re-assumed such harmony recently and it wouldn't be fair on him after the worries he had had about the meeting he was to have that morning with the new clients they were hoping to poach from their rivals. There was still a vulnerability about his moods in the present economic climate: he would be depressed if the meeting went badly and, alternatively, probably would not thank her for taking him down from Cloud 9 if the reverse had occurred. In the former case he would need her support and empathy and a loving bed to retire to, untrammelled by the trivia of home concerns. Neither would it be right to bring it up again with Jamie: Matt always took the stern father approach when in automatic-parent mode and Jamie might be miserable all night. Then he will creep into our bed … and these days Matt hates that, so a molehill will be turned into a mountain and, really, what good would that serve? She vowed to herself that she wouldn't make an issue of this with him after all, resolving that she would not re-open the wound, either for Jamie or herself. A phrase her mother was always quoting sprang into mind: 'Let bygones be bygones'. Sarah comforted herself with the feeling that she had handled the situation well and the issues discussed with Jamie must have left their mark on his consciousness.

Perhaps she herself had been too hard, too brusque maybe, with Jamie today. It would definitely be wrong to drag it all up with Matt tonight: the consequences could be dour. Hadn't she read the article in *The Times* by that currently popular parenting expert, confirming what she believed herself, that any form of punishment or criticism should be meted out as soon as possible after the misdemeanour has been committed? Left too long, the child will have already moved on from there, will bear a grudge and the admonishment will not change the behaviour it was supposed to. Or was that the advice in *Country Life* relating to training dogs?

She let herself return to the world Jamie was creating so eloquently. But not for long.

Parents' Evening tonight suddenly came into her thoughts. After the mortification of this afternoon when she had wished the floor would open and swallow her up, it would be most gratifying to hear her son's praises inevitably sung by Miss Griffin in relation to his star qualities in all the basic skills and his broad general knowledge, especially of all things scientific. Sarah could already feel the pride welling up inside her, secretly wondering if Miss Griffin had ever had such a gifted pupil. Maybe she could enquire about the school's predictions for SATs at the end of the year – or perhaps that sort of question would be regarded as too premature and indicative of the sort of pushy parent she had always tried to avoid in her dealings with Freya's teachers. No, she would be a model parent, meek and grateful. It would, nonetheless, be useful to ask her opinion whether she thought other children shunned Jamie because his interests and ideas were so different from theirs but she realised she would have to phrase that topic carefully. In her career she had met some teachers who belittled children who clearly were more intelligent than they were themselves. She hoped that was not the case with Miss Griffin but rumour had it amongst the mothers-at-the-gate that she had favourites and could be unkind to those not within her inner circle. 'One of the old brigade', one of the grandmothers had said appreciatively. 'Stands no nonsense and none of this play-learning for her, thank God.'

Wondering if time had mellowed Miss Griffin's jealousy of her or whether she still felt animosity towards her as the woman who had usurped her all those years ago by being the successful candidate for a senior appointment, Sarah recalled catching sight of Miss Griffin at one of the district conferences where she showed no sign of recognition, nonetheless appearing to go out of her way to avoid any direct contact. Sarah vowed to steer clear of confrontation this evening and impress upon her how delighted they both were as parents with the tuition Jamie was receiving. If the conversation went well, she had intended to ask his teacher if she could keep a watchful eye to foster the mercurial friendship but now the burgeoning comradeship between Jamie and Dominic was becoming more established, there was less need for this intervention. She would not mention Jamie's occasional faux-pas either; best to maintain the discussion on an academic level. Should such indiscretions have been happening in school, she would have been bound to have heard of them.

Once again Sarah returned to the moment. Sighing deeply, she again comforted herself that her son was almost theatrical in the way he was able to put expression into the characters, even though this story was completely new to him. For Mr. Wonka, he was making his voice sound really spooky, so much so that she could feel the shivers running down her spine. Croaky Grandmother Josephine sounded a real old crone (there, perhaps the incident with the lady in the library had been internalised and he had morphed her into an ancient, wizened mockery of old age). Alternatively, she hoped he wasn't modelling her on her own mother; she secretly thought it more likely to be Eleanor he was caricaturing. Sarah recalled Jamie's characterisations when he made the little girl in the story appear as if butter wouldn't melt in her mouth. The personification of Jamie's feelings towards his sister, perhaps??

Certainly Freya appeared to have little in common with her brother, sometimes giving the impression she despised him. Was the feeling mutual? Her social circle was ever-widening and she often went to one or other of her friends' houses straight from school. Mobile phones in the possession of most children these days enabled dutiful sons and daughters to leave a trail of their whereabouts in a mutually satisfactory manner. Freya was becoming a master of the electronic world and Sarah made sure to give Freya hers when she collected the children from school: it was safely stowed in the glove compartment of the car and she would come to claim it if going to any activity after school. When pressed by Sarah to return her friends' hospitality, she always muttered vaguely about Jamie wanting to interfere in their activities to the extent that her friends were annoyed and irritated by his behaviour, a comment Sarah found disturbing. Thus she was becoming more and more distant within the family, perhaps to be expected now she was in the winter netball and summer rounders teams, choir and orchestra, and not only was a member of the scouting movement but also of Stage Coach where she had a leading role in the forthcoming play. Were all nine-year-olds as occupied, she wondered? Was it important for Freya to become almost invisible within the home? As often as she could, it seemed, Freya also rejected offers for Sarah to collect her friends from these out-of-school events, hastily naming a mother who 'does the school run on her way home from work' and adding chillingly that, anyway, no one likes sitting in their Range Rover with Jamie in the back, 'He's so embarrassing, Mummy'. Did all girls despise their younger brothers?

How Sarah wished her children were more amiable towards each other … but on reflection she realised that it was Freya who was out of kilter, not Jamie: she showed no tolerance towards Jamie, three years her junior. On the occasions he had a friend round when Freya was at home, she complained that he plagued her to watch what he was doing all the time. 'It's always, "look at what I've done; look at me".' Not, Freya had added, that the 'activities' had been anything other than Jamie monopolising his dinosaurs and doing his utmost to interest his so-called friends in some esoteric feature of the Jurassic period. Somehow, Sarah sighed to herself, when invited again, the 'friend' was always otherwise engaged and a return invitation for Jamie to their house was never forthcoming, a source of serious disappointment to her. She herself had always got on well with her only sister but Matt had said wistfully that he had hated the constant bickering and sibling envy in his family. Not a situation Sarah wanted to prevail in her home and, in anticipation of the distance widening not only between her children but also between Freya and themselves, resolved she would in future look more carefully at the behaviour Jamie brought to playdates.

Sarah again attempted to bring herself back to reality. Enough of this discontent, she chided herself: I should have been more attentive during the sessions we had on child development in post-grad teacher training; nothing seemed relevant to the classrooms of Upper Primary years. In her formative mind at the age of twenty-one and in her probationary year, she wished the course focused more on classroom management skills. How many aspiring middle school teachers needed to know the importance of understanding the emotional needs of a young *infant*, the nature of the first babbling sounds, when the first steps were expected to be made, or how bonding developed. Wasn't this something one would be interested in during ante-natal classes? Bollocks, she'd thought at the time. Now she realised why the course had spent time on attachment theory and relationship issues, actually needing these now for her own child at first school level: Sarah bitterly deplored the fact she had baulked at such sessions which she'd regarded as inappropriate to the years she intended to teach. All her subsequent in-service training had been at this level, too, leaving a great gap in her knowledge, now so much regretted. The memory of hamming up a session of group practical work by filming her fellow students' feet, only to be outsmarted embarrassingly by the canny tutor who chose her production to be the one demonstrated to the year group was still vivid. Hadn't she got egg on her face on that occasion, despite brazening it out! Be sure your sins ... Sarah reflected ruefully.

Dreamily, Sarah returned to more positive, optimistic predictions. Perhaps Jamie will be an actor one day. Already she could see his name emblazoned in lights outside the Haymarket, lines of awestruck girls awaiting his presence outside the side-door to sign their programmes and perhaps honour him with a complimentary remark. Maybe The Aldwych? Sarah could remember being taken there as a very little girl to see a revival of a Brian Rix-type farce, the originals being popular in her mother's childhood. Absolutely hilarious, every grown-up said: side-splitting. But she recalled wondering why it was so funny that the actors and actresses had to chase each other all round the rooms and you never knew whose wife was whose because just as you'd sorted it out, the wrong ones kissed each other and got into the bed you thought was someone else's so you had to work it out all over again. Yes, she'd laughed all right when the audience did; you had to, really, because it was nice to do grown-up things and she might not have been taken again if she had not shown she had seen the humour in the racing round bits – which seemed to her to be all the play was about. She had wondered afterwards whether she had not laughed enough because she was never taken to an adult play again and had to be content with pantomimes (where at least you knew when to laugh because it all bubbled up inside you and you didn't have to look to see when others were about to split their sides). She remembered being upset later when she overheard her mother explaining to a surprised neighbour that she and Philip had had to take their daughter as the babysitter had let them down. Claudia had then been quite shocked that her daughter, who she'd thought was too young to understand the plot (which was expected to go over her head), was so amused and often burst into gales of laughter before the adults did.

A little more insight into her son's plight suddenly flashed into Sarah's mind as she recalled perfectly that that had been the first time, in all probability, that she had realised that adults could tell lies with impunity whilst telling children to be honest. She had felt very hurt that the real reason she had been taken to the theatre was not to give her 'a special treat because she'd been so good', but to suit their own convenience.

With a start, Sarah realised Jamie had stopped. She looked down: it was the middle of a sentence.

'Read on, Jamie, read on. That was absolutely super reading.'

'No, I can't, Mummy,' Jamie firmly replied. 'You said "two pages". I have got to the end of page two and that happens to be two pages that I have read to you. Now, you must tell me what the story was about.'

Sarah smiled. The lesson of this morning had certainly been learned: Jamie was falling over himself to be obedient, otherwise why stop when the sentence was not finished? Without a doubt, she would not bring the issues up with Matt. It would be totally wrong and possibly counter-productive. She again re-assured herself that her husband had quite enough worries at the moment. Why worry him unduly when she had, in all probability, taught their son a timely lesson in courtesy? And wasn't there the parents' evening they both had to attend that night, too? If she piled her concerns on to his shoulders, he would probably not thank her for it, especially if his meeting had not turned out in the way he wanted; he would probably end up in a foul mood and 'have a go' at the teachers unnecessarily. After all, she believed her son had done what a six-year-old would think was right and, just because he could read so well, she had falsely assumed he was worldly-wise beyond his age. One lesson she had learned from her child development course she reminded herself of again: emotional ages do not necessarily equate with high intelligence.

'Turn over the page, darling, and read to the end of the paragraph. See, it ends there.'

Jamie sighed. Parents are very odd, he thought, his bewilderment of the afternoon returning. Sometimes what they say is not at all what they mean. Double-thinkers. No, double-crossers, that's what they are, the light of clarification dawning in his mind. And parents are a very good example of those sorts of people, he determined. I wonder if they know that they muddle you up. Flashbacks of his day tumbled into his mind: cruel ladies who don't wipe their noses; mothers who tell you that you should wipe yours but don't allow you to give the same advice to others; assistants in shops whose bottoms are not in the right place and don't like you asking about them even though bottoms are supposed to be rude things you don't show to anyone; grown-ups who tell you how to get on a bus which, when you do as they say, gets you into trouble; mothers who tell you to do one thing and then expect you to do something else. Jamie sighed long and deeply.

He did what he was told, wondering at the same time how many years it would take before he had turned into a double-crosser himself.

Chapter Three

Matt arrived home looking pale and drawn. 'Keep your resolve', Sarah told herself, 'and don't bore him with your own trials and tribulations. Bring out your best line in sympathy'.

Yet like a gremlin dancing devilishly around her, the trying events of her day darted in front of her unwelcoming eyes, despite her determination that her irritations were inconsequential in comparison with those likely to have been experienced by the only breadwinner. The school run, chequered by the freak late-summer storm which had caused flash floods, inducing hysteria in Jamie that the necessary diversion would cause the loss of his attendance mark due to late arrival. Driving the car whilst endeavouring to stifle both the shrieks of said hysterical small boy and the sarcastic rebukes of his sister. Negotiating the bends and oncoming traffic through the resulting melee in which a multitude of vehicles aborted their normal routes and descended upon a single-track side-lane. The washing machine, now in its tenth year, choosing today to breathe its last. Her futile stupidity in alerting the Zanussi engineer to fix the problem, only to have to cough up money she had not got for the extortionate, and in the event unnecessary, call-out fee, only to be told, 'Nothing I can do, Ma'am, which would be cheaper for you than buying yourself a new model. Had its chips, this one has.' In her frustration, not noticing the gunge on the underside of the iron which imprinted itself indelibly upon Matt's best business shirt, needed for the Big Important Meeting early next week. Scalding her finger badly when she upturned the iron in her stark horror to investigate the cause of the problem. The cumulative effect of these mini-disasters causing her to be rebuked by the mechanic for delivering the Range Rover to Dexter's forty-five minutes beyond its scheduled appointment time. Dealing with Jamie's indiscretions in the library, on the bus, and when collecting the car from its M.O.T. Accordingly having to abandon preparation of her economical, slow-cooked casserole intended for the evening meal, instead frantically defrosting ingredients for their forthcoming anniversary dinner into a rapidly assembled fish pie. Not the day to serve up a lavish supper, bound not to be appreciated. The only good thing she could think of was that she was not a depressive, otherwise she would surely be on her way to a sanctuary for bipolar treatment.

Sarah could not extinguish these intrusive memories ... but do so, she must, in the interest of harmony, however artificial. Two bad days don't make a good, she reflected grimly. But her efforts at hauling herself out of her introspection neither relieved her mood nor stemmed the flow of her disgruntled feelings. Even well after the dawn of the second millennium, her husband had again reverted to the expectation that his housebound wife would be at his beck and call when he came home. Good grief, she mused, long gone are the days when smart sneakers (perhaps heeled shoes being the more acceptable footware) should be ready by the door, starry-eyed wife with make-up refreshed, sashaying to offer an unblemished cheek of welcome, clad in uncreased, gunk-free sweatshirt, crisp, curvaceous Levi's in fashionable indigo. In this credit crunch, when was the last time she had contemplated buying herself even a new tee? 'What's wrong with your other ones?' Matt would sniff now the Agency was experiencing hard times and the executives had had to accept a pay freeze, going ape if he smelt the whiff of a credit card. Under normal circumstances he would never notice if she was wearing Victoria Beckham or something from the church jumble sale – 'You are still the same "you" underneath, whatever you wear, darling,' he would say hastily when she petulantly pointed out he hadn't commented on her new designer dress or hairstyle.

As Sarah walked into the kitchen to finalise supper for Matt, her mind once again sped back to years past. She longed for a return of the earlier days when they were both establishing their careers. Matt would encourage her to refresh her wardrobe, delighting in the admiring glances she was attracting from friends and, especially, his colleagues. Whilst they enjoyed joint incomes, in their social world she was aware Matt regarded her, albeit somewhat out-datedly, as representative of his own status as a provider. Not that he took any pride or interest in clothes shopping with her. Sarah had learned very early on in their marriage that a maximum of fifteen minutes in any boutique was ten more than Matt could tolerate: he would examine the dresses, complain about preposterous prices, choose the skimpiest and announce for all the world to hear, 'What! Daylight robbery: 350 quid for this trash the size of a snot rag?' She would feel in her bones the situation would only get worse: a rapid departure was thus indicated.

Her wayward thoughts transported her back to Macy's, New York, after a delirious child-free Christmas. She had been examining some perfume when a supercilious Chanel saleswoman attempted to persuade Matt to buy his wife a New Year present. Adroitly avoiding the sprayed sample and told the price, he offered to buy six of the perfumes demonstrated, one for each of his poodles. If, in a crazy city like New York where anything goes, the saleslady was uncertain whether her leg was being pulled, her doubts were expelled when Matt added, 'And by the way, have you got any horse shampoo?' With her eyes to the ceiling and an expression on her face which said it all, Sarah grasped her husband's arm and yanked him smartly out of the store, saying firmly over her shoulder, 'And we haven't even got *one* dog.' Needless to say, behind the counter, three expensively perfumed, manicured and peroxided young assistants were beside themselves with laughter. 'Made someone's day there,' Matt had grinned as the sharp chill of the New York air hit them once again and they waltzed arm in arm up Fifth Avenue, downed a Manhattan cocktail in The Plaza before spending the afternoon in the Guggenheim. Even disgruntled Sarah, her greatly looked-forward-to shopping spree disappearing before her eyes, saw the funny side and the remainder of the day had passed in perfect communion.

That night as they had snuggled up together in their plush bedroom in the Royal Tower hotel, Matt whispered to his wife, 'You know I only sent up those up-your-arse salesgirls for your benefit,' before pulling her to him in a passionate embrace, the forerunner to what was to be an ecstatic and unrestrained demonstration of their love for each other. 'Our last night, darling, before the world of work reclaims us.' It was always a delicious moment when Matt almost apologised for past behaviour – for this was the nearest he ever came to acknowledging actions which were quite over the top. 'I'm sorry,' never passed his lips.

Sarah snapped out of her unhealthy reverie. 'Heavens knows I am becoming more and more self-centred these days.' She shuddered at the thought she might just be 'losing the plot'. No time for morbid self-pity. On the kitchen dining table she carefully placed her unintentional 'special meal': fish pie with crusty mashed potato topping, non-dairy cream sauce, with lashings of Flora (although she daren't tell Matt it had never seen the inside of a cow for fear of him calling her a food-faddist), haddock, tiger prawns, scallops and mushrooms. As Matt threw his jacket round the chair back, she could tell the day had not gone well for him because he omitted his usual practice of going straight into the playroom to spend 'quality time' with the children before having a quick shower and change of clothes from city suit into chinos and sports shirt.

Amy felt an overpowering wave of sympathy washing over her, her nihilist feelings now exorcised. As Matt slumped into the chair, she put her hands around his shoulders and wordlessly pulled his limp body towards her. How could she expect him to add a parents' evening to what must have been a frenzied day? No question; she would go alone.

They remained clasped together for some minutes before Matt broke the silence, weariness exuding from every word uttered.

'Darling, please don't ask me to go over how my day has gone. It's just been hell. All I can say is I still have a job. That's all I care about … and coming home to my family.'

Sarah couldn't help wishing Matt had mentioned her personally as his main desire but, yes, she supposed the family unit undoubtedly included her as a key element. She would postpone the reminder of the appointment at school, despite this being discussed this morning during breakfast when the expression of pride that his parents were to visit his classroom that evening had shone from Jamie's face. For Matt, 'first in, last out' was being replaced rapidly with 'first in, first out': younger, more inexperienced executives were less expensive to hire than more senior staff who commanded high salaries, pensions, remuneration packages and other benefits such as fat bonuses. Not only that, the younger employees had not got institutional memories to draw attention to and hark back to practices enjoyed 'in the old days'. Then long-serving staff enjoyed business lunches extending through to as late as four in the afternoon under the pretext of courting customers, were encouraged to attend lunchtime meetings of Rotary or Round Table for similar purposes, and no one checked expense accounts more than cursorily. These customs were best forgotten and wiped off the slate as, undoubtedly, this made more economic sense in the present climate and you couldn't really blame the directors who had to appease their shareholders.

Once again deep in her troubled thoughts, Sarah quietly eased herself away from Matt, still sitting with his elbows on the table, hands clasping his head, and moved towards the hob to switch the adjacent kettle on and the oven off. Thus she was unable to halt the tornado which was their son from bursting into the kitchen and leaping onto the back of his unsuspecting father.

'Daddy, Daddy, Daddy, this is such an exciting night: you are going to see my classroom and see my teacher. Oh, oh, oh; I'm so-o happy. She's Miss Griffin, you know. Conor says griffins are dragons but we haven't seen any fire coming out of her mouth yet. Perhaps you will as you are all grown-ups and can share secrets.'

Matt flinched as his son threw himself on top of his sagging body, bounced up and down and continued: 'She says she's going to talk to you and tell you all about me. Please, please tell her about my dinosaur collection – she says she doesn't like me keeping on about them but I think she'd listen to you.'

'Sit up, Daddy,' he urged, noting his father's silence and hunched position, 'You've got to get ready. Or are you going in your suit? All the daddies will look smart tonight, though Alfie's daddy might not and Freddie's daddy digs graves, I think, so it will be ever so funny if he goes in his work clothes, too.' Visions of a man with mud, flower petals and gravel clinging to his cycle-clip clad trouser legs started him off in a fit of the giggles.

Matt made no movement as his son calmed down and continued,

'I don't think you will be able to sit in my chair, though.' Jamie's bright face clouded over. He looked doubtful and somewhat perplexed, his voice faltering as he added, 'And the room won't be big enough for everyone's parents 'cos there will be twice as many people as there are children in our class. You will have to sit on the Ducks' table with Alfie's and Conor's parents; there won't be room for anyone else 'cos Conor's mummy is a bit fat,' adding wistfully, 'Domino's will sit on the Swans.'

'Daddy, Daddy, are you listening to me? And Miss Griffin won't be pleased if you sit like that in the chair she's put for parents to sit in. She gets cross if we do what she calls slouching.'

With that, Jamie tugged at the sleeves of Matt's shirt in an endeavour to pull him from his chair and returned to his earlier theme. 'Daddy, come with me and choose some dinosaurs to show her. I bet she'll like my bestest pterodactyl 'cos she helps us to feed birds outside our window, you know. My pterodactyl is probably a million times bigger than those titchy ones we get on our table. Blue tits, they are.'

Jamie sniggered as he added, 'Conor likes just calling them "tits", but Miss Griffin gets cross with him when he calls out to us to look at them tits out there. Yesterday she said he must call them by their proper name, great tits, 'cos they were bigger than the ones we normally get. I don't know why she got even crosser when he did what she said and told us to look at them great tits and pointed at her boobies. She made him lose his playtime, which wasn't fair 'cos its true what he said.'

Sarah deftly steered an unwilling Jamie out of the kitchen, surprised that in his excitement Jamie had not noted his father's unusual posture as indicative of distress. How could he be so self-centred? Needing to get back to Matt as quickly as she could, she exhorted him not to bring out any more of his collection as it was almost time for bed, and not to come back into the kitchen as Daddy was very, very tired. To her retreating back, Jamie murmured anxiously that it would not be the same for him if his daddy did not come to the playroom as he usually did. It was going to be really nice tonight, without Freya. Daddy sometimes spends more time doing things with her and he tells me to keep out of the way when I want him to do things with me instead.'

Again Sarah was alerted to the fact Freya was spending more and more time away from home these days. Freya was conspicuous by her absence more and more frequently, to the extent that it was becoming obvious that home held little attraction for her. She made a resolution to find a way of determining whether there was an ulterior motive of some description or Freya was just exemplifying a new phase of development.

Back in the kitchen Matt was attempting to recover his composure. With supreme weariness in his voice, he confessed to Sarah that attending a parents' evening was the last thing he felt capable of doing. 'Look, Sarah, I really am shattered tonight and, seriously, think I would be a liability to you and Jamie if I went with you. Could you possibly hold the fort on your own? I know it's an awful lot to ask of you …' his voice trailing off as Sarah moved to put a hand on his shoulder.

'Darling, don't think twice about it,' Sarah responded, squeezing his arm in a surge of compassion. 'We know Jamie is making fantastic progress and the only issue I want to mention to his teacher is why it is that he doesn't seem to be able to keep any friends. It's beginning to worry me.'

Matt raised himself in his seat, momentarily reassured by his wife's sympathetic tone; his own exuded a paralysing lethargy beyond his control. 'Well I certainly don't need to be flattered by the praises from some old battle-axe and I'm sure you'd be better at the friendship bit. I met her once when I took Jamie to school that time you had a dose of shingles and she reminded me of a teacher I had in my prep school. It looked as if a smile would have cracked her face.

It was as much as she could do to say she hoped you'd soon be better.'

Sarah gave a wan smile. 'A sense of humour is, I think, certainly lacking in Miss Griffin. I guess she was jilted at some stage in her life and has never got over it.'

'Just tell her from me that Jamie can tie me in knots with the speed of his number crunching and that seems pretty good for a child who must be one of the youngest in his class. That should puff her ego up a bit.'

Biting back her disappointment that she was not going to be shielded from a potentially difficult interview with the woman who was so put out to lose her coveted deputy headship to such a young competitor those years ago required supreme effort. On the occasions she had come across Miss Griffin at local schools' sports activities or county in-service meetings in the first year after her appointment, this teacher had studiously avoided her, to the point that it was abundantly clear she was being cold-shouldered. Would this be a golden opportunity for her to exercise her superiority over her as the teacher of the son of the woman who had obtained the post she had coveted? Resisting powerful feelings of simmering dismay that domestic matters were nowadays firmly and squarely loaded onto her shoulders, Sarah continued with her outward support of Matt's decision. Matt returned the pressure of his wife's hand as he confirmed his need of a restful evening.

'You're a breath of fresh air, Sarah. I've brought home a report to finish and I promised myself I'd watch the England/ New Zealand match tonight first. Christ, I need to wipe today out of my memory and a win over the All Blacks would help to erase that.'

Nonetheless, Matt felt a seething resentment welling up inside him. He reflected back on his own schooldays and, however hard he tried not to vocalise such thoughts, could not stop himself from adding, 'I honestly can't remember my father trotting up to open nights, Sarah, or whatever they're called nowadays, for God's sake. Why can't we leave teachers to do the teaching without parents breathing down their necks? That's what they're paid for, isn't it? You ought to know.'

As the familiar mantra so often rolling off the lips of her father-in-law was repeated by his son, Sarah bit her lip. She again put her hand on Matt's arm, only for Matt to pull his arm from under her hand. Silent tears welled up in Sarah's eyes as she moved to serve the dinner which would surely spark some memories for him. Although on this occasion hastily thrown into a pie, seafood was always the basis of special celebrations for them; they had their first date in a Devonian fish restaurant whilst watching the tide swamp the sandcastles they'd made earlier, each vying with the other to demonstrate their sculpting skills. Holiday romances never last, her friends had warned her, but Sarah had proved them wrong. Matt pushed the plate away across the table, with hardly a glance. How mercurial were his moods these days: a switch from a loving intimacy could change in minutes to the growling of a smouldering lion.

A long drawn out sigh from Matt.

'You certainly know how to turn the tap on, Sarah.' He only used her Christian name and not an endearment when he was pre-occupied with inner worries. 'Being an advertising manager isn't like teaching, you know: easy hours, long lunchbreak, coffee time gossiping in the staff room, home by four thirty, ridiculous holidays and talking to kids who have to listen to every word you say. You don't know what it is like to work in the real world … and now you are at home all day filing your nails to keep you busy.'

Sarah predicted the litany now about to pour from the mouth of her husband and not that of his father. Was she really, really hearing the same dyed-in-the-wool opinions coming from Matt's lips? Each time they had had to listen to Desmond's entrenched views, even outdated when Matt's parents had begun their married life, they would exchange knowing glances at their outrageous nature. It sounded even more poisonous coming from Matt, she thought, pressing back the tears which threatened to engulf her. These seemed to come so easily when Matt reverted to autopilot. No point in stoking the fire; she mustn't retaliate. Nonetheless, even remaining silent could wind Matt up into an apoplectic tirade when he felt the world was against him. Fight or flight: Matt was a past master of the former and with the desperate need to keep up with the mortgage repayments, the times when he would quickly realise the unfairness of such bitter and uncalled for remarks and snap out of it with his style of loving apology, sweeping her into his arms, showering her with kisses, were long gone. Then evenings would be delectably sweet: the tenderness of his caresses would assuage his remorse for taking out bilious feelings on his wife and the rug by the fireside would be testimony to the love he felt for 'his beautiful bride' as they sought solace in each other. Oh, what sublime memories that rug held for her. Now it was all too apparent that in his desperation to maintain a sense of masculinity, he was reverting to the stereotypical male of a long-gone era. Doing her best, nevertheless, to ensure Matt did not notice the effect his brusque manner was having on her, Sarah, fighting back the tears welling up, reflected to herself that the recent honeymoon period was in its dying days. That day Sarah had learned yet a little more concerning her husband's short fuse.

Without a word, Sarah controlled herself and quietly slipped into the playroom, mustering up an outward show of masterly command of a steadily deteriorating situation by informing Jamie sharply that he had better clear his dinosaur collection away and get himself ready for bed. He had played assiduously with his models since they'd had tea together, Freya being at the home of a friend.

SHEILA SHAW

'No, you can't have another five minutes more tonight.
I have to see your teacher and I want to tuck you up before I
go. Daddy has some work to do so won't be coming with me.
He'll switch your light out.'

A puzzled look crossed Jamie's face.

'Mummy, it's *parents* night; that means two people. Daddy
has got to go if it says two. Will Mr. Holmes tell you off if
Daddy doesn't go? He might write to you again.'

Jamie remembered the horror he felt on the occasion his
father was angry when a letter from Mr. Holmes had said that
they would be prosecuted if they went on holiday in term time
again and a shiver ran down his spine. He hadn't known what
'prossicuted' meant but didn't think his parents would like that
to happen because Daddy had got in the car straight away and
went to give Mr. Holmes a bit of his mind which made him,
Jamie, sob and sob and sob until he couldn't cry anymore.
When his mummy had asked him what on earth was the matter
and he had to gasp for breath so he was able to hear her, he had
told her it was really horrible that his daddy would not be able
to think with only a bit of his brain left and he wouldn't ever,
ever, ever go near Mr. Holmes again if he did anything nasty
to Daddy. Mummy then said 'minds' were not quite the same
as 'brains' and 'give him a piece of my mind' was just a way of
speaking when you were going to say exactly what you thought
to someone. Jamie, who had pondered over this a little, didn't
think that would be a white lie as it seemed like the truth but
it was hard to tell when funny words were used. How difficult
it was to understand what grown-ups meant: they spoke in
riddles, Conor told him but he could never find the riddle bit in
what they said. Theirs were not like the riddles he knew, like his
funniest one which he liked but Grandma Eleanor didn't: what
is the difference between an elephant and a post-box, where if
they say they don't know, you say, 'Huh. No use sending you to
post a letter then.' Grandma always said that each time he told

52

it he should use a different animal and then it wouldn't be quite as boring as hearing it exactly the same. Obviously she didn't understand. Thank goodness, he concluded, children didn't seem to say things which meant something different from what you thought they meant (though Alfie was quite good at that, he reflected, still smarting from the punch he had received).

Swallowing hard and at the same time taking a sneaky look at his mother's hand, he began to place each dinosaur figure very carefully into his very special wooden box, once containing a collection of Daddy's "shatto" wine. This action reminded him what his mummy had said about Daddy when he opened the case one Christmas: she said his eyes had popped out of his head. That had made him scream in horror but Freya had squeezed her mouth up 'as she sometimes does when she looks at me,' and explained that was a saying people said if someone was amazed. It had seemed an unnecessarily frightening way to show you know someone is excited about something and he had wished fervently that adults didn't tell lies about things when children weren't allowed to. Daddy had been given it by a client, whatever that was, as he didn't think he worked in the sort of place where clients went. Alfie mysteriously said a little while ago that his daddy went to a place where clients go to and he had had to wait outside in the car with a packet of crisps for quite a long time once for him to come out. His daddy said he'd murder him if he told his mummy. At the time, Jamie had wondered whether he ought to tell that policeman who came to the school to watch children in Year 6 ride their bikes that his friend might be killed by his father but he hadn't got any evidence as proof so decided he'd better be, what was it, more 'discreet', and 'bide his time', whatever that was. It was a dilemma, he felt, because if the murder happened, would he be in danger of being put in prison for not reporting his friend's life was in danger? If he did so, anyway, he'd be called a tell-tale-tit and that wasn't a nice thing for people to think about him. The shatto box was not as special to Daddy as the syrupy looking stuff in the bottles it had contained and he understood why because the dinosaurs were more precious to him than the box, too, although he would never let anyone take it away from him as it was now the home of his pets. Still, he didn't know why Daddy liked that drink-stuff so much; it wasn't as nice as the Robinson's he drank. He knew how horrible it was 'cos he had tasted it one day when he found it behind a sitting room curtain in the morning after his parents had had a dinner party and he had to run to the cloakroom to spit it out fast. He had to tell his mummy what he had done, because he wasn't like adults who seemed to be allowed to tell lies, and when she told Daddy, he had had one of his fits and said he wasn't going to give that – and he had used a very bad word then – any "shatto-mutton" ever again. Not that he had ever heard the word Daddy used instead of his friend's name, but he knew it must be very bad because Mummy told him never to use that word again in front of us and keep it for his rugger friends. That was a funny thing to say, unless they all say rude words to each other when the match is on instead of watching it.

With gathering irritation in her voice (hadn't she had enough of today, already? Why did he have to be so precise and particular about putting his toys away when he knew she was in a hurry to go out?), Sarah hustled up the last few figurines, bundled them up into the plywood box and stuffed it into the toy cupboard. So much for Château Mouton Rothschild, she reflected grimly, memories flooding into her mind of balmy summer days drifting through Rheims, arms round each other, on the holiday in which they were celebrating their fifth wedding anniversary and just six weeks before they had the confirmation of her pregnancy with their beloved first-born, Freya. What fun they had had debating names over their first ever tasting of such a perfect aperitif before deciding Sarah would make the choice if a girl, Matt if a boy. Oh, how they had laughed when they realised they were breaking their own vow to avoid stereotyping at all costs. They conceded to tradition on this one and promised to accept each other's choice. 'Unless it is ridiculous, like the name of a town or a fantasy name from *The Lord of the Rings* or some sci-fi thing,' it was agreed wholeheartedly. 'So I can't have Sidmouth (Sid for short), even though we met there,' Matt had said mischievously. 'And I promise I won't call a girl Vodka, even though I remember consuming rather a lot that week,' had been Sarah's swift response.

Sarah ignored the agitation in her son's voice as he accused her of messing up and upsetting the order the dinosaurs should be replaced in their 'home'.

'They have GOT to be in their right places, they've G-O-T to.' Jamie ran to the cupboard like a demon possessed, screaming over his shoulder, 'The pterodactyl goes at the top because it's a BIRD, the diplodocus goes underneath and the Tyrannosaurus rex stands where the wood-shavings are at the bottom 'cos that's GRASS and his neck is so long he can reach the TREES up there. You have got to put them in properly, you do, you DO, YOU DO-O-O!'

'I've had enough of this, my boy. We are not going into tantrum mode now. Get up to bed straight away. I am very cross indeed. Clean your teeth, wash behind your neck as well as your face, get undressed, jim-jams on and get into bed immediately. I am starting to count *now*: one, two, three … four …'

Sarah slowed a bit as she saw Jamie was getting flustered and withdrew to the kitchen (my rightful place she thought through clenched teeth). Keep calm, hold your nerve, you're the only one keeping this family together at the moment and a full-blown meltdown needs to be avoided at all costs.

Calming down from the tragedy of the past five minutes when he had witnessed his mother committing sacrilege, and now totally confused as to how he could carry out all those actions simultaneously, Jamie was only too well aware that Mummy was going to be very nasty indeed if he didn't at least try to get them all done at the same time. He would try his best. A brilliant idea crystallised in his mind: dip the toothbrush in water, put soap on it at one end and toothpaste on the brush part, run into the bedroom, get under the duvet, gently scrub his face with the toothbrush handle, making sure the bristles didn't prickle him, brush his teeth, stick the toothbrush under the pillow, dry his face on the sheet – he could do that if he untucked it from under the pillow a little bit – then get properly undressed in bed. Smarting from the taste of soap (he had used the wrong end of the toothbrush at first), he thought that was the least of his worries and with the feeling of 'mission accomplished', he relaxed. Whoops, jim-jams; nearly forgot to stuff them under the sheets. One more thing then to do, he thought, sliding out of the bed. Pulling a book from its shelf, he opened a drawer to take a longish, round black object from inside, then streaked back to the comfort of his duvet.

Meanwhile, Freya had arrived home. 'What's up with Daddy; he hardly looked at me when I went to give him a kiss. He's just leaning on the mantelpiece. You and Dad had a row? I'll help you clear up the kitchen – or would you rather I made you both a cup of tea?'

Sarah accepted her daughter's offer gratefully; she was always so intuitive, and had been even at the age Jamie was now. Sometimes she felt Jamie would crash into a conversation even if there was a dead body on the floor – and ask if anyone would come and play with his dinosaurs. She mechanically put the dishes in the dishwasher, then tidied away the saucepans previously washed whilst endeavouring to conjure up as much interest as she could to contribute sensibly to Freya's account of her evening. To no avail: she heard Freya harumph, with a note of resignation in her voice, that her mother wasn't really listening so in that case she would go upstairs to finish her homework. With a surging feeling that she could be fighting a losing battle with sanity, and not noticing the unexpectedly rude tone of her daughter, Sarah dully took herself upstairs, applied make-up afresh, changed into more suitable clothes and returned to attempt to make her peace with Matt.

'Enjoy the match. I shall be as quick as I can, Matt. I'll take your car; mine hasn't got much petrol in it and I need to see my mother tomorrow: she says she thinks she's got 'flu coming on.'

'Bloody hell. Don't let the old bat give you her bugs to pass on to me; I'm in an important meeting with the Board next week, as you know, and that would be just the time the germs need to incubate. And if you run my car out of petrol,' (why did his wife not keep her tank full; she had all day to think about it), 'I won't be happy. If you go to the pub with the others like we usually do afterwards, have a beer, not a G. and T.; we can't afford to keep up with the Joneses anymore, and don't have Britvic, that's daylight robbery. Have some barley water here instead when you come back.'

Gritting her teeth, Sarah ignored her husband's caustic remarks, doing her utmost to ensure Matt did not notice the effect his brusque manner was having on her. What was the point in being drawn into a slanging match; it would only serve to give Matt more to fester over. Better to allow him time to be more appreciative of her magnanimity by so readily letting him bow out of the school appointment. She hoped fervently that he would not feel as disinclined next week when it was the Class 5 parents' evening, so important as this is the precursor to the 11 plus exams the following September and they both needed to be assured of Freya's position on the head's list of pupils expected to gain a selective school place in 2011.

First, with artificial chirpiness belying the heaviness of

her heart, she walked down the hallway and up the stairs into Freya's room, kissed the bowed back of her neck, and spent a minute casting her trained eye over the homework she was completing. She promised to read her creative writing when she came home from seeing Jamie's teacher. 'Thanks, Mum. It's an imaginary story about life in England if Hitler had won the war in 1945. Wouldn't that be dreadful?' Momentarily buoyed up, Sarah vowed she would not go under; she was made of far stronger material and would find her way through. There was too much to fight for.

The doorbell rang. Oh God: Hannah! Racing downstairs, she grabbed her handbag, hastily removing £10 and thrust the note into the surprised girl's hand as she opened the door, hurriedly explaining why, after all, she would not be needing a babysitter that evening. 'No, please do take it: you will have put yourself out to spend time here and it is our fault we are cancelling at the last moment.' Just in case Mrs. Chilton changed her mind, the cash quickly disappeared into Hannah's pocket: as an impecunious student, it was great to receive remuneration without doing any work for it.

The final thing she had to do before leaving was to tuck Jamie up and explain to him that his daddy would not be coming up to say goodnight to him that night after all. Already running late for her appointment, she made the prediction that it would be just her luck to find all the parking places in the playground already filled and would have to park on the street miles away. Entering his room, with some alarm she noted merely the curve of his body under the clothes. She placed her hand on top of the head she could make out under the duvet, panicking ever so slightly that he would be unable to breathe. Perhaps he had already stopped. Had she been too harsh with him? She felt the constriction in her throat as she endeavoured to pull back the cover. There was some resistance before the top of Jamie's head appeared, his hands clutching the sheets around him, and a pair of eyes was visible.

'Darling,' Sarah said with mounting relief overcoming her anxiety, 'you should never cover yourself up like that; you could suffocate.'

In an instant, Jamie pulled himself up, at first clinging to the duvet still covering his chest whilst holding the long black torch for all his might, endeavouring to keep it hidden. Strangely, he grabbed Sarah's hand and looked intently at it.

'Mummy, why do you spend all day filing your nails? It doesn't do very much good; they are still long.'

Chapter Four

Mutinously reflecting that this would have been the car they would have driven had they gone together, Sarah put Matt's car into gear and reversing carefully out of the garage, she turned sharply to avoid scraping the wing mirror of her Range Rover (more like a refuse cart, Matt often grunted through tight lips on the rare occasions he was able now to ferry the children to the recreation ground). The Advertising Agency was demanding more of his weekend time as they sought accounts further afield and he daren't refuse the assignments. He would use Sarah's vehicle to maintain his company-owned Mercedes in pristine condition when it was going to be muddy underfoot and the children likely to skid, their wellies infuriatingly transferring the worst part of a putrid cow pat, or worse, onto the backseat carpet. Sarah was well aware of the profound stress he was under and, accordingly, did her best to suppress any feelings of disappointment that he was reneging on their earlier promises to each other, made with such conviction, that theirs was going to be an 'equal partnership' marriage. She tried to push the thought out of her mind that Matt could also be losing his cool at the Agency in the same manner as he was so short-tempered at home. If that was the case, there was little hope that he would hold down his position in the firm: his was such a cutthroat business. Hadn't she read that not only the Research and Development departments, but also Advertising, were amongst the first to pare down their executives?

The idea of taking up part-time teaching to help out their

budgetary problems floated into her mind; there was always supply work available in their area and she was sufficiently experienced to walk into any classroom and seamlessly take over where another teacher had left off. The alternative of setting up a coaching service for the selection tests was out of the question, however lucrative. Although there was an abundance of parents determined to move heaven and earth to obtain a grammar school place for their child, such intensive tuition was morally and professionally anathema to her: many who were taught, like Pavlov's dogs, to jump through hoops entered, starry-eyed through the portals, to find themselves completely out of their depths, to the detriment of their emotional development as well as their progress. Instead of succumbing to such traitorous ideas, Sarah sharpened her resolution that their solemn agreement would be honoured: she would resume her career only when their second child was settled comfortably in the junior phase. They had made this decision together shortly before Jamie was born. Having started their family after securely establishing their careers, they were firmly of the opinion that one child of each sex was sufficient and the seal of agreement had been put on this when Matt underwent a vasectomy. With Claudia and Philip babysitting Freya, the amazing gastronomic evening they treated themselves to in order to celebrate her subsequent freedom from 'the pill', (and the anxieties of occasional blips which had frightened them both after Jamie's birth) was brought back to her mind with astonishing clarity. Would they ever afford to pay a return visit to Le Manoir, Sarah mused wryly?

Chastising herself for parking her own car at such an awkward angle in the drive, she excused her stupidity by recalling that she had left it in that spot because of the ease of taking the shopping straight through the garage into the kitchen, fully intending to move it later before Matt came home. He liked to have a smart getaway in the early mornings and was never very pleased when she 'stole' his place. Like those of most families these days, the garage was full of garden machinery, handyman tools, paint pots and ladders and there was no question of using it for vehicles other than the sit-on lawn mower. A shed was not high on their list of priorities.

Compounding the deleterious effects of her time-consuming and complicated manoeuvring, next door's tomcat shot out from the somnambulant position he had been keeping in the shade of Matt's car, hissing in terror, and disappearing Sarah knew not where. Sarah was only conscious of a ball of fur launching itself into the blindspot of the Mercedes. Quite apart from not wishing to assassinate the animal (although many had been the time she had made dire threats against its continued existence on occasions when its plumbing habits had offended her delicate nostrils, or her newly sown seeds had been scattered to the four winds as a result of the creature's unwelcomed calls of nature), she had even less of a desire to incur the wrath of her particularly tetchy neighbour. Leaping out of the vehicle to check its whereabouts, she just sighted it disappearing to safety beneath the ground-sweeping branches of the spruce tree. Lecturing herself to calm down and keep cool, Sarah settled herself back into the driver's seat, jerking it forward so that her feet could reach the pedals more comfortably, and eased her way into what she fully expected at this time of day to be a clear road.

Not to be. Yet again, and despite her best intentions, Sarah felt panic arising in her: the rush-hour traffic had no need to use their narrow country lane as a rat-run and, in any case, should have cleared half an hour or so ago. This would be the night that the notorious M40 had jammed up once more, causing the snarl-up so near to home. Ten minutes to go before her appointment with Miss Griffin was due: no chance of meeting this deadline as, even without traffic chaos, the school was twenty minutes away and she was bound to have difficulty parking unless some early leavers vacated a space. What a hellish start to an evening: inexplicable tantrums, short-tempered husbands, fearsome cats, all behind her, now the likelihood of grid-locked roads.

Despite confidently expecting praise in respect of Jamie's remarkable abilities, the prospect of this personal face-to-face meeting with an erstwhile rival, renowned amongst the chatterers at the gate to have a sarcastic tongue, was not pleasant in her present frame of mind. Sarah had confidently expected to have the buffer of Matt's presence to maintain the status of the meeting as what it was intended to be: feedback of children's progress. Huh, would that now be the only item on the agenda? Recalling the valuable insight she had gained on that day course she had attended before taking up her deputy headship, she vowed to maintain the mindset recommended when dealing with very difficult people. Yes, she would force herself to be up to the occasion. Sarah told herself to be careful to interpret any subtle early warning signs of a coming confrontation and keep her composure, whatever was thrown in her direction. She would brush off any criticism levelled at her like water off a duck's back.

As she cursed the tailback she found herself in and with nothing better to keep her mind off the slow journey, she thought back to the time she had had the misfortune to become acquainted with the dragon she had tried thereafter to avoid in her previous professional life: the years between Freya's birth and Jamie's. Memories flooded back of sitting beside Miss Griffin on those awful, straight-backed chairs gracing the waiting room of the divisional education officer's room alongside five other short-listed candidates some eight years ago. How superior the older woman had looked as she'd exchanged knowing glances with the four men assembled, each of whom portrayed an impression of scarcely concealed amusement that the youngish-looking interloper in their midst had the effrontery to be seated alongside them. Their forced conversation of the past quarter of an hour or so had betrayed the false nature of their interest in her teaching career to date. 'Most impressive,' one receding-haired candidate for the deputy headship had said in response to Sarah's forced confession that she had held the position of senior teacher for just two years. 'And obviously, you had held a key post before that?' Sensing the undisguised disdain in this rhetorical question, the simultaneously sucked in cheeks and lowered eyes directed at the length of her skirt, she had replied tartly, 'I was finishing maternity leave prior to that appointment.' The irony was not lost on her that ageism and sexism were still rife within the middle-aged generation, even at the turn of the millennium. No problem: she could cope with that. If anything, the chauvinistic attitude of the assembled candidates fired her up to a determination that she would present her views on education in as child-centred a manner as within her power. If the interviewing panel wanted staid managers in their schools, it would appear they had a good choice in these they had called up today. Now, she had chided herself, don't become as bigoted as these people are.

At this point the man in the next seat, sensing the need to move the subject on, had taken out his *Guardian* from his brief-case, settled back into his chair and accompanied his opening swish of the paper with a contribution to conclude the unwelcomed inquest on Sarah's career to date:

'At least another quarter of an hour to wait before any decision is made. I was called up two weeks ago and it took them forty minutes to make up their minds. Even if it's a foregone conclusion, they like to make us all wait, the bastards.' He had then cast a glance at Sarah with the kind of expression which meant that if she wished to apply for a post which should be held by a man, she did not deserve an apology for bad language.

Mr. Brantwich, the owner of the broadsheet, had looked round the group with a smug expression stealing across his face which he'd made no attempt to hide. Equally, he made no effort to disguise the reason which followed.

'Beats me why they've put me on the shortlist again so soon. Costs money to pay for a relief teacher every time.'

He had then covered his smirking face in his newspaper, the front page of which Sarah noted was now upside down. By then, Sarah's reminiscences had become so vivid, she was actually reliving them. In her mind, the drama unfolded:

The door of the D.E.O.'s* office opened. His secretary, glasses on the end of her nose in order to peer over the top at the expectant faces, scanned the group. Receding-hair sat up sharply, Mr. Brantwich made as if to stand up, the 'other token female' candidate returned the gaze and the remainder looked decidedly anxious. Sarah hoped she was reflecting an air of indifference.

'Mr. Richards would like Mrs. Chilton to return to the Panel, please. Mrs. Chilton, come this way.'

Sarah, in her first experience of an interview for such a senior position, felt her knees collapsing beneath her. What had she said that they had doubted? Had she made a complete fool of herself? Was her present post now in jeopardy? She knew not to this day how her legs bore her through that green beige door (beige to mask confidential conversation), didn't hear the sound of chairs scraping behind her or the harsh noise of five pairs of feet stomping down the stairs. Through the open door she only noticed the leers on the faces of the interrogators as they waited to clamp their jaws on her. She walked uncertainly to the proffered chair she had vacated only an hour before. The divisional officer rose and, to her consternation, held out a claw. The Panel stood, then sat, seemingly in one movement.

---

*   D.E.O. = Divisional Education Officer

'Mrs. Chilton,' Sarah almost closed her eyes in anticipation of the character assassination she was about to undergo. Could she withstand the onslaught about to descend upon her ears?

'Mrs. Chilton, the Panel are unanimous in their decision,' (Sarah's heart could not sink any further) 'and would very much like you to accept the deputy headship of Greybrook Combined School.' In her mind, his voice echoed and echoed as if in a cavern, stalactites glistening from the roof to scalp her, stalagmites to trip her up. It seemed as if hours had elapsed before the D.E.O.'s firm voice registered on her consciousness.

'Mrs. Chilton, do we have your acceptance?'

Sarah's mind was in a turmoil. Was this a dream? Should she pinch herself? Slowly (it seemed to her an eternity), she reinterpreted the leers as welcoming smiles of encouragement, the extended claw as a hand of friendship. The true significance of the situation began to dawn on her. From what seemed countless miles away, she heard a voice remarkably like hers thanking the Panel for their consideration of her candidature, the honour they were bestowing on her and the fervent hope she held that she would never give them occasion to regret their decision. The distant voice ended by confirming her very great pleasure in being offered such a prestigious appointment, a position she would be immensely pleased to accept.

'We are, ourselves, indeed delighted and urge you to aim towards making a substantial contribution to the head's target of making Greybrook Combined the flagship primary of the county. You came across to each of us as a most dedicated teacher, confirming for us the highly complimentary references we received on your behalf. One of our Panel members is chairman of governors of Greybrook and was a strong advocate of your appointment during our post-interview deliberations. I must add myself that Birch Hall's loss is most certainly our gain.

'Now, Mrs. Chilton, whilst our Panel go their separate ways, I have some forms for you to sign.'

Grimly forcing herself back to reality and briskly discarding reminiscences flooding into her mind of the intervening years since that fateful interview, Sarah's attention returned to the present with a jolt, the horn of the car queuing behind her jerking her into action to close the twenty-yard gap between her and the car in front in the slow-moving column. Some five tortuous minutes later, she left the dual carriageway, ignoring the speed limit on the assumption that all self-respecting citizens would be indoors watching their nightly fix of *EastEnders* and unlikely to make a mad dash for freedom across this residential road. Finally coming to a screeching halt some hundred yards from the school gates, Sarah gathered her breath as she almost fell from the car, one of her heels catching on the rubber mat in her haste. Remembering to lock it, she sprinted across the playground as fast as her M&S shoes would allow before adopting a sedate manner she somehow did not feel. Glancing at her watch, her heart sank as she realised she was now some twenty minutes after the scheduled time for her parental interview. (Shouldn't it be teacher interview, with parents grilling the teacher as in his day, Matt had enquired earlier, his voice heavy with sarcasm.) In through the front door she strode, past the displays of clay, collage and artwork which, had she noticed, would not have disgraced a secondary school. Now to manage the face-to-face meeting with the candidate from whom she had unwittingly usurped the plum post this teacher had coveted so dearly. She did not relish the thought without Matt at her side to ward off any insinuations that might relate to the shortness of her tenure as a deputy head of the school to which Miss Griffin had aspired. Sarah joined the remaining parents of Year 2 children, to be addressed by a cheerful couple in the desultory queue in front of the teacher's desk.

'Miss Griffin is running to time tonight – actually a little ahead, we believe, as there has been a "no show" of the 8.10 appointment. You must be her last, at 8.50?'

'I am the 8.10 "no show". Partner late home from work,' Sarah lied through gritted teeth.

'Oh,' came the disappointed reply. 'You had better go in front of us, then. We are the 8.40 slot. Isn't your hubby coming then?'

Sarah could not help her irritation of this impertinent and intrusive remark showing on her scandalised face and was about to enquire what gave her the certainty to imply she was a married woman when her husband hastily interjected,

'Lucky man! I wouldn't miss it for the world, though. Very important, I always think, to keep in touch with the little lass's progress.'

The heavily sugared voice of Miss Griffin, emphasising assumed empathy, now cut across the room:

'Mrs. Chilton, I am so pleased you have been able to come to our parents' evening. However, as the 8.10 "no show", you will not mind, I'm sure, waiting until I've seen all the other mums and dads, all of whom have been able to come to time, and I would not like to keep them waiting any further. Do feel free to leave if you are in a hurry to go. We can always make another appointment.'

Sarah wished she didn't feel riled by this intended sarcasm, delivered with a forced, fixed smile, but in fact she felt sick to the bottom of her stomach. She knew that, had Matt been there, he would have walked out after such a carelessly camouflaged welcome. Sarah became painfully aware that she must be sure not to rise to any bait which might be dangled in front of her, however thinly disguised. Attempting to appear nonchalant and certainly not affronted, she nodded assent and wandered across to the poetry display. Her practised eye detected the unashamed doctoring up of children's efforts, so obviously to her a re-distribution of teacher-generated phrases written up on the whiteboard for children to select and portray as their original work. Skimming the six-to-seven-year-olds' scripts in the display headed, 'Year 2: Original Creative Writing', Sarah felt silently scandalised at how easy it was to pull the wool over the eyes of gullible parents who lacked the knowledge she possessed in relation to window dressing a classroom for such occasions.

Her eyes alighted on one, scruffier by far than the other items of perfection:

> *The sun is big.*
> *The sun is yell-ow.*
> *The sun is ver-y hot.*
> *I like the sun on me.*

Even more unbelievable to Sarah, this was captioned 'You are trying hard, Jamie. Keep it up.' By its side was displayed,

> *I am big.*
> *The sun is in the sk-y.*
> *The sky is bl-ue.*

Next to a scribbled 'Alfie' in wobbly script was attached a silver star.

What, for Christ's sake, was going on? She knew that Jamie was unhappy at school, a cause she could only put down to a teacher who was possibly finding it difficult to accept a child whose innate intelligence, despite the age-gap, was probably much higher than her own. Even as a young teacher, Sarah herself had experienced the undisguised jealousy of colleagues who had resented the fact that she spent time ensuring her classroom was a pleasurable and stimulating place to be in by maintaining a constantly changing wall display of pictures relevant to the topics being studied. One uninspiring teacher in the first school to which she had been appointed was particularly spiteful in his remarks: 'It is OK for you: you don't have children of your own and can spend time in the evening preparing for lessons,' adding venomously, 'and have ready cash to buy materials.' The school was close to a trading estate which enabled her to call at printing and fabric factories to ask for waste card and furnishing remnants which would otherwise be dumped. Sarah could feel the opprobrium now as she recollected her own experiences of the early days following her entry to the profession as a probationer. Would this feeling of 'not quite fitting in' ever go away? Now, clearly, she had produced a child who was floundering in his search to fit in with the norm. Was there a genetic component to Jamie's character which made others shy away from him?

Again a raw nerve was tapped. Memories of her final school practice in her training days flooded back. Her appointed supervisor at the school on a sink-estate was the head of the college P.E. department who expected free-choice activities. Paralysed with fright when she found the all-boys eleven-year-old class to which she had been allotted had been managed by an ex sergeant major who had taught 'Physical Training' in a regimented style, Sarah had felt in her bones that a similarly rigid P.E lesson would not receive even a pass mark, let alone the overall distinction she was striving for. Her preparation earlier that morning for the lesson to be examined was to place baskets of small apparatus in each corner of the playground. As the rowdy boys assembled noisily in a mad scramble to beat each other down the corridor, ready for a lesson which had not required them to march in military style to 'P.T.', Sarah had felt all semblance of her even shaky control withering away from her. Not surprisingly, when invited to select a basket, take an item and 'explore what could be done with your chosen equipment', the resulting chaos was unbelievable. Sarah still shuddered as she recalled balls landing on the roof, skipping ropes being used to strangle one another, bean bags hurled over the wall into the street, with just one lonely boy attempting to hula-hoop properly. Despite the supervisor's clear awareness of the invidious situation Sarah had been placed in, the debacle had done nothing towards the maintenance of Sarah's self-esteem as a prospective teacher. Shuddering with a memory best re-buried, she speculated whether she had passed on to her son the dominant need to please authority?? Was an inherited factor the reason why he did not transfer his skills from home into the classroom, his teacher being the powerful deity in his world of school?

Signalling the next parents, Miss Griffin pressed the kind of bell usually placed in unattended reception areas where members of staff are conspicuous by their absence and only after three or more abortive rings does a desultory assistant resentfully honour you with their presence. A surly, 'Can I help you?' clearly signifies the diametric opposite of their intention. Sarah's new acquaintances responded to the call-to-arms. Ten minutes then elapsed during which Sarah did her best to calm her racing nerves. Eventually, the classroom cleared until she was the only other person present and then came the valedictory remarks:

'So nice to speak with you, Mr. and Mrs. Hobson. Ruby is an absolute delight to have in my class and I wish there were more like her.'

The ingratiating tones expressing unconditional praise floated across the classroom and through the open door for all to hear as the gloating parents made their way from Miss Griffin's desk. Sarah would not have been surprised if the father had backed away with a tug to an imaginary cap and a bow from the shoulders in dutiful obeisance.

'Give her a big kiss from me,' Ruby's teacher added, casting her eye at Sarah. The well-satisfied parents passed Sarah a smug look.

'Not politically correct,' Sarah fumed to herself. 'Matt would probably have checked her CRB listing later had he been a witness to the conversation.'

The bell for the last interview sounded.

The silky smooth tones used by Miss Griffin to other couples seemed to turn to granite as she called Sarah's name. Reminding herself of the valuable lessons she had learned, and had implemented in her career following attendance at the course on the Management of Difficult People, Sarah determined to suppress even a glimmer of visible reaction to any caustic comments from this sadly embittered woman. Sarah, hand offered in greeting, shook the other's firmly and took her place in one of the two chairs placed side-by-side in front of the formidable Miss Griffin's table. Her overriding thoughts centred on the inclusion of an appalling contribution by her son to the poetry display and she cursed herself for not thinking to bring Jamie's book reviews along, his holiday diary and his account of their family trip to the History Museum where he had insisted on remaining in the dinosaur section with Matt who had stayed with him while she and Freya had moved on to see the WW1 exhibits.

A glacial smile losing the battle to warm her face, her pen poised above the final 's' in the list headed 'Parents' Evening: Autumn 2008', there was an initial pause as Miss Griffin couldn't help but notice Sarah's reddened face (a diffusion which always betrayed her inner anxiety and over which she had no mental or physical control); she had lowered her head momentarily to observe the slash through 'Mr. and Mrs. Chilton: 8.10.' There was no doubt about the pleasure which was taken over correcting this entry to 'Mrs. Chilton, only: 8.50,' the 'only' being heavily underlined with what Sarah took to be a triumphant flourish. The teacher's introductory remark, so sweetly uttered, chilled Sarah to the marrow. Any lingering preconception that this interview was going to be a pleasant experience evaporated in an instant. Outwardly, she kept her cool. Her vow not to be pulled into a probable no-win situation when Miss Griffin had the clear intention of putting her down, primed her decision to allow her unwelcomed adversary to deliver an inexplicable catalogue of Jamie's academic shortcomings. An inwardly stunned Sarah determined to provide her with enough proverbial rope to hang herself if Matt later suggested a complaint about unprofessional conduct should be made. It flashed through her mind, however, that there were no witnesses to this demoralising demonstration of parental intimidation and it would be her word against Miss Griffin's. The school would probably close ranks in the dragon's defence and, as a parent, she would lose her case. What the hell, she thought, better to pity this hard-bitten woman instead rather than giving her free rein to damn herself with her own bigoted opinions of a child she should be nurturing. There would be other means of handling the outcome of this unpleasant interview.

Certainly, Sarah's determination not to take on the challenges thrown at her to enter into a debasing argument riled Miss Griffin into further, and more intrusive, realms.

'It is such a shame that your husband has not taken this opportunity to discuss his son's progress, Mrs. Chilton, as I do need to talk to both of you.' Her pencil ran down the list as she murmured, ostensibly to herself, 'Mmm, only one single parent has arrived without a partner of some description.' Lifting her head, she continued in a firmer voice, 'Nonetheless, it is appropriate that you are my *final* appointment for this evening as it is necessary to assure you of my sadness that Jamie is so behind with his work. He has made no progress since he left Class1, as far as I can see from the records, as I am sure you must both be aware.'

Sarah thought her ears must be playing tricks on her but

before she had time to gather her thoughts, Miss Griffin decided she should now adopt a more concerned tone.

'Indeed, I am so concerned about him that I shall be discussing the wisdom of keeping him down a year to repeat Year 2 if he isn't able to catch up with the rest of the class. I am very aware he is the youngest but one in the class and, with a late July birthday, he wouldn't feel uncomfortable. Our special needs teacher and I are considering whether to place him on our register of those children who are finding it hard to keep up with the curriculum so that we can give him some individualised support. We have a budget allocated for such purposes, of which you yourself, as a former teacher,' she emphasised the penultimate word, 'will be aware, of course.'

Totally bewildered by this turn of events when she was only expecting accolades and quite apart from her decision to allow Miss Griffin to take control of the interview, Sarah was lost for any form of words which could defuse the deteriorating situation in which she found herself. Miss Griffin continued:

'Mrs. Chilton, this must be difficult for you to accept but, rare as it is for this school to have to make such a suggestion to parents, we feel it not only our duty, but very much in Jamie's best interests. With your agreement, we would place Jamie on "Action Plus" which will enable us to have additional support from any outside agencies that might be helpful for him. Of course, you know the procedures only too well. So it is our intention that if insufficient progress is made between now and Christmas, we shall go ahead, with your approval. Meanwhile, our special needs co-ordinator will draw up an Individual Plan of Action for him to which you can contribute.'

Sarah could contain herself no longer.

'Miss Griffin, I am absolutely astounded to hear you speak so of Jamie's attainments. You must be confusing him with another child in Class 2, surely, not our son.'

But Miss Griffin's monologue, despite hardly veiled

criticism levelled at her assessment, was unstoppable. She continued as if Sarah had not spoken.

'I must also add that whilst we feel very concerned for Jamie, we both are of the opinion that he could put in more effort each day. He seems entirely in his own world at times, the only topic interesting him being dinosaurs.' She paused as if searching for kind words. 'Sometimes, you know, he daydreams so much and seems so spaced out that we wonder if he is sleeping well.' Sarah felt she fell short of phrasing this in a more accusative manner by refraining from suggesting that they were keeping Jamie up too late at night.

Miss Griffin's eyes lit up as if a profound thought had just crystallised in her mind. Thankfully she thought better of expressing it, which was just as well, for her lack of professional integrity, already in question by Sarah, was even impacting on the teacher herself and she was well aware of how close to the knuckle her barbed comments had taken her already. What was in her mind was to have been thinly disguised as whether the family kept their medicines in a locked bathroom cabinet, out of the reach of their children. However, she did attempt to keep carefully within the bounds of propriety whilst savouring the moment of superiority.

After a pregnant pause for the significance of her remarks to sink in, Miss Griffin hastily moved on in a valiant effort to appear genuinely concerned (which, in actual fact, she was – if only she had the character to override her pangs of jealousy).

'Maybe he has a low blood count, perhaps? An iron deficiency, maybe? Your doctor could check this out for you. We do worry about him so.'

Although having been prepared to an extent by the appalling example displayed of Jamie's work, Sarah could not believe what she had heard. She had fully expected commendations in abundance, tempered possibly by veiled accusations that Jamie's homework had been primed by her

SHEILA SHAW

and was not his original work … but this tirade lambasting a little boy who was clearly under-functioning, and certainly not a slow learner, bore no relation to the Jamie she knew so well. The astounding description of a special needs child was impossible to reconcile with her experiences of Jamie at home.

'Miss Griffin, I really must again suggest that you must be talking about another child, not my son. Jamie has no learning difficulties whatsoever and his accomplishments are far above those of the friends he brings to our house from time to time. Indeed, our next door neighbour's boy does not read or write as well as Jamie and he is in Year 3.'

It was as if she had not spoken. Following her personal agenda and rising to the opportunity to show superiority over the candidate whom she felt in her bones had stolen her rightful appointment to a deputy headship those years ago, Miss Griffin continued to throw as many poisoned arrows as she could in the direction of her one-time rival. Wishing that it would be acceptable for comparisons to be drawn at this point between the skills required for teaching first school children as opposed to those necessary for developing the abilities of the middle school age range, nonetheless Miss Griffin felt that discretion was the better part of valour in these days of 'political correctness' and confined her comments to drawing attention once more to Jamie's limitations.

'I am sorry to say that we have now come to the end of our range of pre-reading materials with Jamie and he is still unable to apply what we, as teachers of the "Early Years", call "sound-syllable correspondence" to help him decode even the simplest words. We teach phonics in this school, absolutely vital for our children to write down their own thoughts; Jamie does not seem to have grasped even the most basic alphabetic sounds and cannot yet write to dictation.

'I am sure that you will have been devoting considerable time at home, and the level of patience we offer here, to

76

bring Jamie's basic skills up to scratch, but Jamie is one of the two Year 2 children who have barely started on the Reading Scheme.'

Sarah exerted tremendous effort to maintain her composure. She had warned herself before the meeting that it would be hard indeed for Miss Griffin to sing the praises of any progeny of hers; this would be anathema to a woman who was clearly consumed with envy. Sarah was prepared to be the recipient of some sort of retaliation, but assumed this would be in the form of repressed commendation. Phrases such as 'outstanding promise', 'pleasure to teach' would unquestionably stick in her throat but this diatribe? This denial of her son's well-nigh prodigious talents was tantamount to slander. What could she say to correct this woman's erroneous and mistakenly harsh appraisal of a boy whose reading age she had herself measured to be the equivalent of a twelve-year-old?

Miss Griffin was in her element, cherishing every moment of her long-awaited opportunity to put this young upstart in her place. Revenge, so long in making its appearance, was as sweet as nectar.

'There is also the problem that he does not know his clocks.'

Sarah, internally chilled to the bone but outwardly steadfast in her intentions to avoid any danger of getting caught up in the heat of the moment, mentally recalled how accurately Jamie observed his bedtimes at 7.10 p.m., his prompt reminders of the minutes left before his favourite TV programme on the Discovery Channel and for which he was allowed to stay up (with the proviso that he wrote an account at the weekend of each episode he'd watched). She cast her mind back to when, at the age of two-and-a-half, he would creep into their bedroom in the morning to count how much time there was to wait before the 'bellgoes had gone', as he would say when they would sleepily enquire what he was doing in their bedroom, having been told he could come into their bed 'when the bell goes'. By now even more baffled, Sarah wondered what on earth Jamie was trying to do; why, why, why was he conning his teacher into believing that he was so incompetent? Did that keep him in a safe comfort zone? Did he fear the bullying would start up again if his class knew he was a talented, even 'gifted', child? Sarah again felt a sense of deja-vu: she had imparted the genes of conformity to her dearly loved son.

'Let me show you his maths book.'

Page after page of stamped clock faces requiring the times noted to be written underneath by the child. Nothing more complex than o'clock, half past, quarter to/past, with not a single tick by the side of sloppily written figures, many numerals reversed, and the crosses of the teacher revealing rising anger as the pencil pressure accentuated as the errors increased. The scruffy, dog-eared pages also contained examples of simple addition sums to ten/twenty bearing ridiculous answers, sometimes to four figures and often showing number reversals.

'We provide him with cotton-reels, beads, buttons, any apparatus we have, but understanding is totally lacking and our inspiration running out,' the sour voice continued, with an assumed weariness to disguise joyous retribution, so long in coming.

Was Sarah hearing about the child who readily calculated her shopping bills before they reached the check-out or cash register? The child who only last week at the Farm Shop, where the assistants did not use a calculator but wrote items down on a notepad, told her the amount to pay was actually 50p more than she had been charged and the blushing young girl, rechecking her calculation, agreed Jamie was right. The manager, Mr. Ellis, had offered him a punnet of strawberries as a reward for his honesty but Jamie had said it wasn't right as the shop's profit would 'go down' and that would not be fair. At the time she had laughed with the others when Jamie had thoughtfully asked Mr. Ellis if his assistant would have to stay in at breaktime to write the sum out again. Her thoughts moved on to wondering whether perhaps Jamie's own playtimes had been curtailed; she would ask him tomorrow. Perhaps, also, that was the reason he had not been complaining lately of being victimised, a factor of the previous term: he would have relished the opportunity to stay indoors, well away from the perpetrators. Maybe he had found his own method of evading the bullies.

Sarah knew she had nothing to say which would make the interview more positive. She consoled herself that she had staved off the danger of being drawn into the anger which must be driving this frustrated teacher to such limits. In a steady voice she did her best to rise above the horrendous situation she had found herself in whilst feeling it essential to cause Miss Griffin to question her own judgment.

'I hear him read every night. He has just finished *The Lion, the Witch and the Wardrobe* and we are currently working through a Roald Dahl book. Jamie writes a paragraph for his book review before bedtime most nights. He has his own analogue clock by his bedside and has no difficulty in keeping the time limits we set for him. He keeps a running total of the items in my shopping basket before we get to the check-out unless I am doing a "big shop" when there are too many for him to keep pace with and, instead, he has his own list to collect and price up for me.'

'I make sure he keeps in the same aisle as me,' she added, to neutralise any charge by Miss Griffin that she could be endangering his safety in a public place. 'Also he is able to tell the time better than his nine-year-old sister. I simply don't agree with your view of Jamie as a child with learning difficulties and I shall take the matter up with the headmaster as soon as possible.'

Stung, Miss Griffin threw caution to the winds whilst adopting an empathetic tone as a cover for her accusations.

'Mrs. Chilton, my dear, it is possible that you are blocking out the true nature of the capabilities of your son. I know that sometimes children are helped by illustrations and have a gift for making plausible stories up to fit the pictures. This may be happening. You may be engrossed with preparing the family supper and hear a really great composition which sounds accurate. But I can tell you there is no comparison between Jamie's competencies and those of all but one of his peers. Not only is the comparison invidious, I cannot recall any child since I have been at this school who has been so much out of his depth. The account you have given me of his prowess shows he is covering up for his difficulties.'

In an attempt to ignore Sarah's steadily increasing pallor, she continued, unsuccessfully, to aspire to a modicum of placatory compassion in her approach:

'You may be "feeding" ideas into his head unconsciously: you are probably unaware of your own actions and comments which precede the conclusions he draws with regard to the supermarket bill, for example. As for telling the time, maybe he hears this given on the radio which enables him to mention the time to you. Probably he is not looking at the clock at all. Are all your clocks analogue?'

Sarah was speechless. Nothing she could contribute to this travesty of the justice due to her son would serve any purpose whatsoever.

'I suggest we meet again on a date which suits your husband's busy schedule as well, perhaps in a month's time, and certainly before we embark upon preparations for Christmas plays and concerts. Meanwhile, give some time urgently to Jamie's needs.' She paused (in order to stage-manage reflection, Sarah thought), before continuing:

'By the way, did you take him to see the film of *The Lion, the*

Witch and the Wardrobe? Mr. Holmes reads a chapter of a story to the children on the day we all prepare our lesson schedules for the next week and I know he has introduced them to C.S. Lewis.'

Sarah made a vain attempt to call upon all her fast diminishing reserves of diplomacy whilst simultaneously feeling sick to the bottom of her stomach, failing miserably to summon up the rapidly departing vestiges of resistance she no longer had the power to feel without considerable effort. She retorted that if these face-saving behaviours were indeed being used by Jamie, these were clear signs of innate intelligence, riskily adding tartly, breaking her rule that she would not be provocative herself, that perhaps classroom management techniques and teaching style should be examined as a cause of her son's inexplicable behaviour. But a niggling doubt was creeping into her mind which had surfaced before and now was welling up to the extent that it could not be ignored. Was the fault within Jamie himself? Should she blame herself, as now was Matt, for producing a child who doesn't fit easily with peers? Or could he, perhaps, be playing the dunce to avoid attention being drawn to his knowledge and skills? Does he believe that dumbing down and showing stark incompetence would endear him to the bullies in his class and make him one of them?

Swallowing hard to repress her near-overpowering sense of shock that an unfathomably different picture of her child's capabilities had been presented to her, Sarah then controlled herself sufficiently after this aberration to thank Miss Griffin for her care during the first half-term, refraining from imparting the fact that their son intensely disliked being in her class but did, however, like the children on his table. It struck her at that precise moment that there might be some significance in the name given to the group sitting alongside Jamie. She had not given it a thought before although Matt had humphed, perhaps with accuracy and not the perversity she had attributed it to when made, that 'Ducks' could be a polite synonym for 'Runts'. 'Swans, Moorhens, whatever, and Jamie is a Duck?' he had snorted in disbelief when Jamie had mentioned his placement on the table in front of Miss Griffin's.

Miss Griffin had appeared throughout to relish each syllable of the message she had been imparting but decided it now prudent to turn to more sociable conversation. She re-gathered momentum to enquire,

'And, do tell me, how are the fortunes of the advertising industry progressing at this time of economic disaster? All this credit crunching must be having a salutary effect on your lives at the moment. It really is a pernicious time in which we are all living. Here in school we are having to work within a very limited budget nowadays.' She smiled benignly. A seething Sarah assumed that Miss Griffin's verbal assassination of her son would now be replaced with more missiles flung for her to catch on her husband's behalf. Ignoring the disguised but clearly malicious question relating to Matt's salary, she made no comment. The preposterous nature of the woman's bile could not sink any further. Miss Griffin was aware she had overstepped the mark and returned to Jamie.

'Before you leave, Mrs. Chilton, do take the trouble of looking at all of Jamie's books. The caretaker is waiting to lock up as he has signified we are the last to finish but I will have a word with him to hang on a bit. Oh, and the poem on the wall. Jamie was guided to write the sentences you see there; he cannot manage without help. I was very pleased with his attempt but I must mention that this was his third copy; the first two had too many errors to enable me to put it on display,' adding reflectively, 'We do like to celebrate all children's best attempts, whatever their ability. It does, as you well know, instil in them a sense of pride to see their work on the wall. Mr. Holmes always makes a point of noticing new additions.'

As a shaken and dumbfounded Sarah could add no further comment which would not be perceived as confrontational, Miss Griffin added as an afterthought: 'Maybe you could also tidy his desk for him before you go; I have lost count of the times he has been asked to put his things in order.'

With a despairing feeling of utter bewilderment, Sarah turned the pages of scruffy, corner-torn exercise books bearing Jamie's name in large teacher-writing. Nothing she had heard or seen made any sense whatsoever to her. Looking vainly along the walls for any other sign at all of his accomplishments, she caught the gaze of the Smarty-Pants who had taken advantage of the late-night extension to the parents' evening to examine as many books of other children as time would allow and gave her the thumbs-up sign in recognition. They were still luxuriating in the apparent compliments shining on every page of the books they scanned belonging to their daughter.

'Not a day goes by and she gets a gold star. Phew! Never got a single one in my time, only mentions in the Black Book, mostly for being lazy, I think, but really it was all too 'ard for me. Wouldn't let me do science but said I was good with me 'ands and me mouf ... but never at the right time, they said.'

They made their exit, but not before adjusting the table sign containing their prodigy's exercise books so that the significance of 'Table 1: Eagles' was not lost on Sarah. Leaving time for them to reach the car park before her, she followed suit. She had no spirit left to call upon to withstand an invidious comparison of their feedback of accomplishments with that which had rained down upon her own ears.

★

Sarah had no recollection of leaving the school or of the journey home in the October gloom, reminiscent of her own despondent mood. She could not help a niggling doubt creeping in to her mind, however, that truly, the teacher had been performing her duty: had Jamie really been a child exhibiting moderate learning difficulties, Miss Griffin had imparted nothing more than it was her duty to do. Had she really made outrageous insinuations – or was everything she said appropriate in the context of a slow-learning child? This was a salutary thought as, under those circumstances Miss Griffin's remarks would not have been taken as offensive but helpful and she must not overreact except with respect of Miss Griffin's total underestimation of Jamie's true abilities. It was only the long-standing memories which they shared which had irrevocably coloured the conversations they had just had together.

Thus still reeling from irrepressible shock and not quite knowing how to convey to Matt the unnerving events of the evening, she gathered her courage to walk into the sitting room, priming herself to break the news gently. His open-jawed head, from which guttural sounds issued through the doorway, told its own story. Added to this spectacle, a half-filled whisky glass on the coffee table beside her slumbering husband, a rugby scrum in full spate on the TV, did not present an appealing sight but at least enabled the postponement of the 'inquest on the inquisition' and inevitable recriminations as to how she had allowed herself to be so brow-beaten.

Would Matt take the embittered teacher's side and quiz her as to why she, as a teacher, had not spotted that their son was falling so far behind his classmates? There was very little these days, Sarah reflected wanly, that was not her fault. What use was she now: promotion to a prestigious deputy headship at such a young age and against tough opposition, then an unplanned pregnancy within twelve months of taking up the appointment, and now the mother responsible for a failing son. Leaving Matt well alone, deaf to the television pundits now holding an inquest on England's misfortunes, she removed his hardly touched plate from the coffee table, took it into the kitchen, covered it and placed it in the fridge: her lunch for tomorrow. Dimming the downstairs lights, Sarah took herself wearily to bed.

The recent honeymoon period was short-lived indeed.

Chapter Five

Sarah had no idea at what time Matt had eventually awoken from his deep sleep on the sofa and climbed upstairs. He had not slept in the marital bed but had retired to the spare bedroom, probably in a huff rather than to spare her from being disturbed, she thought. Surprisingly against her prediction that she would go over and over in her mind the horrors of the previous evening, she herself had slept the sleep of the dead, or the just, although feeling none the better for this when she woke to stretch over to Matt for a morning endearment. Not that any intimacy had been any more than perfunctory these days. Finding herself alone in the bed, she waited in vain for a surprise cup of tea which she would have perceived as a sign of apology for the rather callous indifference shown to her on his return from work the previous evening, not to mention his blunt refusal to attend the parents' evening. Remaining under the normally soothing duvet until the alarm sounded, Sarah fought back salty tears – how easily these came these days – as she wearily threw back the clothes, later making three beds instead of two. Freya was old enough to make her own, only needing to pump up the pillow and straighten the cover. All too often this hid a multitude of sins which lurked beneath the neatly smoothed comforter: crisp packets, forbidden teen magazines and, heaven forbid her mother ever seeing, a sachet of Sun-In, a freebie hair-lightener attached to the most recent copy of Mandy which awaited a trial run when summer arrived and she could claim her hair to be bleached by the strong sun.

A dull ache in the pit of her stomach as she arrived in the

kitchen to prepare breakfast was almost stronger than Sarah could bear. The despondency she felt that Matt had chosen to desert their bed compounded the nauseous effect of her humiliating experience at the hands of Miss Griffin, causing her face to drain of colour, not unobserved by Freya. Matt had left an hour ago, Freya told her, 'to beat the worst of the rush hour.' She had added that her father had seemed out of sorts and had downed a handful of pills to cure a headache. Casting sidelong glances at her mother, Freya was undecided whether a friendly, sympathetic hug would be appropriate or would only add to her mother's obvious discomfort. She was only too aware where her father had spent the night: she had awoken to hear expletives as he tripped over her 'cello case left on the floor of the spare bedroom, shutting the door after him none too quietly. Freya hated it when her parents were out of synchrony with each other but never before had she been witness to separate sleeping arrangements and she did not like the feeling of uncertainty it created in her mind. What could she do to help? What had caused the rift? Is it serious? Will they get divorced? Crazy thoughts, Freya chided herself … but she would try to think during the day what she could do to help them get back to being happy with each other again. She knew they argued about Jamie and his foibles and Daddy often told Mummy to be stricter with him but, surely, that couldn't be the reason they had fallen out? She walked round the table and put her arms round her mother. 'I love you so much, Mummy, and Daddy, too.' Should she add, 'I'll always be here for you, Mummy,' but if she said that to Mummy, what could she say to Daddy without letting Mummy down? The dilemma was too difficult to solve on her own … but to whom could she turn for advice on such a personal matter? She considered the idea of the Samaritans – that seemed a bit drastic and she could find herself talking to a neighbour or someone who knew her parents. Should she ring Childline?

The lady who runs Kids' Club that she had read about which helps troubled children? Either of those would be less personal than confiding in her teacher and she wouldn't be betraying confidences. She would find the numbers to ring by googling the organisations tonight. Oh no, not a good idea: Mummy could find out what she had looked up because there would be traces on her computer, however hard she tried to eliminate them. Freya felt in a complete quandary.

Gripping her daughter to her wordlessly, not trusting herself to speak, Sarah sensed that Freya was acknowledging the tensions in her parents' relationship and not wanting to break down in front of her. Freya was too young to take on the burden of a grieving mother. It was a few seconds before she was able to express her feelings as they clung together. 'Thanks, Freya, you are a wonderful daughter.' She pulled herself together, snapped back into action, squeezed Freya's hand and moved to the door of the kitchen.

'Jamie,' she called from the hall. 'It's time you were downstairs. Breakfast will be on the table in fifteen minutes. A clean shirt is by your bed.'

'Mummy, to be honest with you, I need more time than that,' came a worried small voice from above. Sarah disliked him using a phrase more suited to an adult and rather precocious for a six-year-old and told him so but Jamie continued without acknowledgment of his mother's rather testy rebuke, cautioning truthfulness at all times.

'You see, it's quarter past seven now. It takes three minutes to clean my teeth, four minutes to get washed, five minutes to get dressed and then I have to get all my things ready in their proper place by the door to take to school and that takes five minutes as well. I can't get everything done until 7.32, it's just impossible. Please let me have the extra two minutes I need to get it all done.'

Sarah smiled in quiet satisfaction that Jamie was providing

a perfect, although strangely pedantic, example of assessment of the passage of time. Belatedly she warmed to the prospect of the day she had planned, and felt rather pleased that her son was becoming a stickler for punctuality. Nonetheless, she felt a niggling disquiet that Jamie's growing passion for accurate timekeeping was becoming a little intrusive, even obsessive. She returned to the kitchen to fill the cereal bowls, making sure that the blueberry topping covered the surface of Jamie's, another irritating obsession he was forming. With time at a premium this morning of all mornings when, to her, there was so much at stake, it would not be an appropriate moment to take him to task about the ridiculous nature of his insistence that no cornflakes should be visible. Ever since his class had had a lesson on nutrition, Jamie had paid far too much attention to what he insisted had to be 'a balanced diet,' with the emphasis on starting the day with fruit, 'the redder, the bedder,' he would state, adding, 'Breakfast like a king, lunch like a prince and dine like a pauper,' emphasising the last syllable. He had given a withering reply to Freya when she had snorted that he clearly didn't know what a pauper was: 'Course I do, stupid: it's a short way of saying "a poor person".'

A wail descended from above.

'Mummee! I forgot to add in the time that it took to ask you to give me more time. Now I'll be later than I said. Oh, oh, oh, oh! I can't be downstairs for another two minutes after the time I told you I'd be in the kitchen for breakfast.'

Sarah benignly reassured him there was enough time if he'd just concentrate on getting himself ready. Why was he becoming so punctilious? Freya was the reverse, rather too lackadaisical.

At precisely 7.33 a red-faced Jamie burst into the kitchen, triumph seeping from every pore of his small frame. He pointed to the clock.

'Look, Mummy: I beat the time I said I needed. I was wrong but my mistake has worked to my advantage. I s'pect the reason was it wasn't a two-minute talk we had, only a one-minute one.' Relief shone from the expansive smile lighting up his face but as his gaze moved to the table, a frown crossed his face.

'You haven't put the cornflake box on its mat properly, Mummy. I tell you it's wrong every day and it's not kind of you to keep on being so careless.'

With meticulous care, Jamie shifted the box so that it was parallel with the edge of the table mat before sitting down. Sarah noticed with increasing perplexity each morning that Jamie lined his chair up with the grouting of the floor tiles and did his best to do the same with the spare chairs on each side of the table so that they were in a perfectly straight line. He did not seem to be concerned about hers or Freya's for some equally unaccountable reason which she had not cared to fathom. Not for the first time optimist Sarah, rather than acknowledging the disquiet she was increasingly feeling that Jamie was developing rather strange habits, cast her son as an embryonic architect, his mind alive with intersecting lines and angles at balance with each other. Freya broke her reverie:

'Mummy, Jamie is being ridiculous. You know he is. He seems to have got a stupid idea in his head and you are doing nothing to stop it. It's not a game, you know. Why do you allow him to do it? He gets really angry if I tell him not to be so idiotic.'

Although Sarah knew Freya often stood up for her brother at school, it was a different matter at home. Whilst deep down she shared her irritation, she knew, however, that to draw attention to unwanted behaviour was often tantamount to forcing an increase in it. When teaching she had worked on the alternative principle of rewarding reduction so, with this in mind, Sarah signalled Freya to come into the hall where she quietly suggested neither of them should comment upon this growing obsession but offer a distraction. She would put a rug down to cover the floor tiles and each morning Freya could attract Jamie's attention away from the floor with one of her jokes – he always laughed uproariously whenever she told them, however many times he had heard them before. Freya was secretly pleased that her mother, usually so occupied with her brother, had taken her into her confidence. She now knew that she, too, was worried about Jamie's oddly developing mannerisms which were, to his detriment, becoming intrusive into everyday life. Before they returned to the kitchen where Jamie had straightened the table to his satisfaction, mother and daughter gave each other a meaningful hug.

With her children seated, she waited until Freya excused herself to practise her 'cello for the customary fifteen minutes before leaving for school. Although this was no pleasure for Freya, who would have preferred to give the ghastly instrument up, it got this chore out of the way for the day. Unknown to her mother, however, Freya had devised her own method of completing this heinous task. At the beginning of the term, innocent little Freya had sweetly asked her music teacher to demonstrate the correct manner to play the pieces whilst she recorded the recital. 'So that I can have a perfect example of how they should sound.' The cunning child was thus provided with the ability to repeat snatches ad nauseam whilst lying on her stomach on her bedroom floor, fingers on the on/off button of her recording machine and nose within her girlie magazine, until Sarah called her 'dutiful' daughter to pack away her instrument and jump in the car.

With Freya out of earshot, Sarah took the plunge. 'Jamie, Miss Griffin told me last night that you are still on the pre-reading books. Why is this? I really don't understand.'

Jamie's face crumpled immediately, early triumph draining from his face. In an instant, tears streamed down his cheeks.

'I can't do it. I can't do it like the others do it. I can't, I can't, I *can't*. And Miss Griffin says I'm getting worse at it, not better. I can't read the same way as they do, it's so difficult. You never make me do it like that. I do try, I do … but Miss Griffin says I don't and she's the teacher so she must be right which only makes it even worse 'cos that means I can't try 'cos she says I don't. She said she would tell you how lazy I was but this just isn't fair of her. I'm definitely not. I looked lazy up in the dictionary and it says it means "sluggish". That's a horrid thing to call me. Slugs are nasty slimy creatures and I'm not.'

'I just don't know what game you are playing,' sighed Sarah, weary of the day already, despite her determination to expunge the events of the night before. 'You can read all the books we get from the library without me helping you with the words and you have read all the ones you had for your birthday. Just why are you pretending you can't read the books they give you at school? Just what is stopping you from showing you know a lot of things already that they are teaching your class? Why are you pretending you can't make any sense of the print?'

'I'll answer your first question first and the others, if we haven't got time, in the car. The games we play in my class with sounds are horrid and I'm no good at those either. Miss Griffin says anyone can play the snakes and ladders she makes us play to learn sounds, and why did I tell a lie when I said I could? I told her her game was nothing like snakes and ladders and she said I was not to argue with her. But she didn't tell the truth herself: it wasn't snakes and ladders 'cos although you have a dice with numbers, like you do, you pick a letter out of the box when you reach a rung on a ladder. She said we went up if we said the sound the letter made and down when we got it wrong. I did try to do it: I hissed when I got on the snake but then she stopped the game I was in when I tried to make the clacking noise a ladder makes when you shut it up. Do you know, she said she'd like to put me in her book – but I don't think she did so that made me very sad.'

At the time Jamie had puzzled over what she had meant: was he to be a character in a story she was writing? That would make him very proud, he had thought. Perhaps there would be a film and he could ask if he could play his part in it. How pleased his mummy and daddy would be … and all his friends might want his autograph like someone had Daniel Radcliffe's and charged everyone to see it.

He continued to answer his mother's questions.

'Miss Griffin said I was being very silly and I said I wasn't because I tried very hard to make a ladder sound. I had to sit by her side during assembly which she makes us do if she is cross. Mr. Holmes asked me why I was sitting there and I told him Miss Griffin said I'd told a lie when I'd told her the truth. Mr. Holmes said I'd have to see him at breaktime but I said it wouldn't be necessary because the optician you took me to said I'd got good eyesight. Do you think Mr. Holmes wants me to wear glasses? And, Mummy, all the children in my class laughed and at breaktime they told me to hiss at Mr. Holmes but I wasn't able to because he didn't ask me to play snakes and ladders with him.'

Not for the first time in just twelve hours, Sarah felt faint. This jumbled account of why he was not reading at school was incomprehensible. Jamie continued his monologue unabashed.

'So I can't read because I'm no good at it and no good at any of the games either. There's another one called hopscotch but we don't hop on the squares as we do in the playground although I always fall over which makes my friends laugh and there's a stupid one called Magic E which I don't understand because Miss Griffin says we should leapfrog over the last consonant before the Magic E and when I got out of my seat and asked someone to bend down so I could do one, she said

I'd be the death of her and I cried because you know people who murder people get put in prison for all their life so I've refused to play Magic E ever again. I don't know why she asked me to the next time because I don't think she really wants to be dead. My friend wasn't very nice: he said no one would mind very much. It was lucky Miss Griffin didn't hear.'

Jamie's voice began to tremble as he recalled the tyranny of having to read 'like the others on my table do'. He explained through his tears, with Freya, 'practice' over, now standing transfixed in the doorway and simultaneously stifling giggles, how you had to 'sound it out'.

'Listen, Mummy, I'll try to do it with the book we were reading last night before you went out.'

He rushed to the sitting room, returning with *Charlie and the Chocolate Factory* and opened it at the chapter he had read so eloquently to his mother earlier. He began:

'K-h-ch-a-rer-ler-ih-eh: charerlerieh; a-ner-der: anerder; t-h th-eh: the; kh-ch-oh-ser/ker-oh-ler-a-ter-eh: choser/ kero – oh, I don't know what it is … It is so … o … o hard, Mummy. You must help me.' Jamie's voice trailed off. 'That's how they do it on my table but all except Alfie can do it better than me. Miss Griffin says I don't try but I do, I do, I do. She says I must blend all the letters together but I don't know what she means. She keeps on telling me to blend, blend, blend and then I have to do it when Sam's mum comes in to help us. I asked Sam's mother if she could bring her blender-thing in to help me but she said she was here to help me read, not cook, and that got me all muddled up. Miss Griffin then helps Sam and Sam's mum says Sam is getting on better than me so Sam runs round the playground shouting out he's better than me and I'm a rubbish reader. I'll never do it like she says I have to.' Tears streamed down the mortified boy's face.

A glimmer of understanding was beginning to form in Sarah's bewildered mind.

'Look at the clock, darling. What time is it?'

'It's 8.14 or do you want me to say nearly quarter past eight? It's very hard to know which way Miss Griffin wants me to answer clock questions, so tell me which you want,' Jamie responded through shuddering sobs.

Aware of the passing time, Sarah ignored his questions and quickly drew two clock faces on the paper she had hurriedly taken from the dresser.

'What is the time on this clock?'

'Mummy, I can only do clocks when I look at Daniel's clock. He gets a tick sometimes but he often covers up his work so I can't see and then I look to see what Alfie has done. I had one tick yesterday and Miss Griffin said I was trying only because I knew she was going to speak to you tonight and I probably didn't want her to say I never got any clocks right. Daniel gets more ticks so I try to copy his when he lets me; sometimes he gets a star when he gets more than one right.'

There was no point, Sarah thought, in giving Jamie a written calculation to do: she knew what to expect. Everything was now only all too obvious to her. My poor, poor baby, she almost cried to herself as the torture her child had been going through, unbeknown to her or Matt, was beyond belief. Sarah pulled herself together swiftly and suddenly began firing on all cylinders. No need to conjure up a superhuman effort to drag him to school.

'Collect your things, children, and stand at the gate. We leave in five minutes. Remember to take your 'cello, Freya, and Jamie, your recorder.' Why hadn't that hapless teacher not shown surprise that a child who she thought could not read was able to play quite advanced tunes on the recorder, she mused. Could this narrow-minded woman not question her initial snap judgments?

Arriving at the school gates, correctly parking well behind the pelican crossing and the pitch of the lollipop lady, aka Sam's mum, Freya was despatched to the junior playground.

'You and I, Jamie, are going to see Mr. Holmes.' Jamie was about to explain that he had told her he had seen Mr. Holmes in assembly and didn't need to see him in his office because it was assembly every morning so he would soon be seeing him on his stage-thingie (he stands up on great big blocks of wood the caretaker has to get out each morning for him so that everyone could see him very clearly, he would have told her), but Sarah cut in:

'I have your library book with me and I shall ask you to read a page to him in the same way just as you do with Daddy or me, not as Miss Griffin expects you to.'

Jamie's face lightened as he warned his mother: 'I mustn't miss my 'tendance mark, though, Mummy, or the welfare officer might come to talk with you like he does to Alfie's mummy sometimes. Quite a lot, actually; Alfie is often too late to get his mark.'

Inside the entrance hall Sarah sidestepped the teacher-enhanced 'Exhibitions of Children's Work' and rang the bell to speak to the secretary. Another face which could turn the milk sour, with a manner to match. Why doesn't the headmaster realise what damage a surly secretary, the first introduction to the school for visiting prospective parents, can do to the image the public holds of a school, she reflected. The unwelcoming voice of the secretary asked curtly and pointedly whether she had an appointment. It was not in her diary of engagements for the day and Mr. Holmes was a busy man. Sarah responded with equal firmness that she was prepared to wait as long as was necessary to have a private conversation with him and when he could find a spare few moments from his packed schedule, she would not take up more than ten minutes of his time which she knew all too well was precious. No, she didn't mind that Jamie would miss his attendance mark if he did not join his class before 9.15; he would wait with her. She was shown to a seat in the corridor; the absence of grace in the action was palpable.

Jamie sighed with relief: he would miss having to demonstrate his ignorance to Sam's mother that morning. Today was Wednesday, one of the days she came in to class when her lollipop duties were over. Why was it called a lollipop, the pole she held aloft to stop the cars? It was a silly name; it wasn't even spherical like a ball. A dinner plate would be a more appropriate name. 'Dinner Plate Lady / Lollipop Lady'; he really didn't think he would like to be given either title if he was her.

He felt a thrill of spine-tingling excitement. He wondered whether Mr. Holmes was too old to enjoy listening to what Charlie was up to. How he would love to make him happy and pleased instead of cross with him. It was a good thing, really, to be able to see him again and not just in the hall or on his occasional visits to the classroom when sometimes he talked to Miss Griffin at the back of the class and Miss Griffin told him not to turn round, so he was never able to see him very much at those times.

Mr. Holmes' door opened and he appeared in front of them. His mother stood up. Jamie rose to his feet, too, and said in a sing-song voice, as used in his class, 'Good morning, Mr. Ho-o-lmes.' The headmaster nodded at Jamie in reciprocation.

'Mrs. Chilton, I am not sure what I can do for you. I am sure Miss Griffin enlightened you last night of our concern. At this stage I can only reiterate her opinion which, of course, has been backed up by our well-qualified special needs co-ordinator, Mrs. Ackroyd. She will be sending you an appointment shortly to discuss the matter more fully with her.' He transferred his gaze to Jamie. 'Jamie, of course, should be in his classroom right now, not here with you. Does he have a doctor's note?'

'Several matters of considerable concern involving Jamie need discussing with you, Mr. Holmes,' Sarah replied, ignoring Mr. Holmes' veiled reprimand as to precisely where her son should be, 'and I should appreciate doing so in the privacy of your office. As a matter of urgency, if your school is going to continue to be responsible for my son's education, which, in the minds of my husband and me at the moment, is in doubt, I wish to clarify your understanding of the status of Jamie's proficiency in basic skills.' Sarah used poetic license to include Matt who, as yet, was in blissful ignorance of the school's unfair condemnation of their child's abilities.

Unused to being addressed so curtly, a somewhat taken-aback headmaster ushered both Sarah and Jamie into his study, indicating to her the low chair in front of his desk. In time-honoured style, he remained standing (page 6 of the manual on how to belittle parents, crossed Sarah's mind).

'Mr. Holmes, I learned with astonishment last night that, in Miss Griffin's opinion, Jamie has not yet progressed beyond the pre-reading stage. I have brought Jamie to you this morning with the purpose of enlightening you as to the true nature of his literacy proficiency. You have *The Times* on your desk. To Jamie, it is upside down. Jamie, what is the heading?'

Jamie looked for assurance that his mother wanted him to read the leading headline. Why? Could Mr. Holmes not do this for himself? He was the headmaster, after all. Grown-ups were strange so often you could not predict what they would ask you to do.

'Bank rates falter for the third day in a row. Mummy, that is row, not row, isn't it? I didn't think the bank men would be rowing a boat but I expect they get cross with each other some of the time. Daddy says they do, so I'll say "row" as in arguing with each other. What does "falter" mean? Is that something to do with getting something wrong? Everyone in my class says it's my fault when something's not right.'

Mr. Holmes' eyebrows were reaching the ceiling. Sarah corrected Jamie's misreading, explaining the word causing him problems meant 'in a line, one after the other', in the same manner as he lined up his dinosaurs, putting them all in a row. Jamie explained, to the disconcertion of his mother and astonishment of his headteacher, that as he didn't know what 'falter' meant, he had forgotten the other alternative meaning of 'row.' 'It's very hard to work it out, you know, when there are so many to choose from. It would be better if they had different words for each meaning, like the Eskimos have ever so many words for different sorts of snow. Did you know that, Mr. Holmes?'

'I expect Mr. Holmes did, Jamie,' Sarah interjected hastily, to ward off the possibility of the unfortunate man being treated to a soliloquy on arcane facts. One of Jamie's recent passions was to explore general knowledge books and bore everyone with his latest discovery, not always at the appropriate time but more likely to be when the family was in a hurry to go out. 'Now ask Mr. Holmes which page of your book he would like to hear you read.'

Jamie swelled with pride. Did he just hear Mummy say Mr. Holmes wanted to hear him read? She must have whispered to him when he was talking just now. He dutifully passed *Charlie* to Mr. Holmes who opened the book at random in silence and passed it back to Jamie. Jamie cleared his throat.

'It is in the middle of a sentence. Shall I go back to the end of the last page?' Mr. Holmes nodded, almost lost for words. Jamie stood up and read the continuation sentence … and on … and on … and on.

'Well done, my boy. Well practised. Did you learn that off by heart? I expect the book fell open at the page you wanted,' he said, with suspicions of trickery solidifying in his mind. 'Now,' he said decisively, as if to end the matter, 'let me hear you read from this book on my shelf.' He passed Jamie a copy of *The Lion, the Witch and the Wardrobe*, smiling benevolently as he did so. With all the administration work and red tape associated with headships these days, he hardly had time to spend in classrooms and depended upon feedback from his SENCo* in respect of children under-performing, trusting her judgment. Clearly, he was facing a parent unwilling to face the reality of her child being below par and would have to ease her into a greater understanding. 'Barking at print', was a phrase one of his mentors in his early days of teaching had called it when children had little awareness of the text they were reading by informed guesswork.

Jamie read the first page faultlessly and with expression. His mother suggested he read another page. Mr. Holmes intervened to retrieve the book while Jamie enquired,

'Do you have any books on dinosaurs, Mr. Holmes? They are my favourite and I've written in my journal about the Tyrannasaurus rex I saw in the History Museum and my best programme on The Discovery Channel is *Life in the Jurassic Period*.'

Warming to his subject, he was beginning to see Mr. Holmes as a friend.

'Do you watch the Discovery Channel? I'm asking Father Christmas to put the CD in my stocking and I could lend it to you when we start school again after our holiday if you would like me to – the CD, I mean, not my stocking!' Jamie giggled as he pictured in his mind the image of Mr. Holmes struggling to put on a child's footwear but composed himself sufficiently to add, helpfully he thought, 'As I was explaining to you just now, it's so easy to get muddled up with sentences sometimes, isn't it?'

Mr. Holmes indicated weakly that whichever he would lend him would be a kind gesture. Sarah picked up a receipt from Mr. Holmes' desk.

---

*   SENCo = Special Educational Needs Coordinator

'May I?'

Not failing to notice the store was Laithwaites and the individual purchases were greatly in excess of those she made at the same store, and her request not being vetoed, she folded it in such a way so only the prices were visible.

'Jamie, here is a list of ten items Mr. Holmes has bought. What did he have to pay at the check-out?'

Jamie took the somewhat crumpled sales voucher and scanned the items with a practised eye.

'There are an awful lot of ninety-nines in these numbers, Mr. Holmes, eight of them, actually, so it's easy. Pretend those items in the pennies column cost 100p each, it's easier that way. That is £1, so that makes £8. But you must take away 8p for the 1p each you have counted too much. So that is £7.92. I'll add up the £'s now and then add on the £7.92. 4 add 8, add 9, add 6, add, ooh, four lots of 8 which makes 32; that is £59. Can I write that down, Mr. Holmes, please? I expect you think I've left out the two lots of £16. Well, I haven't. Mmmmm. That is a lot of money! Just wait and I'll tell you.'

Jamie's eyes swept heavenwards for a moment while he silently mouthed a few calculations.

'It is £91, plus – was it £7.92, Mummy? I think it was. So altogether I think it's £98.92. If you let me have your calculator, Mr. Holmes, I will tell you whether my answer is right.'

What a great day this was turning out to be, Jamie thought, excitement mounting. Perhaps Mr. Holmes would let him come to his office every morning to read to him, tell him what he owed in the shop and remind him of the time in case he couldn't see the clock from where he was sitting and had forgotten his watch. He wondered if Alfie or Sam could come, too; they were his friends. Dominic, although already becoming his very special friend, was still a 'new boy' and would have to earn the privilege first.

Suddenly looking agitated, Jamie glanced at the clock on the wall of the study. 'Mr. Holmes, you have to take assembly in eight minutes' time. Shall I go back to my classroom now otherwise I will not be in time to take my proper place in the class line?'

Mr. Holmes, not knowing how to take the startling revelations of the morning, shuffled to his feet and held the door open for the child whose teacher had told him was so far below the rest of the class that he would probably need a Statement to enable him to be admitted to a special school for children with moderate learning difficulties. Reaching the corridor, Jamie turned, proffering a hand to his headmaster in farewell and said how much he hoped Mr. Holmes had enjoyed his narration of the stories and would be happy to continue any time Mr. Holmes wished to hear more. Did that six-year-old 'dimwit' actually use the word 'narration?' He had never been so stunned in all his years of teaching.

Alone with the head, Sarah fired her parting shot.

'Now, Mr. Holmes, you must explain to me exactly why the staff of your school hold the opinion that my son cannot read, tell the time, write his name or perform the simplest of calculations. I would like to know precisely why they think he should be placed on the Special Needs Register, I assume to be fast-forwarded to Action Plan Plus?'

As an ex-deputy head, Sarah was well up on the hierarchy of procedures available to schools and, also, of parental rights.

'Matt and I will await a formal, written explanation whilst considering whether to make a complaint to the chief education officer in relation to the neglect of our son's clear abilities.'

Had she been a lawyer, Sarah would have prefaced her final remarks with

'And thereby I rest my case.'

Eyes glued to Sarah's departing back, feebly, Mr. Holmes called Mrs. Lawson to make him a cup of strong coffee, simultaneously withdrawing from his filing cabinet a half-empty bottle of Bells.

Chapter Six

Mr. Holmes downed two strong mints to disguise any lingering, tell-tale aroma of alcohol before entering the Hall to take the morning's assembly. Unbeknown to him, however, the smell of peppermints rarely deluded the staff, who would pass knowing glances to each other and assume he had found his secretary rather overbearing that morning.

To his immense relief he remembered in time that it was the weekly 'Show and Tell' morning, to be taken by Year 6. His only contribution, he reflected, would be to praise the class for the quality of their performance, whatever the outcome. A vital function in this was, additionally, to avoid treading on the toes of the respective class teacher responsible for the production. He often felt he was walking on a tightrope: too excessive praise could hurt the feelings of the previous week's teacher whereas insufficient could act as a demotivator to the current one. This particular morning he noted it was the turn of his deputy, Peter Danesfield, whom he would have to placate. He took his place amongst the staff, wafting the telling odour of peppermint to his right and left as he did so.

The story of Grace Darling was enacted, following which a feisty rendering of "For those in Peril on the Sea" brought the production to a close. Mr. Holmes, aided by the whisky, felt rather pleased with himself for bringing to heel any lingering thoughts of the unsettling encounter which had come close to shattering his normal joie de vivre. His acting ability to utter trite laudatory phrases complimenting Class 6 for linking their assembly so aptly with Trafalgar Day before publicly inviting Miss Griffin to take her coffee to his office during morning break was worthy of an Oscar. Conversely, a rather baffled staff wondered why the life-saving exploits of a plucky young girl linked with Nelson's victory in the head's mind, one saying under her breath that perhaps the need for peppermints had something to do with it, whilst Peter Danesfield cursed himself for not actually capitalising on the day's date, 21st October, which celebrated England's Day of Glory. Next week, he knew the Reception class would celebrate Diwali, always a gift for the class whose turn it was; this year every teacher would be on their guard for candles, held by quivering five-year-old hands, toppling frighteningly to the ground. He would be more careful to check the useful notes in his diary next time it was his turn to demonstrate the burgeoning dramatic talents of his class, nurtured by him alone.

Miss Griffin did not enjoy her breaktime talk with Mr. Holmes. She felt the insinuation that she should have detected signs that Jamie was a super-intelligent child was grossly unjust. She was, of course, convinced that Jamie's mother had played some part in encouraging her child to play dumb in class whilst she taught him at home herself. As she strode back from the humiliation of a dressing down by the head, Faith Griffin reflected that she had totally disagreed with Jamie's mother when listening to her at a teacher conference giving a lecture she had been invited to give as an exponent of child-centred teaching. No doubt this had something to do with her misguided perception of her son's basic literacy and numeracy skills.

The shrill sound of the bell for the continuation of morning school forced Miss Griffin to come out of her reverie. She hurried to the playground to marshal her charges into the classroom, ignoring the questioning glances of her colleagues, all agog to learn whether she had received a put-down. Once indoors, the children took their place on the carpet, the first four claiming a seat on the sofa. Arms folded, they looked expectantly at their teacher who, belatedly on that morning, checked for absentees.

'Yes, Miss Griffin,' 'Here, Miss Griffin,' each child intoned as names were called and duly ticked in the register, silences being accompanied by the jerking of heads as each looked to their right, left and backwards, to seek the child who should have responded and hadn't. Did they think an apparently absent child would suddenly spring out of nowhere like a Jack-in-a-Box? A sharp tap on the door signalled the unexpected entrance of their headmaster.

The class, having greeted his arrival with a sing-song, 'Good mor-ning, Mr. Ho-ol-mes', looked expectantly at the two adults. Mr. Holmes addressed the assembled group.

'Year 2, Miss Griffin and I have a surprise for you this morning. You all know Jamie: he is a very special member of your class. Miss Griffin has been encouraging Jamie to work very, very hard and this is exactly what Jamie has done: he has worked so, so extremely hard that he is now able to read almost any book he likes. And, moreover, he has made such a tremendous effort that he has learned all his tables and his number bonds and can tell the time correctly by looking at the hands of a clock.'

'And in relation to the last point,' coldly interrupted Miss Griffin, 'that is more than even some of the Eagles can do. I have threatened to confiscate their digital watches.'

With a hurried mental note to speak to her later of the likelihood of parental complaints should she put that threat into practice, Mr. Holmes continued,

'Now, in my hand is a very special Headmaster's Award Gold Badge. Whose shirt do you think I should pin this on?'

Mr. Holmes surveyed the expectant faces.

'Ruby, your hand was the first up. Who do you think has

earned my special Gold Badge? Absolutely! Jamie, you have done so well to take notice of all the advice Miss Griffin has given you. Jamie Chilton, you are my Special Golden Boy of the Week. And, what is more, I think Miss Griffin has a prize for you, too. Miss Griffin …?'

A strained smile on her face, Miss Griffin steeled herself to convey a symbol of her praise. Her face draining of colour, she turned to pick a card from the table behind her, steadying herself as she did so.

'Jamie,' she said stiffly, 'I present you with an Eagle's table card.'

As a single unit, the class gasped. Never had anyone been moved up four groups in one day. Eagles were the brightest children, the teacher's pets of Year 2 and, if you were lucky, you might move up one table during the year. After Ducks came Moorhens, then Herons, then Swans and finally Eagles: five tables with six children on each. Yet Jamie seemed unmoved by the attention he was receiving.

'What do you say to Mr. Holmes, Jamie?'

'Good mor-ning, Mr. Ho-o-lmes,' Jamie responded in the lilting tones and emphasis as practised by children over the generations, fortunately deciding that reminding the headmaster that he had already wished that he would have a good morning and didn't need to do so again was, perhaps, not the right thing to say. Miss Griffin interrupted him in barely suppressed irritation.

'Jamie, Mr. Holmes has given you a very special Gold Badge. I meant, what should you say in return?'

'Thank you, Mr. Ho-o-lmes', Jamie intoned, his eyes focusing on a bird which had just landed on the window ledge.

'Mr. Holmes, is that a house martin? Or a swallow? We have house martins nesting in our porch, did you know? We are lucky 'cos they come back each year.'

Miss Griffin, eyebrows raised quizzically and regaining

her composure, caught the gaze of the head. In a conspiratorial undertone that only her headmaster could hear, she remarked,

'We shall see how long he can keep his place as an Eagle, Geoff. You have just witnessed an example of how this child cannot keep his mind on anything for more than a few seconds.'

Conversely, Mr. Holmes reflected silently that he had actually always been mightily impressed by this little boy's quiet obedience during assembly times. Unlike a number he could name on the Ducks' table in Miss Griffin's class, this one sat perfectly still, hands tightly clasped in his lap and looked directly at him (admittedly, sometimes rather disconcertingly), whilst he was giving a little homily or emphasising some rule of the school which had recently been infringed. It did not matter how frequently he ordered his flock to sit very still, keep their hands to themselves and their eyes on the speaker's face, reminders which he particularly emphasised before the vicar's weekly visit, there were always wrigglers. And there was always at least one Duck who found something in his pocket to play with. Not that the vicar, generally lost in his unctuous homily, would notice, was it not for Miss Griffin's attempts to call the miscreant to order by clicking her fingers and glaring at the child whose neighbours would then poke him in the ribs, with obvious unfortunate consequences.

Mr. Holmes' distracted mind then strayed to the current incumbent of the church to which the school was attached. St. Michael's was a C. of E. school after all, and the chairman of governors, therefore, was always an honour held by the vicar, who had to be impressed at all times. The present one was new to the parish (indeed, it was his first incumbency), rather wet behind the ears, Geoffrey Holmes felt, a man who was over-earnest and anxious to fulfil his duties to the letter, unlike his predecessor who had reached retirement long before the official age. That man's apathy was such that even in his mid-50s he had dozed off during meetings, preferred to give in to the loudest advocate (whatever idiotic nonsense they were spouting), and did not keep to the agenda. He would often forget to bring his reading spectacles on the weekly religious assembly day and lost his place in the biblical text he was quoting, stumbling incoherently then carrying on several disconnected paragraphs later, the only benefit to his bored listeners being that he got to the end of his 'sermon' rather quickly.

A good relationship with this new vicar was essential: he held the casting vote in times of a stalemate and Geoff Holmes had the feeling that he would no longer hold the reins which, as head, with a weak chairman, he had been able to do in the past. Without doubt, being allowed to appoint his own wife as school secretary during his tenure would definitely have been a no-no. Margaret was soon to replace the formidable Mrs. Lawson, whose husband, he was mightily relieved to learn, was about to bundle her off to the West Country, there to inflict herself on another unsuspecting head. He wouldn't even need to give her a good reference to get rid of her: the relocation was now a fait-accompli and, my, what he would confide to any distant colleague should they telephone him for a testimony as to her character didn't need any preparation: it would roll off his tongue, an accompaniment to any reference which could be required. This, he planned, would only amount to an arid statement of the length of her employment. Turning his mind abruptly to reflect on the newly appointed chairman and his incurred responsibilities, he hoped fervently that the new vicar/chairman was not going to be too assiduous in reading the copious guidelines for governing bodies. There was much in there of which he would prefer him to be in blissful ignorance.

With a start, Geoff Holmes became aware that the startled eyes of Class 2, as one, were focusing upon him and brought his wandering thoughts sharply back to the present. With a nod to Miss Griffin, a pat on the head to Jamie and an exhortation to the class to work as hard as Jamie and do their very best to copy his outstanding example, he turned to leave. An Eagle had preceded him to open the door.

'Mr. Holmes,' piped up Jamie, 'you have left your Gold Award behind. May I get up please, Miss Griffin, and give it back to him?'

Mr. Holmes stopped in his tracks. Miss Griffin's expression was blank. A frown crossed the head's face, not a fleeting one but one which for at least thirty seconds, seemed permanently etched on his forehead. Indeed, any wrinkles still in their formative stages appeared like gullies on a parched plain. The humiliation he had suffered earlier that morning under the supercilious tongue of that creature who had had the presumption to insinuate his headmastership of the school was lacking, was now being reinforced by her insolent offspring having the temerity to throw his award back in his face.

'Are you telling me you are rejecting the highest commendation the school can offer, turning down what other Ducks would give their eye teeth to be given? I don't understand you: I can only say you're a very rude, ungrateful little boy.'

'Mr. Ho-ol-mes,' Jamie counteracted, oblivious of the rebuke, 'Mummy took me to the dentist last week and, luckily for me, he said there was one nearly ready to fall out. Mummy said the tooth fairy would come if I put it under my pillow. She – fairies are girls, you know; elves are boys – would take away my tooth and turn it into bread, replacing it with a £1 coin. Now, if you would like to wait a week or so – look, see how it wiggles – I would give you that tooth instead and I could then have your Gold Award. That would be fair, wouldn't it? Gold is better than £1, I think,' adding dubiously, 'I'm not sure though.' Nonetheless he nodded his head in obvious pleasure at the prospect.

Looking around him, Jamie could see how impressed his class was with him: they were staring at him, open-jawed. He puffed himself up in importance and resumed his soliloquy.

'I don't actually think my tooth is an *eye* tooth,' he mused, as if to himself. 'I didn't know eyes had teeth in them. That's a very strange thing: you can't see them, but then you can't see your heart or lungs either, so I'll look them up in my 'cyclopedia. Would it matter if it's just an *ordinary* tooth? An insider, maybe?' Jamie paused to waggle his tooth so that Mr. Holmes could see it then, after reflection, corrected himself:

'But to be honest with you,' (Jamie liked to confirm his truthfulness, just in case it was ever in doubt) 'I think I would prefer to have the Tooth Fairy's £1 coin, though, because Mummy said I could spend it on anything that I want that costs a pound and I might like that better than a gold badge. As a matter of interest, what value is your special award?'

An intrigued Miss Griffin watched with some concern as Mr. Holmes looked as though he was about to have an apoplectic fit. Never had he ever been addressed in such a strange manner by a child so young. His parents were clearly to be blamed for creating such a pompous prig, one who doesn't seem to have any idea of the boundaries to be kept between adults and children and whose obtuse logic was completely baffling. Controlling himself with a real effort, the shaken headmaster cast over his shoulder as he left the room,

'Miss Griffin, perhaps it is the moment that your young charges need to be reminded of their manners. A lesson on their choice of appropriate remarks to people in authority, how to discriminate which adults to be jokily familiar with and *when* to do so should be high on the agenda.' Striding down the corridor, his head reeling with the shock of the sequence of the day's events, he toyed with the notion that perhaps he would himself call round to the child's home one evening to discuss just these matters. Mrs. Lawson could make an appointment for him. He would be able to tell quite a lot about their management skills by meeting the parents on their home ground.

The class most certainly did need calling to task for their reactions. Starting with the Eagles, spreading through the Swans down to the Moorhens, Class 2 shook with suppressed laughter until they could hold it in no more. The carpet was soon full of writhing children, collapsing in mass hysteria, much to the Ducks' irritation and bewilderment and Miss Griffin's stern recriminations.

'Get off me.' 'You're hurting me.' 'Ouch, ouch! Miss Griffi-in, he kicked me.'

Seeing everyone's uncontrollable mirth, but not understanding why it was funny that Mr. Holmes should give away his gold award, Jamie had no idea of the absurdity of the pictures in the minds of the class: elves and fairies circling round with baskets of teeth, others in baker's shops milling incisors, filling ovens with strange-looking loaves. The Eagles were doubled up with laughter but the Ducks looked as puzzled as he was. Now an Eagle, he must do as Eagles do: Jamie began to laugh, but in a high-pitched, forced, and exaggerated manner.

A crack of a ruler hard down on the table … and another … but it wasn't until a third, that Year 2 came to its senses. Miss Griffin ordered each child back to its allotted table, then directed them to put their hands on their heads and to sit in silence for two whole minutes. These minutes would be taken from their lunch-hour, which, for Class 2, would therefore begin two minutes after the bell to signal the end of morning lessons.

★

The class completed an hour of maths in silence. Jamie sat as usual, but rather perplexed, at the Ducks' table, Miss Griffin not yet having decided who to demote in order for Jamie to take his place with the Eagles. He was sharply told that a place would be found for him all in good time but that he should be thankful that Mr. Holmes had not told him to lose his breaktime play for being so disrespectful and downright cheeky to him. His head in a whirl, he wondered for the hundredth time why adults did not always do what they had said they would do: what was the point of being given an Eagle card and then being made to rejoin the Ducks?

Out in the playground the Eagles gathered round Jamie.

'I would not have dared to say to Mr. Holmes what you did. You're really cool! He looked as though he was about to explode!'

Another Eagle added,

'I am so glad you are going to be on our table: you come out with such funny things.'

Chapter Seven

Miss Shadbolt, duty playground teacher for the day, didn't set the same rather rigid standards as Miss Griffin, and was seen by all the school to be rather lenient; the latter always gave a sharp reminder when she was on duty that any talkers en route would have to come to her room at lunchtime. As Year 2's turn came to enter the building and as they came in sight of their classroom door, the chattering along the corridor miraculously ceased: few children had any desire to incur the displeasure of their dragon-like teacher. In the classroom, Miss Griffin had rearranged the seating.

The now seated class looked about them expectantly.

'Jamie,' Miss Griffin fixed a stern gaze on the hapless little boy, 'as you all heard from Mr. Holmes this morning, you have earned your place on the Eagles' table. I would like you to sit in Brendan's seat from now on. Brendan has not been trying very hard and he is to join the Swans. There has been an empty seat there ever since Habil left so that makes a very convenient arrangement. Now be aware,' she added darkly, 'no one's place is set in stone, so work as hard as you can, young man, as I can very easily make more changes.'

'I am glad they're not stuck in concrete,' Jamie confided to Millie, his new neighbour. 'They would be very difficult to get in and out of if they were.'

Millie nudged Flora, Flora repeated Jamie's aside to Freddie, Freddie to Ruby, Ruby to Charlie, who surreptitiously poked Jamie in the ribs and whispered,

'Get some superglue from home, Jamie, and stick it under your chair legs. That would be a laugh.'

Jamie felt pleased he was being accepted so readily in the Eagles group. This was going to be real fun. When his Daddy got home that evening he'd ask him for some of his Poxy stuff for a project at school. Not quite sure why, he thought it would be wiser not to explain exactly what he was intending to do.

★

It was Faith Griffin's intention the following morning to introduce Class 2 to the Structure of the Earth, in preparation for later primary years when they would be taught that erosion, volcanic action and earthquakes would alter surface terrain. From her portfolio of pictures saved from the moment she had made the decision to undertake post-experience training for a B.Ed degree, she had scoured educational periodicals, responded to advertisements selling past copies of *Pictorial Education* and amassed a considerable collection which, before she displayed on her classroom wall, she mounted on stiff backing card. The spare bedroom in her small flat overflowed with a copious quantity of labelled cardboard boxes kept on their side for ready access. Stripped of furniture, she had no use for the room for its intended purpose: no one ever visited Faith Griffin. Her parents had a 'box-room', the name Faith gave to the home of her treasure trove.

The night before her lesson she had withdrawn from her prized collection a picture of Mount Snowdon. Neatly securing this to the whiteboard she began her lesson.

'Now later on in Year 5 or 6, you will learn lots of exciting things about how land changes. Where we live today, just outside Greysbury, it is rather flat, isn't it, but not far from us are a number of hills. Some of you live on roads that have the name "Hill" in it: Clumber Hill, Castle Hill, Grange

Hill,' (Jamie's unwelcomed interruption suggesting Clot Hill Avenue was corrected as Clo<u>th</u>ill Avenue which was flat, not hilly, he was smartly told) 'and I expect your little legs get a bit tired when you walk uphill to your house. But we have to drive quite a long way, or go by train, to a really big lot of hills, so big that we call them mountains. Jamie, put your hand down.'

'Miss Griffin, I don't need to wait for Year 5 or 6. I know how mountains are made. They are made out of molehills.'

The class screwed up their faces, as of one, and the Eagles did their best to stifle giggles, passing knowing looks across the table.

'We have got some in our garden but Daddy doesn't want them to grow up as big as that one in your picture. There is usually a hole nearby so my daddy puts paraffin down it and sets it on fire. He only does it when I'm in bed but, if I am awake, I see a red glow on the curtain and get up and peep through. I don't let him see me because he doesn't want me to watch him doing it. Do you know, when I asked him once what he was doing, he said he was warming Mr. and Mrs. Mole up because it was a cold night and it was cold under the Earth and ...'

Miss Griffin's mouth tightened in exasperation as Jamie seemed to be warming to his topic, never mind the temperature of the moles.

'Jamie, it is extremely rude of you to interrupt and with such nonsense. Fold your arms and take the trouble to listen to what I am saying. When I want to ask you a question I will but I shall demand a sensible answer. For heaven's sake, stop that ridiculous giggling, Brendan. Pull yourself together. It's not funny.'

The lesson continued with a puzzled, but subdued Jamie, with Eagles occasionally choking back a snigger punctuated by sidelong looks at each other.

'You are a real joker, Jamie,' his neighbour whispered to him, giving him an appreciative smile which made Jamie feel warm inside. Perhaps that was like the moles felt when the fire his daddy made to stop them from freezing got going. As Miss Griffin drew her narrative to a close, the class was instructed to draw a hill they knew in the range around them called the Chilterns. Despite Miss Griffin's warning, Jamie could not stop himself calling out that his name was Chilton, too, and perhaps that was why the moles liked his garden. He also could not resist including a small molehill at the bottom of his hill with a little mole peeping outside.

★

At the lunchbreak, having had first sitting, the boys drifted into their friendship groups which were remarkably akin to the seating plan of the classroom although there was some cross-referencing, generally when children, whatever 'tables' they were on, were neighbours of each other and friendly outside school. Eagle boys tended to discuss the rival merits of the Action Man figures they had brought out from the inner depths of their pockets, while Ducks seemed to enjoy playfully jousting with each other, sadly often with some discord requiring the intervention of the duty teacher. Football was only allowed under supervision (health and safety restrictions), during summer months when the field was in use but boys would do their best to flout this rule when autumn days were sunny. Much more intermingling could then occur as ball skills were most certainly not the preserve of the brighter children in the class. The girls from each table generally associated according to their preferred activity: they swapped beads, played hopscotch, skipped or merely sat on the steps, talking happily; some squabbled noisily. The teacher in charge kept a watchful eye as she walked around, usually holding a Duck or two by the hand, often that of Wayne from Year 3 who was one of a few children qualifying for free school meals.

Although he still found himself ostracised by his table mates (regarding him as the class joker was one thing whilst actually fraternising with this irritating boy was another, to be avoided at all costs by all the unfeeling rejection strategies six-year-olds could muster), Jamie rushed up to the Action Man group.

'Shall I tell you all about our molehills? I could tell you which day my daddy does the paraffin thing. And what my mummy says. Mummy has shown me in my 'cyclopaedia all about moles and I am going to get a book about moles from the library tonight.'

But his words fell on deaf ears. With a collective shriek the boys raced off with their possessions to a bench which had just been vacated, one dropping from the group en route to complain to the teacher on duty, bursting out:

'Miss Shadbolt, Jamie is annoying us. He won't leave us alone.'

Miss Shadbolt sauntered over to Jamie who was advancing towards a group of girls who, as they saw him approaching, began to stick out their tongues and waggle them.

'Miss Shadbolt,' enquired Jamie, 'do you know how mountains are made?'

Lucy Shadbolt looked at her watch in relief, then raised her whistle and blew three long blasts.

Chapter Eight

As the children seated themselves for the start of the afternoon's lessons, a messenger came into the classroom, having knocked politely on the door and been given the go-ahead by Miss Griffin. Miss Griffin frowned as she read the message written in what the staff called the Little Red Book which contained the Orders of the Day but could circulate at any time. LRB, so-called for short, was a crib from a Communist dictator, Chairman Mao's book of the same name. Secret police would raid a house in the middle of the night and frogmarch out any infringer of his rules, never to be seen or heard of again, and the staff felt Mr. Holmes' missal – which had to be initialled as read and agreed – spanked of the same regime. As one young staff member put it, 'I even have to think about whether I have washed behind my ears that morning when he comes into my room – and it is more than I would dare to question anything written in the LRB.'

Turning to the messenger, Miss Griffin said tartly,

'I see there has been a change to the timetable this morning. I note that I am the last to receive the book; is there a reason for this? With the young children in my care, it takes longer for us to get ready when there is any change in plan. Why am I the last today to be shown this?'

All eyes were on the messenger who was eyeing the floor with embarrassment.

'I am very sorry, Miss Griffin. I didn't know that 'cos it's not me what usually takes the book round,' adding somewhat lamely, 'I went to my class first and then backwards to the other classes.'

Noticing Miss Griffin's attention was directed towards the messenger and not the Eagles and luxuriating in the welcome he was getting from his new friends, again Jamie confided in Millie.

'I wonder how many things she bumped into doing that. It would be particularly hard walking backwards round corners.'

Jamie's remark was again passed from ear to ear, each being greeted by a choked snort until reaching Charlie.

'You had better tell her what a dangerous thing that is to do next time you see her,' Charlie urged as he winked around the group.

A real glow of pleasure engulfed Jamie, swelling with pride with his new-found status. All the Eagles were his bestest friends. Better to tell her now, he thought; I might not see her for a long time and Year 6's don't take any notice of Year 2's. Miss Griffin didn't seem to be realising what danger the messenger was in so it was his duty to warn the messenger now. He put his hand up and waved it furiously, wriggling in his seat. Curtly, Miss Griffin told Jamie to sit still and stop waving his arms around as if he was part of a wind farm.

'It is very important, Miss Griffin, what I have to say. If that girl walks backwards down the corridor she could walk into something really hard, like a corner of a desk. There are some desks outside Year 4, you know. Or she could crash into someone and one of them could get hurt.'

Warming to his subject, he continued, 'and she could knock someone's cup out of their hand. As you must know, teachers send for their coffee when it is wet playtimes.'

The messenger's jaw had dropped; her eyes had widened. She put her hand over her mouth to keep herself under control. Miss Griffin's own jaw tautened as she snapped,

'Jamie, you're a very cheeky little boy. You know perfectly well what she means,' (Jamie nodded his head fervently in agreement) 'and if we weren't late to the Hall already, I would write a note to your mother to tell her exactly how you have behaved since you have joined the Eagles.'

Extremely perplexed by this rebuke, Jamie mused over the mixed statement made by Miss Griffin. I'm told I am rude one minute, then the very next thing she says that she will say to my mother how kind I was to warn that girl. She really is a very funny lady. Still, the last remark was nice so he thanked Miss Griffin very much indeed and told her his mummy would be pleased to receive a letter like that. The messenger left, casting a sidelong look at the class as she did so, most of whom had shoulders heaving with mirth.

'Pull yourself together and line up quietly by the door,' ordered Miss Griffin sharply. 'Father Harrold has come unexpectedly to run a preparatory practice for the Christmas Carol Service.' St. Michael's C of E. was attached to a local High Anglican church where all clergy were called priests and carried the title 'Father', one the new incumbent insisted on being called instead of the term 'Vicar', which Mr. Holmes far preferred, that of 'Father' sticking in his throat and taking much time to get used to.

'Blimey,' muttered Charlie under his breath, 'he is starting early this year. We haven't had Fireworks Night yet.'

As they filed into the hall to sit in the space left behind by the Reception class, each was given a Children's Hymn Book. Father Harrold (Christian name Percival, but he only used that on very formal liturgical occasions) stood on the platform beside Mr. Holmes. He had put together a Christmas concert but as this was his first as the newly appointed representative of the church, he thought an early, preliminary run-through, enabling him to iron out the wrinkles, would not come amiss.

'We are very grateful to you, Father, for giving us so much of your precious time,' unctuously intoned Mr. Holmes although he still regarded this whippersnapper as hardly out of his cradle. However, Mr. Holmes liked to keep in with the

Church as he called it, was a regular worshipper, although not by choice but to be noticed by the congregation, most of whom had, or intended to have, at least one child at his school. At the end of every prayer it was notable that he said 'Amen' rather loudly, either two seconds before or two seconds after everybody else. He had stealthily wormed his way into the respect of the previous incumbent, so that he was now a member of the Parochial Church Council. He had no wish to be a churchwarden as that would mean going to church at least twice on Sunday and faithful attendance was expected on Saints' Days, of which, he felt, there were too many. Even if the school had a day off, that had to be made up during statutory school holidays which he thought grossly unfair.

'It is our practice, Father, to start with carols the young ones can sing. They can then return to their classrooms whilst Years 3 to 6 can sing the more difficult ones and the choir can add the descants. The orchestra will join us the week before the dress rehearsal.'

Ooh goody, Jamie thought to himself, we will all look very smart in our best clothes. Or did this mean they would all be dressed up as kings or shepherds? He fervently hoped he was not told to be a sheep – he'd felt all itchy in his cotton wool outfit for the Nativity play in Reception. The audience, on that occasion, had been highly amused by the realistic bleating with which Jamie had enriched the manger scene and thanked Mr. Holmes for 'the best Nativity ever'. Earlier they had been entranced by the little sheep who fell flat on his woolly face at the arrival of the angels as, more suitably, had the awed shepherds. As the director of ceremonies that Christmas, Faith Griffin's face had been crimson in embarrassment. She'd already transferred him from the role of innkeeper as, at the first rehearsal, Jamie had spread his arms expansively on the arrival of Joseph and Mary and told them he had plenty of room. '*Inn* you come,' he had declaimed merrily. 'That is what inns are for,' he had explained indignantly, in mitigation of what was deemed to be an insolent manipulation of 'the greatest story ever told', punishment for which aberration his demotion to a sheep seemed to Jamie to be really unkind. 'You have to make room in inns and I was giving them mine.' He felt glad it was only carols this Christmas.

The pianist began the first notes of "Little Donkey". Mr. Holmes pointed to the number on the board beside him, there was a rustle of paper and the Early Years children began to lisp their way through the first two verses. Father Harrold left the platform and waved his arms about just as Jamie had seen when his parents put the Last Night of the Proms on their TV.

After a re-run, as Father Harrold had looked a little pained (which made Jamie wonder whether he had toothache and whether Mr. Holmes should tell him to go home to bed), and had asked them to sing with a little more brightness in their voices, the Early Years class were encouraged to twist to and fro in their seats in a 'baby-rocking' motion to add a little more authenticity. Unfortunately, their movements were neither very well co-ordinated nor realistic and a few 'ouches' and unnecessary retaliation rather spoilt the atmosphere. Nevertheless, Jamie thought the little donkey carrying Mary and her unborn baby on his back must have felt very, very proud.

The next carol was announced as "Away in a Manger". This was chosen especially for Year 2 to sing. At the second repeat, Father Harrold walked down to the Class 2 line.

'Mr. Holmes, this little chap here has a beautiful singing voice. Do you agree it would be a lovely entry to the carol if he sang the first verse as a solo, then the remainder could be sung by his fellows?'

He pointed out Jamie.

'Little man, would you like to sing the first verse on your own?'

The class looked expectantly at Jamie.

'I do know all the words. Would you like me to sing them to you now?'

Father Harrold beamed. 'Yes, yes, do. That would be lovely.' Mr. Holmes warily nodded assent. The pianist played the opening bars softly. Jamie began, in a pure, piping voice,

'Our Wayne in pret a manger,
No crumbs for his bread,
The little Lord Jesus
Lay sweets on his bed.
The stars ...'

Mr. Holmes looked as though he was about to blow a gasket. He signalled to the accompanist who, by that stage, was playing at fortissimo to drown the words; the notes for the fifth line died in the air. Realising the horror of the situation, there was not a single snigger from amongst the assembled wide-eyed and dumbfounded children.

'Go to my room,' thundered Mr. Holmes in Jamie's direction.

'Don't you want me to sing all of the first verse?' enquired a very puzzled Jamie, showing by the aggrieved expression in his face that the order to leave the hall was unfair.

Miss Griffin pushed past the children trying manfully to hold in their tummies so that she could pass, took Jamie by the hand to guide him through the row of seated children and onwards towards Mr. Holmes' room. Her explosive tones could be heard even after the hall doors had swung closed behind them. Explaining to his incensed teacher that these were the words the Eagles sang and now he was an Eagle, he'd thought Father Harrold would want him to represent their more advanced thinking, he marched stoically alongside his angry escort, adding that as Wayne was his friend in the next class, it seemed right because he didn't have much to eat and he didn't think he'd have many presents in his stocking. Tears began to run down Jamie's cheeks as he asked Miss Griffin to think how kind Jesus was to give Wayne sweets to fill him up on Christmas morning. He got his handkerchief out and blew his nose noisily straight into her face just as she bent down towards him to take him by the shoulders. Miss Griffin, fuming, wondered whether there was any end to the insolence of this outrageous child.

Back in the hall, scarcely a pin could have been heard had it been dropped. Sitting cross-legged in the Year 5 line, Freya had wished the floor would open up either to swallow her, or her brother – she did not mind which. What was it about her brother that he always said anything that came into his head instead of first thinking about it? The rest of her class would be bound to mock her at breaktime: they often did, calling Jamie stupid and where did they get him from? One of the boys had once suggested they had picked him up from under a monkey puzzle tree. Freya, never lost for words, had smartly retorted that with a nose like his, he must have come from the parrot enclosure in the zoo, 'so kindly keep your nasty comments to yourself 'cos you'll get back worse than you gave.'

A hasty exchange of words by the two men, and the next carol was announced as "O Little Town".

The first-year children were then dismissed. The gravity of the situation was not lost on any child. Miss Griffin, who had returned, grim-faced, to the Hall was the next to usher her class back to their classroom, where she curtly instructed all Eagles to stand in front of the class while she gave vent to her profound displeasure. Jamie was conspicuous by his absence: he had been told to await Mr. Holmes outside his door. The head would, he was told, give him a piece of his mind in no uncertain terms.

The bell to signal lunchbreak clanged resoundingly. Miss Griffin discharged her class with the exception of the Eagles; these were left standing, hands on heads, facing the whiteboard. A full ten minutes later, with a final confirmation of how ashamed the group had made her feel, instructions were barked for them to join the queue for lunch. Charlie asked permission to speak; he needed to tell his teacher 'something else Jamie said'.

'When the others have gone,' he was smartly told.

Four Eagles filed out of the room.

'You know when we say the Our Father, do you know what Jamie says? He says, "Our Father whose art is in heaven, Harrold be your name". He says those are the proper words because of Father Harrold being important. He does, really he does.'

Miss Griffin sighed. Enough was enough for one day and it was hardly lunchtime. She took out her notebook entitled 'Jamie Chilton: Record of Behaviour' and added another paragraph to page 6.

★

Back at home that night, at Sarah's request, Matt wearily cross-questioned Jamie about his solo part in the carol concert, rescinded as soon as delegated. Sarah had heard confusing accounts from Jamie, who seemed to have been chosen to sing a verse on his own then, apparently, disgraced himself. Sarah felt aggrieved that Matt otherwise grumpily left all the upbringing of the children to her nowadays, blaming her for any transgressions either of them made: 'You're at home to keep them in check: you should know how to control them,' being a refrain she had to choke over far too often these days. What had happened to the women's rights supporter she had married?? He had changed so much since their decision she should remain at home and not resume her career until both children were secure in school. Did he feel emasculated that he was now the sole provider, but in these times of austerity could not bring the benefits they had both enjoyed? Was it that he resented having to work such long hours so that he was deprived of giving the children the attention he would not only have wished but had fully intended? There was also the aspect that there were times when she felt Matt did not even *like* their son; the way in which he was developing seemed to be a disappointment to him.

Sarah had thought Matt, once a rugby player who, together with his mates, knew alternative words to a number of well-known songs, would perhaps be more empathetic on this occasion. Conversely, Matt, as had recently been his custom, silently criticised his ex-deputy head wife for being unable to handle problems like this which cropped up with her precious child. Why not, for God's sake, she had held a very responsible job in school; why is it she cannot deal with minor tiffs and the usual scrapes boys get themselves into? Didn't all boys sing about shepherds washing their socks by night while sitting round a tub? What else would you expect? Matt felt rather pleased that his son had had the courage to sing rude words in front of that po-faced, foppish new vicar – I bet that man was crucified at school, he thought uncharitably and with some latent spitefulness, remembering he had not been guilt-free of that crime himself. Boys like that, he felt, were always ready victims and the only career possible for them was in the Church, hiding under a cassock and strangled by a dog collar.

Matt was even more reluctant to attend St. Michael's on Sundays now that both his children were in the school they had worked so hard to get them into, buying a house in the catchment area although it initially stretched their means. He had solemnly confirmed that he was indeed a practising Christian, which he professed himself to be when filling in certain official forms, despite utterly disliking what he called 'organised religion'. Until Sarah had forced him to go with her, the last time he had been inside a church, apart from weddings, baptisms and funerals, was as a reluctant thirteen-year-old choirboy. Without knowing why at the time, he had found the unwelcomed, single-minded attention of the choirmaster rather overpowering and when this creep had offered to teach him how to play the organ ('you could stay behind after choir practice'), he had firmly put his feet down and refused his parents' pleas to continue in the choir. His parents had told him that turning down such a kind offer was really ungracious of him. 'He said he would teach you for free? That was extremely generous of him and you are a most ungrateful boy.' Although he had felt uncomfortable about the idea of sitting close to a man he didn't actually like, without knowing why he had this feeling, it was some years later when Matt realised that it was not the church organ he was expected to play … and he felt quite sick. It was around that time he 'went off' organised religion. And he certainly was not enamoured with those churches where you had to address the vicar as Father; what rot. The stuff that was splashed about all over the place didn't make for a pleasant atmosphere, either: fair made you choke.

His mind wandered to other incidents of that nature he had had to confront. On an earlier occasion, one which should have forewarned him about the organist's intentions, he had been asked by the art master of his grammar school if he could paint his portrait wearing his choristers' ruff. On arrival he found a boy in his class who they all felt to be too effeminate lolling in a chair without a stitch of clothing on. Matt had fled from the house before even crossing the threshold into the studio. His mother had been particularly angry with him for opting out as she had treasured the thought of having an oil painting of her second son to hang above the fireplace. Matt had not dared to give her the reason he had made his decision at the very last minute: she would neither have understood nor thought it was anything other than his imagination playing tricks on him. And, much later, there was that corporal in the Air Cadets who had propositioned him – at least at seventeen he was able to recognise when he was in danger of being caught up in something abhorrent he would most certainly regret and dealt him a swift uppercut. Needless to say, his membership of the Cadets was short-lived. Again his mother was furious as the uniform had only just been bought but he daren't explain the reason for his decision as he knew his word would not be believed against that of a trusted senior. Confiding in his brother George was no good, either: he was already living away from home in his first job after graduating. Instead, Matt gave the excuse of pressure of A Level studies and his determination to apply to Oxbridge, Durham or Bristol. He was on a sticky wicket there, however; he had already given his word to his parents that the Cadets would not be a passing notion.

'Well, Jamie, what's all this we hear about you being caught out singing rude words to carols?'

Matt was more concerned about the fact his son was caught out and said so; he had no problem with the choice of language.

'Daddy, the words weren't rude and it wasn't outside at playtime and I wasn't playing Catch or Tag. I didn't say any words beginning with "f" or "b" or "s". I think there are some "c" words but I don't know those. And I didn't say the "sh" one, either. I think it was because I sang about Wayne, one of my best friends; they were the words the Eagles sing and it didn't take long for me to learn them 'cos I'm on their table now. I think it was because it was about Wayne, you know. He likes to play with me and he is sometimes my bestest friend. He's very clever and he likes talking with me. Boys in his class often tell him to buzz off, which isn't very nice so he finds me and I find him. It's grown up to have a friend in Year 3. I don't think his parents give him much to eat 'cos he always asks if there are any seconds at school dinners so as I am an Eagle and was asked to sing all by myself, I sang what Eagles sing. I'll sing you the lines they said were rude. They didn't let me sing all the verse.'

Matt gave a long, drawn out sigh. Why did Jamie always have to go round the houses in any explanation? Was he trying to put him off the scent?

'Jamie,' he interrupted sharply, 'I am not asking you to give me a description of all the stray dogs in your school – just keep to the point, for Chris'sake.'

'Mummy doesn't like you blasphing, Daddy, but I won't tell her what you just said. The carol doesn't have anything to do with dogs, either. I don't think there are any, actually. Or about cats, either. Do you know some?'

His father did not reply so Jamie took this lack of response to be the signal for him to sing. As he finished, Jamie enquired,

'Is the word "pret" rude? I don't know what it means. It's the only word I don't know. Is it a polite way of saying "prat"? Alfie's mother calls him a prat – and a brat, sometimes,' he added, eyes to the skies in mock horror.

'Well, for a start, it's "Prêt a *Monjay*"; it doesn't rhyme with "danger" in the way you sang it,' Matt shot back, grim-faced, the thrill of pride which had engulfed him when he incorrectly believed his son was being audacious at last and doing his best to be the 'real boy' he had yearned for as a son having long gone. Instead, his child seemed to have few masculine qualities and no idea that his version was a stupid revision of a carol. He appeared to be completely unaware that he was exposing himself to ridicule, not peer approval.

'And what do you know about Prêt a Manger?'

'Well, it's the name of the sandwich shop Mummy and her friends get their sandwiches from when they go for coffee. I go, too, when it's half-term or holidays and the other children are there who Mummy knows. Most of them are Eagles or Swans.'

Matt groaned. He was becoming increasingly frustrated that the family would not be able to afford a holiday if Sarah continued to spend all her surplus housekeeping on frivolities. He had still not abandoned the hope that he could slip off on a boys' weekend to Amsterdam that was being furtively discussed by his rugby pals. Perhaps he could manage this under the pretext of a business conference. But it would require funding and, as they shared a bank account, he would have to be very, very careful to pay by cash and not credit card. He knew how much Prêt a Manger sandwiches cost – and he assumed she'd have the smoked salmon or avocado and effing bloody crayfish. He sometimes had these himself for lunch when out of the office, a perfectly acceptable thing to do as you could hardly arrive at a client's with a baguette, some butter, a couple of slices of ham and ask for a knife, and the only edible sandwiches, in his opinion, were from there. Apart from BLTs, of course. Also, he could put it on expenses sometimes, when he would buy himself two. Being at home, he thought with a stinginess which actually repulsed him as it was diametrically opposed to his previous pleasure of being the main breadwinner, Sarah could make her own and should be more thrifty.

'Anyway,' added Jamie, 'Father Harrold gave me a piece of his mind. Mr. Holmes said I should be grateful for that and I am. Very, very grateful. I expect I shall know more about the Bible stories he tells us now I've got some of Father Harrold's mind. Mummy told me that having a piece of someone's mind was when you told someone exactly what you thought about something so I hope he's given me that bit because he seems to have lots of different thoughts about ever so many interesting things. I know quite a lot of them. Last time he told us about a "Prodical" son and I'd like to be one of those. There was one about a Smartie who walked on the same side of the road as someone who'd had an accident so he'd helped him.

It would be a nuisance if you were down on the ground and people were not on your side, wouldn't it? I know! I'm going to tell Mummy to cross the road to where other people are walking so we shall always have someone to help if we fall over and break a leg or an arm or something. My friend, Freddie, well he's on the Eagles table so he must be my friend, fell off his bike and hurt himself so I'll ask him now whether there were people on his side of the road. Having a piece of Father Harrold's mind will help me to know a lot more than that, you know.'

As the disjointed monologue continued to assault his ears, Matt came as near as he ever had to throttling his son. Didn't his child realise that he was out of order to make light of a serious misdemeanour? But Jamie was unstoppable.

'Miss Griffin said I was lucky because I only got a ticking off. It's nice to have a lot of ticks in your book. I expect Mr. Holmes wrote something nice about me, too. He writes about people in his Black Book and shows it to one of his visitors. I think his visitor is an important person because he works at the Educational Office, you know, that big building in Greysbury. Miss Griffin is always saying that about something that we do. She says then that we will be written up in his Black Book. Do you have one in your office to write about people and put ticks in your book about them?'

Matt felt the one-sided 'discussion' was getting very out of hand, long past the point of irrelevance. Was this his son's tactic; change the subject at every opportunity? It *had* to be his clever ploy to get himself off the hook. Wearily, he attempted to get back on track.

'I expect she also tells you to wash your mouth out when you say rude things – your great aunt used to say that to me and carried her threat out one day,' he added with feeling, not one he wished to recall. 'She said it was Vim – but I know it was the flour she made bread with.'

'Oh,' said Jamie with interest. 'She was your great aunt as well, was she? We don't see her very often, do we? Mummy says that when she sees her, she asks her to have a cup of tea, calls her nurse for one, and then asks Mummy again if she would like a cup of tea and keeps on saying that over and over again. She also asks her if you have been a good boy and eating up your dinner nicely and it doesn't matter how many times she asks her and Mummy tells her you are, she keeps on and on asking.'

Matt's aunt was in her mid-eighties and had had symptoms of dementia for the past ten years. He refused to visit. 'What's the point? She asks me the same questions as you, so clearly doesn't recognise me. You've got the time to go so if it makes you feel better, you go by yourself,' he would say testily. He took a deep breath, deciding there was no point in pursuing any further the introduction of this red herring by Jamie.

'Jamie, you've upset your mother, not me. I don't suppose this is the last time you will get in trouble for saying the wrong thing at the wrong time but just try thinking things through first. What might be alright in the playground is not right in school or where there are adults around. Get yourself into bed and put your nightlight on. Make sure you apologise to Mummy in the morning for being so thoughtless.' Saying this brought to mind a vivid memory of one of his masters at school who used to bark at students who'd not done their prep and would give an inane answer to a question: 'Engage your brain, boy, before opening your mouth.' Matt sincerely wished his son would do just this.

Sarah was none too pleased later when she found Jamie in bed without having washed his face and hands or cleaned his teeth and stoutly remonstrating in response to her question that he'd done exactly what his daddy had asked him to. 'He did not tell me to do those things: just go and get into bed, he said.' She was even less pleased when she learned Matt had told him Mummy didn't have any brothers so wasn't quite up to the mark with understanding how boys behave in private. Did not her twelve years of teaching count for understanding the young male point of view? Whatever the feminine word for 'emasculated' was, Sarah was feeling this more and more often.

Chapter Nine

Jamie's best friend and who had been his next-door neighbour on the Ducks' table, a boy who was flagged up by the school as in need of individual support from a teaching assistant at certain times during the day, was Jamie's role-model for his performance in class before his promotion. It was Alfie's clocks he had copied when Daniel kept his covered by his arms, Alfie's halting reading he had done his best to match (after all, the T.A.* always told Alfie how good he was and how pleased he made her feel when he 'sounded out' the letters so nicely), and whose sums were always marked, 'Well tried, Alfie', sometimes with a star next door to the comment from Miss Griffin. Alfie had been very proud to call Jamie his friend, even though he had had to thump him once when Jamie had said it looked as if his hair had been cut by a lawnmower. With Jamie by his side, he always had a friend to play with as neither he nor Jamie were included in the games of others. Anyway, Jamie always had nicer things to eat at breaktimes like a tiny cake with round red sticky things on top and Jamie would give him that and Alfie would give Jamie his salt and vinegar crisps, albeit rather squashed as Alfie had sat on them in the classroom. He always asked Alfie what else he had got in his pocket and held firmly on to his cake if Alfie's pocket had also been the receptacle for a piece of lavatory paper which he'd been provided with to use as a handkerchief. He only ever swapped if the crisps had been wrapped up in that silvery paper Mummy used, although it was never as smooth as his mummy

---

* T.A. = Teaching Assistant (Teeaye in Jamie's mind).

kept hers. It was always very wrinkly and sometimes smelled of something other than crisps. Jamie was rather guarded before the exchange took place; there were a number of occasions that he thought he'd keep the cup cake for himself. Not that Alfie liked the cake part, it was the red thing he lusted after: it wasn't like the nice shop cakes he was sometimes given at home. He was thankful his friend didn't seem to mind if he put that bit in the waste bin, even though he tried to do it when Jamie wasn't looking. Now Jamie was sitting with the Eagles, he would have to find another friend to show his work to so that they could copy from him and perhaps play with him.

As the term went by, Alfie's mother wondered why her son seemed to have lost his devil-may-care attitude. Even Miss Griffin was aware that happy-go-lucky Alfie had become so listless in class. Without warning and without the usual appointment to ensure his teacher would be available, Tracey Smegley stormed into Miss Griffin's classroom after school one day, dragging Alfie behind her. Looking up from the pile of exercise books she was hoping to mark before her bus was due, Miss Griffin was startled to find herself suddenly and unexpectedly being taken well out of her comfort zone. Certainly she was unused to being the recipient of the torrent of pent-up rage which was about to rain down upon her.

'My kid says you're his teacher. Well, I've just come to let you know I've had enough of this. He's being bullied, that's for sure. Wees his bed every night, he does, and I'm just about sick of it. I want to know what your school is doing about it.'

Before Miss Griffin had time to collect her composure, the flow continued unabated as the young woman rose to her theme.

'I've heard you have to have a sheet on this what parents can see and I want ter see it. Me 'usband was talking to 'is boss and he said there was a proper name for this and it was my right to have a look at it.'

Alarmed that there was a mild accusation in this intrusive

encounter, Miss Griffin expressed concern that something of which she had no knowledge had been occurring in Year 2 and pressed for the basis of the complaint.

'Alfie said his bestest mate didn't sit wiv him anymore and so he didn't play wiv him and no one else will. My poor Alfie ain't got no one now, he says, to go around wiv – they all tell him to clear orf. It's not right, I tell yer ... Know what I mean?'

Tracey almost thumped the table but, suddenly remembering her own schooldays when much of her time was spent on a corridor outside the head's study, realised such action could get history repeating itself. She satisfied herself with her theme, soon relaxing into her more natural mode of speech.

'Lee says he'll come up to see yer if I don't get no satisfaction from yer ternight.'

Miss Griffin, now well aware of the identity of the fireball (Alfie had hidden himself behind the door but sufficient of his body had remained visible), had no desire to engage in a 'discussion' with Mr. Smegley who was known to be belligerent in the extreme if you got on the wrong side of him. It was not exactly a pleasant experience, she had been given to understand, if it was the right side, even. Rumour had it that the last time he was 'away on business for three months' his assignment had been at the Queen's pleasure ... She made a firm vow to watch a few instalments of TOWIE to bring her up to speed on the East London / Essex accent assaulting her ears if she was to meet the two parents at any time in the future; she could not recall any of her previous pupils whose parents hadn't picked up the technique of using even a few aspirates and glottal stops when speaking to what they always referred to as 'Authority'.

To save a further blistering tirade, she offered to go with Ms. Smegley to the secretary's office to get her another copy of the St. Michael's bullying policy, sent to the parents of all new entrants, Ms. Smegley having denied all knowledge of ever seeing anything of the sort.

As an afterthought, mischievously Miss Griffin also made the suggestion that Ms. Smegley could invite Jamie to tea one day, as that would be a means by which the two boys could re-establish friendship (that would put Jamie's mother on the spot and reveal the genuine nature of her liberal attitudes; in all likelihood she would not know how to refuse without getting a mouthful of swear-words and being called a stuck-up pig). Miss Griffin said that, on the school's part, the duty-teacher would be asked to keep an eye on Alfie at breaktimes. She, for her contribution, would be watchful in class for any unkindness towards him and, for example, make Alfie the captain to pick team members when the occasions arose. In that way he would not be the last child chosen, which he usually was. Meanwhile, she would see that any other encouragement for the boys to sit near each other, say at lunch, for example, would be given by the well-trained and kindly dinner ladies.

★

Thus it was that some days later Sarah drove Jamie to Alfie's house some distance away in the housing sector estate. She had been pleased to get the invitation, especially as she had heard so much of merit from Jamie about the boy who was, apparently, his 'mentor' in class when Jamie was a Duck. She had put two and two together about the status of the family in the local community and wanted to do her best to integrate a re-housed family into the life of the school. It must be very hard, she mused, to be uprooted and find yourself out of your depth amongst a neighbourhood unwilling to accept you into their midst and she felt proud of Jamie that he was going out of his way to show friendship. Jamie had not got an unkind bone in his body and, so far as she was aware, treated all he came in contact with on equal terms. She was only too pleased to accept the invitation, carefully written on lined exercise paper in an irregular script but also showing that spelling was not one of Alfie's mother's accomplishments.

Perversely, Matt had not approved of the idea (middle-class snobbery, Sarah had thought with a note of despair; how was it she had only found long after their marriage how bigoted and prejudiced her husband could be privately at times, despite espousing to believe in a classless society, a contradictory factor she put down to his upbringing). 'You can take the man from his background, but you can't take the background out of the man,' was an aphorism she vaguely remembered. For her part, she firmly held far more liberal ideas about social flexibility and was only too happy to make acquaintance with the Smegleys, about whose son she had heard so much of a positive nature from Jamie. Yes, she had heard the pernicious rumour that the family had been re-housed from Peckham to give them a fresh start in life away from the street gangs and drug pushers they had been involved with, but democratically-minded Sarah had dismissed the gossip, feeling sure that social engineering had to be given a chance and what opportunities for this would there be if the family was damned before they had settled in? The Smegleys' tenure was now into its second year and Sarah had continued to close her ears to the apparent fecklessness of the not-yet-thirty Ms. Smegley and the extended absences from home of her partner, as constantly and maliciously voiced by the chattering mothers waiting to collect their children.

Ignoring, therefore, the trashed packing cases in the overgrown dandelion and rose bay willow-herbed front garden, the clutter on the doorstep (obviously in preparation for a visit to the tip, she reflected charitably), Sarah could not help herself feeling thankful, however, that it would be her, not Matt, who would be collecting Jamie at six. Reflecting on the damning nature of gossip, destined to prevent upward mobility and maintain societal barriers, she attempted as best as she could to bang the knocker dangling from its

RIPPLES IN A POND

socket without entirely dislodging it. The door shuddered
on its hinges as it opened, revealing the squalid nature of the
Smegley home. Sarah was aware it was not in keeping with
the vast number of neatly kept homes on the estate re-housing
impoverished families from Tower Hamlets and other less
salubrious areas of London, clearly signalling that incumbents
previously living in what could be described as 'sink' areas
had been effortlessly absorbed within their new, shire-county
surroundings in which they had been only too pleased to find
themselves, leading her to the conclusion that this family must
be in the throes of a 'good turnout'.

'Pleased to meet yer, I'm sure,' was the greeting she
received from a youngish woman with rather too much make-
up on than was customary for Sarah or her friends to use
and a blouse with significantly more cleavage than generally
displayed by the mothers at the school gate during the daytime.
She declined a 'cuppa', despite her avowed intention of staying
a while to make friends with Alfie's mother, excusing herself
by saying she had a daughter at home she did not like to leave
too long (the actual reason being the smell emanating from
the house which was a mixture of seriously wet dog, cat litter
trays and stale cooking fat).

'Please yerself,' Tracey Smegley responded huffily – she
knew only too well the opprobrium in which their family was
held within the district (not that she was aware of the word for
the loud remarks made in their hearing and the rapidity with
which neighbours crossed the road as any Smegley passed by,
not to mention the visits from the social services lady which
caused comment from the neighbours).

'But you'd h-ave to take us as you find us. Perhaps when
you fetch h-im?' Tracey bust a gut to 'speak proper', sniggering
as she did so.

Seeing that what to Tracey had appeared to be a blatant
refusal to show intimacy with her had hit a raw nerve, Sarah

thanked her rather more profusely than she felt but again declined the very kind offer, with many additional thanks. She explained that this would not be possible, unfortunately, as her husband was working late that night and there was no other adult in the house to take charge of Freya. No, Freya was not her dog but her daughter, she corrected Ms. Smegley who had questioned the ownership of a name she had not met before.

With unabashed excitement, Jamie cursorily accepted his mother's kiss and followed Alfie down what passed for a garden path to a scruffy area his friend described proudly as his sandpit. En route, he thrilled with the carnage of broken bikes, wheel hubs and the vast accumulation of cables and pipes, which were liberally sprinkled over what had clearly never been flower beds during the Smegleys' tenancy. He enquired if Alfie's father was an inventor; if so, had any of his inventions been shown at the Design Centre in London to which he'd been taken by his daddy one Saturday? A mangy-looking dog sitting by the side of a cracked old lavatory stretched itself, yawned and strolled over to sniff Jamie in inappropriate places. Fortunately for the cowering Jamie, a well-aimed stone by Alfie in the direction of 'Rozzer' sent him yelping, tail between the legs, back to whence he had come. Tracey shouted from the kitchen door that there was to be 'no muckin' abaht', and 'no frowin' sand in each ovver's eyes', but her smoke-cracked voice was lost in the last whines of the mongrel, to which was added the mewling of a pair of scraggy, ill-fed kittens.

The boys set to to build an 'anshent British thort,' they'd seen in a video in school (Alfie's suggestion, as it was his house), scrabbling at the sand until their fingers were scraped raw. Jamie felt it had a rather musty smell unlike seaside sand. Alfie then 'had a good idea': he ran back to the barely standing fence which protected their treasures, he explained, from 'being nicked by them nutters next door', and brought what looked to Jamie suspiciously like broken-off pieces of car bumpers which, Alfie confirmed, 'woz given me by me cousin wot said he got 'em off a bluebottle's car.' Blinking in amazement, Jamie said he had no idea flies could drive and did he mean a wasp's car 'cos his daddy often went to watch Wasps and was going to take him there when he was older but only if he learned to play rugby. He confided that his daddy had said that would be a real surprise for him so he had every intention of 'googling' the rules to demonstrate that he knew them, and wrapping up the print-outs as a surprise present for his daddy's next birthday. He was not much wiser in respect of the nature of the specified insects, however, when Alfie retorted that he, Jamie, was nuts because he didn't know bluebottles was rozzers. It did remind him of that horrible dog, though, and he thought it might be useful if he mentioned that he would prefer it if Alfie could keep Bluebottle away from him when they went in for tea. Alfie had confirmed that he didn't expect no bluebottles would be round for, as far as he knew, his dad had been going straight ever since he 'came out them Scrubs last year'.

Jamie was proud his friend knew so much and wondered if Alfie would also be promoted to the Eagles table; it was probably only a matter of time. After all, he was so clever, he had his own special teacher, called Teeay by Miss Griffin. She didn't like the way Alfie's socks were always down by his ankles though (and with holes in them), and Jamie felt he could help his friend by reminding him privately that he should remember what she had told him on a number of occasions recently but without any success.

'Alfie, if you want to come up and sit next to me, you really had better pull your socks up, you know. They are always down at your heels and Mrs. Bennett tells you about it.'

In response, Alfie let out a scream of scornful laughter, then spat out:

'Y-ou-ou p-erv. People say that when they mean yer've gotter be more careful, or summat. Not do it, or such like. It's got nuffink to do wiv wot your socks are like. I pulled mine up once when I was abaht four when my sister was telling me how to draw somefink and she gave me a right clip rahnd the ear for cheekin' her.'

Jamie trusted Alfie's knowledge: he had learned a lot from him and would continue to do so even now he was on a different table. He also had lingering memories, none too sweet, of looking to see where Alfie's dad had put clips in his ears: Alfie was always saying that was what his dad had done when he had come home from his holidays. It seemed to him to be funny that his sister did the same thing to him, yet they had never been visible at school. Just as well: you weren't allowed to wear jewellery in school because of Elven Safety, though what that had got to do with elves he wasn't able to work out for himself and must remember to ask Freya some day. Elves had a lot to do with a number of restrictions that Mr. Holmes reminded them of from time to time: playing conkers, going out to play when there was ice on the ground, playing that Bulldog game – which he didn't like, anyway. Fairies were supposed to live at the bottom of your garden; did Mr. Holmes think there were some in the playground as well? Weird.

Alfie liked to play with Jamie because no one would include him in their games – they said they didn't like the way he smelt, which Jamie felt was an impossible thing to know, any more than anyone but Alfie would know exactly how he could hear or could taste things. When an amused Eagle had mocked Jamie when he had asked him how he knew about Alfie's smelling ability, explaining there was always a nasty smell around Alfie, Jamie expressed the view that sometimes there certainly was a smell of chips around him and probably Alfie liked to smell that because it made him think of dinner.

Now Alfie had used a new word, one he had never ever heard before but, as Alfie had said it, he must know what it meant. Alfie did:

'Me dad says some people are pervs. It's a word you use when you fink they're stoopid. He always says that abaht two blokes up our road. When they walk by, he sez, "there go them pervs" and my mum says he should shu' up and keep his rotten language to hisself. So it's a cool word to use, really. Oh, and he called Mr. 'Olmes a perv when he told me dad what a sweet girl my sister Chantelle woz 'cos she gived him a bunch of flahrs when she left to go to the commun'y college. Me dad said she'd probably nicked 'em from the churchyard she walks frew as they were them Christmas 'mums or somesuch: all white droopy petals wiv stinky leaves. Me nan hates 'em; sez they make her fink of death. So, when me dad is narked wiv her, he sends her a bunch. Makes her mad. He grows 'em speshly for her so he's always got 'em when he wants 'em. But ones you can get from churchyards you can get anytime. Me dad can't pick his 'til near Christmas so I 'speck that's where they get their name from.'

Jamie wondered why Alfie and his mother didn't seem to be able to pronounce some of their letters. He hadn't really noticed before because he and Alfie just chased each other round the playground at school and Miss Griffin got cross if you talked in class. He wondered whether this was a polite thing to ask but decided to risk it and asked Alfie why they didn't say 'h' in his family and swapped their 'th' with a 'f' or a 'v', but not the other way round, though, strangely, he did say 'thort' for 'fort.' But why didn't he say 'deaf' for 'death'? He wished he hadn't mentioned his concerns because he got a sharp thump in the ribs in response. So that's what missing those letters is all about. No wonder Alfie doesn't omit those letters as much at school, he reflected ruefully as he thanked him for the demonstration. Perhaps he had better not try to do the same. He moved away to the edge of the sandpit, deciding to give Alfie a wide berth.

The fort was taking shape nicely. Keeping a safe distance, Jamie filled his piece of bumper and flung the contents across to Alfie, maintaining a good rhythm and momentum in this manner, which enabled Alfie to build up the walls at twice the speed as when they were getting in each other's way.

A screech came from the open kitchen window.

'Oh my Gawd – I fought I'd told you little brats not ter frow sand in each uvver's eyes.'

Tracey Smegley thundered down the path as quickly as her frayed mules would let her, apron (depicting a busty nude female) flying in the breeze. Jamie's eyes were transfixed on this apparition; it certainly had to be seen to be believed. At that moment, Alfie rubbed his eyes with his sandy fingers, wailing,

'Mu-um, there's sand in my eyes. Jamie frew it at me. It 'urts like stink.'

'Get' aht of that sandpit, you little devil. Get aht. Get aht.'

Tracey jerked Jamie out by his shoulder, just as her daughter, Chantelle, fresh from her P.S.H.E.* class at the college, shrieked from afar,

'You ain't allowed to touch kids, mum, you child molester. They'll have yer up in court if yer don't look aht. Yer'll be fahnd guilty of child abuse.'

'Let 'em do wot they like. I won't take no insult from snooty kids, or their muvvers – stuffed up creature. Looked as if she'd got a nasty smell under her nose and couldn't breathe proper.'

Jamie looked perplexed at that point, thinking what an odd comment to make as everyone had to have their noses breathing in air otherwise they'd die. Chantelle made the observation that Mrs. Chilton, 'prob'ly goes to them pilot's classes they have down the village hall.'

---

* P.S.H.E. = Personal & Social Health Education

Tracey Smegley didn't even pause for breath.

'Do yer know wot he just said to me? Almost called me a liar. Said I'd not told 'em to frow sand at each other, only not in each other's eyes, and he hadn't. How else did Alfie get it in, then? Tell me, go on, Mr. Clever-pants. How? Look at Alfie: he's screaming wiv pain. Do yer fink he did it hisself? Don't rub it, yer stoopid effing kid. Chanty, take him in and wash his eyes out.'

The colour drained from Jamie's face. He was being accused of throwing sand in his friend's face – which he hadn't: he'd thrown it carefully onto the pile where Alfie was kneeling – and now Alfie was going to be made blind. He most certainly had not asked his friend to bend down when he threw the sand across to him: Alfie had bent his head down himself; it had not been forced down by Jamie. He ran after Chantelle.

'Chantelle, Chantelle, please, please don't do it. You'll never get them back in again; they could even be the wrong way round. Please, oh please, just wash out the sand, not his eyes. Leave them in, please, please do.'

Chantelle turned to give Jamie a scornful look.

'You mad or summat?'

Deftly she swung her little brother under her arm on reaching the kitchen, twisting his head to face the ceiling. The cold tap was turned on, adjusted, and Chantelle swilled the water as gently as she could, showing a compassionate side to her which her parents had neither witnessed before nor would have welcomed had they done so. Still holding him, not an easy feat as Alfie struggled wildly to cope with the pain in his eyes, she 'shushed' him soothingly and did her best to flush every grain out as speedily as she could. Not for the first time, Chantelle marvelled at the rich chestnut colour of her brother's hair, often calling him 'ginger nut,' which she knew would make him mad. There was some unspoken doubt in her mind as to Alfie's paternity but since Lee, her dad, had got other girls 'in the Club' as he called it euphemistically, he didn't ask questions of Tracey, even though the date of conception was when he was driving his truck for a two-week stint on the Continent. The unexpected presence of copper hair, which no-one in either of her parents' families possessed, gave much support for suspicion. On occasions, however, when he wished to rile Tracey, her dad was not averse to questioning his 'son's' parentage in quite vulgar terms. At its mildest, he would refer to Alfie as the son of a bitch but the choice of maternal proclivity could become far more insulting. Lee was otherwise only too pleased to call Alfie his own, feeling Tracey would then never dare to check up on his aptitude for straying from her bed.

Hopping up and down on one foot, oblivious of the kicks he was receiving from Alfie's jerking legs, Jamie repeatedly urged Chantelle to leave his friend's eyes in. Eventually, a triumphant,

'I can't see no more sand in there, Mum. It's all washed aht. Alfie, can yer feel any's left in? It will be sore for a bit but I 'spect you're not going to go blind, as your useless friend here finks.'

Chantelle turned to the still sobbing Jamie and felt a surge of pity for the boy who clearly came from quite a different background from theirs, not that he could help that, she thought. A sense of relief flooded over her that she had done a good piece of work with her troubled little brother and could therefore feel charitable towards his friend who obviously hadn't injured Alfie intentionally. She knew how quick her mother was to cast blame on anyone other than any member of her family, let alone her precious son, who seemed to be the 'apple of her bleeding eye.' Chantelle giggled at the mixed up meta-wotsit, or was it an 'idiot', or one of those 'smiley' things? She never was any good at English.

'Go on, look at 'im. Still got 'is eyes in, see?'

Jamie moaned they were now all red and not proper eye colour at all and the class would laugh at his friend with eyes which weren't blue or brown or green.

Dismissing this as irrelevant, Chantelle added,

'Dunno what you was finking of. What else do you fink you have to do if someone gets somefink in their eye? Probably should've taken him dahn the surgery: the nurse there would've washed his eyes aht with a proper eye bath, she would,' and with an aside to Tracey, 'We'd better get one of them for the 'ouse now we've made that bleedin' sandpit for the kids.'

At least Chantelle's remarks had turned Jamie's concern away from Alfie's dilemma: he now had other unpleasant images chasing through his mind. His vivid imagination had conjured up visions of his bath at home swilling around with eyes of all colours and sizes and he thought he was going to be sick. He put his hand to his mouth to hold it in and to his horror, he noted his hands had bits of nasty-smelling blacky-brown stuff crusted on them. As he held these up for the others to see whilst simultaneously swallowing the contents of his mouth, Chantelle squawked,

'Oh my gawd, his hands are all covered in cat shit. I told you we needed to put a cover on that sandpit 'cos those damn cats fink it's their litter tray. Come 'ere, yer little perisher, and I'll scrub 'em for yer. Phwaar!'

Hands duly scrubbed by Chantelle in the kitchen sink, which was doing overtime even though there was a water shortage, Tracey then sniffily gave it an extra flooding to make sure all traces of faeces had disappeared. Had she got any, she would have sprayed it with disinfectant like they made her do at the offices she cleaned, but the milk-bottleful she had appropriated some time ago without anyone seeing her had been used up by Chantelle a long time ago after one of her college hygiene lessons had made her go round the house disinfecting everything in sight with such abandon that her father had thought he was 'back in that Scrubbing place again.'

At last normality, if that could ever be ascribed to the Smegley ménage, had been restored. With only an occasional shudder, Jamie kept close to his friend, just in case there was a chance that one, or both, of his eyes worked their way loose and dropped out. He'd felt faint as he watched the water flooding across Alfie's forehead and eyes; could they still fall out? He must be brave for his friend. A friend was a person who would give his life for you and you for them, a person who was 'there for you' through thick and thin. Which was this episode: 'thick' or 'thin'? You stood up for a friend, too. Well, Jamie was certainly 'there', and he would continue to stand up for Alfie until Alfie felt well again. Obviously, that was the best a friend could do, he told a stupefied Chantelle who had asked them both to 'sit dahn for tea.' Chantelle said that was all stuff and nonsense and he should do what he was told when in someone else's house. Her parents made the rules in this house, she had added. This provided Jamie with another dilemma: two opposing orders. Should he continue to stand up for his friend or should he obey the rules set in Alfie's house? Weighing up the pros and cons of both (without knowing this was what he was doing in effect), he chose the latter, deciding that adults must also be obeyed, yet a third thing to remember. Oh, how difficult life is, he agonised. It was so much easier when you were in a buggy and didn't have to make any decisions at all.

'Ooh, burgers and chips for tea and we're sitting at a table like we do in the school canteen,' grinned Alfie who had almost forgotten the earlier disasters in which he had played a prominent part. 'That's 'cos you're here. Only usually have take-aways when me dad gets paid' … 'and afore he gets blind drunk and ain't got no money left,' Chantelle added darkly. Alfie continued as if there had been no interruption,

'Me mum says Burger King costs too much so we have 'em for a treat on a Friday if me mum goes up the parade and afore me dad goes up the Dog and Pot. She does get 'em dahn the market on Tuesdays sometimes and sticks 'em in the freezer. Burger King is best though.'

'My mummy makes burgers herself,' Jamie volunteered helpfully. 'She minces up the steak in a mixing thing – I think it's called Ken Wood, or maybe Magic Mixer, probably that's because it seems like it magically changes the meat into stringy bits, quite long ones really. Then she allows me to pick a handful out – after I have washed my hands, of course,' he added hastily in case his standards of hygiene were questioned, 'and pat the lumps into roundy shapes. After that, I roll each one in crumbs she's made in that mixing thing – she puts a sharp blade in it and chops slices of bread up to very small bits for me. She tells me to put the burgers, 'cos that's what they are now, side by side in a straight line on the grilling pan thingy then she grills them. We've got a deep, fatty fryer to do the chips in,' adding reflectively, 'Does your mum have one as well? Ours is electric.'

Chantelle, her charitable sense vanishing fast, threw him a withering look which had no effect upon Jamie's demeanour. There was more than a trace of envy in her voice which overlaid the sarcasm:

'Oh, fancy pants, and I s'pose your mother bakes them poncy little cupcakes with sugary stuff on the top and coloured bits and flippety pieces of chocolate round them bulging over their flouncy cases. And I 'spect you get a roast on Sunday, don't you?'

'Your voice has changed, Chantelle. You just spoke like most people do. Oh yes, lots of nice things. Usually she prides herself on giving us something different to eat every day. She lets me look at her favourite cookery book, written by somebody called Dahlia … Smith, I think her surname is,' adding as an aside, 'Or is it only men who have their last names called "sir-names". Are ladies' last names called madam-names, can you tell me?'

Not having received an answer, the Smegleys having lost interest and engaging themselves in alternative pursuits, Chantelle checking her lipstick, Tracey scraping raw mince from the sink whence it had fallen and slapping it back in the frying pan, Alfie being the only one remaining partially interested in the monologue, Jamie continued his theme unabated. 'And lets me choose a menu sometimes. Then she makes me make a list of the ingredients. She crosses some out because she says we've got plenty of that in the larder and takes me to Waitrose and tells me to find everything, put it in the trolley and add up all the costs. Which supermarket do you go to in your family?'

Chantelle mumbled something about there being nuffink wrong with the Sat'day market, only posh people go to super ones. There was no mistaking the ice in her tone.

Neither was there any stopping Jamie, now not only warming to his topic but positively roasting in the excitement of having what he thought to be a captive audience.

'Then I wheel it to the checkout counters. Are there any in your market, Chantelle?' Not receiving any more than a glazed look, Jamie pursued his theme. 'The lady packs it into those bags we have with ladybirds on (actually, that's from Tesco's but Mummy says Waitrose won't mind us using one from a rival shop: it shows them the Tesco customers change where they go), and I take it (the trolley, I mean) to the car. The best bit is when I take the trolley back to stack it with all the others: it makes a great bang. Whoosh, it goes! I like doing that in M&S best, though, because I can get the £1 coin back Mummy had put in earlier. After the whoosh it comes straight out but you have to pull it a bit and that is quite tricky really. Actually, I don't think it's the same coin exactly, to be honest with you. Sometimes she lets me keep it for being so helpful.' Jamie's forehead creased as he reflected on a thought which had occurred to him as he was soliloquising. 'Oh, I saw a trolley in your front garden, by the way. You couldn't have got your £1 back on that one, Chantelle. Did you? Mmm, I s'pose it's still in the slot so you haven't actually lost it. Won't be easy to get out now, though, it looks a bit squashed up.'

'Cor, how some people live.' Chantelle's compassion having disappeared long ago whence it had come, she looked derisively at this unspeakably horrid little kid. She turned to Alfie.

'Where did you get your friend from, Bucking-harm Palarce?' she enunciated in her best elocution voice which, up to that time, she had been doing her best to redeem from the depths of her memory. She almost choked as memories of primary school lessons for those posh children who wished to enter speaking competitions flooded back. Huh, how she and her friends mocked those girls who did. As for any boys stupid enough to take these, the ribald remarks they would receive every time they passed Chantelle and her friends were enough for them to opt out before their enrolment had been confirmed.

'Well, I will explain to you. Would you like me to?' Jamie enquired, politely. Without waiting for an answer, which undoubtedly would have contained heavy sarcasm, he continued:

'I was Alfie's best friend when I was on the Ducks' table. Now they've moved me to the Eagles but no one on that table likes to play with me because they say I don't kick the ball straight. I think I do, actually. When I kick it, it doesn't wobble any more than it seems to when they kick it but they still tell me to go away; and they don't like Alfie. They say he is smelly so Alfie and I stay together and chase each other. Anyway, I like the smell of Alfie; it is of chips but the only problem is, it makes me feel hungry.'

Chantelle knew only too well what smell emanated from her little brother: she had to put up with all manner of taunting in primary school until one of the teachers bought her a deodorant stick and told her to put it under her arms each morning. That didn't do the trick and the teacher in Year 6 taught her how to wash her blouse and put a clean one on every second day. She also told her to change out of her school clothes when she got home and never hang them near the kitchen. Now at the community college, Chantelle was very careful to ensure she didn't offend anyone's sensibilities and she firmly resolved to look after Alfie's clothes for him in the future as well. Therefore all she added to the discussion was a sniffy, 'Lame ducks more like it,' and nobody spoke for quite a while, Tracey busy with the chip pan, Chantelle combing her hair, Alfie looking shifty and Jamie taking in the stark differences between the Smegleys' furniture and that in his own home. At last he broke the silence:

'You haven't got a tablecloth on your table,' he offered up by way of conversation as no one seemed inclined to add any further comments as to the culinary expertise, or hygiene, of his host's family. 'Eating here will be like having a picnic. Do you have picnics every day?'

This question receiving no reply, Jamie continued with his appraisal of the kitchen/diner. 'And those flowers aren't real, are they? Mummy won't have artificial flowers in our house. She says they gather dust. I know she is right now 'cos I can see layers of it on the leaves from here even, and the colours are all faded so you must have had them a long time. Mummy buys some fresh ones each week when we go shopping.'

The scandalised Tracey, for once, was lost for words.

'Oh, and could I have another glass for my coke, please? This has got a chip in it. Hey, isn't that funny – we're eating chips and I've got one in my glass!! That's a coincidence, isn't it? I know they are different words, though, but I think it's silly that you spell them the same way. Do you know, when I was just six – that was about three months ago – Mummy told me I shouldn't drink from the cup they gave me in a restaurant as it had a chip in it and that breeds germs.'

Jamie paused and looked thoughtful.

'Mmmmm. Funny, that. How could a piece of china breed? It's not an animal or any living thing: not an insect or a reptile. Strange thing to say. Oh, well, I will have to ask my daddy. He's a clever man, you know. He went to Oxford and they gave him a degree in science. That was good of them, wasn't it? But they only give them to very clever people, my mummy says. It's an award, like Mr. Holmes gave me.'

'I fink I will squash this bleeding worm in a minute,' Chantelle interjected, in an effort to break up this unctuous, and in her eyes unwarranted, criticism of her family's domestic practices, and miming a strangling motion with her hands. To no avail: Jamie returned to his discourse on cracked china.

'That was when I learned there were two sorts of chips. As Daddy said, you learn something new every day. I told Daddy that Mummy must have very good eyesight because I couldn't see any chips in my cup and I sniffed in it and said it didn't smell of chips, either. At the time I didn't know why they all laughed at me. Well, actually, not all of them: Freya said something like it being the stupidest thing she'd ever heard. That wasn't nice of her and I told her so at the time. My brainy daddy explained some words have two meanings and a whole potato is cut into chips – just like the bits that come out of a cup or glass or vase or plate or, or, or anything like that when you break it and a chip of that sort could be any shape you break it into, or it does it itself. Mummy added that you could eat potatoes when they are cut into chips but you mustn't drink from things when chips have broken off them because the piece where the chip was before it was broken off and was properly in the cup or glass or whatever, collects nasty germs which could make you sick.'

'Lord save us!' Chantelle gasped fervently, eyes to heaven. 'And we don't wan'cher being sick in our house. Fucking 'ell, I've had to clean up after yer already and I'm not doing it again. 'sides, we ain't got no more glasses. You got the only one we have, I fink. Wot's wrong wiv a bottle, anyways?'

Tracey brought another glass, wiping it with a cloth which Chantelle had been using to dry Alfie's eyes.

'Inspect that first then I'll pour your coke into that one.' Tracey was so choked with fury that she spat the words so sharply, she even pronounced the glottal stops.

'Oh no, Mrs. Smegley,' (Jamie always put the 'r' in) 'that would mean I would be drinking coke which had already been contaminated by germs.'

Alfie was beginning to think it had not been such a good idea of his mother's to invite his friend over. Somehow, and he had no idea why, neither his mum nor his sister seemed to think as much of him as he did and there was a danger that Jamie and he would never get back together again after this. He had hoped so much that his mum going up to see Miss Griffin would have made her put him up to the Eagles with Jamie. His hope was receding fast.

Chantelle snatched the first glass, downed the contents and snarled, 'If yer don't like our food, don't eat no more and if I'm sick – which I won't be – you can clean it up. I won't offer yer any cake: we've had it a fortnight and I saw flies on it in the kitchen. Probably from that cat shit yer brought in on yer hands. They were b-i-i-g … and FAT … and shiny blu-u-u-u-ue,' she added darkly, her face close up to a cowed Jamie's, her eyes as large as saucers.

'That's very kind of you to warn me, Chantelle. To be honest with you, unless you see the insects, you can never tell what's landed on food. My mummy says it should always be covered up. Alfie, when you come to my house I'll show you some bluebottle spit and poo under my microscope which I got for Christmas last year. They were on slides that come with the package – oh, by the way, I don't mean the slides you slide on, or what we're not to do when there's ice on the playground but ones where you slide samples onto the glass and put another piece of glass on top and that is why the microscope slides are called slides, just in case you didn't know, which I didn't until last Christmas. English is funny, isn't it? The leaflet which comes with the microscope tells you what each slide is. The bluebottle poo looks disgusting and that's what is probably in your cake if what Chantelle saw was actually a bluebottle. They can be mistaken for meat flies, but I s'pose they only go on meat so it was definitely likely to be a bluebottle, Chantelle. Do you do science at the community college?'

Ignoring the facetious comments directed at her personally, while Jamie pondered on whether anything could be 'definitely likely', and whether he should rephrase his last statement, Chantelle interjected with relish:

'Oh, and I 'spect they spat and pooed on the burgers, too.' Chantelle warmed to her topic, 'It should be alright though, 'cos I squirted everyfink wiv fly spray wiv DDT in it – that kills orf everyfink, humans as well, I fink.'

Teeth tightly clenched, swallowing back hard the unspeakably awful ingredients of his tea which had suddenly returned to his mouth, Jamie left the table, knocking over the second glass, fortunately empty, in his rush to find the cloakroom. It did not cross his mind that a downstairs toilet was not a feature of this sort of house – not that he was aware that the home of his friend, apart from the decor he had felt obliged to mention, was any different from his own. The first door of a room he opened, the stench greeting his nostrils before he had time to close it again, merely contained an ill-assorted collection of putrefying trainers, workman's stinking boots, boiler suits covered in paint of all colours, smelly socks, the whole reminiscent of a rubbish tip. A squawk from the direction of the kitchen met his ears at the point at which it had crossed his mind that it wouldn't be spotted if he heaved up into a wellie boot, but thought better of this idea as his presence near the cupboard had been noticed. He, most fortunately, remembered the story he had heard at Sunday school when the vicar had told them about their sins finding them out, ruefully expecting this would be classified as a sin.

There might not have been much of Jamie's hair left, or even his head, had he followed his first instinct. Unbeknown to him, Lee Smegley had walked into the hall. Undoubtedly, the final outcome would have been another holiday for Mr. S. at Her Majesty's pleasure.

'If yer looking for the bog, yer young 'ooligan, it's upstairs in the bathroom. 'Spect yer've got a fucking hundred of 'em in your house but we've only got one. And mind that effin' dawg.'

Scrambling up the stairs, it was not a difficult task to locate the loo; the stench guided him. He stuck as many fingers down his throat as he could, an unnecessary action, however, as the vision which greeted him as he bent over the open bowl was enough to make him retch up not only a mixture of Burger King and chips, fly-blown cake and coke but the contents of his school lunch as well. It goes without saying that neither his hands, nor what passed for porcelain, were sights to be recommended. Shaking with combined shock, horror and disgust, he turned on the tap, encrusted with the grime of ages, releasing a fierce jet of water which bounced on the dingy yellowing plastic of the basin and right back into Jamie's face. Howling with built-up distress, he buried his face in the tattered cloth which passed as a towel in the Smegley household.

Meanwhile, downstairs, Chantelle was being given a reprimand for 'taking the piss out of a little kid', before the four-letter studded harangue turned to the wisdom of allowing Alfie to play with a stuffed up horror such as Jamie. What Alfie could learn from Jamie filled them with a mixture of fury and scorn. The best thing to do would be to go 'up the school' and ask Miss Griffin to keep them apart as Jamie was 'not doing our Alfie any good wiv his nasty manners and rude behaviour.' Alfie's overwhelming dismay at the way the evening had gone was unbounded. He shuddered as the final epitaph was delivered by Tracey, confirming the friendship was doomed for all eternity.

'Fuckin' hell, he sounds like a fuckin' teacher the way he talks at yer.'

Body still racked with silent sobs and shuddering as if shell-shocked, Jamie returned, sporting a very puzzled look on his face.

'There is a very funny rubber thing in your bathroom that I've not seen before,' said Jamie. 'What is it? It's a sort of rabbit-shape and buzzes and wobbles if you press a button on it. Does it float in the bath, like the plastic duck I've got in mine?'

Chantelle fled upstairs, her mother hot on her heels.

★

At 5.45p.m., Tracey Smegley, Jamie by her side, rang the doorbell of The Firs, Cedar Gardens. Sarah opened the door.

'Jamie was a bit sick after his tea so he might need a dose of somefink. Couldn't have been anyfink he'd ate when he was wiv us as it happened in the middle of tea. Yer oughter put him into bed early, I fink.'

With profuse thanks for accompanying Jamie home and profound apologies for Jamie's untimely indisposition, Sarah closed the door.

'Oh my poor darling! Whatever did you have for lunch at school today?'

Chapter Ten

Tracey lost no time in letting Miss Griffin know that the suggestion she had made had not been a success, bursting into the classroom before Friday lessons had started, interrupting the teacher's preparation for the lessons of the day: Jamie had no manners, his behaviour was rotten and would Miss Griffin please stop Jamie from going anywhere near her poor Alfie. The last thing she wanted was for her son to turn out like that revolting little prig. Would Miss Griffin like it if her son had a friend like that who made rude remarks about the way she kept her house? She was going to take her complaint to the authorities and see if an injunction could be made against that Chilton woman – is that her name? – if she dared to come anywhere near her house again with that horrible boy. And, in future, if she didn't think Alfie was being protected by his teacher, she would report her as not doing her job properly.

Ms. Smegley thought she knew all about injunctions: she had 'had enough' of those brought against Lee over the years and it was about time she used this herself as a threat against any person she came up against who happened to offend her. As outwardly patiently as she could, Faith Griffin directed her towards Mr. Holmes' office, doing her best to remove her from the inquisitive eyes of her pupils, soon to be taking their places in the classroom.

With as much determination as she could muster, Faith steeled herself to remain calm. Her vendetta against her rival could yet be resolved in her mind through another agent: Mrs. Smegley could still be the means whereby Mrs. Chilton was

brought down to size. Yet patience was not a personal virtue
Miss Griffin prized highly; she felt more comfortable when
in total control of her life. In fact, there weren't many that
Miss Griffin felt were necessary although she did profess to
be a person of integrity. Sadly, she had few friends to take her
mind off work and the incidents with the Smegley family
would have benefited from being confided to a sympathetic
confidante. She had always had an ambition to be a teacher,
not to impart wisdom but because she believed that to be a job
which would give her prestige in the eyes of the community. As
an only child born to rather staid, elderly parents – her arrival
at the age of forty-eight was, indeed, a shock to her mother
who felt her neighbours, peeping behind their curtains, would
be mocking her as a lewd woman. You did not engage in 'those
sorts of things' in your forties and, indeed, the Griffins had
kept themselves to themselves 'in the bedroom department'
for many years before even that decade had caught up with
them. Nevertheless, the Good Lord in his Infinite Wisdom
had seen fit to bless them in this way and they set to bring up
their daughter as befitted faithful adherence to the Pentecostal
faith, marking this by naming their newborn appropriately
as a symbol of joyful gratitude and respect. Although in her
own way Faith Griffin had rebelled a little during her teenage
years (incidentally causing particular distress when she broke
away from the religious fundamentalism of her parents), the
profound effect some of the teachings had had on her behaviour
remained with her without her being aware. Gluttony she
despised and was frugal in her choice of food, humility got
you nowhere (she was as good as anybody, better than most),
envy and lust (providing the latter wasn't after men, heaven
forbid) were important values as without either of these one
would lack ambition. Pride was something which sustained
you and kept you from being like those for whom you have
little time, or even loathed. Sloth, well, no one could accuse

her of that. How many virtues was that she had a converse respect for? She'd not kept count.

To her immense chagrin, Faith's pride had been dented once more. Not only wrong-footed by a six-year-old and his mother, now her management skills were being questioned by a young woman almost young enough to be her daughter, had her life taken a different turn and she had married. In her own opinion she, who was a teacher of considerable merit, had not only been pipped at the post by that minx who had charmed her way through *that* interview (probably flaunting herself at the mainly male Panel), but had now been outsmarted by her obnoxious son. Furthermore, her judgment had been called into question when attempting to appease his friend's mother by setting up the idea of after-school socialisation.

Faith had obviously been the victim of a careful plan masterminded to reveal an inability to detect super-intelligence and this latest visitation from Ms. Smegley caused her to firm up her resolve to do her best to demonstrate Jamie was not at all what his mother had cracked him up to be in front of Mr. Holmes. No doubt about it, whilst he might be good at learning parrot fashion under pressure – or, more likely, coercion, Faith Griffin thought darkly – he would not be able to sustain it. She would be alert in the coming term to every whim and foible the child displayed and, where necessary, record its nature. At least, she had an unwitting ally if she played her cards well and managed to convince Ms. Smegley that her vendetta should be against Mrs. Chilton alone and she, Alfie's teacher, was doing her utmost to tame a most unruly child. Would Geoff Holmes call in Mrs. Chilton to explain her side of this debacle? The likelihood was that he would regard a matter outside his school as beyond his jurisdiction, which would inflame Ms. Smegley even more intensely and there would be no knowing how that would affect future contact between the two families.

Faith would then feel in some small way vindicated, however vicarious that relief that might be.

The door to the classroom burst open as an inflamed Ms. Smegley, having spoken her mind and left a time-bomb ticking in the mind of the challenged teacher, ignored Faith's advice and sped homewards through it, almost knocking over Jamie, the first child to enter. He marched up to Miss Griffin, still reeling with shock, in an attitude of importance, holding aloft a letter addressed to his teacher.

'You don't need to open it if you haven't got time: I can tell you what's inside. It's a message from my mummy to say I wasn't very well at Alfie's last night and she thought you ought to know. I'm not sure why whe's written to you 'cos I could have told you myself, as I am doing anyway.'

Miss Griffin sharply told a clearly bemused Jamie to take his seat on the carpet.

'But Miss Griffin, we sit on our bottoms on the carpet. Why do you want me to take my chair? Is it because I'm to do something important?'

What a horrendous start to the day, Faith groaned to herself. Thank God (if there is such a deity), it is Friday. Her mind conjured up visions of the autumn walk in the Chiltern countryside she had promised herself on Saturday, probably ending up at a National Trust estate for a cream tea. Could she get through the remainder of the week before she could claim her well-earned rest period? She snapped back into action.

Sadly, events of the afternoon stretched her patience further before her longed-for weekend, a feature of her working day which was becoming the norm, she later reflected, seemingly 'sent to try her' by some unknown being. Nonetheless, a softer side of her character was revealed.

The calm demeanour of the afternoon class was interrupted when Jamie was late back into class, explaining to his teacher that he had been trying to find Conor's marbles. 'Why didn't

you let Conor find his own marbles,' Miss Griffin said crossly.
'How many times have I told you all that if marbles are lost,
then it is the owner's job to look for them?' adding tartly to the
class, a number of whom were in stitches, 'And there is nothing
to snigger at. At least Jamie was trying to be kind, even if he
did not take any notice of my clear instruction.' Miss Griffin
could never find it within herself to give *unconditional* praise to
Jamie, the epitomisation of her own thwarted ambitions. But
her condemnation of the class's hilarity fell on deaf ears; the
class was convulsed.

'Charlie, please tell me the reason for such uncalled-for,
childish behaviour,' she had continued sharply.

Jamie, who'd thought it was stupid to tell children off for
being children, decided to keep that thought to himself as
Miss Griffin was then getting angry and that had seemed very
unfair when he had been trying to help Conor.

Charlie, the class spokesman at all times, a fact resented by
a number of his peers who thought him to be Miss Griffin's
pet and would tease him for it later, had responded, choking
back his mirth as well as he could. 'Conor said something
we thought was silly and so Millie said he'd lost his marbles.
Jamie felt sorry for him and,' he could barely utter the words
without being overcome with the vividness of his memory,
'and so he obviously went to look for them.'

Ignoring the ludicrous nature of the situation, the teacher
questioned further. 'And what did Conor say to cause you to
be so unkind, Millie?'

'He said Father Christmas was not anyone's dad, it was his
mother's boyfriend who had a van and cleaned chimneys so it
was easy for him to get down them.'

Even Miss Griffin often felt compassion for Conor, a
bewildered little boy who always seemed the butt of class
jokes. Why did Jamie feel it necessary to follow suit? Strangely
in view of her entrenched feelings in relation to his mother,

she felt equal strength of compassion for Jamie welling within her. Instructing the class to pull themselves together, take out their reading books and read quietly to themselves, she gently took Jamie into the book-corner, sat him on the sofa and then explained the intended meaning of the phrase but so softly that Conor could not hear the damning explanation in case it made him feel even more crushed than the bullies in the class made him feel. Conor was probably the only boy in the school who needed help to understand what was happening around him; his 'social skills' were definitely lacking.

'So, Jamie, the boys hadn't realised you thought "losing his marbles" was a true fact until you gave me the reason why you were late into class. As a result, you had them in stitches,' adding as she'd noticed the frown of incomprehension on Jamie's face, 'that is to say they laughed so much, they felt their sides were splitting and needed stitching up. So now, when you hear those phrases again, you will know what each means, won't you?"

Not for the first time or, indeed, the last, did Jamie think that it was stupid not to say what you really meant instead of saying things which were, frankly, quite ridiculous. Nevertheless, remembering the lesson on white lies, he had nodded assent, clutching his sides to ensure none of his ribs, or lungs or his heart, fell out.

Chapter Eleven

And whilst Faith Griffin was enjoying her well-earned leisure time that week-end, untrammelled by concerns relating to the Chilton family, the family itself had to deal with an embarrassing visit from Matt's relatives.

'That's the second time that doorbell has gone,' Matt bellowed down the stairs from the bathroom where he was hastily shaving. It was bad enough when he was criticised by his wife for his Sunday 'designer stubble'. Sarah described two days of non-shaving as scruffiness; there was no chance of achieving a suave male-model look in such a short time, she said, in a tone of voice which only wives know how to use, and believed he was just being slovenly. Matt had no wish for his ungainly elder brother to make similarly disparaging comments. It was rare to receive a visit from his brother's family, they did not have a lot in common being so wide apart in age, and there had been a time when any intimacy in their relationship had soured to the point of information on the fortunes of either being communicated to each by their mother. Not that this was welcomed, only their wives allowing a modicum of family gossip to seep in to their respective homes, unbeknown to their husbands. It was actually the sisters-in-law who healed the rift eventually, taking the bull by the horns at a cousin's wedding where extending a stupid feud could have marred the day.

'Who the hell is going to answer it?'

'Jamie, darling, you're the nearest. Answer the door,' Sarah called from the kitchen.

Busy straightening up the cutlery on the dining room table, his 'Sunday job' which he had proudly taken on as his responsibility 'now I'm six', Jamie carefully moved the condiment set to his satisfaction, the salt to the left of the sharp crease in the centre of the tablecloth, the pepper to the right.

'Jamie, stop fiddling about with the things on the table. Hurry up and answer that door before they think we're not back from church yet and go away.'

A perplexed looking Jamie wondered whether his mother had lost a few marbles. There was not a fiddle in the house.

'Jamie, for God's sake, do pull yourself together and stop daydreaming. Answer that door immediately.'

Up to her elbows in crumble for the rhubarb pie crust, Sarah was fast losing patience with the family who seemed to be leaving everything for her to do or delegate. Unthinkingly Sarah, using the nickname used in private between herself and Matt when discussing his affluent much older brother, George (who ate far too many business lunches yet returned home ravenous), added, 'It will be Uncle Porker.'

Rather perplexed that in less than forty-eight hours he had been warned twice to guard against the collapse of his body, Jamie emerged from his reverie.

The bell now rang continuously. Making a throaty brrrrring noise sound in answer to the ring of the door, Jamie looked through the quarter-light to see what was there which could be making such a sound. There stood Uncle George, Matt's rather overweight brother, looking somewhat out of sorts and cross, his cousin Max and his Aunty Julie. He opened the door.

'Oh, hello, Uncle Porker, Auntie Julie and Max. It's good you've got here now 'cos Mummy said if you don't get here soon, she'll give you a cold dinner so it's lucky you are not any later because we don't like cold pork. Ooh,' Jamie's eyes lit up with dawning recognition, 'I wonder, Uncle Porker, if that is why Mummy has cooked pork today – we don't have it very often as Daddy says it's not his favourite.'

Puce-faced Uncle George, slamming shut the front door which missed his wife's fingers by millimetres, strode past Jamie straight into the kitchen, to face his wide-eyed, frozen-to-the-spot sister-in-law.

Matt, who by this time had joined Max and Julie in the hall, merely gave each a cursory welcome as his main intention was to grab his son by the scruff of his neck and whisk him into his study. Some minutes later a deeply bewildered child, released from the onslaught of his father's wrath and with his father's stinging phrases ringing in his ears, emerged to meet his uncle, still smarting with indignation in the hall. Suffice it to say that amends were not made when a crestfallen Jamie attempted to make his apologies for repeating the name he had heard his mother refer to him by:

'As mummies are always right, I thought your name was Porker, not George after all. Daddy says I have to remember it is George, George, George and I must never say Porker again because it's very rude.'

Turning away from his now completely lost-for-words uncle, Jamie went rapidly upstairs, straight to his bookcase, immediately selected a book and stuffed it under his mattress, shifting it to the centre until it stopped alongside a dog-eared copy of one entitled *Busty Beauties*. It was really weird that Conor's mummy had given her son a rude book, he had thought to himself at the time, but it was kind of Conor to pass it on to him. There were quite a lot of rude pictures in it and the title was certainly rude. The book, which now was also hidden in his secret place, had Porky the Pig's name coming up a lot in the story, so it was best to do what Conor said and keep the rude books in a place where your parents couldn't find them. That's what he'd told him to do, anyway, when he'd given him the magazine which he later said he'd actually nicked from his mum's boyfriend's van; his mum had no idea he had it in his possession and would have murdered him had she known.

Shaking his head as if he would never understand adults, especially the violent thoughts they harboured, Jamie returned to the family gathering, now icily exchanging what are usually called 'pleasantries', a descriptor far from the truth in this case.

Throughout lunch, Jamie barely uttered a word, afraid the wrong name would come out of his mouth without him being aware. He tried hard to work out what his father actually meant when he said he didn't want to hear the wrong name drop off his lips: did words make a bumping sound when they hit the floor and how did a word stick on your lips in the first place? Was that the same as 'eating your words'? Jamie had little to say, speaking only when spoken to and then only in monosyllables, being careful not to address anyone by their first name.

'How are you liking school, Jamie?' his aunt enquired kindly, having beaten Sarah to introduce a neutral topic of conversation. Sarah had just begun to open her mouth with another comment about the extent of the wintry weather.

'The classrooms are a bit small, Aunty.'

'Maybe there are too many children in your class,' responded his aunt. 'It's all to do with the cut-backs. What do you like doing most? History? Are you good at sums?'

'What are sums, Aunty; I don't think we do sums, and I like the end of the afternoon the bestest.'

'Fancy, a school that doesn't do arithmetic,' growled Uncle George, aside.

'Oh, but they do,' interjected Sarah, 'but they call it maths nowadays.'

'So what lesson comes at the end of the afternoon, then, Jamie? Art? P.E?'

'Oh no, it is not a *lesson*, otherwise school would go on and on until the evening and we'd all be asleep by then. We can go home when our mothers collect us and that is what I like doing the most at school.'

Feeling that the Sahara Desert could prove a more stimulating theme, attention switched away from Jamie but, after such an inauspicious start to the visit evoking unfortunate memories of the Cold War, conversation remained at a very mundane level with continued awkward intermissions, livened each time courses were changed. The topics then focused on choice of starter, main and dessert, respectively, ingredients, cooking, the merits of Waitrose over Tesco and vice versa, each discussed with false heartiness by the women, the two brothers studiously avoiding the gaze of the other. Even though the ten years separating the two men were less significant in their middle years, Matt still felt aggrieved that his brother liked to put him down as often as he could. Sarah had suggested that George had resented losing his 'only child' position when he had been born: the lavish attention he had received for a significant portion of his childhood would have dwindled when another came on the scene to share parental affection. Matt felt the years drop away as, back in his childhood, the inferiority he had then been made to feel surfaced once again. Damn it, he would stand up to George with all the vigour he could muster: he would not allow him to stir up the old feelings of insignificance; he was his equal and the first to show a sign of contrition would be the weakest.

It wasn't until mid-afternoon when the port was offered that the frigid atmosphere warmed a little. An early chance of a thaw had gone into remission when Max had declined the smoked salmon roulade and announced he was a vegetarian. He would prefer to have beans or cheese on toast (several slices in fact as he was rather hungry), because he was of the opinion that the seas and rivers were now over-fished. It was wrong to indulge in buying salmon: if everyone stopped doing so, the world would be a fit environment for all creatures of the deep to enjoy a long life. There was a scarcity of cod in the North Sea, would you believe? In relation to meat, he did not wish to encourage farmers to breed animals for slaughter and he would stop those 'killing machines' (he was now warming to the opinions he held so fervently) who prided themselves on being 'good shots' by shooting pheasants, grouse, partridge or pigeons. 'Even harmless mallards on village ponds,' he spat explosively in the direction of Matt whom he suspected had taken part in a duck-shoot on at least one occasion.

To a stunned audience, and rising to his theme, Max withdrew a number of pamphlets from his pocket, copies of which were quickly declined by his bemused hosts. Freya accepted one of each as Class 5 had been discussing the merits of vegan and protein diets in R.E. and she would be well in advance of her friends if she was able to memorise some of the data before the next lesson. A delighted Max complimented her for her interest and promised to send her others on his return; perhaps she would like junior membership of his Vegan Society? She mumbled her thanks, declining the latter offer 'with thanks all the same' and his delight that he had found a convert being short-lived, Max resumed his theme.

Julie, clearly embarrassed, ever appeasing, interrupted the all-too predictable diversionary flow of his favourite gripes: greenhouse gases, vivisection, to which had lately been added the indignities to the human race of aborted foetuses. It all sounded so unbelievably idiosyncratic, and therefore added protectively, 'Max is such an animal lover, you know. He even rescues ladybirds he finds in the house and not only takes them outside but finds the exact bush loved by aphids to put them in.'

Sarah was somewhat amused by the fervour of this young man's views: he seemed to expect that his proselytising would gain disciples. She could not help herself feeling pleased that his monologue, delivered in a dull monotone until giving real vent to the opinions he held so fiercely, was eventually nipped in the bud by Matt. Sitting next to his nephew and lifting the tablecloth to peer under the table, he enquired why Max was not wearing plastic shoes.

'Shoes are quite different,' Max retorted cuttingly. 'You don't eat those. They are made from the skins of animals which are already dead. They haven't been killed just for the sake of providing gratification for humans.'

Thankfully, Matt's intervention had the good fortune of diverting his nephew from his eccentric soliloquy.

Nonetheless, despite her secret delight that the pomposity of their nephew was being challenged, Sarah gave Matt one of her glares which were put to good use in her days as a deputy head, signalling discreetly, she hoped, that this conversation must be closed as soon as possible if family relations were not to be irrevocably impaired. She was only too aware that, given half a chance, Matt would have capped Max's support for the tannery industry with some unnecessary riposte relating to scurrilous Third World exploitations. Weak smiles all round followed, with Matt merely satisfying his own honour by coughing loudly into his napkin. Julie asked if someone would kindly pass her the salt. The set of Sarah's mouth now conveyed the less than subtle message that Matt was not to enquire whether any condiments, ingredients of the meal, items of clothing were to be put through a similar inquest.

Staring shiftily at his plate most of the time thereafter, Max waited for his toast to appear. It didn't, Sarah having intercepted her husband's glare across the table which said, with all the full force subsumed within that evil glower, that if anyone left the table to make beans or cheese or anything at all with dairy products, especially butter, in or on it, the whole collection of relatives would be despatched home instantaneously without passing 'Go' and receiving £200 for doing so. The only concession to the cause was in fact made by Sarah who ensured Max was the first to be handed the vegetable tureens, ignoring the 'Are these locally grown?' in case a diatribe on carbon emissions of aircraft bearing Kenyan beans, Peruvian broccoli, Canadian apples for the apple sauce, Italian chestnuts for the stuffing was forthcoming.

A further rebuff to Max came from his mother when he sought to draw attention to the times of the buses to either Tesco or Waitrose and had enquired whether Sarah would like him to tell her her quickest method of alternative transport should she wish to save the environment by not using her own petrol during her shopping excursions. Before Max could present a treatise on greenhouse gases (callously nipped in the bud by Julie), he was told in no uncertain terms to drop the subject instantly but it was only when the port and liqueurs were passed round that his voice was eventually drowned in the general melee of collecting plates and serving cheese. Matt intercepted the cheese board to ensure it was not accessed by his nephew. It mattered not one jot to Matt that Max was now regaling his relatives with the virtues of 'dairy' as it didn't involve the death of any animal, repressing the urge to enquire whether Max would like his nipples squeezed roughly each day. Even Matt occasionally acknowledged the bounds of propriety.

Leaving the men and boys to the dubious pleasure of their own company, Julie and Sarah withdrew to the sitting room and settled stiffly into opposite armchairs, exchanging a few commiserations that the lunch had turned out as it had. Excusing herself, Freya had disappeared to her bedroom, mentioning something about the masses of homework she had to get through. Whilst she had been grateful for the pamphlets, she really found her much older cousin incredibly boring and thought the remainder of the afternoon would be better spent by updating her Facebook and Twitter entries. Unbeknown to her parents and together with her friends, Freya, good-little-butter-wouldn't-melt-in-her-mouth-Freya, still underage for membership of social media, had managed to find a loophole to gain entry. They stealthily communicated with each other, always removing any evidence which could be intercepted by spying parents. The two male cousins, likewise, showed their preference for each other's company rather than that of their respective fathers, and repaired to Jamie's bedroom.

Sarah did her best to smooth ruffled feathers by explaining to her sister-in-law that nicknames in her book were only given to people whom one loved dearly; these remained within the family and, after all, George had gone through a rather overweight period when he was having to entertain so many clients and it was so nice to see today he must have lost quite a few pounds which was no end of an improvement and … Sarah's voice trailed off as she realised she was getting deeper and deeper into the mire and her best intentions were being thwarted because, quite frankly, she had no excuses or rationale to offer which could possibly ease the situation which she knew was entirely of her own making.

'Oh for heaven's sake, Sarah, don't let's lose any sleep over this. It wasn't pleasant for any of us when we weren't talking to each other and we don't want to go through a period like that again. George is just a little bit sensitive over his tummy at the moment, having been in denial for so long. None of his shirts fit around the neck now and only this morning I told him I would order some 18½ neck-sized ones when I'm next in Piccadilly. Make me a cup of tea, Earl Grey if you have any, please, and let's start the day afresh.'

With a rueful laugh, Sarah gave Julie a hug and the two women, each wiping their damp noses, went into the kitchen. Sarah would have liked to concur with her sister-in-law for solidarity's sake but, quite the reverse, she was actually becoming a little concerned that the reverse was happening to Matt: you could almost see the pounds falling off.

Julie continued:

'At his latest B.U.P.A. check up George was diagnosed with type 2 diabetes and told to cut out sugar ... but he refuses to acknowledge hidden sugars in wines, spirits, sauces, feeling virtuous that he no longer has the beastly stuff in tea or coffee. He is his own worst enemy. Says I'm always nagging and in any case, there will be another study next month saying how good sugar is for warding off heart attacks or strokes or some other dastardly disease. He's also supposed to cut down on shellfish but I suppose we will have to deal with one thing at a time if any useful improvements in lifestyle are to be made eventually. But let's change the subject of male health.'

'Well, we are getting increasingly more worried about Max's job prospects,' confessed Julie in answer to Sarah's question as to how Max's career was progressing for such an exceptionally bright young man.

Whilst she was piling the dishes ready to fill the dishwasher and preparing tea for themselves and a large cafetière of Lazy Sunday for the men, Sarah's mind went back to the accounts imparted by her in-laws years ago in relation to their son's decision to embark on a career in education following university. Still fresh in her mind, having been treated to Max's interminable self-justifying reminiscences over the years, it had been unlikely that there was any fabrication in Julie's recall. As Sarah listened to the depressing update, her sympathy went out to her sister-in-law who had always held such high hopes for her gifted son's career, now seemingly so far off course that it couldn't have been more in tatters had he been an academic wastrel instead of the most academically brilliant student his public school had ever nurtured.

'Do you remember how proud we were at Max's graduation? Everyone spoke to us of the glittering future an Oxford 1st Class degree held for him, yet nothing but embarrassing disasters have blighted his career path ever since. We have just not known what to do to advise him,' Julie confessed. 'The problem has always been that his head is in the clouds.'

Sarah herself had never found it easy to have a conversation with Max, even when he was a teenager, and had wondered why he had undertaken a post-grad teacher training course immediately leaving university. Knowing how intense he was in all his conversations and how difficult it was to introduce another topic to break the monotony, she had felt him to be a most unsuitable candidate for the profession. As a newish sister-in-law at the time, certainly one in awe of Max's family, the epitomisation of a captain of industry's household, Sarah had felt it was not her place to offer any advice when they learned that Max's first teaching post had broken down. Astonished that George and Julie had excused his failure by persuading themselves that any son of theirs, with a father held in high esteem in the business world, would be unlikely to have possessed the 'street cred' needed, she had merely offered the opinion that, naturally, time and experience would be needed for him to acquire such skills. In any case, she had not thought it her business to ask questions at the time which could have been considered intrusive.

'In our dreams,' continued Julie, 'we had projected ourselves eventually to the platform of some distinguished public school, applauding Max's inaugural speech to parents. In retrospect, we should have seen the light when the outcome of his final teaching placement graded him in the "Questionable Failure" category. Did we tell you that the expertise of an external examiner was needed to decide in which direction the decision would be made?'

Sarah thought it wiser to deny knowledge that Max's school practice had ended in farce; it did not seem appropriate that her memory for the detail of his downfall had intrigued them at the time. Matt had remarked to her then that it was about time the smug look had been taken off his brother's face and his precocious nephew taken down a peg or two.

'I don't like going back over old ground,' Julie resumed, 'but, apparently, Max had taken the trouble to read from sheets of his own notes that he'd made for the Third Form bottom set on the subject of Shakespeare's sonnets. The class had complained that his lessons were so boring and he was advised by his supervisor that he must "bring them to life". Well, dear Max interpreted this to the letter, intending to whet his students' appetite for the study of Sheridan's *The Rivals*, next on the syllabus.'

While Julie paused in reflection, Sarah recalled privately that she knew that the ensuing chaos had disturbed adjacent classes so much that the deputy head had been sent for to calm the students. Only too well she remembered that Max had brought in a tea-chest containing a motley collection of theatrical cast-off period clothing to the next lesson, instructing the class to dress themselves 'in character'. She and Matt had thought this hilarious but a most incautious action for a trainee teacher to undertake.

'Oh, the aftermath was so painful,' Julie continued. 'George insisted on attending an interview with Max and the deputy head. Max flatly denied that the class was out of his control: he said he thought they were entering into the spirit of things extremely well. Really, I am not exaggerating but, Sarah, you can imagine the scene, I'm sure.' Putting her hand to her head and rubbing it across her forehead, she gratefully accepted the refreshing glass of water Sarah handed her.

She put her arm around Julie. Her sympathy with her sister-in-law was acute and she had no wish to evoke unpleasant memories for her any further. In her own mind she held vivid memories of the mayhem which had been described to them at the time: girls with tousled periwigs falling over their eyes heaving doublets over their buttocks, boys fighting over an assortment of wimples, poke-bonnets, bustles and God knows what, one of the miscreants trying to clap a codpiece onto a nonplussed student's nether regions in an uproar which had resounded the length of the corridor. How she and Matt had split their sides later, envisioning the scenes of pandemonium.

With a wry smile, and recovering her wavering composure, Julie paraphrased her reminiscences, adding, 'Max had to write a full explanation in the Log Book but he was not allowed to speak with the parents who apparently sought some sort of reprisal for their precious child being put in detention as a result of a teacher's folly, we were told.'

'Yet,' Julie continued, 'the better judgment of the member of the Examining Board called in for a final opinion was overruled. He had advised that allowing Max to pass would be an indictment of the university's quality standards but the final decision had been left to the chair who decided that a young man with such intellectual promise and so much wisdom to impart' (Julie preened herself at this memory) 'should not be lost to the profession but nurtured.' The rest of the account which she re-told, had been gleaned under later questioning of Max as his 'career' had unfolded and Sarah had little doubt in her mind that the narrative had not been embellished throughout the course of time.

'Thus,' Julie said, returning emotion and indignation creeping into her voice, 'Max was appointed after a cursory interview, to a 1500-pupil comprehensive school to teach history, *not* his own subject, to the lower sets. I ask you, would you believe it? Such an outrage.' She paused for breath, appreciatively noting the concern on Sarah's attentive face before resuming.

'For the first two terms he taught set C but the head of history then told him that he would like to see him teach a lower set because he thought he would be better suited to less able pupils as they would benefit hugely from his knowledge. Continuing to teach the more average pupils, as he'd put it, was apparently wasted on them as they would now be better advantaged by working in the library, researching topics for themselves. Max said it had been explained to him that he'd "transformed their attitude to learning during his time with them and they would now certainly be capable of learning independently." Still only in his probationary year, you know, he had felt really proud that his teaching had been held in such high esteem.'

Sarah, sensing the irony in these statements, was surprised that Julie had not interpreted the sentiments in a similar manner to that in which they had struck her. Somewhat bemused, she allowed Julie to continue without comment, intrigued by Julie's accounts of his lack of acceptance amongst his colleagues. Sarah learned, contrary to the glowing reports penned on occasional holiday postcards, that no one befriended him. 'That said it all,' Julie added darkly, setting the scene for more disclosures in relation to the misplaced appointment of her beloved son to a school unworthy of his presence.

Over the intervening thirteen or fourteen years since Sarah had been first introduced to Matt's family, there had been a dearth of detailed information relating to Max's career misfortunes. She and Matt had long suspected events had not turned out for him as well as his parents and relatives had predicted but they had been given little to go on from sparse notes in Christmas and birthday cards. Neither she nor Matt communicated with friends via Facebook, nor did they Twitter, and so far as they knew, George and Julie steered clear of any social medium other than sending brief messages by e-mail. It now seemed to Sarah that the ice having been broken in respect of the conveyance of her true feelings, the older woman was grateful to bare her soul in newly restored intimacy with her sister-in-law and she felt a wave of compassion engulfing her as Julie made to continue with her sad revelations. So involved were they with their exchanges of confidence and support, it startled them both when Max suddenly burst into the kitchen.

'Mother, Aunt Sarah, Jamie has been going through his collection of prehistoric creatures with me. He really does have a most comprehensive knowledge of the Jurassic period.'

This statement was delivered in a conspiratorial tone, with no sign that he had noted the astonishment on the women's faces that he should have the temerity to intrude on what should have been clearly apparent as a private conversation. He continued, 'But I must say, his pronunciation of some of their names is inaccurate. I have corrected these for him, Aunt Sarah, and I suggest one or other of you as his parents should hear him practise the proper stress on the syllables until he has them off by heart.'

An embarrassed Julie attempted to steer Max gently back through the door from whence he had come. Max had other ideas. He sauntered to the fridge to get himself a drink, carefully rinsing the glass Sarah had given his mother earlier when she had felt a little faint. 'Just in case she's sickening for something. You can never be too careful: there are a number of strange viruses about. All brought from overseas, I have no doubt. Do you have any TCP or other germicide, Aunt Sarah? I would feel safer.'

Ignoring her son's pomposity, Julie summed up for Max:

'Thus ended Max's first appointment. The governing body held a meeting the following week, and permanent exclusion was ratified.'

Max had to have the last word. 'Mother, Aunt Sarah, it would be helpful for you both to read the transcripts of my meetings with Mr. Johnson and with the governors. I was very proud of the way these meetings went: they praised my work very highly and asked me a lot of questions which I answered very clearly. They're in my bureau at home, together with the letters they sent me. They recommended I apply for a position in higher education and said my teaching would be very suitable for that type of institution. I'll get them all out for you one day if you remind me. I was really pleased when the chairman said I should be eminently suited to teaching a class of A level students who would, no doubt, they all thought, be inspired by my teaching, and sincerely appreciate being taught by a tutor with a 1st Class degree from Oxford. I thought deep down they must be really sorry to lose me, in fact.'

Julie passed a wan glance across to Sarah in gratitude as she confirmed that she would be happy to do that when they were at home. Sarah's knowing smile, accompanied by a comforting hand on Julie's knee, expressed commiseration and solidarity with her sister-in-law.

'And that, as they say, was that!' pronounced Max with finality. 'Would you allow me to look in your fridge for a snack or something, Aunt Sarah; I am feeling a little hungry. Actually, a piece of fruit would satisfy me, if you have any. Not white grapes, though. Diabetics mustn't eat them so what's not good enough for diabetics isn't good for me. Diabetes might be genetic and you can't be too careful in your choice of nourishment. May I?'

Obtaining the agreement he sought, he thanked Sarah profusely and left the kitchen in what, Sarah noted, was a rather ungainly, awkward gait.

'But that was not the end of our woes and disappointments.' Julie choked back tears as Max departed. Her composure had fragmented as the sad revelations of the afternoon had moved on through the passing years, evoking seriously painful memories for her. 'He managed a series of short assignments, each designed to help him find his niche.' Resignedly, Julie quietly filled in Sarah with Max's exploits thereafter, a further catalogue of disasters, summing up the lacklustre jobs for which Max had been accepted 'on trial'. Sarah made the sensible decision to bring the confessions to an end.

'Julie, I think we both deserve another cup of Earl Grey. I'll put the kettle on. You have been incredibly brave in sharing all your worries with me and I am so grateful for such confidences. I just can't tell you how sorry I am and do wish we could see each other more often. Now you are living so much closer, we must not leave it so long before we get together again.'

★

At this point, the men, excluding Max, having demolished more port than permitted George to safely usher his family to the car for their homeward journey, requested a 'coffee fill-up' and agreed it was 'time the ladies joined us'. Together with a fresh cafetière of coffee, the tea tray was carried back to the sitting room and the box of Bendicks mints Julie had brought as a gift, was opened. Sarah was thankful that George's hand was on the shoulder of his younger brother and it seemed that the air had been cleared. Remarking thus to Julie, she was a little perturbed by Jamie, who had obviously overheard, rushing in and telling her that it was thick with cigar smoke in the hall and should he get the Airwick?' 'Little piggies ...!' commented Julie, only too pleased that her sister-in-law's son, as already demonstrated at the outset, was no stranger, either, to the commission of embarrassing faux-pas.

Matt pressed the plunger down into the cafetière and enquired,

'Well, Max, we're all looking forward to hearing of your exploits at the clothing store. How's it going, old chap?' The last Sarah and Matt had known of his occupation, and this only hazily, was as a shop assistant.

'Oh no, Uncle Matt, they don't need me at the gentlemen's outfitters anymore.'

Putting two and two together, it transpired from Max's rather convoluted explanation that the usual calamity had not been long in causing 'marching orders' to be delivered. The conversation was then adroitly changed by Sarah who could see Matt close to exploding with pent-up disbelief. Seeing Julie's crestfallen face and to avoid Max disclosing his latest misfortunes for his uncle's sharp tongue, pitted with sarcasm, which would have, in all probability, demolished Julie's composure entirely, she intervened:

'Jamie, it would be nice if you took Max up to your bedroom right now and practised those Latin names he's taught you to say properly. I believe you have already made a promising start.'

The eyes of both cousins lit up. Max asked politely if his uncle and aunt would excuse him, thanked them profusely for lunch which he had enjoyed very much and said he wouldn't mind the baked beans he'd asked for earlier, if it was not too much trouble to send them up for him.

'So if you will excuse me again, I want to rejoin Jamie. He has also requested me to give him the Middle English names of his dinosaur collection. I told him the names were Latin so it would not be too difficult. I am not sure whether I will know all of them but I will do my best, as I always do, whatever I am called upon to undertake.'

With a slight bow, and thanking his aunt and uncle for their company which he assured them he had appreciated enormously, Max departed, an air of importance glowing from every pore.

Matt, now dispensing tea and coffee whilst Sarah passed round the chocolate mints, thanking Julie again for them, puzzled silently over his nephew's strange, stilted speech, so often delivered in a monotone and whose peculiar manners and posture were almost Dickensian. A similarity with an eccentric relative suddenly struck him. He recalled an ancient great uncle whose peculiar behaviour caused much mirth amongst the younger members of his family, not the least to him. In respect of Max, Matt reflected, his brother and his wife had certainly brought their only son up in an old-fashioned manner to allow him to speak and act in the odd way he did: he seemed an old man already in his posture and conversation, strangely discordant with what one would expect of a twenty-seven-year-old in the first decade of the 21st century. Perhaps Great Uncle Edward had had a similar upbringing.

Possibly starting university before his seventeenth birthday had not been a good idea either, Matt reflected, exposing him to ideas probably well beyond his capacity to absorb and question. Such an unconventional character, quite unlike any other young man he had ever encountered. Over-familiar in many ways, encroaching on one's personal space by sitting or standing too close and always interrupting, often with a totally different topic to the one you were discussing. He made you puke with his constant references to Chaucer; why did he assume everyone else was enthralled with his boring stories? He also thinks himself an authority on Shakespeare with his bloody First in literature. He would wax lyrically on any aspect of the bard, always a signal for Matt to make an excuse to leave the room but even then he had to lock himself in the lavatory or his study. Max would follow him wherever he went, still spouting his views on his life, plays, sonnets, actresses and actors who had distinguished themselves over the years by playing their respective parts superbly or outrageously badly, critiques he had agreed with or opposed, Stratford/Old/Young Vic productions of note he had reviewed for his university alumni magazine as 'excellent,' 'formidable' or 'reprehensible in the extreme'. Matt could feel his blood boiling; perhaps a heart attack was coming on – he had been warned about high blood pressure, causing him to do his best to lose a little weight, perhaps too much. No, it was impossible for that irritating nephew of his to take any hint, he was so bloody thick-skinned and why his parents couldn't cure him of that was beyond him. If he had a son like that he would knock some manners into him. Had Max ever been disciplined in his life? That wet Julie was always making excuses for him; the woman ought to have been hauled before a Child Protection Board. Matt hated his nephew's habit of 'talking over' him and the manner in which he corrected him when he was talking of the journeys he made for the advertising company he worked for. Did it matter one jolt if he did not give the exact mileage or precise route? Had he been cooking the books, his insolent nephew had enquired primly. The man was out of order and his parents should be ashamed that they had not curbed his impertinence.

Matt, walking towards the door, announced he'd bring in more port, just at the moment at which Sarah found it necessary to make excuses for her husband's seeming pre-occupation from the family discussion carrying on round him. She now intended this to be steered away from contentious issues.

'Matt is working so many late nights this month. Seems you are either out of work in this recession or worked off your feet. He is so often exhausted at the weekends.'

Matt shot a glance at his wife before he reached the door which could have frozen the sun as George growled, 'He is not the only one,' and Julie interjected, 'Not home before ten, and that is if I am lucky.' Matt's muttered rejoinder was, unfortunately, not so inaudible that Julie did not smart under the jibe, 'Can't do much for your sex life, then, supposing you have one.' Tears once more prickled the back of her throat and brought anguish to her heart but she managed a wry smile. It would have been worth more than a penny to Matt had his sister-in-law been aware of his concluding thought, 'Conceiving Max must have been a fluke.' Thankfully, she wasn't.

Max's pleasure showing his intellectual superiority to his young cousin was short-lived, however. George had decided he'd had enough of the references to his son's waning career, and it was time to call a halt to this inquest which nakedly exposed Max's feelings. To George, every reference was a cruel slight on his own aspirations for a son to add prestige to his name.

Thankfully, George used the excuse that he wanted to complete the return journey to Leamington before sunset as frost had been forecast for later in the evening. As they collected their belongings and were helped into their coats, Matt could not help enquiring with heavy sarcasm why Max needed to muffle himself to the eyebrows in a thick woollen scarf, one of those ghastly bobble-style hats the Jamaicans wore and a heavy overcoat which looked as if it had once been the property of a Siberian goatherd. For Chris'sake, a family car as befitted the chairman of a large manufacturing company in the Midlands was the most comfortable and well-heated limousine on the market. At least 300 grand, his brother enviously surmised. When they reached their home, their status symbol Bentley would be parked in their driveway immediately in front of the massive front door, itself covered from the elements by a wide canopy held up by Grecian columns on the limestone terrace. Their butler (huh) would later drive the Daimler directly into the garage (well, one of their three). Was there really a need for all this feather-wrapping molly-coddling?

'Uncle Matt, it is almost winter. The temperature outside is 10 degrees Celsius; approximately 50 degrees Fahrenheit.'

Really there was no answer to this but Matt could not resist a raised eyebrow and a further question:

'When will you learn to drive, Max, and save your father such an onerous journey?'

Max's reply made reference to the fact that George had

a chauffeur to drive him to the office and his mother always drove him, Max, to appointments such as his frequent need to visit the job seekers' office or would call a taxi to enable him to attend interviews. There was, therefore, no need at all for him to drive.

Matt's rejoinder that maybe some day a girlfriend might expect her escort to drive, was rejected by Max who thought he'd find one who had her own car like his dad's girlfriend did. There would never be a necessity to get a driving licence: 'She always drives when Dad takes her to the theatre or out to dinner and the chauffeur has his day off. I used to see them when I walked to get a taxi home from the outfitters shop when I was working there; it was not far from my father's office. Dad said I was to tell Mother he was working late; I'd supposed he had a meeting with his colleagues at the restaurant or in the theatre and so I told Mother exactly what Dad told me to.'

Without noticing the astounded look on his aunt and uncle's faces, he shook their hands with excessive formality. An impatient George, the engine already turned on, oblivious of the bombshell his son had just exploded, urged Julie to get into the car and stop letting the heat out, for heaven's sake. Thankfully also well out of earshot and awaiting Max to get into the car so that she could shut the door for him, Julie excused this overprotective action by calling over her shoulder,

'Max doesn't like to get his lambskin gloves dirty; he bought them at the outfitters where he was working. They really are the bee's knees.'

'Yes,' Max said in a parting shot, 'I carefully cut the voucher from *The Times* and only paid a quarter of the real price, £28 reduced to £7.'

Closing the door with a long, drawn out sigh of relief that the dreaded visit which had started on such a low note had

had such an unexpected and revealing ending, Sarah looked at Matt in disbelief.

Matt stood, staring at the car receding into the distance. Turning to Sarah, his head slowly turning from side to side, it was evident he could not get his mind around the significance of the words uttered by his nephew, a raw indictment of infidelity if ever there was one.

'Bloody, bloody hell. For Chris' sake, what was that pompous ass doing, letting his father in the shit in his wife's hearing. Is he mad? He's stark, staring bloody mad, in my opinion – unless he wanted his mother to know or intends to blackmail his father. What on earth goes on in that idiot's mind?'

Sarah collapsed into Matt's arms.

'Thank goodness the philanderer is your brother, not mine. I would never hear the last of it. Matt, darling, there will be no recriminations about the way things went today.' For some minutes they clung to each other in mutual support until Sarah gently pulled herself away and turned to face the waiting chaos in the kitchen. No surface remained free of used crockery, crystal glasses, crusted pans and the dishwasher hadn't been emptied yet of the clean breakfast and food preparation dishes. Sighing, she pulled on her Marigolds. Matt followed her and slumped into a Windsor chair, shaking his head in renewed disbelief that his nephew had been so disloyal.

'Sarah, weekends are supposed to be for recharging batteries. I feel drained. Last week was hell; next week is unlikely to be any better and how I am going to get through it, I just don't know. Could I leave you to clear up all this mess, I just must have a couple of hours' break.

'Would you mind? I'll make it up to you.'

Sarah moved over to Matt's chair, signifying by the hug she gave him that he had her support. 'My darling, darling Matt, next weekend will not come too soon and we'll make it up to each other. Only,' she added mischievously, 'providing you don't kid me you have any meetings with clients in restaurants or theatres.'

Jamie's puzzled, 'Daddy, how many bees' knees do you need to make a pair of gloves?' went unanswered.

Chapter Twelve

Jane's promised invitation for Jamie to come to tea was set for an early evening in mid-November. It had been arranged by the respective mothers as they passed each other at the school's Bonfire Night party.

'Send him round in his play-clothes, Sarah, they'll be out in the garden so he'll need an anorak: the grass is full of worm-casts and somewhat muddy, the ancient swing is a bit rusty and even if I clean it, he'll only dirty it up again. Dominic likes to swing standing up: he says he can work it up so much higher when he is standing – you know what boys are. Oh, and by the way, Mark cleared a wasp's nest from the eaves a couple of weeks ago: all inmates dead so there's no worry that Jamie will get stung again by a lazy one. What a relief it must have been that the allergy test was negative.'

Bypassing the last remark, Sarah replied that Jamie always managed to get all his clothes in such a mess that it was now difficult to distinguish best from worst. There was no point in buying new unless there was a special event to go to as he was now into a growth phase and it would be throwing good money after bad: he would not get any proper wear from anything she bought for him. 'The only people to benefit would be the charity shops.'

For reasons best known to herself, Sarah decided to omit any correction of the true cause of the hysterics on that fateful day: better to leave Jane in blissful ignorance of the actual trigger of the tantrum. A physical reaction was plausible, a misunderstanding of language could signify a slight stupidity, certainly weirdness at the very least, in relation to her son's sagacity. Heavens knew there was a growing oddity about Jamie's reactions to events other children would accept without demur; so much better not to broadcast this. Nice as Jane was, she was known to be the fount of all knowledge in respect of the peculiarities or indiscretions within the neighbourhood and rumours, once started, quickly gathered momentum without any help from the Chinese. Sarah smiled a wry smile to herself; she would protect her son's integrity with her last breath.

'This is the first time I have walked to your house on my own,' Jamie announced. 'My mummy walked me to the corner and watched me until I got to your house. She said she wouldn't, but I kept turning round and she was still there. I did try not to let her see me, though, because that was catching her out in a lie and she wouldn't like that. What I did was to go behind a hedge and peep out but the funny thing was, it was then hard to see her: I had to look sideways as I came out.'

Hardly pausing for breath and ignoring the astonished look on Dominic's mother's face at this outpouring of unnecessary detail, he continued: 'I forgot to tell you when you took us to Legoland that it was very good to note you were still alive, Mrs. Broadbent. I was so pleased to see you for myself, even though Dommie had pointed you out one day after school. At the time I didn't think I ever would again and Dominic wouldn't have a mother. My mummy didn't really mean what she said, you know; I now understand because my daddy told me, that she was really sorry she had to stop talking to you. She didn't mean she was going to cut you up. Do you hear what I am saying?'

Not only totally bemused by this peculiar information that her friend could have had murderous intentions, she felt intensely irritated by this child whose unusual turn of phrase often startled her when the two families had met at school functions or walked part of the way home together. On this occasion his last ill-judged question riled her. Far too much adult

RIPPLES IN A POND

conversation surrounding him at home, she thought. All too often teachers' children were over-coached to stand out from their peers by having vocabularies and stock phrases which were too sophisticated for their age and actual understanding. What was it they had laughed at when they had invited this strange-mannered boy to join them at Legoland at half-term? Oh yes, it all came flooding back: use of the word 'incarcerated'.

Jamie had told them his family had been incarcerated on 'that awful motorway; you know, the one they call the biggest car park in Europe. We were jammed up solid for half an hour.' Jamie had giggled as he related his thoughts which had formed in his mind of all the cars stuck together with Bon Maman strawberry or raspberry compote. When Dominic's taken-aback father, ignoring the extent of Jamie's fertile imagination, had asked him what that big word he'd used meant, Jamie had responded in a scandalised tone, 'I thought you would know! Being kept inside our Range Rover, of course.'

'You mean you would have been "held up" then,' Mark had corrected him. 'No,' Jamie had replied, 'we were all sitting down in our seats.'

Unbelievably, this bad-mannered little six-year-old had then shaken them by remarking that their faces looked funny when their eyes got really enormous: their eyebrows then disappeared under their hair. Well, perhaps not Mr. Broadbent's; he had such a tall forehead that his eyebrows could still be easily seen but it made him have wrinkles and, 'Could I have one of those chocolate biscuits, please?'

On the present occasion Jane thought Jamie had gone too far and needed to be taken down a peg or two. His precocious attitude should not go uncorrected, even if it was not her job to teach him manners. She would put him in his place.

'Jamie, has your mummy never told you to mind your "p"s and "q"s? I wonder what your headmaster would think if you asked him if he heard what you were saying.'

'Mrs. Broadbent,' a puzzled Jamie answered, 'Mr. Holmes doesn't wear a hearing aid. So far as I can tell, he can hear perfectly well what I say to him. In assemblies he often asks us all a question and sometimes it will be a Year 6 boy or girl who will answer and they sit right at the back of the Hall. From Mr. Holmes' response to him or her, it means he can hear from quite a long distance away, too far for me to say exactly, and we haven't done metres properly yet in Year 2, have we Domino, so I can't really make a sensible estimate. Do you know what I mean, Mrs. Broadbent? Oh, I'm sorry: you don't like me calling him "Domino", do you? It just slipped out.'

Dominic, who had been tugging at Jamie's arm impatiently with the unnecessary distraction this conversation was causing when all he wanted his friend for was to play in the garden, had shaken his head and added he had already done them in his prep school and what did it matter, anyway. Jamie continued,

'It is the same when we are in the playground when the teacher who is supposed to be on duty to look after us is away and Mr. Holmes has to blow the whistle for us to stop playing and line up when he blows it again. There is always someone who doesn't stand still and quiet – it was you once, Dominic; I expect you told your parents or did you get a letter about it, Mrs. Broadbent? – and he then says, "Are you deaf?" in a very nasty voice and they tell him why they didn't stop straight away. Mr. Holmes then says, "You go to my room right now," and it sounds like a dog barking when he says "now", like that. They go and he says, "And take that look off your face or I will do it for you", which seems a strange thing to say. I don't know, either, why he wants them to go to his room as he is not very pleased with them and if he is going to give them a house point, or something, which he would mark on his chart, he could have chosen one of us who were standing still exactly as he meant us to do when the whistle blew.

'As a matter of interest, Mrs. Broadbent, how can another

person take a look off someone else's face? Come to think of it, I couldn't take one of mine off. Can you do it? I think it is only possible if you have one of those masks on like we had at Hallowe'en.'

Jamie began to chortle and then noticed a look on Mrs. Broadbent's face he didn't quite like.

'Oh, I've got it! I think I know what to do. If I put my hand up like this, Mrs. Broadbent, and wave it, will it take off the look you have just put on your face?'

'Enough is enough,' an astounded Jane thought, and if thoughts could pass through gritted teeth, this is how they would have come to fruition. Good grief, Sarah's son makes a speech every time you ask him a simple question. She felt exhausted already, yet all she had done was to open the door to the infuriating child. Jane made up her mind to discourage this burgeoning friendship; she most certainly did not want this insolent boy's influence to rub off on Dominic. Thankfully, she noted that Dominic had already slid away and was swinging as high as it was safe, she thought, for him to go. But the ordeal was not over yet: Jamie still intended to continue his oration.

'Oh, and I nearly forgot, Mrs. Broadbent; silly old me. I thought about what I said just now – well, a few minutes ago – and my memory tells me I did not use any "p"s or "q"s in the sentences so I said all the words correctly. I will, however, try very hard to say them properly when a word has these letters in them. Had you noticed when I had been here before that I had a speech impediment? My mummy hasn't told me I have and she was a teacher so she ought to have heard me if I hadn't been able to say those letters.'

'Is this child doing his best to send me up?' pondered Jane in some bewilderment, reluctant to think the worst of a six-year-old and preferring to put it down, as before, to too much adult companionship. Still, she thought, suppressing her indignation, Jamie was not yet seven and still a six-year-old at heart. What a dreadful shame he was being taught to adopt a pseudo-adolescent style of conversation. She called Dominic.

'Dominic, Jamie is ready to play now and it is time for him to have a go on the swing. Come along and take him out into the garden, will you please. It will shortly be tea-time and if Daddy is going to set up the train track for you before bedtime, we will have to get a move on.'

'Oh, don't you worry yourself, Mrs. Broadbent. I know where your garden is and it's not necessary for Dominic to take me there: I can walk there myself. Don't forget: I came along your road without my mummy with me so it will be easy for me to walk along your path to the swing. I expect the floor plan of your house is exactly the same as ours. My daddy got ours out of his burrow-thing he keeps his special papers in and showed me a little time ago.'

'Off you go,' hastily interrupted Jane, wondering why this child was so erratic in the way he used some advanced words in near-correct context, pronouncing them correctly, but had not mastered others. She avoided a reply to Jamie's quizzical,

'Do you mean "off I have to go" to my home or "off I have to go" to the swing? It's not easy for me to tell precisely what you mean.'

Hand on his shoulder, without comment Jane ushered him into the hallway and along the passage, still protesting his proficiency in finding his own way, until Jamie found himself the other side of the kitchen door leading to the garden. He was then able to draw his own conclusions from this action because he could not see a way round to the front of the house. He was aided in his decision by a shout from Dominic that it was his turn and he'd better be quick.

Jamie sat down on the muddy swing, pushed off from the ground and then began the motion to enable him to swing as high as he could. The arc he was making was pitiful in

comparison with Dominic's. He continued whilst Dominic
went back into the house to get iced lollies for them both,
the unseasonably warm sun in their secluded garden being the
incentive.

'Don't lick mine as well,' shouted Jamie as Dominic
returned, seemingly unconcerned in which direction his
tongue went as long as it was hitting something cold and
raspberry-ish. 'You might give me germs.'

'You are a sissy, Jamie, and you are not going very high.
When you get up to the top, pull your legs right in as you go
back and shove your bottom on to the seat hard and then push
your legs forward as far and as hard as you can. Do all that
when you have come as high as you can get towards me. *Now.*
Aaaaaargh! Aaaaaaargh! Oh, oh, Jamie!'

Jamie had followed the instructions to the letter. Taking
his hands from the chain at the height of his forward-swing,
he had grabbed hold of his legs in an attempt to 'pull them in'.
The seat tilted as, simultaneously, Jamie pushed his bottom
down hard. Jamie overturned and hurled backwards headfirst,
curled up like a snowball, to the ground. Twisting and
untwisting, movements caused by the abruptness of the loss of
load, the seat swung dizzily back then forward. Dominic, who
had dropped the lollies and raced to try to block Jamie's fall,
just missed receiving a violent thump on his head by having
the presence of mind to duck.

At her son's tortuous scream, a terrified Jane flew to
Jamie's assistance, her mind covering every eventuality from
mild concussion, through paraplegia to imbecility. Thank
heaven she had finished her St. John's Ambulance course.

'Don't touch him, don't touch him, Dommie.'

Heart pounding, she almost fell over in her haste to reach
the moaning child. With what relief she realised he had, for
the most part, been catapulted onto a pile of sodden autumn
leaves covering rain-saturated soil. As he had fallen he had

somehow unwound himself and the force of the landing had been diffused by the spine being relaxed and as straight as it could be under the force of the impact.

'Dommie, fetch me my mobile, quickly, quickly. Jamie, can you hear me? You are going to be fine. I'm not going to help you up, you must stay there until a doctor arrives. I am going to call him.'

Jamie had stopped moaning and was lying still. His eyes were shut. Staccato sentences descended from his quivering lips.

'What are you going to call him? ... Dr. Foster – he goes as far as Gloucester ... Can he hear? ... Is he in your house? ... What did he come for? ... Is your husband ill?'

White as a sheet, Dominic ran back with the mobile. With practised hands, Jane dialled NHS Direct, at the same time ordering Dommie to bring the rug from the dog's basket in the kitchen; that was the nearest place to find one. Having been assured the medics were on their way, the operator asked her to remain on the phone to answer some questions. She was instructed to feel Jamie's pulse (already done; possibly a little more rapid than would be expected), not to move him from the position in which he fell (confirmed had not), cover him with a warm, thick blanket or coat (this was being done as the order was given), the operator constantly repeating her assurance that the ambulance would be with them in a few minutes and questioning the caller was not holding up the arrival of the medics. Dominic, whimpering as he went, was despatched to the gate (another instruction) to guide the way to and through the house.

In minutes the familiar sound of the ambulance tones was heard. Two medics bearing a stretcher, oxygen cylinder and other paraphernalia which might be needed, burst into view and, instantaneously, everywhere was controlled action. Jane explained she was not the little boy's mother. Dominic, trying to be brave as his mother had asked him to be, explained the events leading to the accident, tears streaming down his cheeks. The medic who appeared to be in charge, and apparently called Fred, asked Jane to cuddle him a bit: 'You are still not too old for a cuddle, young man – neither am I,' he said, winking at his mate.

'No bones are broken, pulse and blood pressure are fine and there is just a slight cut on the back of his head which probably occurred when he grazed that bush there – I'm not a gardener so don't know what it is called. Some nasty prickles on it here, see; I should re-site the swing. Set it on bark chippings – a deep layer, four to six inches or so. We will have to take him to A&E as there seems to be a spot of delirium and possible slight concussion, therefore. He's been rambling a bit. Said he could smell a big dog. Asked if it was a German shepherd; said he only liked little dogs and white ones but big ones had enormous tongues and could eat you. And some maniac' ('No, I didn't say that, I said Dominic,' the medic was corrected by a pitiful voice from under the blanket) 'had licked his lolly and told him to grab his legs so that was what had made him fall off the swing. Had the dog had his lolly? Something about the alphabet – didn't understand what he was getting at – said he had some speech lessons when he was younger. Oh, you've got all those down, haven't you, mate, and the one about having a mask on your face and waving your hands about?'

'Mate' had, and some more, he said.

'Only to be expected that a serious fall like that would produce some concussion,' the medic called Fred explained.

In much trepidation, Jane had then gone back into the house to telephone Sarah, putting the kettle on en route. Sarah did her best to keep the alarm out of her response as the carefully measured tones (but which at the other end sounded quite glib) broke the disastrous news to her. The early-evening-before-Matt-gets-home glass of Chardonnay slithered out of her limp grasp as she heard her voice, as if from a distance, thanking Jane for doing everything necessary and said she was on her way right now. Hastily scribbling a note to Matt, telling him to call her on her mobile as soon as he got home, shouting up the stairs to Freya and telling her she was just going to fetch Jamie from Dommie's but 'might be a little while: you know how we mothers natter,' she fled from the house. She had quickly resolved the dilemma of whether to take her daughter with her, exposing her to the possibility of seeing her brother's injuries, which could be very serious indeed, for all she knew. If not sufficient for the medics to do any more than bandage him up, then she was only leaving her for a very short time and, now ten, Freya was a responsible enough child. She blocked out of her mind the lessons of the film they had watched together a short while ago, *Home Alone*; this was an altogether different situation, she told herself firmly,

Ignoring Freya's cheeky, 'What, nattering again? You only had coffee with her this morning and you were going to check my homework, remember?' she sped down the drive and ran down the road, crossing it without looking, to the screech of tyres and a loud, 'Look where you're going, you stupid bitch. Is your house on fire?' Hurtling round the corner, she just avoided crashing into a small crowd on the pavement opposite the ambulance.

'Ooh, that's Sarah Chilton, isn't it? What's she in such a hurry for?'

Hurrying through the house, the door to the garden open for her, the paramedics had already lifted Jamie onto the stretcher, a gauze dressing on the side of his head just above his ear. The paramedic called Fred quietly explained that her son was perfectly alright.

'Quite robust is the young human frame; still supple

bones at six. Only a precautionary measure to get him properly checked out and he'll probably be home later tonight. Docs might decide to keep him in for a night, just to keep their eyes on him. Does seem to be rambling a bit.'

Indeed, robustness of lungs, at the very least, were demonstrated at that point.

'No, no, noooooo. I won't let anyone put their eyes on me, ever, ever, ever.'

Both Fred and 'Mate' looked at each other in astonishment. Another example of delirium but no one suffering slight concussion would shriek out like that. 'Mate' added another statement to his notebook.

'We would like you to be in the ambulance with your son,' Fred said to Sarah, still suffering the effects of shock and, in a quiet aside to 'Mate',

'Be a good chap and go and move the nosey bystanders away before we leave this house,' and kindly to Sarah, 'There's just time for you to down that cup of tea your friend has got for you.'

★

On her way to A&E., it was not easy for Sarah to break the news to Freya on her mobile that her brother had merely had a 'bit of a tumble and only needed a quick check-over by a doctor.' Even without being able to see the flashing blue lights, the sirens blaring would belie the low-key nature of the message, added to by the early return home of her father. On his arrival Freya flung himself into his arms, beseeching him to drive her to the hospital. Matt, who had also been concerned when asked by phone to leave the office as soon as possible and hold the fort until his wife's return, did his best to allay his daughter's pessimistic feelings by putting the landline on 'speaker-phone' when Sarah's voice of controlled calmness came through at that moment to say all was well under the circumstances.

Once in hospital Jamie was quickly through the triage process and seen immediately by the duty registrar, duly X-rayed, blood sample taken ('Mummy, please, please tell me, will I have enough left?'), and then given a dose of Calpol to ease any headache. The immediate intention was to keep him in for one night in the Children's Ward, only as a precautionary measure as predicted, but nurses reported continued delirious responses to their questions, later substantiated by the young houseman during his evening ward-round and no indication as to when he would be sent home was given. Sarah had protested that the reason why he had thought the doctor was a butcher was probably because of his white coat, also worn by the assistants on the supermarket butchery counter. Furthermore, she tried to explain that 'seeing how warm you are' was the expression used in their home when temperatures were taken; he had been upset by the usual phraseology when he was younger, thinking something was being removed from him that he did not understand, and so they had hit upon this more friendly substitution. The nurse muttered something about six-year-olds not being expected to shriek with fear, however, when terminology perhaps implied extraction. To Jamie, she spoke in a kindly manner, 'Just putting a swab under your arm, my love.' In her state of shock, however, Sarah was unable to justify in a satisfactory manner the manner in which he attempted to pull his arm away, sobbing that it would be horrible to feel a squab there and he wasn't going to let anyone do that to him. Sarah's lame, 'I think he thinks you are slipping a baby pigeon in his armpit,' only intensified the nurse's opinions that she was dealing with a delirious child. Further fuel was supplied to establish this as a working hypothesis as, later, Jamie continued to engage the staff in 'rambling, rather weird' conversations encompassing a variety of subjects relating to his life, of which they had no knowledge.

Sarah was naturally disconcerted when it became apparent that an overnight stay, at least, was planned. Had there been a more severe injury than the paramedics had led her to believe? Fortunately the hospital was within a quarter of an hour's journey from their house so she could slip home to placate the family before returning with night clothes, cuddly toys and the necessary toiletries.

Although Sarah had been allowed to sleep beside Jamie in a roll-away bed provided, naturally she had to leave during parts of the following day to care for Freya. Thus she could not enlighten the consultant, whose decision on discharge was sought, on the rationale behind what was perceived as providing evidence of delirium. Even Sarah's assurances that Jamie was actually a very bright child who loved nothing better than to draw adults into conversations about matters which fascinated him, this accounting for why nurses and doctors felt he was suffering mild concussion, did not ease their concern. 'Jamie always surprises people with his advanced language,' adding that it was probably because of his tender age they had regarded it as symptomatic of delayed concussion. She also endeavoured to explain, rather ineptly she felt, that Jamie seemed to *prefer* the company of older people and speaking with the nursing staff was likely to be his way of making friends and seeking reassurance that he was in kind hands. Never having been in hospital before, he would not have realised the medical and cleaning personnel had a heavy workload to get through and little time to talk.

Early in the morning of the third day after his admission, Matt, who had grudgingly taken a day off work on the assumption that he would be able to take Jamie home, arrived at the wrong door of the hospital ('Are you an emergency?

This is A&E'). Smarting with the curtness of the desk clerk who had implied stupidity in his choice of entry and nearly choking from unaccustomed nostril-clogging antiseptic, he lost no time in retracing his steps to read the large sign he had been directed to.

Not surprisingly, he was also not best pleased when politely told by the staff nurse when eventually locating the correct ward, 'No, your son cannot be discharged until the consultant has given his approval. Mr. Watson does not make his rounds until at least 11.30 and that is dependent on whether he is in theatre. Would you like me to check the day's list?' Thus Matt, still with his nose feeling very much out of joint, the reason for which he laid blame fairly and squarely on the shoulders of his wife who had assured him 'discharge' was on the notes she had read, had had to make do with a lesser mortal, the junior houseman appointed to the Children's Ward.

Dr. Angus Robertson, told by 'Staff' that the parent was 'raring for the verbals', awaited Matt in the ward sister's office. The bright welcoming smile on the recently qualified house officer's face as he greeted the tight-faced Matt masked the trepidation he felt at this, his first confrontation since his transformation to fully-fledged doctor status. Starred A's at every stage of his public school education, graduating at the highest level and regarded by his contemporaries as of astounding intelligence ('but with the interpersonal skills of a frightened rabbit'), he was now to realise the wisdom of attending the interpersonal relations course recommended but which he had turned down. Suffice it to say that his somewhat insensitive bedside manner had cost him the coveted 'Student of the Year' prize in 2008 which had, otherwise, been his for the taking.

Dr. Robertson's social clumsiness got him off to a very poor start in the discussion which Matt had intended to use as an opportunity to ascertain the true state of health and prognosis for his son, finding it hard to believe the nature of the concerns Sarah held. Instead of awaiting his 'opponent's' first move, the young houseman jumped in with both feet, and ill-clad ones at that.

'Pleasure to meet you, Mr Chilton. I'm Dr. Robertson, Children's Ward.' He extended his hand which Matt shook in a conspicuously abrupt manner. 'I understand that you are very unhappy that your son has not been discharged after his fall. You are quite at liberty to make a formal complaint should you wish and I have a form here for you to complete. Here, let me lend you my pen.

'I am extremely sorry that you feel we have mismanaged your son's...'

'Hey, wait a minute, wait a minute,' Matt exploded, cutting the raw recruit to the medical profession short: 'Wherever did you get the ridiculous idea we had a formal complaint to make? I assure you, there would be a lawyer by my side at this moment had I wished to do so. Merely as the boy's parents who had been told four days ago that he would be kept in overnight as a precaution, I am here to find out why, in this hospital-bed-shortage era, he seems to have taken up residence. My wife and I are beginning to be perturbed that there might be a sinister reason for the hospital to feel it necessary to continue to 'keep a watching brief.'

Matt shuddered as he ruminated on how gauche and wet behind the ears some high-flying medics could be. Dr. Robertson crashed on unwittingly, the sound of shattering glass being almost palpable as he attempted to win over his adversary with sophisticated medical knowledge.

'Mr. Chilton, we have to consider a range of possibilities and to make sure that any trauma is temporary and not caused by a tumour or other lesion. And if so, we should lose to time in embarking on the right course of treatment, for instance radiotherapy, in the hope of halting the progression.'

Hardly noticing the father's scandalised expression, he

blithely continued with his exposition. 'Before we take such risky action our nurses are logging your son's seemingly bizarre remarks and egocentric conversation in which he engages any passer-by. This even extends, unfortunately, to the mothers of our really seriously ill patients who are not best pleased with being asked whether their child is about to die.'

The directness of the young houseman reduced even the usually self-controlled Matt to a jellified shadow of his normal adversarial persona. Was this man talking sense? Had the nursing staff listened to Jamie's admittedly unorthodox ramblings and put a deviant slant on them? Should they at home have been concerned at his sometimes outrageous remarks? Sarah had always explained to him that the emotional and social development of highly intelligent children was often ill-matched and you could not, therefore, expect Jamie to be able to put into practice all the advanced theories with which his mind experimented. Whilst Matt's personal opinion, often unfortunately voiced to the detriment of marital harmony, was that anything uttered which was offensive should be smartly overruled, Sarah preferred his 'emotional literacy' development to take its own course. Undoubtedly their differences in opinion in the upbringing of their son was impacting upon Matt's temper, fragile enough as it was when maintaining an executive position nowadays often felt like running up the going-down escalator. Was it now too late? Swallowing back the unaccustomed feelings of paralysis which were steadily engulfing him since first hearing the dreaded 'c' word which, of course, the man meant when he mentioned 'tumour', and without his usual bombastic manner, Matt faintly asked to see the logs being kept by the hospital staff.

Dr. Robertson called for Jamie's file. Several sheets were extracted by the Houseman, now feeling more in charge of the situation whilst being totally unaware of the effects on a father of his blunt explanation for the tardiness in discharging his young son.

Matt began to relax as he read the listed entries, now running to well over twenty, all so recognisable as the out-of-order remarks and incomprehensible rants of an undisciplined, exceptionally bright child whose mother failed to curb his outspoken rudeness.

Clasping the papers with uncustomary shaking hands, his eyes flickered over several typed pages in disbelief that the incongruous questions and remarks of a six-year-old could cause such alarm. The first one to strike him had resulted in a Nigerian nurse being given a day off to recover. Wouldn't it have been more sensible to have asked the nurse herself to spend a minute or two chatting to the child about her home country? Over-sensitivity to a young child's misunderstanding also needed someone to calm the nurse down and ensure the innocent questions were not regarded as indicative of a mental disorder. The entry was ridiculous:

'Enquired whether Nurse B came from Ghana – they had learned about that place in school. Did she do witchcraft 'cos he'd read they did a long time ago? Had she got any bones in her pocket: a hospital was a good place to collect them, wasn't it, and she could post them back to the witch doctor. How long did it take to do her hair like that, all knotted up? Could she run on hot coal?

Another concerned the interest any small boy, never having been in hospital before, might have about standard practices. 'Frequently calls across ward to ask what is in bedpans and can he look at it. Were they the same as the metal dishes their food was served in? Said his poo will have tomatoes in it because that is what he had for dinner.' Shouldn't all Children's Wards have picture books with information as to what to expect to see when in hospital? Was it so surprising that everyday items to hospital staff need explaining to young patients? And why had they not followed up his interest in bedpans by describing the type of illness of patients who would need to use one?

Had they done so, the feelings of a newly admitted child with burned legs would not have been hurt so badly as Jamie's question asking whether he could walk to the toilet or whether he would 'have to have one of those frying pan things to do his poo in', would have been unnecessary.'

A later entry shone out as further evidence that the hospital was at fault by not providing an informative booklet aimed at relieving the likely misunderstandings of young patients: 'Wants to know each day what movie is on in the theatre and do they do pantomimes there at Christmas? Rambled on to the Polish cleaner about beanstalks, glass slippers, giants, spirit lamps, funny ladies called windows who'd lost their husbands and could not find them which was not surprising 'cos they didn't look for them and mice who drove coaches.' For the cleaner from the EU who had no knowledge of English pantomime and fairy stories, was it really necessary to transfer her to another ward when suggesting she borrow a book from the library for her own enlightenment would have been more appropriate? Clearly there had been no attempt to satisfy Jamie's interest in hospital theatres; had they done so, they would not have been treated to constant requests to know the day's entertainments he presumed were being shown. Surely, the nurses only had themselves to blame by not spending a little time explaining the difference to him. Could volunteer auxiliaries not be employed to assist if nurses did not have time to talk to their young patients?

These gems were interspersed with accounts of conversations which did not make any sense unless you knew the context. Matt recognised disjointed accounts of a holiday where everything had gone wrong which could have gone wrong. Whilst he could make sense of the events recorded, to anyone not having the time – or perhaps inclination – to explore these reminiscences with him, the jumbled memories of Jamie would no doubt sound like the disconnected ramblings of a deranged mind. Why were they not discussed with Sarah when she was visiting? For example, Sarah could have thrown light on another entry, Matt thought, relating to Jamie's experiences at that depraved family's house, the one which ought to have been condemned (certainly unfit now for other human habitation): scrubbing brushes, cat shit, coke cans, sandpits, strange voices, all sounded familiar.

As Matt shook his head in disbelief, Dr. Robertson, who had withdrawn to take a call on his bleeper, came back to join Matt. He recoiled a little as he looked expectantly at the father now bristling with hardly concealed anger.

'So you now understand our concerns that your son is presenting many worrying symptoms which need investigating, I am sure.'

Matt drew in his breath before he returned the shot. 'Dr. Robertson, far be it from me to question your superior judgment as a paediatric clinician but as a mere layman with ten years' experience of the upbringing of my children, six years with a child with an inquisitive nature not unusual at his age, I do feel that the vast majority of the entries in your log could be described as the examples of an insatiable (and rather endearing, some people might say), appetite for knowledge about the strange environment in which he finds himself unexpectedly. Put it this way, I would assume if you were suddenly and inexplicably transported to an island in, say, the Andaman Sea which, I believe, is populated by tribes who still lead a hunter-gatherer lifestyle and repel attempts at contact by outsiders, even welcoming shipwrecked sailors with poisoned arrows, you would also have a number of questions you would ask in order to help you make sense of your surroundings. Would you not be utterly bewildered by such an alien and utterly confusing turn of events?'

'Put like that, Mr. Chilton, I am beginning to understand the source of your anxiety. You must appreciate, however, that we are making clinical judgments based on available observations of our patients.'

'Which would be better informed should your staff take the time to talk with some of them, in order for you to understand where they are coming from,' smartly retorted his adversary. 'Especially the younger and therefore the more vulnerable ones who find themselves in strangely novel situations without warning. As a case in point, I see from one of your entries that you have a psychologist of some description around who you indicated was to be called in to dispel Jamie's suspicions on something or other. Where is it … ah, here it is on page 6 of your comprehensive notes. I quote:

'Would the police send the doctors to prison if they knew they had drugs and gave them out to people? Against that entry, you have written: With parental permission, clinical psychologist to explain differences to patient.'

Matt ignored the attempted interjection of the out-of-depth junior houseman at that point in the interview; he was fired up and unstoppable. His sarcastic tone emphasised his point precisely.

'Tell me, why is it there is only *one* entry as far as I can see which has any reference whatsoever to support to be offered to my son to further his understanding of hospital practices?' He paused before throwing in his final insult: 'Because of the mention of police involvement?' Matt sucked in his cheek as he looked at the doctor through lowered eyelids, awaiting a response which did not come.

His eyes flicked down to the last entry. 'Must say you would have been lacking in humour if you were not amused by this one.' He passed the book across to the now blatantly discomfited young doctor.

In fact this entry, when it was originally drawn to his attention, had caused him acute embarrassment, not amusement; it was the ward nurses who had found this incident uproariously hilarious. 'That one will go down well at the Christmas drinks party,' Dr. Robertson had heard the ward sister chortling. Dr. Robertson felt the hairs on the back of his neck bristling as the printed words brought back the bitter memories that statement had aroused:

'Asked Dr. Robertson which trolley he'd fallen off. Was it the tea trolley or the medicine one? Said he'd heard the male nurse who was strangely called a sister, not a brother, say that and hoped it didn't hurt when he fell off. What was he doing on there, having a ride on it? I gather the unfortunate nurse in question had to be given tranquillisers and lost a day's pay for insubordination.'

Enough was enough of this mental torture. Baptism by fire could not have had a worse effect on him. His initial surge of self-importance when first told he was to deputise for the consultant, Dr. Watson, in this potentially tricky and delicate discussion with a dissatisfied parent had dissipated long since. Dr. Robertson desperately tried to bring the conversation to an end which would be satisfactory enough to restore his self-esteem. Sadly, this was a losing battle, particularly as Matt had offered the sarcastic opinion that it was probably the houseman himself who needed the tranquillisers, not the nurse.

'Mr. Chilton, I must explain. These bizarre remarks are not genuine questions a well-brought up child would make. Many members of our nursing staff are mothers of similarly aged boys. Indeed, I believe most have been on the Children's Ward for a number of years and they have been taken aback by what they hear on an hourly basis. Quite frankly, manners are acquired by good parenting skills and we are all convinced that is what you and Mrs. Chilton have always used. Although not a father myself, I have witnessed my nieces and nephews in their homes and these are always polite and would know when to ask a certain question and when not. It is therefore our duty to consider context and relevance and we are united in questioning whether these are the remarks of a child suffering neurological damage of some sort which needs investigating. I am sure the paediatric consultant will tell you the same. We are in the process of referring to him for his opinion.'

'Well,' said Matt, rising and resuming control, 'I shall be delighted to relieve you from this irksome task. No, I don't want a Complaints Form but if you will be so kind as to give me one in which I can take full responsibility for my son's discharge without leaving you in the proverbial shit,' (Dr. Robertson blanched) 'I will sign it here and now and make arrangements for my wife to pick him up later today. If these entries are your reason for keeping him in as a patient under observation, then, believe me, I will sign to say these are nothing compared with some of the outrageous remarks he makes daily, odd ideas he gets hold of, etc., faux pas from which his mother does not dissuade him from making. Meanwhile, I thank you and your team for being so solicitous in regard to his welfare and I bid you good day.'

Dr. Robertson cleared his throat, feeling that this roller-coastal discussion, if you could call it that, had become exceedingly stressful. 'Mr. Chilton, it is clear you have every intention of removing your son: this is your prerogative as doing so would not be life-threatening. As you are clearly aware, hospital protocol rules that in such cases the next of kin must sign a discharge form indemnifying the hospital against any future harm to the patient should that occur post voluntary removal. It is also imperative for you to sign the agreement that has been fully explained to you.' He rustled in his drawer and found the necessary form. Matt signed, almost without reading it, cursorily shook the houseman's outstretched hand and strode from the interview room. When this crisis was over, he would try to get some sense into Sarah. By Christ, he would insist that she brought Jamie into line with his peers. Indeed, the comments Dr. Robertson had just made, summed up his own feelings. Perhaps this young, clearly inexperienced houseman, had more sense than he had originally credited him with.

★

A mentally exhausted Dr. Robertson collapsed unceremoniously into the staff nurse's chair, not noticing the scuffle of feet which preceded Matt Chilton as he strode out of the door and along the corridor, not even aware, as were the collective staff, that the father neither remembered to seek out his son nor heard the wailing cry of, 'Daddy, Daddy, Daddy' in his haste to leave the premises. Matt had much on his mind.

Entering his office building, surprising the chief executive he met on the stairs of Branksome and Co., Advertising Agency, who mentioned something about a 'short day off', Matt nodded at his secretary, sat down briskly at his desk and wearily phoned Sarah to give her a synopsis of the events of the morning.

Sarah, bearing flowers as a heartfelt thank-you gift for the ward staff, duly collected Jamie at four o'clock.

'Ooh, these chrys's-and-their-mums smell like a graveyard. Do you think the nurses will like them? Oh, and by the way, Mummy, the nurses had very funny nicknames for each other. One was called Hospital Bicycle but they got cross with me when I said I liked the hospital bicycle nurse best and said I must not use that name; it was a secret one which I must not say to her. Just like when I called Daddy's brother that name he didn't like. Another one was called Scooter and I know why 'cos I heard someone being cross with him and asking why he was always scooting off when a bedpan needed emptying. He wasn't very nice to me once when I said he should be called Brother not Sister. Silly to call him that, isn't it?'

Chapter Thirteen

By the end of Year 2, Miss Griffin's notebook, with tightly written sentences on each page, also reached its end. Miss Shadbolt was the teacher for Year 3. A more lenient, but kindly, teacher, perhaps a little less observant, far fewer items of difficult behaviour were recorded, even though under Lucy Shadbolt's more lax management, the class could become quite unruly. Juicy Lucy, Matt unfortunately referred to her as, a term which embarrassed her enormously when she overheard Jamie use this nickname to an amused Dominic one day.

Was Jamie becoming more conformist now he was a member of a class approaching eight years of age, many already having done so? Or was he adapting to the set routines? The year rolled on, Miss Shadbolt not finding Jamie to be quite such a handful as Faith Griffin had predicted. Secretly she felt rather pleased: she often felt daunted by the more experienced teacher's brusque cut-down remarks during staff meetings when she, Lucy, had had the temerity to make a contribution (or so these seemed to her as she bit her tongue and tried to hide the crestfallen state which Faith's negative comments always left her in). Whilst other members had made more supportive statements in relation to Lucy's suggestions, Mary Ackroyd often proposing Lucy's ideas should not be condemned out of hand as, after all, brainstorming sessions always threw up some very interesting ideas, absolutely no interjections, however tactful or kind, could assuage the hurt Lucy suffered. A concerned staff member, worried for her stressed feelings, brought in a letter to a national newspaper in which an expert was answering the question from a reader one day about sleepless nights her child had been having because of a teacher who constantly made disparaging and humiliating remarks to her charges. The response was to make this known to the governing body and certainly to bring it up at an OFSTED inspection. Lucy, however, was not appeased: she thought that like victims of playground or cyber bullying, it was often the case that harassment only happened to those who were incapable of resisting the pressures; why was she the only staff member to be the recipient of a vitriolic tongue? Just as a teacher/parent had to inculcate self-defence tactics against bullies in their children, the same should be the avoiding strategies of adults in similar situations. She made up her mind to enrol in a professional course at the local Teachers' Centre on 'How not to be a Victim.'

There was an incident later in the year, however, which very nearly catapulted Lucy into such a state of impotence that she was nearly lost to the profession.

One playtime Charlie and Freddie were particularly friendly towards Jamie. The three of them walked arm in arm, whistling as many war songs as they could think of. 'We like the one about World War II,' said Charlie. 'Do you know it, Jamie?' As Jamie didn't, Freddie asked if he'd like them to teach him. Jamie said he was good at learning words so thought he'd soon be able to join in with them.

'We'd better go behind the shed,' Charlie said, 'then no one else will hear. You know Miss Shadbolt said she wanted us to find out songs they sang in the war for our next history lesson? Well, you've got a good voice, Jamie, so you could sing it for her. You might get a table point for us then. History's this afternoon.'

The two boys exchanged knowing glances as they both mentally recalled the carol incident last year, not that they had had any direct input into that scenario, at least not the carol part and Charlie chose to have a conveniently blank moment about letting on about Jamie's rendering of the Lord's Prayer. It didn't take more than ten minutes of the lunchbreak for Jamie to be word perfect.

Back in the classroom, Miss Shadbolt asked the children to contribute names of the songs which cheered up the soldiers and which they'd sing in their canteen. She had already awarded a table point to Millie who had announced that she knew who the Forces Sweetheart was. Vera Lynn was duly written up on the board in a separate space above "The White Cliffs of Dover". "Roll Out The Barrel", was contributed by Freddie and "Pack up your Troubles" was volunteered by Ruby, tossing her chestnut hair back with a swish as she made her contribution. Jamie often stroked it, to her annoyance, especially when he told her that if she painted it yellow like some ladies did, she would turn into Rapunzel. And Miss Shadbolt had laughed when Jamie asked what a 'Rary' was that was that had to be tipped a long way away, but her expression had looked a bit severe when he had continued to ask whether the place the rary had been dropped from was Snowdon as that was probably the nearest mountain high enough to throw it down; it had to be steep, obviously. She underlined the full word when she wrote it up and all the class laughed too; in fact, Jamie hadn't been the only one who had wondered.

Miss Shadbolt then produced a funny-looking box which she called a gramophone, together with a thin, round, black thing with lots of grooves in it which she said was a 'record', a 78 one. This puzzled Jamie who wanted to know what record it had won, was it in the Guinness Book of Records, for example, but his waving hand to attract her attention she wisely thought best to ignore. The class listened in amazement to the croaking voices, the crackling, tinny sound and how Miss Shadbolt had to keep winding what she called a crank handle. Several others were put on the turntable until all of the songs the children had listed were included.

'Miss Shadbolt,' Jamie called across the room to Miss Shadbolt's back as she was closing the lid down. 'What breed of dog is that on the lid? Why is it sitting on that 'phone thing?'

'Jamie,' hissed Freddie, 'ask if you can sing the one we taught you. She'll be ever so pleased with you then. It looks as if she is not going to answer any more of your questions so that might put you back in her good books.'

Puffed up with importance, Jamie felt it would also restore his name in the book teachers keep for saying what he mistakenly thought were nice things about children. He had not seen Miss Shadbolt write very much about him so it was something to cheer her up.

'I know one which wasn't on those black things, Miss Shadbolt. It's on the River Kooee, though,' he giggled at the connection and made the sort of hand wave you might give if saying 'coo-ee.' 'This is the first verse. 'Shall I sing it to you? We could all sing the chorus as I could teach the others if you like.'

Without waiting for an answer, Jamie stood up from his seat and began in his clear lilting treble, head swaying jerkily from side to side as if marching:

'Sergeant!
He's only got one ball.
The other's in the Leeds Town Hall
And now his mother,
She wants the other,
So he won't have no boll-ocks at all!
Dah de dah dah dah dah.'

'The last bit, the dah-dahs, is the main chorus. Shall we practise it?'

Miss Shadbolt's jaw dropped. She blushed; her cheeks turned tomato red. The class was silent, waiting for their shocked teacher's response. Warming to his topic, but a little unclear as to the meaning of one or two of the words, he asked for clarification.

'They did have cannon balls in World War II, didn't they? Is ball-ocks the collective noun?'

'That is ab-so-lutely dis-gus-ting, Jamie. It is the sort of thing that if my brother had said that as a child he would have been told to scrub his mouth out. Go and stand by the door.'

Miss Shadbolt looked frantic, almost as if she was about to pass out. She was uncertain how to deal with this situation, which clearly could get out of hand. Charlie put his hand up.

'Miss Shadbolt, he was singing that at playtime. We told him he should stop but he said he liked it because it was about cannon balls in the war and he'd been to Leeds as his daddy's great aunty' (he enunciated the word 'daddy' to intimate that any seven-or eight-year-old who didn't refer to the abbreviated version was a sissy) 'lived there in a big house which could, perhaps, be the Town Hall but he'd never seen things like cannon balls when he'd been up there.'

Jamie called from his station by the door that he would ask next time he was visiting his great aunty, 'who also, as a matter of fact, is my daddy's aunty. Isn't that funny?'

The lesson continued, Jamie enquiring several times whether Miss Shadbolt still wanted him to stand by the door. Not at all sure of herself, Miss Shadbolt was dumbfounded when he'd given her the information that it was not possible for him to see what she was writing on the board from where he was standing, her desk was in the way and did she want him to continue monitoring the door or to copy down the titles, adding that if someone wanted to come in, he could leave his seat quickly to open the door for them? In that way, he announced triumphantly, he would be quite capable of killing two birds with one stone, a phrase he had learned when Matt was watching a football match at the same time as he was hearing him read. It had seemed such a weird thing for his daddy to say to his mummy when she'd accused him of being more interested in the match than listening to his son. He had remonstrated with his father that that was a cruel thing to do and if anyone saw him, he could be reported to the RSPB, he could be put in prison and then what would become of them all? His father had not been kind to him on that occasion but at least he had learned the strange thing you say when you did two things at once.

Miss Shadbolt had decided that the audacity to sing a rude rugby song in front of her was not a matter she could deal with on her own. Her brother had taken her to a Wasps' party many years ago where the loudness of the rousing singing as more and more beers were drunk had shaken her to the core. But if she invoked the support of senior staff, it could count against her and she was due for an appraisal interview in the near future. Jamie was clearly taking advantage of the fact that he probably knew what a soft spot she had for him. One of the youngest in the class, but the brightest by far, she generally found his naïve personality most endearing. In previous years, she had often sought him out when on playground duty, mainly to save him from the victimisation of others which she had put down to jealousy and the tendency of peers to gang up collectively when there was a distinctively different child in their midst. Being the victim of others' hostility herself sometimes, her heart warmed to this rather 'unusual' child, certainly not one out of the mould of 'twenty-four tins, all contents portion-controlled'. Basically, she knew that young children were often afraid of 'differences' and acted cruelly towards the outsider in an effort to feel safe themselves and, without children of her own, she felt particularly protective towards this child with his quaint ideas.

She studiously ignored a muffled comment which she was supposed not to hear but was meant for Jamie's ears, which

Jamie's shuddering body
could no longer withstand
the pressure. . . .

for large or small lies

PURE BRILLIANT
White

PROFESSIONAL

© TimBaynes 2011

.. Do liars carry paint pots around in their pockets and do they paint their lies before they say them?

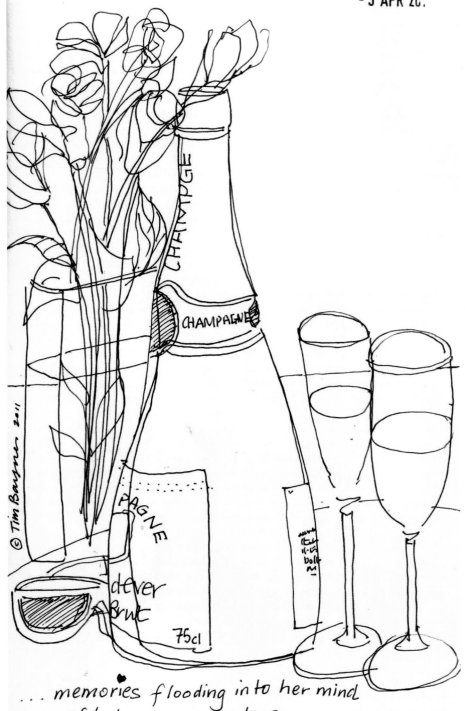

... memories flooding into her mind
of balmy summer days
drifting through Rheims, arms......

'Now let's get your book checked out.'

There's time for you to read a page
or two to me before tea if we go home now.

caused the children within earshot to do little to hold back
their giggles:

'Cool, Jimmy-Jammie, you really took the mickey out of
old Shagdrawers.'

Lucy bit her lip: she mustn't break down, only the pressure
she felt under controlling some of the sharp-witted members of
her class, together with the looming SATs tests, was beginning
to get to her. It didn't help that her mother seemed to be
morally blackmailing her. As the only unmarried daughter, she
was demanding more and more of her time. Eventually, having
responded to her mother's pleas to come to live with her ('You
know it makes sense dear. It is silly to heat the house just for
me now your father has died, and two can live more cheaply
than one'), she bitterly regretted making such a decision. Lucy
Shadbolt felt her heartstrings tugged whenever she went out
with her only friend, Margaret, to hear the bleating farewells
of her mother, 'You go, dear. I'm all right here by the fire with
my cat. I'll just have a boiled egg on toast and go to bed early.
There's nothing I want to watch. Don't you worry about me,
just go and enjoy yourself.' How could she enjoy herself with
her mother's sacrificial sanctimoniousness ringing in her ears?
Even the use of the word 'boiled' was a veiled reminder that
she would never poach one without her daughter there to see
she didn't scald herself.

How to manage the present situation? She quelled her
rising panic and forcefully told Jamie he would remain exactly
where he was until the end of the lesson. The assignment she
was giving the class to do for the last quarter of an hour, Jamie
would have to do at home tonight. She was writing to his
mother to tell her the reason why.

'I would like it if you would also write that I earned a table
point for singing the River Kooee song. She will tell my daddy.
He always says, "I don't believe you", so he might if he sees it
written down.'

Wondering if Jamie was still trying to 'take the mickey', as Brendon had helpfully suggested to his friends, she realised he was probably taking advantage of the attention she had given him when on playground duty last year. She had often walked around with him to keep him company when he had complained nobody would let him play with them. Sometimes he had brought a game for others to play but had been rebuffed when attempting to persuade them to give up whatever activity it was they were doing in order to let him demonstrate the rules of *his* game to them. Sometimes Miss Shadbolt would draw some of the younger children round; these children would be impressed by an older child seeking their friendship. Unfortunately, however, Jamie made the rules too complex and it would not be long before one or other was crying his eyes out because Jamie had chastised them for breaking one which, of course, had been too hard for them to comprehend. Girls would frequently ask her to 'Tell Jamie not to keep tugging our ropes / spilling our beads / kicking our balls away from us,' and she had walked around with him. Surely holding the hand thrust into hers was acceptable in a public arena; yet she was well aware not even her CRB check could protect her from charges of child molestation if these were maliciously brought against her. Intrigued by his eccentric view of the world, Lucy was often amused by his engaging chatter which she thought to be rather old-fashioned or too adult, reminiscent of a child who seemed far more at ease in the company of adults than was good for him. She was often gratified that he seemed to take it for granted that she already had background information about the incident he was relating to her, as if she was well into his confidence and, in his estimation, more than just a teacher but a true friend. Sometimes she would make a comment which he would regard as incongruous. 'Oh no, Miss Shadbolt, to be honest with you, the orange youtans we saw in Sepilok aren't wild, you know.' Miss Shadbolt had resolved on that occasion to access Wikipedia to locate the city she had never heard of and whether 'youtans' were what she assumed they were.

The class had not been easy to manage for the rest of the history lesson and Lucy Shadbolt was, as were her charges, glad to hear the bell signal the end of the school day. She had had to stop a ruler fight amongs the Herons, stopping in mid-sentence and directing what she felt was a withering look at the offending boys who simply continued until a neighbour snatched the rulers from them. Why did this technique work wonders for Mr. Bolton – she'd seen him do this successfully on more than one occasion when she shared a lunch-duty with him? For Miss Shadbolt, as any good teacher could have told her, not even shouting quelled any bad behaviour. Her heart sank as, at the first jarring trill of the bell, desk lids had clanged upon exercise books quickly thrust inwards, there had been a burst for the door even before Jamie, still believing himself to be the door monitor, could open it. 'Come back Year 3, come back,' she screeched out but to no avail, the departing backs were already clad in anoraks or jackets: Year 3 were out into freedom like bees swarming from a hive.

'Would you remind me of the homework you have given me, Miss Shadbolt. Do you want me to do it on paper, for the wall display, or in my social studies book? I would like to write something about the Battle of Britain. I have a poster which would go with it and you could put both up in the space over there. Oh, and could you hurry please; Dominic is waiting for me and his mother is doing the school run tonight so I ought to go right now.'

Miss Shadbolt was lost for words. She handed him a piece of paper which she had already headed, 'Evacuees in World War II.' She then withdrew from a desk a sheet of school-headed notepaper on which she wrote:

Dear Mr. and Mrs. Chilton,

I regret to tell you that I am getting increasingly concerned that Jamie is becoming a very outspoken boy, now to the point of rudeness well beyond an excusable level. I would be very pleased to discuss this matter with you both and I am available after school at any time between 3.30 to 3.45 but would prefer you to make an appointment.

Yours truly,

Lucy Shadbolt (Miss)
Year 3 Class Teacher.

She told Jamie to get his coat and accompany her to Mrs. Ackroyd's room. Passing an anxious Dominic in the corridor, she told him to tell his mother Jamie was on his way. After all, she knew that the school run included Jamie's sister who, being in Year 6, would not be out of class for another five minutes. After a quick, furtive discussion with the more senior teacher who was responsible for special needs, the letter was countersigned and duly placed in the already-named envelope. Jamie was told to give it to his mother immediately when he reached home. Jamie assured the two teachers that he would 'lose no time in doing so'.

Dismissing Jamie, Lucy Shadbolt then spoke of her rising concerns about Jamie's strange disregard of correct respect for adults.

'Sometimes he addresses me as if we are on an equal footing and the liberties he took today made me wonder what is going on at home.'

She asked if the SENCo would join her in the discussion she proposed to hold with his parents. Actually Lucy Shadbolt was feeling quite faint at the prospect and wondered whether she'd have the courage to face them, even with Mrs. Ackroyd's support – could she call in sick that day? Had she been too pro-active in sending that letter?

'In your role as SENCo, it is probably really important that you do. Am I right in thinking the County Handbook has something about it under "Disciplinary Measures"?'

Mary Ackroyd felt important: Mr. Holmes generally asked her to 'sit in' on such meetings but never gave her a role of responsibility on such occasions, which she thought he should do in her position; now her chance was about to come. But facing Mr. Chilton? That was another matter. She was unsure which would be worse: confronting Mr. Chilton or Mr. Smegley, a possibility often discussed in staff meetings and which she had so far circumvented by keeping both of their offspring on 'internal watch' only. She also wondered whether she should call in sick on the day? However, if she asked Gordon to attend, he would be bound to steal any thunder which could accrue to her if the meeting went to her satisfaction; you never know. She steeled herself.

As the after-school discussion relating to Jamie's misdemeanours gathered momentum, Mary Ackroyd had to recommend that Jamie's name should be entered on the list of 'School Action' children, a proposal which would be made to Mr. and Mrs. Chilton. Glad of her support, Lucy Shadbolt determined that she would not let her apprehension take hold of her: she would face her fears head-on.

★

'Mummy, I have an important assignment to do at home tonight. It's going to have a special place on the wall and is to do with our World War II project. I was chosen to do this – the others wrote about it in the lesson. It's all about children in that war Great Grandpa, yours I mean, not Daddy's, was always telling us about before he died. Do you remember? He told us how he worked at a garage where they had big balloons. I suppose they were to advertise to people and get them to go for their petrol there, weren't they?'

Taken aback for a moment as her grandfather had not been a car mechanic, ever, Sarah then realised her young son, who was only four at the time he had passed into oblivion (Matt's expression; he had never got on well with the Old Man, as he called him), had misheard the initial letter, exchanging a 'b' for a 'g'. She had always felt a little perplexed when Jamie would make allusions to the fact that Grandpa would have been able to fix their car instead of Daddy always groaning when he scanned what he called extortionate bills from 'that blood-sucking Mercedes garage'. Sarah, correcting her son's malapropism (not for the first time she had had to put him right when he used a word inappropriately), explained the significance of barrage balloons and that Great Grandpa had been a flight lieutenant in charge of a group of balloon sites defending the north of England from bombardment by enemy planes.

Jamie interrupted her by adding that he'd been door monitor during the history lesson and he thought Miss Shadbolt had written her a note to say how pleased she was with a war song he'd sung.

'Do open your letter, Mummy; it's for Daddy too but he probably won't mind you reading it first.'

Having digested the contents with a sinking heart, Sarah was mightily relieved Matt was going to be late home that evening. Her self-respect as a mother couldn't sink any lower. She was finding Jamie to be increasingly more difficult to understand, Matt was becoming more and more irritated with his son's 'girlish' attitudes and the early promise he had shown seemed to be over-shadowed by strangely eccentric behaviour.

★

Sarah had replied to the letter explaining (by telephone so that there would not be any incriminating references to the school's rising concerns on her personal computer – Freya was not the only devious member of the family in this respect) that she would be coming on her own. She had realised there was 'some urgency' and felt it better not to await the time when her husband's schedules of work were not taking him up to the Midlands on an almost daily basis, as they would be doing for the foreseeable future.

The eventual meeting, dreaded by both teachers and Sarah in almost equal quantities, outwardly passed very smoothly, not the least reason for this being the absence of Jamie's father.

Thus, with the absence of both Mr. Holmes (who, most opportunely, had 'found' he had a Diocesan meeting to attend – which he had, but early enough in the afternoon for him to have been back at school in time) and Matt unknowingly 'unable to attend' for aforesaid reasons, the special needs conference proceeded without acrimony or confrontation on anyone's part. Sarah was inwardly anguished to have to listen to the catalogue of instances in which Jamie had been reprimanded for apparent rudeness, albeit delicately expressed by one or other of the two teachers in attendance, and at a loss to provide valid excuses for his behaviour. Any maternal explanation of his innocence, his thoughtlessness, his unwitting cheekiness, was foiled by Mrs. Ackroyd who assured her that an intelligent near-eight-year-old definitely knew the differences between what was correct and what was insulting. They kindly suggested what they thought were mitigating circumstances, however: Jamie, in all probability was 'playing to the gallery' in order to gain the attention of his classmates.

Agreement was reached that Jamie should be formally placed on St. Michael's' Special Educational Needs register at 'School Action' and an Individual Education Programme would be devised to guide his oppositional behaviour in a positive, not condemnatory manner. This would be reviewed at the end of the term and consideration then given to procedure to the next stage of the Code of Practice or Jamie would be withdrawn from the register altogether. The government regulations to give support to a wide range of children, including those 'behaviourally challenged', were explained to Sarah. (A box of strategically placed tissues were a benefit at this point to white-faced Sarah, appalled that a conduct disorder was clearly on the teachers' minds). 'We do know you are aware of these but it is also in the regulations that we make it quite clear to the parent what this entails,' Mary added.

Thus, Mary Ackroyd had had her first experience of chairing an S.E.N. discussion and of supporting a colleague in what they had both presumed would otherwise have been very trying circumstances. Sarah, however, far less triumphant, drove home with a sinking feeling crushing her heart. Was Matt right in his judgment of her parenting techniques? Was her trust misplaced in her assumption that Jamie was a victim of his own advanced intelligence not being a match for his interpretation of what was right to say, to whom and when? She was finding Jamie to be increasingly more difficult to understand and was running out of excuses for his eccentricities now he was a 'rising eight'. Matt was becoming more and more irritated with his son's 'girlish' attitudes and the early promise he had shown seemed to be over-shadowed by strangely 'different' language and 'unusual' reactions which should be outgrown now. In a sense she was mightily relieved the school was going to keep him in the spotlight. She understood that examples of idiosyncratic behaviour would be recorded and another meeting would be held at the end of term.

Her car safely in the garage, she unlocked the door and,

mustering up a cheerfulness she did not feel, paid off and thanked the babysitter for overseeing tea and homework, called the children to say their goodbyes and joined them in the playroom until bed-time for Jamie was reached. Freya, noting her mother's unaccustomedly distant mood, crept into the kitchen, returning on Sarah's completion of her vague night-time valedictions to Jamie, to present her with a cup of tea. She had been aware from Jamie's earlier excitement that a meeting with his teacher had been called ... and she had predicted the worst. Dominic had spilled the beans in the car about the WW1 fiasco and recalling her mother's artificial brightness as she paid Hannah, she wanted to comfort her.

Sleep for Sarah did not come easily that night. Even Matt, usually dead to the world until the alarm went off, complained her tossing and turning was keeping him awake. Must she change her approach and adopt Matt's curt recommendations as to how to bring up her enchanting, very special son?

Chapter Fourteen

The year progressed without further hitch and Year 3 steadily transmuted into Year 4. Sarah found it hard to believe Jamie would be nine at the end of the school year. In many ways he was grown-up for his years, in others he still remained innocent of so many aspects children of his age took for granted.

The family's excitement that academic year had been intense when the secondary selection procedures had determined that Freya's average score of 132 had put her firmly amongst the group of Year 6's who were deemed suitable for a grammar school education. Christmas was therefore doubly exciting, as was the Easter holiday when the specific school was identified and uniform and equipment were chosen. Sarah felt their decision not to have Freya coached for the exams was vindicated, as to have done so, being herself a teacher in state school education, would have been against her principles. Matt, too, was all for allowing natural merit to shine through, or otherwise. Jamie joined in the subdued delight – Sarah was anxious to avoid Freya feeling a sense of superiority over those in her class who had been regarded as appropriate for the local senior, not grammar, schools. Freya was forbidden to use the terms 'passing' or 'failing', although Sarah sensed she was on a losing wicket there because she was only too well aware of the neighbourhood's fixation with the 11 plus being an indication of success. On the day that the letters were received, shrieks of 'Have you passed?' 'Have you passed?' 'Oh my God, you've failed, have you, you poor thing!' at the school gate were indications of the hysteria the results had caused amongst the children. As for the parents, the coffee shops were witness to a different level of hysteria or abject misery. Even the doctors' surgeries were crisis centres with scenes of despair which required medication to relieve severe depression. Sarah worked hard to prevent her daughter making any contribution to the hysteria but knew that, by doing so, she was causing her daughter to feel 'different'. One in the family was enough, she thought bitterly, and did not chastise her when she discreetly observed Freya using the commonly accepted terminology.

★

The phone call from her sister-in-law was not unexpected. A return of honour went without saying. Intuitively, both Sarah and Julie knew that they had left much in the air on the occasion when the two families met almost a year ago and both women regretted having left it so long to reconvene. Perhaps the passage of time would have allowed the dust to settle.

'Sarah, George and I, well me really, would love you all to come over for lunch one Saturday soon. The time has gone by in a flash. I feel we have so much to talk about that doesn't interest men – well, our men – and I, for one, can't have such a "no holds barred" chat with anyone else as I am able to have with you.'

'I feel the same, Julie. Let's make it soon. I'll get the diary.' Julie offered another, more telling reason for proposing a lunch date.

'I've been so worried about Max, Sarah. He is still living at home and really doesn't seem to want to move to a flat of his own. It doesn't occur to him that a twenty-eight-year-old living with parents is most unusual and seems scandalised when I put the question to him that it is time he became independent. Seems to be so wrapped up in himself.'

Whilst Sarah was in complete agreement, she thought it

more sisterly to comment that she often read articles in the dailies that this was becoming a trend now graduates were taking time to find employment and mortgages were becoming impossible to obtain. Without a job, how could they apply for a loan and, similarly, how could rent be afforded?

'You're so right, Sarah, but all George does about it is to criticise, criticise, criticise. Max is so thick-skinned he takes it all in his stride and merely proposes counter arguments,' Julie sighed, the crack in her voice revealing the pressure she was under. 'George then ends up by saying that his behaviour hurts his mother. I often just feel like the piggy in the middle.'

Commiserating with her sister-in-law, Sarah realised she was feeling an empathy with her that she really could not fully understand. Was it because Jamie seemed to show facets of his cousin's rather eccentric behaviour at times? Was the reactive behaviour of the two brothers similar in nature – both certainly seemed to have short fuses and an intolerance of individual differences in the characters of those with whom they came in daily contact. A lunch date would not come amiss. Offering a sympathetic ear, she was pleased to hear Julie's profession of solidarity in their relationship. Julie continued:

'I really couldn't bear the atmosphere in the house created by Max's inability to keep a job and often thought about coming over and pouring out my heart to you,' adding reflectively, 'He ought to be thinking of finding a girlfriend, too. Certainly joining an organisation of some sort could help but any suggestions in that direction are rebuffed.'

'Any Saturday in the next three weeks would be fine for me,' returned Sarah, who felt that any further comments in relation to Max's intransigence could release pent-up emotion clearly at risk of spilling. Not a good idea for that to happen without eye contact and devoid of the physical warmth of human compassion. Diaries were checked.

A date mutually agreed by the two sisters-in-law as a possibility was left for each to check with respective husbands and after the usual sharing of current family news, they promised to get back to each other within the next couple of days.

Not before Matt had shown his true family colours.

'Absolutely no go,' he expostulated on being told of the girls' plans. 'Count me out for whatever weekend that's on offer until, at least, the next millennium. What I had to stomach from my pompous, trumped up, nauseating fat slob of a brother when they were over here, was enough to last me until the next but one decade, thank you very much.'

What's in a few dozens of years, Sarah sighed, her husband's excesses in considering the passage of time emphasising the rivalry between the two men. As if wound by clockwork, Matt continued expressing his strong feelings on the issue of further contact.

'Even though months have passed, it seems like yesterday. And as for that good-for-nothing pup of theirs, I wouldn't lose any sleep if I never set eyes on him again. It will be golf, golf, golf for me whenever she sets a date. Sort it out for you and the kids but I just have better things to do. As the old saying goes, you can choose your friends but not your relatives. For Chris'sake, we don't need to live in their pockets now that the ice has thawed.'

Strangely, George was also 'otherwise engaged' for the foreseeable future and beyond when the return visit was proposed to him by his wife. Sarah and Julie agreed to go ahead, secretly thankful there would be no need to avoid treading on eggshells: 'The two boys, after all, get a good deal out of each other's company despite the vast age difference,' the older woman commented.

'Freya will be at Guide camp that weekend so we will really be able to put the world to rights without anyone breathing down our necks,' summed up Sarah's stance entirely. Sarah had no heart for a losing battle with Matt anyway, merely to preserve family unity. Where was the even-tempered man who was so mild-mannered and thoughtful until recent times?

★

So it was that Sarah and Jamie found themselves cruising along the motorway at 11 o'clock that Saturday morning on a day miraculously unfettered by roadworks. The journey was accomplished in record time, Jamie amusing himself by counting the number of Eddie Stobart lorries which were travelling in either direction. His excitement knew no bounds when he had reached twenty. 'Oh, Mummy, I wish they said on them where they are going, you know, like buses do.'

Once at her sister-in-law's house, following the renewed exclamations of pleasure that the families were meeting again, the two cousins lost no time sharing the eclectic treasures of Max's bedroom (still more reminiscent of a teenager's than that of a near-thirty-year-old, Sarah reflected, having accompanied Jamie to the 'den' to which Max proudly escorted them). Max firstly drew their attention to the notice on the door: 'Entrance forbidden. Password required', reassuring them that not even his parents were allowed access; he did the vacuuming, dusting and tidying himself adding, especially for Jamie's benefit, 'I really cannot abide anyone disturbing any of the objects I have so please ask, Jamie, if you wish to touch or hold anything, won't you.' Jamie's stout assurance having been given, his mother retired downstairs, privately musing on her nephew's peculiar attitude and quaint use of language. She couldn't help shuddering at the possibility that some of these eccentricities might be adopted by her own son who was at such an impressionable age. Max and Jamie were thus left in private intimacy, enabling them to indulge in shared interests of a strangely unorthodox nature, Jamie hanging on every word Max uttered and Max puffing himself up with importance and the hero-worship he had never in his life before commanded.

Not only was Jamie beside himself with excitement that he had been accorded such prestige by being allowed to enter the 'Holy of Holies', he was overawed at the size of the room and the incredible array of artefacts, many of which, he thought, deserved their place in an exhibition. Around the walls were Greenpeace, Smoking Kills and Ban the Bomb posters, the latter dating back as far as Greenham Common days of mass protest, framed photographs of marches to animal rights group meetings, coloured thread linking to the unmistakeable bobble-hatted figure of Max himself, foremost in the crowd scenes. The biggest of all, one of riot-geared, shielded police holding back a motley crowd of enraged anti-vivisectionists, had place of honour above the marble fireplace.

Noting Jamie's fascination, Max explained the importance of standing up for your principles and that you were never too young to form opinions to protect the underdog. Jamie, having been struck by a particularly large picture of beagles ostensibly smoking cigarettes, said he understood perfectly, well, almost perfectly, as he craned to see which dogs were being sat on which needed special care to be taken. Personally he thought the dogs' throats should be the first and foremost point to be considered protectively.

Max's bed next took Jamie's wide-eyed attention, the bed-head of which being carved into an enormous pterodactyl shape, the wings curving forward over the pile of pillows. 'I commissioned that as a twenty-first birthday present from all the guests at my party who gave me money. Now I come to think of it, Uncle Matt and Aunt Sarah contributed so I expect an amount from your pocket money went towards it as well, as your name and Freya's were also added to their card. So I must give you a belated thank you for your share, cousin,' he concluded, smiling benevolently, patting Jamie on the shoulder in solidarity and ignoring Jamie's, 'You look like Wally in "Where's Wally?" books. Are you the model for him?'

Jamie's question as to the underlying reason behind sheets and duvet made from camouflage material was explained as necessary in case of any personal attack by any of Bin Laden's associates who could be living incognito in this country and planning an attack. 'You see, my father is a very important businessman: he is the chairman of his company and could be a marked man. It would really affect the economy if he was blown up and I'm concerned that the attackers could come through my room first.' Jamie's eyes could not have opened wider had the lids been kept apart with toothpicks. He fervently hoped Uncle Porker – oh, no! – he had given him the forbidden name; perhaps it was because he had visions of Uncle George marked with Melton Mowbray stickers like the ones on those pies they ate sometimes on picnics. After all, the pie factory was not all that far from Leamington's Spar shop. That must have been how Leamington got its name. Funny that, he reflected. Was there a town named after Woolworths or Boots or Tesco's, perhaps? He resolved to look up in Daddy's atlas of Great Britain he kept in his car for the occasions that his sat-nav had taken him up a dead-end road when he didn't want it to.

Jamie was so alarmed by the immediacy of the manner in which Uncle George's nickname had sprung into his mind that the vivid picture Max was creating vanished as quickly as it had come. Not to worry: another one was being graphically painted.

'Of course, if a World Trade Centre-type incident occurred,' Max continued earnestly, 'if, for example, they went for the Birmingham Bullring or the transmission masts in Daventry, then we would only be affected if the planes fell short of their target.'

'I've got an idea which could save you,' exulted Jamie, jumping up and down. ' My mummy's daddy's daddy, that is my great grandpa, was in the war we had a long time before she was born, I believe, and he helped put lots and lots of lights up in very big fields near the city where he lived. They were so big they were called 'mores' – more big than any field could be. That was to make the enemy think that was where the factories were so they would bomb those instead. The city people were made to keep their lights off at night and put black stuff on their windows, Mummy said. Perhaps you could put lots of lights up in your big garden. Daddy said you had a blooming park: that means you have lots of flowers, too, so that would be a good camouflage as well, wouldn't it?'

A shiver ran down Jamie's spine as he wondered whether maybe his home could be near any missile target. He knew they would not be able to distract anyone determined to terrorise the area where they lived: their garden was not big enough for it to make much difference to their safety even if they covered the ground in lights. He could ask his daddy tonight when he tucked him up if they had any room to put up a nuclear shelter, though. That could solve the problem. He also vowed to look in the fancy dress shop to see if there were any dressing-up clothes for soldiers so that he could wear a camouflage suit to bed as pyjamas. Then the terrorists would be scared off. The relief he felt was palpable. It was good to have a brain.

Careful to ask permission to touch anything in the room, Jamie wondered whether it would be acceptable now for him to move around the spacious bedroom or whether those interesting things he could see should be viewed from a distance. He was effusively thanked for his enquiry, too effusively, Jamie thought, but grateful nonetheless that his wish was granted. Restraining himself from hopping in hopscotch fashion along the length of the chequered rug on which giant chess pieces stood, Jamie moved enthusiastically towards the display of pre-historic figures positioned below a map of the world, coloured pins marking where remains had been discovered. His joy knew no bounds as, hardly able to suppress his excitement, the two discussed the finer points of each model. Nuclear threats, al-Qaeda attacks, Death by Smoking, were relegated to the insignificance they should hold in the minds of children.

★

Downstairs, over pre-lunch gins and tonics, Freya's induction into her grammar school was given full rein, Julie showing unrestrained delight that her niece was showing considerable academic promise, had made many new friends and joined many after-school clubs. She had been selected for the hockey and netball teams, an accolade for St. Michael's who had provided a third of both junior teams. This topic aired, Julie then had a further opportunity to express her deep concerns relating to the peculiarities of her son to a sympathetic ear. Sarah listened intently but could not help herself making connections in her mind, she fervently hoped unnecessarily, with her own son.

The topic turned to husbands. Sarah, of course, could not forget the faux pas Max had made in commenting about his father's 'girl friend', and sincerely hoped he had kept his counsel in front of his mother. Delicately, Sarah thought she would make a broad attempt to bring her brother-in-law's indiscretions out into the open. Should Julie be aware of these, it might be helpful for her to unburden herself to a close relative: it must be heart-breaking for her to have no one with whom she could share her misery. She found a way in to this by, seemingly, using Julie as a confessional.

'Since we last met, Julie, Matt has almost undergone a complete character change. Oh, I have a good idea why – but his behaviour towards me has altered so much …'

Eyes widening, Julie put out her hand to touch Sarah's knee. 'Sarah, don't tell me Matt is having an affair, please don't. Oh, I can't believe it. I can't believe it. Tell me it's not true.'

The vehemence of Julie's interjection in turn startled Sarah. 'Good God, that hadn't occurred to me. No, no, I sincerely hope not. It's nothing like that at all.'

Julie sank back in her chair, her hand withdrawn. 'Oh, thank goodness. I just don't know what I would do if George was unfaithful to me. It would be the end of my world.'

In a sentence, Sarah had her answer. But now she was left having to divulge the present nature of her husband's unwelcomed character traits, she couldn't help feeling pangs of disloyalty surging over her as she was only using this subject as an introductory ruse to allay her concern that Julie was having to cope with the knowledge that *her* husband was compromising her.

'Well, Julie,' she responded, in relief that Max had not let any cats out of the bag, 'your reaction has made me feel better already. Nothing, I am sure, to do with an affair. It's really a mixture of how he criticises me for my handling of Jamie and how he expects me nowadays to be the devoted housewife, never helps out as he used to do, notices every speck of dust and wonders what I've been doing all day while he is slaving away in the rat race, working his fingers to the bone.'

'Oh, is that all. He's not the only man, you know, to think housework beneath him. Only the other day I read in *The Times* that men were four times more likely not to have done any cleaning in the past month. If I remember rightly, it said that women are the most likely to clean toilets, mop the floor, clean the oven or do the ironing. You're not alone.'

Sarah's gaze drifted out of the window to see what she could only describe to herself as a fleet of gardeners beavering away at the flower beds as Julie concluded,

'After all, I think George imagines Marigolds are what grows in the borders. It wouldn't occur to him to load the dishwasher on a Sunday when our housekeeper has a day off.'

In the far distance Sarah noticed a machine akin to a combine harvester cutting a lawn and couldn't help defending Matt's position a little. 'I must say, Matt does regard taking out the garbage for recycling as his job and he does mow the lawn.' To hear Julie allying herself in some way with Sarah's life was incongruous.' Did she even do any household shopping? If so, it would be to buy designer clothes for herself. Now, now, jealousy gets you nowhere, she chided herself.

'Oh, and I also read that many fathers do not take their paternity leave allowance. So much for the emancipated man of today …'

'And the emancipated woman,' Sarah added wistfully. 'Absolutely typical.'

'I agree,' ruminated Julie. 'Clearly what men profess to openly isn't matched by their actions. We'll never know really what happens behind closed doors.'

At that point, Max appeared in the doorway, ostensibly to enquire whether he could have a plastic bag to put the fossils in he was giving Jamie.

'For heaven's sake, you know where they are, Max, you've lived here long enough. Go and find yourself a couple,' Julie responded with irritation in her voice, the conversation they had just had sinking in. Was Max taking after his father and expecting spoon-feeding all along the way? Sarah, who wondered why a twenty-eight-year-old in his own home had no idea where to look, was even more astonished when he questioned whether it would be acceptable for his mother to allow him to take a sandwich bag from the kitchen drawer. He was sharply told by Julie to work that one out for himself.

Suppressing her irritation that Max was displaying his quirkiness so soon in the visit, Julie suggested it was time for lunch: their cook would be concerned the salad would be going limp – 'as limp as I usually feel, having to explain to neighbours why, yet again, Max's job is up the swannee. I hate listening to the outpourings of their barely disguised simulated sympathy,' she added, waving acceptance to their old retainer, fortunately out of earshot, to serve their meal in the orangery immediately.

Full of reciprocal pleasure in each other's company and 'not in the least hungry', Max and Jamie reluctantly sauntered through the Smallbone kitchen for lunch which, being a warm Indian-summer day, was to be taken on the covered terrace. First Jamie investigated the jam jar filled with honey dangling from the rafters whilst simultaneously being exposed to the all-too-familiar lecture from Max on the horrors of vivisection, animal rights and in which setting it is acceptable to take the life of 'creatures which have the same right to be on this planet as homo-sapiens have'. Apparently in Max's book, wasps come into this category but it would need another encounter for him to explain this fully and to his satisfaction, so his offer to do so was brusquely curtailed by his mother, only too aware that an unstoppable stream of pomposity would inevitably follow. Max, perplexedly enquiring why his mother was looking at him like that was finally squashed by Julie's firm announcement that the four should sit down to eat before Cook cleared the plates away.

Sarah drew a suitably crestfallen Max back into the conversation. She was intrigued by this inept, socially gauche nephew and bursting to learn how the salesman's position in a gentlemen's outfitters mentioned at the previous 'get-together' had come to an abrupt end. A year ago she had adroitly terminated the topic in order to avoid Matt taking a further opportunity to unleash heavily veiled sarcasm in the direction of his brother, merely for the purpose of appeasing his damaged feelings when Jamie had unfortunately called him Uncle 'Porker'.

'Aunt Sarah, that was quite a long time ago now. I didn't stay long as Mr. Daniel was making mistakes, not working the hours he was employed for and he didn't like me telling him that sort of behaviour was fraudulent. He didn't want me to stay there if I didn't like how he was running the store so I had no option under the circumstances but to leave. You can't work for a person who doesn't obey the rules of the company, can you?'

Feeling it necessary to do so, whilst Julie visibly cringed under the supercilious attitude her son had been unable to suppress, Sarah assured him that he had obviously done the right thing. Max unctuously reiterated that consciences had to be obeyed. He adroitly changed the subject.

'May we leave the table now, Mother? I think Jamie would appreciate seeing my workshop, wouldn't you Jamie? You told me you before lunch that you would.'

Jamie's shining eyes told a story in itself. Both left the table to walk through the garden together, Max's arm conspiratorially around Jamie's shoulder.

Grinning as the notice on the door of a building the size of a small bungalow loomed ahead, Jamie commented, 'You know, Max, you ought to have the same notice as they have on unused doors in Tesco's: "This door is alarmed". I saw it last week. Do you get it?' His cousin's expression was quizzical as Jamie continued: 'I said to the manager who was by the information counter that it was silly because doors do not have feelings, whatever Tesco's might think,' he paused in reflection, frowning. 'Mummy said he'd think I was being cheeky but I wasn't. She didn't agree that I was trying to be helpful,' he added indignantly. 'It got worse though, because he said he knew where I was coming from – but he didn't seem to like it when I asked him how he knew where I lived.'

'Did he tell you how he knew?' Max enquired.

'Well, Mummy said it was a figure of speech and he

meant he could see what I meant, which didn't explain it at all, so I just think he couldn't be very good in his managing job if he put silly notices like that up. And most figures, like humans for example, speak, so that was an unhelpful thing for Mummy to say.' Max was unsure how to explain to Jamie any more successfully than his aunt had done but there were more relevant things to attend to.

Three bolts secured the door. That was merely the first hazard for any intending intruder to negotiate. Yale keys were then produced, not just one but, again, three. Eventually, the fire-door yielded to Max's turn of the final lock and the interior was revealed.

Jamie gasped as what appeared to him a real Aladdin's cave revealed itself at the point when his eyes got used to the change of light in the room. Labelled tools of every shape and description hung in an orderly fashion around the walls whilst in the centre of the workshop a conglomeration of strange tubing and boxlike constructions in various forms and an assortment of materials appeared to be in the process of being linked together. Already his idol, cousin Max was showing himself to be a real live inventor ... and one actually in his own family, his very own relative. He turned in awe to his elder cousin.

'You seem intrigued, young Jamie.' Max preened himself almost visibly, delighted to be creating such an impression. 'If you promise to keep a very important secret, I will explain what it is you can see in front of you that is my own creation.'

Eyes almost popping out of his head, Jamie swallowed. He could only nod his head violently in response, causing Max to comment that he reminded him of those wooden chickens on a board that when you shake it, they peck the grain. He must not disgrace himself in front of his clever cousin and make him think he was too immature for the disclosures he believed were about to come.

'I don't expect you know this but my parents will be celebrating their thirtieth wedding anniversary later this year and I am making something for them which will be a real energy-saving device. They will like it much better than a shop-bought present.' Max rubbed his hands in quiet jubilation as Jamie gave his assurance to keep the secret.

'Cross my heart and I never tell a lie … not even a white one, so you can put your trust in me never, never to break a promise.'

'Well, you see, there is a problem in our house with the laundry. Mrs. Timms, our housekeeper and shopper, is not as young, Mother says, as she used to be and she expects me to take all my clothes which need washing downstairs to the laundry. To save Mrs. Timms' legs, Mother says.'

Somewhat puzzled and unsure how saving Mrs. Timms' legs would be an appropriate present for his aunt and uncle's anniversary present, he asked Max to explain how he planned to do this. Unfortunately, Jamie found the ensuing extensive explanation describing a laundry-delivery gadget, despite this being accompanied by reference to a clarifying diagram heavily hi-lighted in fluorescent colouring, very complex indeed to assimilate. Chutes from Max's bedroom would wind down through cavity walls to the laundry room where, by means of some sensing device, the various fabrics were to be separated.

'You see, Mrs. Timms will not have to climb the stairs to collect all our laundry baskets from our bathrooms. And,' he concluded triumphantly, 'she won't get tired legs and will not give her notice in.'

Very early on in the flat-toned monologue, Jamie's interest waned and his attention was drawn to more exciting attractions which he was bursting to handle. Suddenly his thoughts turned to recalling what he had intended to tell Max as soon as he arrived but which had slipped his mind.

'Max, you know those Eddie Stobart lorries, don't you. Can you guess how many I counted? Going both ways, I mean.'

The elation Max felt when he was sure he had a captive audience melted away in an instant. Stiffly and wordlessly he marched to the door, the formerly affable hand on Jamie's shoulder now being a means of propelling him through it. Jamie was aware that the expansive mood of his cousin had changed immeasurably and did his best to ascertain the reason. It wasn't his fault that the functions of each of the intricate components of the contraption were described to him in such an elaborate manner, quite beyond his comprehension, that his mind had wandered to less esoteric matters.

'You seem to have lost your cool, Max. Can you tell me why? Ooh, you've got a swimming pool. Did you lose it in that? I suppose you would if it is heated,' he reflected as he noticed steam rising from the uncovered end.

The two cousins sauntered into the kitchen without noticing the sisters-in-law deep in conversation.

'What about a game of croquet, Aunt Julie, Mother? I'll get the gardeners to set the hoops up on the lawn?'

Julie decided to disregard this most intrusive suggestion. 'You're doing an excellent job with your cousin, Max. Now go back to your room upstairs and carry on the good work. I'm telling Aunt Sarah what an awful time you had at Docklands and we don't want to be interrupted again.

Unfortunately, this last injunction caused Max, who'd already ushered Jamie to the kitchen stairs, to turn on his heels and rejoin Sarah and Julie. Unaware of their visible irritation in this further intrusion, he thought it would be helpful to give them the benefit of his thoughts.

'Oh, that was a most stimulating time for me although I didn't find my colleagues very interested in what I said to them. I'd go into the staffroom — well, that is what it was called, a real euphemism if ever I heard one. For a start, you couldn't see across the room. Honestly, you could choke in it. The teachers were unconsciously making themselves into human beagles – though I'd rather they poisoned themselves than have those awful vivisectionists inflicting their experiments on those poor unsuspecting dogs. Not one of them seemed to want to know about the serious dangers of smoking, not only for themselves, but for me as a passive inhaler of their pollutants. Are you for animal rights, Aunt Sarah? I could send you some leaflets about our next meeting in Huntingdon.'

Julie's further entreaty 'Max, please, leave us on our own. Please,' again fell on deaf ears. There was no stopping the monologue. During his first two terms at Dockside following his appointment, Max had gleaned much in the way of staffroom gossip. Not that he was part of it: in the main he had quickly become a lonesome figure in the smoke-laden converted caretaker's room the staff called their own in the building which first saw the light of day in the mid-'30s, the height of the Great Depression.

'Apart from wanting to tell them details of what I had been teaching so that they could have a discussion about it in registration time – form tutors were supposed to introduce current affairs and items of interest in the first period, a short one, so that they got to know their students, you know – I would mark my books. They just seemed to want to drink PG tips or Gold Blend instant coffee. I took in my Alta Rica and offered it to them as a superior brand but they really were quite rude about it. Said it was too posh for them. What a thing to say! I told them they were looking a gift horse in the mouth but they went back to dreadfully infantile things like putting bets on how long, to the second, Mr. Johnson – Old Jonners, they called him – would "drone on" in assembly. You wouldn't believe another one, it was so crude and I told them so. It was how many times Mr. Johnson would scratch his bottom during prayers. They actually used a very bad word instead of "bottom". I was ashamed that these crassly uncouth people were my colleagues.'

Max shook his head in renewed disbelief.

The images conjured up by these allusions to disloyal teachers caused Sarah to assume they had made themselves a bolt-hole as far from the head's office as they could – she had not been a deputy head for nothing and knew only too well the foibles of any school staff. Julie, obtaining Sarah's promise not even to tell Matt, quietly confided,

'And they weren't puritanical in their language,' adding gloomily, 'Max said to repeat the Anglo-Saxon word used would stick in his throat, so the original had been left to our imagination.'

Taking advantage of a lull in the monologue, Julie chose this point to make a further attempt to eject Max from the kitchen. 'I really must insist you rejoin Jamie, Max. I expect he is wondering where you are.'

Even this further interjection passed unnoticed.

'Oh, another one of their bets concerned one of the governors who would visit quite often. They were very unpleasant in the remarks they made about her: Miss Hanson was her real name but they called her Honey Toothpeg, I think because she talked as if her mouth was filled with sticky stuff and her teeth were crooked. I never saw her close enough to notice those disfigurements for myself as whenever she came, the fire bell would go off and she'd rush off the premises. I heard someone saying that it was Mr. Johnson who set it off because he wanted to get rid of her. The bet they had was how long she would spend in the school before the alarm would sound. Putting two and two together, I think Mrs. Spears, the head's secretary, would measure the time for them.'

Sarah, her mind continuing to note the pedantic nature of Max's speech, was somewhat disappointed that Julie was successful at her next effort to remove Max. She effected the manoeuvre by putting her hands around his waist and propelling her protesting son to the bottom of the stairs. His narrative was illuminating for Sarah inasmuch as it conveyed the unfortunate impression of a societal misfit and she would have been interested, albeit most certainly more than a little intrigued, in the continuation of his conversationally awkward monologue. Also formulating in her mind was the worrying notion that he and Jamie had further characteristics in common: a quaintness in language and sentence construction and an inability to relate realistically to situations around them.

Now alone with Sarah once again, Julie went on to divulge that she and George had been incensed that Max had not been allocated the 'A' forms, especially when they were regaled with the cause of his demise. She continued her tale of woe, recalling the episode she had heard Max relate so many times before.

'During Max's third term at Docklands, hardly into his first lesson with Form 4D, taking as his subject French foreign policy on the eve of the Battle of Waterloo, apparently, it seemed his flow had been interrupted by a voice from the back row who questioned his accent, would you believe, Sarah. Snooty, they called it. Max had been so indignant when he reported this to us that I just cried with the thought of him being in such a challenging school. It shocked me to the core.' She paused to regather her composure before clarifying their own concerns that they had had with regard to coming across to his students as rather superior.

'You see, Sarah, Max had told us that at interview the chairman of governors (he worked at the docks, I believe, loading and unloading cargo) said he would have to rough up his voice a bit, but Max had not been sure how he could do that so we suggested he practised in the mirror. We did feel that his accent had got rather exaggerated at Oxford and he would drop this when he left, but Max wasn't having any.'

'No, I certainly wasn't! The Oxford accent is one of the best there is,' interrupted the unmistakeable voice of Max behind them where they had migrated to the warmth of the Aga. 'But it was quite preposterous. I felt really insulted when this chap told me to "speak in a lingo we understand".'

Wanting to follow up her embryonic hypothesis, Sarah urged Julie to allow him to stay this time. Although she had not had any personal experience of autistic spectrum pupils, she had seen *Rain Man* some years ago, the syndrome had been briefly covered in her B. Ed., and her formative thoughts were beginning to crystallise. Now she badly wanted to hear Max's exposition and attitude towards what was steaming up to be a further career disaster. Why was he not questioning his personality characteristics which were anathema to both pupils and colleagues?

Max assumed an attitude of aggrieved persecution as he continued to regale them with his account, the poor treatment he had received clearly still festering in his mind. Sarah was beginning to feel her head would burst. She did her best to interrupt but was learning fast that once Max had a captive audience, it was impossible to do so. Later she would attempt to paraphrase for Matt so tried to keep alert, not an easy exercise when she was already feeling the stress of the day was getting on top of her. Apparently a general hubbub had arisen. A chant then ensued, following the interruption. Whatever Max had said, the last phrase had been imitated by the back-row boys, mimicking Max's accent. Stoically Max had carried on, thinking to himself that they were using rote-learning techniques. He had heard that using these were the only way teachers were able to drill the slower learners into at least having facts at their fingertips, even if they had no idea what to do with them, but was nonplussed as to why they only repeated the last phrase each time; so disjointed would be their learning as a result, he had felt.

'Aunt Sarah, I am sure you are familiar with George Orwell's account of the schoolteacher forced to desert her creative teaching style and re-impose dull repetition on her class. I believed this pedagogic technique would pay similar dividends. If you don't know it, you really must read *A Clergyman's Daughter*. You might find it helpful if you go back to teaching again. You were a deputy head, weren't you, before Jamie was born? I find it much better to refer to literature than to adopt the "softer" methodologies as espoused in my post-grad teaching course.'

As Max droned on, Sarah confirmed in her mind the incongruity of her nephew's stilted sentence construction. She must google the variations of the autistic spectrum; she was becoming surer in her mind that this was at the root of his clearly idiosyncratic social behaviour.

'Well, some boys in the front row had been faithfully acceding to my introductory instructions but were most unpleasant to those at the back trying hard to speak correctly. I don't like to repeat their rude words in front of ladies but as you are related to me, Aunt Sarah, I think you will understand. They used the word "cretins" and asked them to shut up. I rebuked them for interrupting my lesson but I got what I understand is called "a mouthful" in response. I did my best to continue but they then packed up their books and left the room, so I could only think they had to go to another lesson.'

Under her breath, Julie confided to Sarah, 'Their language got worse, I believe. One of the boys called Max an 'effing tosser'. And he used the Anglo-Saxon word itself. It really is disgraceful that teachers have to put up with such language these days. George was absolutely horrified, as you might guess.'

It was not clear to Sarah whether it was the cut-glass tones in which Max had repeated the insult, or the ignominy which he had been forced to endure but Julie was almost in tears as memories were re-evoked. 'Oh, Sarah, Sarah, I can't tell you how wet my pillow was that night when he told us the first time he came home. My heart just bled for him.'

Without a word, Sarah passed the box of tissues across to Julie, now sitting crumpled on a chair.

'Mother, are you feeling well? It is rather hot in here with this Aga. What do you have to do to turn it down, Mother? Perhaps you could give my mother a glass of water, Aunt Sarah. I would get one for her myself but I don't know where Mrs. Timms keeps our glasses. I think Mother may be a little faint but I'll carry on, all the same – while you are rinsing one of our lunch glasses out – with telling you all about the outrageous behaviour of those rude teenagers into whose thick heads I was doing my best to instil some culture.'

Sarah searched her mind to remember where she had filed that fascinating *Times* article she had read recently in which an expert in the diagnoses of autistic spectrum disorders was discussing a few case studies. She had been particularly interested in individuals described who were called 'idiots savant' because of their outstanding talents in a specific area but who were unable to relate to people in the normal manner – whatever is 'normal', being questionable, of course. Could this be the reason why Max seemed to be out of the real world in his social skills?

'Well, the back row, then the only pupils left, began to leave, pushing and shoving their way through the desks. Unfortunately for them, they had chosen the wrong moment for their exit. The first to make a move sighted our headmaster advancing towards the classroom, turned suddenly and fell into the nearest, as did the others. You'll never guess what happened next. It was an amazing sight: all of them collapsed rather like a pack of cards can do – have you ever seen this happen yourselves? You do play bridge, don't you, Aunt Sarah?

'Anyway, to continue once more; you are listening, aren't

you?' A speechless Sarah wordlessly signified she was. 'What was so strange for me to understand was that Mr. Johnson accused me of letting the class go from my responsibility. Can you believe it? Shocking, absolutely shocking, of him to do that. There was a great big inquisition, quite unnecessary, and the outcome was that I was not allowed to finish my probationary year. It was extremely hurtful to me for them to do this when I was teaching in a most well-prepared manner. Mr. Johnson didn't appear to appreciate this so I showed him my supervisor's lesson appraisal reports. I know they were very impressive. I told him I always researched my additional material from the most erudite sources and he was at liberty to check this with my supervisor if he wanted; he'd always expressed amazement that I had been so diligent.

'Shall I get the reports for you to read now? Oh, I'm so sorry you have to go but I do understand that the Birmingham traffic will be meeting the M40 soon on their way back to Banbury or Oxford. A lot of commuters to the Midlands factories live in those areas, you know.'

★

So, not very long after a lunch, which had had its depressing moments for all concerned, Sarah and Jamie waved their farewells. Thankfully, to everyone's delight, the afternoon had ended on a high note with the good news of the esteem in which Max was held by his latest employers, and with Jamie excitedly clutching a bag of fossils given to him by his cousin. However, this good humour was almost sabotaged by Jamie's parting vote of thanks. The two women had exchanged glances, amused on Julie's side, embarrassed on Sarah's, when Jamie thanked his aunt very much for the salad, enquiring whether she had noted that he had eaten all the lettuce, every bit, 'cos his mummy had told him he had to eat every bit of whatever was for lunch, whether he liked it or not. 'And I really hate lettuce, it sticks in my teeth but I stuck it up between my mouth and my gums when I could and spat it out in the loo, so that doesn't count as not eating it because none was left on my plate, you see. So I was very good, wasn't I, Aunty Julie.'

The departing guests merged into the slow-drifting traffic of the motorway, unfortunately just as the Midlands rush-hour was starting. When Sarah had negotiated her way through the tree-lined avenues of the private estate on which her sister-in-law lived, she turned her attention to Jamie, intrigued to know how he had spent his time with Max. She had her suspicions that not all had been a bed of roses.

'You know, Mummy, I was wondering what Daddy would like for a birthday present. You know he hates putting the rubbish out for the dustmen, don't you. Well, I've got a great idea for making him special chutes which can be fixed to the kitchen window so that he can chuck the bottles in one, the paper in another, then one for the glass and plastic bottles and all the rest that you never know what to do with in another and they can swish down into the different bins.'

'That, Jamie, is a great idea.' Sarah's voice was heavy with sarcasm. 'Now kindly tell me how your father can be saved from wheeling these bins to the gate, clever boy.'

Triumphantly, but after a brief pause, came back Jamie's animated reply. 'Well, for a start, it would work if we put the bins the council give us under the window. You see, Mummy, I never put all my eggs in one basket: I'll work on a railtrack then for his *next* birthday to go alongside the drive. That'll save his legs, just like Mrs. Timm's legs have been rescued. Or perhaps I could do it for Christmas, if he is finding it too much to push them down the gravel drive.'

Another brilliant thought struck the animated little boy. 'And by the way, Mummy, I was just thinking ...'

'Not now, Jamie, please!' Was there ever a time her son did

not have ridiculous ideas flooding into his mind? Inventor, scientist ... ... or just a theorist whose crazy thoughts never materialised into anything worthwhile?

Unused to accommodating the boy-racers intent on reaching home in record time, tailgating, weaving from one lane to another, Sarah determined sadly that the important thing for her to concentrate on was driving safely, not reflecting upon the fact that whatever Jamie had picked up from his cousin was only adding to his idiosyncratic ideas rather than mediating them. She felt chilled to the core that there was something bizarre in the manner that these two cousins, despite their age differences, had so much in common.

Oblivious of his mother's put-down, Jamie continued. 'Well, what I also thought was this. Could I have some really strong netting, maybe chicken sort of wire or something like that. Mrs. Sampson next door keeps chickens, doesn't she, so maybe we could ask her for some. I'd like some over my bed? Just in case the ceiling falls down on me while I sleep.'

Mystified, Sarah icily enquired exactly why he thought such an unlikely mishap could occur. Jamie's reply did nothing towards making her think that the two cousins should spend any other sessions in each other's company.

'You see, it is very, very possible that Alka-Aida' (Jamie's favourite piece of music was 'The Grand March' from Verdi's opera) 'could send missiles or hijack aircraft like they did in New York. Then where would we be if they hit the roof above my bedroom? It is the only one above the garage, you know, and crashes often hit the sides of houses.'

Sarah, endeavouring to manipulate her car successfully through the rush hour traffic which had built up around Greysbury, fortunately had paid no attention to Jamie's idiosyncratic request. Yet another accident on this notorious stretch of road then added another hour to their journey home.

'So it was good we left later than you wanted to, Mummy, otherwise it might have been us in that accident,' Jamie said cheerfully.

Chapter Fifteen

Months passed, as did Year 3, with Miss Shadbolt's previously tenuous hold on the equilibrium of her charges having been strengthened by the support of the SENCo supervising her management of Jamie's erratic behavioural blips. Thus, with one or two exceptions, members of St. Michael's' teaching staff were the unwitting beneficiaries of a little boy whose propensity to accept the outlandish suggestions of peers often led him into trouble: their teaching techniques improved immeasurably from casual, impromptu staffroom discussions.

Mrs. Ackroyd, both SENCo and now Jamie's teacher in Year 4, often sat by him and told him he was better than a tonic with his ability to lighten up the classroom on the dullest of days. He certainly observed all rules of the school and had been withdrawn from the Special Educational Needs register, Mrs. Ackroyd having explained to Sarah's relief at the end of the autumn term that in her position as teacher responsible for the welfare of such children, planning a personal programme for monitoring his behaviour was no longer needed. She assured Sarah that she was able to diffuse any other troublesome situation which could be simmering within the classroom without it festering and fermenting into a full-scale eruption. A watchful eye on playground relationships would continue to be kept and how the year progressed carefully monitored. Should it be considered a helpful strategy, Jamie could be 'put back on it' without causing any hiccups in school routine. Whilst it was true that occasionally he would rub Miss Griffin up the wrong way when it was her turn for playground duty and he would then spend more time then facing the wall with his hands on his head, this only caused low-level dissension. The amusement of the other children who loved to provoke him into some misdemeanour unwittingly was sometimes evoked: 'Charlie's set you up again, has he?' some of his friends would say to him and Jamie would reply indignantly that he didn't need Charlie's help, thank you; he was able to put his hands up by himself. His robust put-down on such occasions usually sent his antagonists packing.

Life in Mrs. Ackroyd's class continued to be relatively smooth as the year sped by. There was no doubt about it, this experienced teacher had the management skills needed to quell any potential victimisation which would place Jamie in an incriminating position. Most significantly, she rarely rose to his unconventional comments, regarding them as irrelevant, which she would gently tell Jamie they were. Oh yes, he would remain behind as others left for break, ostensibly to stress the value of the point he had been attempting to make in class, but Mary Ackroyd would then engage him in some mundane task to take his mind off his persistence. Although it delayed her from collecting her well-earned cup of coffee and having a ten-minute rest-break, this forbearance saved any altercation which, for example, Faith Griffin would enter into or to which Lucy Shadbolt would succumb. Furthermore, the 'let's set Jamie up' brigade found there was no longer such amusement to be got by so doing and found other, more acceptable, diversions for their pleasure. Mary Ackroyd felt it to be a feather in her cap simply to have Jamie sitting close to her table from whence she could offer him a pleasant task to do as a reward whenever he refrained from blurting out answers or said anything which was inappropriate. A finger on her lips was often adequate as an agreed warning. When this was insufficient to stop the flow of inconsequential interruptions and he did not earn his reward (giving out papers/books, collecting finished work or other mundane tasks which he was thrilled to undertake), she felt Jamie was relishing his self-assumed position as 'class jester', and often found it hard not to be amused herself. It did rather 'jolly the day along' and, by sharing the joke with her charges, Jamie, without knowing why, felt proud to be the instigator of their mirth. Thus there were threefold benefits for Mary: she went up in the estimation of the class not only for her management skills but the manner in which she never allowed any situation to get out of hand, and also for the experience she was getting in her role as SENCo. Boundaries were set which each pupil understood and honoured.

On the last playtime of the year when Mrs. Ackroyd's children were due to move up to Mr. Bolton's class, Year 5, she had, nevertheless, warned her vulnerable pupil that Mr. Bolton would most certainly lick him into shape.

'Yuk!' grimaced Jamie, who was extremely alarmed that Mr. Bolton's moustache would be very scratchy. He made up his mind to keep as far away as possible from his new teacher. What shape Mr. Bolton would choose to turn him into didn't bear thinking about: the whole idea made him feel very, very sick.

★

During the summer holiday Jamie became more and more listless as September approached.

'I really do think Jamie is sickening for something,' Sarah confided to her friend. 'He's a bit young for glandular fever, don't you think, Jane? There is quite a lot going around but usually in adolescents in the first throes of a girl/boy relationship. It's called the kissing disease, isn't it? I can't think any self-respecting girl would allow him to indulge that sort of behaviour, even if it crossed his mind to experiment. He's had all his jabs but there always seems to be a nasty virus doing the rounds and Jamie seems to have got it.'

'Of which you are told, "there's a lot of it about; take a dose of Calpol or maybe half an Ibuprofen if he has a headache",' Jane contributed, adding she did not know of any factor which could produce lethargy except, perhaps, M.E. However, she decided not to mention that in order not to prolong the trend of the conversation. Together she and Mark held their own opinions of this strange little boy whose parents seemed to pander to every foible; Jane did not wish to connive with the 'illness' theory when all he needed was to be firmly taken in hand and told to stop his quirky behaviour. She was only too aware of the peculiarities of Dominic's erstwhile friend; even he had found Jamie rather burdensome in the last couple of years and the friendship had cooled considerably, only remaining in rather a stilted style when their two families got together.

'I think I'll take him to the surgery next week if he doesn't perk up a little by the weekend,' determined Sarah.

In fact, Jamie became quieter and less responsive as August drew towards September. He positively shrank away from her whenever the word 'school' was mentioned. He flinched and stubbornly refused to go with Sarah to buy new school shoes, sweatshirts and trousers. Eventually Sarah implored Matt to take him.

'There is to be none of your stupidity, Jamie. It's time you pulled yourself together. Mr. Bolton was a sergeant major in the Army before he trained to be a teacher, so he won't stand any nonsense from you either, any more than he would have done from his platoon,' remonstrated Matt early on the Saturday before the new school year began.

Sarah's worries didn't subside. Jamie had begun to wake up in the middle of the night, screaming. In an instant, Sarah would rush into his bedroom to calm him down. She would find him shaking, sweat pouring down his face, his pyjamas saturated. Recurring dreams of Disney-like monsters, tongues lolling out menacingly, would be licking Jamie voraciously all over his body, occasionally pausing to moisten their lips afresh, until Jamie's shape had been altered irrevocably. These creatures had usually, Jamie sobbed, started off as benign little dogs but, as they approached Jamie, changed from friendly chihuahuas, pekingeses, dachshunds, into the most fearsome beasts with live coals for eyes, bristles as thick as scrubbing brushes flaring out of their nostrils, cavernous ears and furnace-like flames for tails. On the worst night Jamie experienced, a tiny 'sausage dog', as Jamie called the German breed, transformed into a gigantic frankfurter which, rather like those party balloons, could be contorted into grotesque shapes. As Sarah burst into his room on this occasion, her son was violently sick all over his constellation-patterned duvet cover. In the morning Sarah kept him indoors before rushing him up to the surgery to keep the only appointment available.

Dr. Allinson, having performed the usual medical investigations, pronounced Jamie as being perfectly healthy, all indicators of childish ailments and viruses being conspicuous by their absence, and finally enquired whether he had been watching any 'DVD nasties'.

'You might not have any at home yourself, Mrs. Chilton, but you would be surprised how many adolescent boys buy them without their parents' knowledge necessarily. It is all too easy for younger children to have access to these. Parents go out, leave their older sons in charge as babysitters, then on go the DVDs: easy babysitting material. Can happen in the middle of the day – Mum goes out shopping and, bingo: no prizes from guessing what comes out from under the sofa and there you are!'

Dr. Allinson chuckled.

'It happens in the best of homes, my dear. I speak from

experience. When my son went to university and my wife decided to spring clean his bedroom, she took all the drawers out from the fitted chest and in between the bottom one and the floor found a treasure trove of girlie magazines. She was appalled, absolutely livid. I told her it was a natural phase that all boys went through, a part of growing up, and I suggested she replace them where she found them and never mentioned it to him.

'Actually,' he reminisced, 'now I come to think of it, she did give them back many years later, as a memento of adolescent interest in bodily functions. His wife, I must confess, was none too amused.'

Sarah assured Dr. Allinson that there was no danger of Jamie being exposed to horror DVDs in that way: he was rarely invited to the homes of others and when he was, it was to homes where, by chance, Jamie's friend was the eldest in the family. Neither she nor her husband had ever allowed their children to own iPhones and, as far as she was aware from gossip at the school gate, the majority of parents held strict views about limiting their children's use of all-purpose phones and tablets, even if they possessed ones for their personal use. Thankfully, there had been no evidence of cyber-bullying at the school and the horrors of intimate photos being passed around of children in compromising poses still only featured in lurid tabloid press reports and were unthinkable in this neighbourhood. There had been a talk at a P.T.A.* meeting she had gone to about the dangers of permanent loss of the ability to socialise if the trend for exposing every facet of daily life electronically was to escalate. Losses of personal identity, insensitivity to pain, lack of empathy with others, and the need for a wider, but impersonal, audience rather than enjoying live human companionship were the most obvious implicit

---

*   P.T.A. = Parent Teacher Association

dangers which the speaker engaged by St. Michael's warned against. Sarah remarked upon the horror of observing families at restaurants, all with noses in to their phones during their entire meal, tapping away, not even responding to waiters' questions. Eye contact in streets was lacking for the same reason, erstwhile friends could be passed by unnoticed.

Suddenly realising Dr. Allinson was being 'consulted', not acting as a debating partner, she then withdrew from her high horse to await the medic's advice on the reason for their visit.

'The new term begins next week, I believe. Could Jamie be anxious about moving to a higher class? Is he falling behind and worried about the increasing workload? Does he have the necessary level of skill required? Year 5 is his next class, isn't it?' he added, looking up Jamie's birthdate on his medical notes.

'No,' replied Sarah feebly. 'Jamie is the best reader in his class and sits with the most able children.'

'Any friendship problems?'

Looking across to assure herself Jamie was completely absorbed in counting aloud the zebras and mollies swimming through the rocks in the tropical fish tank by the door, she replied softly, 'He says he has lots of friends but I often see him wandering alone in the playground after I have dropped him off at school. He tells me the boys say he is "a great laugh", so he certainly isn't bullied in any way now, so far as I know, if that is what you mean. I'm also sad to say he does not seem to be the child most often invited to parties.'

Jamie chose that moment to rush across to ask for Sarah's help in counting the fish. 'Mummy, the task is quite impossible. The black mollies aren't easy to check because I can't tell if the one who comes out from behind the rock is the one which I saw go into the hole. I could easily count the same one twice. It's really irritating.'

Dr. Allinson smiled quizzically and, ignoring Jamie's

interruption, to Jamie's astonishment advised Sarah to 'keep her ears to the ground' to see if any children, who were frequently the butt of others' victimisation themselves, were pursuing him in any way. A giggle rolled up in his throat as he pictured his mother crawling along, scraping her ears on the playground. Whatever would his friends think? But this was a solemn occasion and you were not supposed to laugh whatever the advice doctors gave you.

'So, young man, you are ahead in your class? Your mum says you are not bullied? There were no things troubling you last term?'

Jamie accepted each of the statements as facts, nodding his head in affirmation as each was uttered: his doctor was bound to be accurate: doctors always were. Your mummy took you to the doctor when she did not know the answer; the doctor gave it to her.

Dr. Allinson left his desk and signalled Sarah to walk with him to the window, out of Jamie's direct earshot. He paused to check Jamie was still otherwise engaged with the tropical fish and mentally praised his secretary for setting this attraction some months earlier: it had already proved its worth and certainly provided the digression he sought for his young patient today. The question he was about to ask was delicate in the extreme, covering a subject he was always embarrassed to address.

'The only other question, Mrs. Chilton, which *has* to be asked, is, is there any possibility of, erm, sexual abuse? Not,' he added hastily, 'that I am querying it within your immediate family, but sometimes an uncle, an older cousin, a trusted neighbour …' His voice trailed off, '… even a teacher. I am so sorry to present this to you like this but we must always take a child's distress seriously and seek the cause. Just keep a wary eye open, Mrs. Chilton.'

The kindly doctor was not mistaken in suspecting that this

mother would be taken aback by the directness of the enquiry and took her wide-eyed, open-mouthed lack of articulated response to indicate that a concern of that nature had not entered into her mind. Brushing aside a half-uttered denial, his voice now reflected a hearty tone.

'Of course, there has been so much in the press lately, with the accusations against so-called celebrities, professional people, many in the Church and the public eye falling thick and hard; I do apologise for bringing it up.' He changed the subject abruptly. 'Above all, don't worry as your concerns will be passed on to your son and exacerbate a situation which will only distress you more.'

He ushered a shocked-faced Sarah back to Jamie's side, bringing the consultation to a close, offering his advice as he did so.

'Lots of exercise before bed, Mrs. Chilton. Milky drinks. Watch his diet: no cheese. A pleasant story after a warm bath. Do come back if the night-terrors haven't become a thing of the past by the end of the month and we'll ask one of the child psychotherapists attached to the practice to have a look at him.'

Jamie, having been left to his own devices and becoming bored with fish that he was unable to count, was now studying the stethoscope on the doctor's table. As he opened his mouth to enquire whether that was the same sort vets used as he'd seen a vet with one on repeats of James Herriot's programmes on TV, his opening sentence was pipped to the post by Dr. Allinson's jovial, stentorian tones:

'So, old chap, stop frightening your mother. Dreams are only dreams, you know. Think of all the lovely things there are in the world before you drop off to sleep and you will sleep like a baby.'

'I will try, Dr. Allinson, but I shan't need to be in a cot, with bars so I don't fall out. Only babies go in those and, as you probably know, I'm older than that. I'll be ten next birthday, double figures.'

Sarah and Jamie thanked Dr. Allinson for his advice, leaving him still chuckling over Jamie's remarks, and left the surgery, Sarah churning over in her mind the significance of the references he had made to contacts within the family and the neighbourhood. Could there be? Were there? It did not bear thinking about but think about it she must.

Behind his surgery door, pausing for reflection before ringing the bell for the next patient, Dr. Allinson checked his computer for the notes sent by the paediatric consultant from the hospital, and the entries which recorded earlier visits to him by Mrs. Chilton in relation to her son's various seemingly psychosomatic ailments and anxieties. He sighed as he made a note on his pad: speak to health visitor and school doctor. Suggest check on whether child does not wish to change for PE/swimming or brings a note to excuse himself. Notice if he flinches on sudden movement of an adult close to him. Look for marks on body and any regular absences suggesting cover-ups for 'unfortunate' incidents. On Jamie's medical notes he recorded: 'Recurrent nightmares; unknown cause. Ask H.V. to check for enuresis. Professionals to keep contact and not shrink from initiating a case conference.'

In a moment of sudden enlightenment it also occurred to him that he should give some thought to the question of Munchausen's syndrome-by-proxy, a little known manifestation whereby an adult seeks attention, not directly, but through a relative, usually a child, by creating 'accidental' injuries or illnesses in order to get sympathy for the personal worry and stress caused. He noted that the hospital records he held mentioned an angry father determined to discharge his son against the advice of the consultant. Was the hidden agenda there that the father was annoyed with his wife for ensuring the child remained an in-patient for as long as possible? He sighed: so much responsibility laid upon the shoulders of GPs these days. He was constantly reading in the medical press about various indications of harm which an alert doctor should notice … or otherwise be in danger of being hauled in front of a disciplinary court for negligence. He added to his notes: 'check frequency of, and reasons for, visits to surgery. Q: M-by-P?' More admin work for after-surgery hours. Did the government have any idea what the medical profession did in their own time when they thought of legislating longer working hours and weekend 'on call' for GPs? Perfectly OK if they allow extra funding for extra staff – but where would the money come from: Defence? Social Services? The judiciary? Robbing Peter to pay Paul, he surmised sardonically, as he packed his briefcase with the confidential letters to dictate and notes of phone calls he would make that evening.

★

Matt groaned when Sarah imparted the main conclusions drawn by Dr. Allinson.

'For God's sake, Sarah, the boy was nine a few weeks ago. All he needs to be told, again and again until it sinks in, is to pull himself together. All that mollycoddling you give him is making him into an absolute wet. You're not to pander to him anymore. If he yells out in the night, leave him to scream. He'll soon come to his senses and realise dreams are dreams, just that. You rush into him at the first sound; he is probably still half asleep. What you are doing is simply giving him the attention most real boys don't want from their mother. "Oh darling, darling, Mummy's here",' he mimicked cruelly, ignoring his wife's shocked reaction at his rebuke. 'What a softie you're turning him into. Do him good, actually, to watch some of those DVDs Dr. Allinson referred to.'

Sarah turned away. What was happening to their marriage? Again they seemed to be drifting apart with no shared views on almost any topic she could think of: money, holidays, child management, friends, relations, politics. She had never felt so hollow inside, yet again consumed by a sinking feeling which was beginning to leave her devoid of all self-esteem. She forced herself to be cheerful in front of Jamie.

'Come for a walk with me, Freya and Jamie. Daddy's brought some work home to do. It's a beautiful evening and the sun will not set for a long while yet. We'll walk through the fields to the stream. Bring your fishing nets. Oh, and a jacket of some sort, it will get quite cold later.'

'I'll get some worms from the garden. Mummy, can I have a can? If you haven't got a spare one, I could ask Mrs. Jones next door; I'm sure she wouldn't mind. I heard her say yesterday when she was talking to Mr. Jones that it was a real can of worms and she didn't know what to do about it, so she probably wants to get rid of it. Shall I go and ask her?'

'Mum, do I have to go with you? Jamie drives me nuts sometimes and I don't think I can stand any more of his stupid remarks,' Freya grumbled.

'Freya, it's not often you are around these days and it would be good if you could take an interest in your brother occasionally,' Sarah scolded with a chill seeping through her bones that the entire family was drifting apart. Was there anyone at all who wanted Jamie's company? Was that the reason Freya spent so much of her time away from home, even more now she was firmly established in secondary education and no longer in the youngest year group of her grammar school?

'Helping Jamie to understand when he gets things wrong would be a sisterly thing to do. Yes, you are coming so take that scowl off your face and go and get some worms from the garden,' Sarah said sharply with a vigour she didn't feel. 'And you can put them in a sandwich box; that will be just as good.'

Jamie giggled. 'Daddy won't be pleased if he finds worms in the sandwiches you make for him sometimes. I'll help you, Freya. I bet I find more than you-ou.'

Picking out a trowel from the shed, Jamie turned the soil over in the nearest border. In no time he had fished out a dozen or so and decided that would be enough. Sarah was waiting for him in the kitchen and told him that Freya wouldn't come after all as she had her 'cello practice to do. Freya had avoided this as much as she could during the holiday but now was only too aware that she had an awful lot to make up before she had her first lesson of the term and Grade 2 loomed. How she wished that her mother would not be so firm in her judgment that once you had started and enjoyed the first month's tuition, it was demoralising for the visiting teacher if the lessons were terminated, a wish always refused by her mother … Perry-something, hers was called; she wondered why his parents had not called him Terry instead … and what a surname he had to go with it. He was anything but 'pathetic' with his commando-style boots and roaring up to the school on a motor bike; Perry Pathetic, indeed. She had been told that as she had promised in primary school when first taking up the instrument that she would never want to give up, if she changed her mind later, she would not be allowed to do so. Just because her Mum was a deputy head before stupid Jamie arrived, she said it would be setting a bad example and it might get round to any school she managed later (Sarah was still ambitious) that the rules she enforced on others were perfectly all right for her own family to break. There were quite a few of Matt's genes in Freya: she was, at almost thirteen, already quite forceful in her own opinions and had a personalised sense of injustice.

'Well, a dozen will be more than enough for me, fishing all by myself. Unless you'd like to as well, Mummy. Go on, do; it's great fun and we could catch a salmon or a trout for tea. I was very careful when I was digging, Mummy. I left no stone unturned. There wasn't always a worm underneath but

I know you have to keep on turning stones over until you find what you're looking for.'

Sarah, preoccupied with her thoughts, took no notice of the irrelevant nature of Jamie's remarks.

As the two walked hand-in-hand across the buttercup-studded field to the stream, Sarah was startled by the manner in which Jamie reacted whenever a dog hove into sight, whether on the lead or frolicking in the grass. Depending on the distance between them and the type of dog or the direction in which it was travelling, Jamie would either grip her hands so tightly that she winced and ordered Jamie to relax his hold, or grab her from behind in an attempt to bury himself in her clothes. Sarah admonished him to no avail: it seemed an absolute reflex action in response to near-the-surface memories of his horrific dreams. In view of the snide remarks made earlier by her husband, she took the more corrective stance.

'You're being ridiculous, Jamie. What on earth would your friends think of you if you shrank away in fear every time you saw a little dog? That last one was not much bigger than a rabbit.'

They manoeuvred themselves through the kissing gate, dutifully kissed, although without much fervour on Sarah's part, and made their way to Jamie's favourite spot where there was a tiny beach of shingle. Sarah sat herself down on a log, her mind far away. The image of her newborn son being delivered into her arms after the unremittingly painful labour she had experienced with her second child flooded into her mind. She recalled the vivid feeling which had swept over her as she looked down on this crumpled, helpless little body still steeped in amniotic fluid and the thought had raced through her exhausted mind, 'What, oh what, will the future hold for you, my precious, so yearned for, little son?' Sarah forced back her tears. Now wasn't the time to have unhelpful flashbacks.

Jamie primed the little cane rod he had manufactured himself with a bamboo stake, garden string and some bent pins, winding each wiggly worm in turn round the hook. Not a successful enterprise as the worm slipped off as the hook hit the water. The significance was lost on Jamie: he was feeding worms to the fish, as every fisherman did, and it wouldn't be long before they nibbled his hook dangling enticingly above their open jaw (or did they only have mouths while sharks, and perhaps barracudas and piranhas were the ones which had jaws? He vowed to look that fact up on Wikipedia). Fifteen minutes later, the dwindling supply of worms evaporated entirely.

Jamie, aghast that he no longer could attract the trout he had lusted after, turned to Sarah whose eyes were staring into the middle distance. He fished into his pocket and dropped a penny into his mother's lap. Immediately, Sarah's thoughts returned to the here and now.

'What have you done that for? Have you just picked it up?'

'It's for your thoughts,' answered Jamie, surprised that his mother didn't know that was what pennies were for.

'It's not a good thing for grown-ups always to divulge their thoughts to children,' Sarah responded, suppressing tears which always welled up whenever she reflected upon the seemingly precarious state of her marriage. She had spent the previous five minutes in a reverie, with the memories of the years before the recession had hit ferociously hard and the children were still in their infancy. How they would 'date' on a regular basis, her mother babysitting. They would surprise each other, often meeting at a pre-arranged destination – even once, she recalled wistfully, under the clock at their railway station, each wearing a carnation in their lapels – Matt would whisk her off to a cherished restaurant, they would creep home and up the stairs, doing their best not to tread on the creaking stair. The way Matt undressed her so very, very carefully and still with wonder in his eyes before her hands would slide under his shirt ... the memory faded with the ebullience of Jamie's demands.

'Well, if I don't know them, I can't help you,' Jamie shot back; he'd heard that response many times from adults and thought it would bring his mother to her senses. You can't have any sensations when you are daydreaming; he knew that only too well as the bites he got from the dogs in his dreams, however fierce and terrifying these monsters were, did not show in the mornings, even though he and his mummy looked for them extremely carefully in the places on his body he pointed out to her.

Ignoring the impertinence, she told Jamie to pack up his fishing tackle, said she would not hold his hand on the way back – he was too old for that sort of thing – when, to her horror and without any discernible warning, there was a tremendous sp-er-lash! Jamie had jumped into the stream. The water, fortunately, only coming up to the lower reaches, had nonetheless soaked his trousers through to the skin. Sarah's reactions moved rapidly from incredulity to fury as the cause of this ridiculous spectacle, a Labrador puppy, tongue hanging out, lolloped along the narrow path, barked a friendly 'hello' at Jamie before loitering excitedly on the edge as if making up his mind whether or not to join him in the water for a frolic. Thankfully the boisterous animal had its mind made up for him by being ordered onwards by his owner. With a lingering look back at Jamie in the water and now safely on his leash, the dog re-joined his master who, casting a scathing glance across at Sarah, offered the unnecessary opinion, heavily laden with sarcasm, that it was lucky the boy had jumped into shallow water, not a raging torrent. His further uncalled-for, unkind rejoinder to Sarah's comment that she would not have expected him to offer his services in rescue had this been the case, indicated that a set of reins might prevent a re-occurrence if the lad was as scared as that of a small dog. Realising he had been too defensive of his pet, he added grumpily,

'Amber wouldn't hurt a fly. Her bark is much worse than her bite.' At that, Jamie, struggling to avoid slipping further into the shallows, encountered a scary vision dancing in front of his eyes of being supper for a hungry animal.

Scarlet-faced from the hideous lack of sympathy, Sarah turned her angry attention to Jamie, now safely back on the bank. 'For heaven's sake, Jamie, you really have to learn to control yourself. Jumping in the water is a crazy, crazy thing to have done. You could have been swept away downstream.'

She held out her hand to steady him and yanked her son onto the path, seconds before an elderly couple on their evening walk, not expecting the dappled sunshine of the waning sun to reveal the unfolding drama as it did, offered their services to help dry the partly sodden, muddy boy. The areas of his body and clothing which had not been drenched, might just have well been as they had got a further soaking as he scrambled unaided up the bank, the sides crumbling as his feet scrabbled for a hold.

'Some dogs should be put down when they attack people,' the woman offered sympathetically, her husband adding, 'and their owners made to serve a gaol sentence, in my opinion.'

'No,' Sarah spluttered, 'it was not the dog's fault; he did not knock my little boy into the water. I think my son was trying to retrieve his rod,' she lied, knowing full well what had precipitated Jamie's leap.

'Should take him home quickly,' the man concluded, 'he's shuddering with cold. It's turning into quite a chilly evening. End of August, you know; soon be winter.'

Sarah, who did not need his advice, and calling him a Job's comforter under her breath, nevertheless thanked him, made her embarrassed excuses and the two, Jamie wrapped in his mother's anorak, wound their way home without further frights. Needless to say under the circumstances, the age-long custom when passing through the kissing gate went unacknowledged, even Jamie realising it would not help matters had he drawn his mother's attention to the omission. His mother, in fact, was recalling memories of the time when Jamie used to implore them to buy him a pet dog to replace his toy one which he pulled along on a string. To their amusement, this wheeled, bedraggled animal which had to accompany him everywhere, rejoiced under the name of Mackit, the origin of which they only realised many years later when Sarah had, as she often did, accused Matt of being 'dogmatic'. When had his desire for a real live one been replaced by abject fear?

A note from Matt was on the table when they reached home:

'Am down at the Red Lion. Starving, so will have a chilli and chips down there. Back after the match.'

★

It was not easy, emotionally, for Sarah to lie awake listening to Jamie's screams as night-terrors continued to engulf him. It was so painful for her not to get out of bed to calm and reassure him: she could hardly bear it and would lie, trembling, until well after the troubled child settled back into what she knew from experience would be a disturbed sleep. In the morning he would look pale, with dark rings around his eyes but Matt was a light sleeper and would vent his rage on her if his night's rest was interrupted. She was sick and tired of his sarcastic remarks about her lack of child-rearing skills and the references to the ardour of his work, the pressure on him to achieve sales objectives, the ruthlessness of the market, the interference of politicians. He, of course, made invidious comparisons between those people on a supposedly 9 to 5 lifestyle – 'though when did I leave the Agency at 5 bloody p.m?' – and the comfortable lives led by women who were at home all day. Surely, since it would not be long before both children were teenagers, she could at least be looking at the educational press to see what jobs were around? His vitriol knew no bounds. She was still smarting from the rebuff she had received when she had not resisted a beautiful 'top' she had previously admired in a local smart boutique when she spotted it in a Blue Cross sale at a 75% discount.

'What's wrong with the tee-shirts you've got?' Sarah had thought Matt would have bust a gut. 'They're not worn out. You don't need it. Take it back; we are not made of money.'

No sale bargain was on sale or return unless defective … and, in defiance, Sarah had no intention of taking it back, even if she could. She'd make up the £15 spent by cutting out lunch for a fortnight. That would be ten days. She doubted if her measly lunches of beans, sardines or egg-on-toast (Welsh rarebit as a treat) would cost more than £1.50 per day so that would enable her to break even on her housekeeping without Matt knowing. Sarah did not even care about the subterfuge to which she was resorting.

Chapter Sixteen

Sarah's heart sank as the day of the start of the autumn term dawned. Jamie, now in his tenth year, said he had a really bad headache, felt sick, very, very, very sick and his legs wouldn't hold him up. In vexation, Sarah took his temperature and immediately felt alarmed: 102.5° Fahrenheit. Yet when she pushed aside his tousled brown hair and felt his forehead, it had not been at all hot, he was not flushed and there were no signs whatsoever of fever. She rummaged in the medicine cabinet, usually kept in pristine order, but she recalled Matt last week being enraged because he couldn't find the size of plaster he needed to cover a shaving cut. She wished she hadn't had a negative reaction to the uproar he caused but, instead, had restored the contents to its usual state: a place for everything and everything in its place was not only a maxim she had absorbed from her mother but, artistically minded, she liked to see well-organised cupboards and drawers in any case. Not for nothing had she had a gap-year job as an assistant to an industrial engineer in a confectionery manufacturing company; she had enjoyed her stint as a time and motion study trainee because of the responsibilities she had been given (one to design a Christmas pack, which gained a prominent place on supermarket shelves, her only reward being the satisfaction it gave her), so much so that the company had encouraged her by offering a greatly raised salary if she would forego her university course and remain with them. The sky's the limit, she was told: 'there is no glass ceiling here in this American company and we are unable to raise your salary until you are on our permanent staff, which you could be in the summer, if you decide to stay with us'.

She found what she was looking for: a thermometer you could place in the child's armpits. She sat with Jamie in case it slipped out of position. Withdrawing it, she was not really surprised to note it read 37° Centigrade. She shook down the older thermometer, replaced it under Jamie's tongue, once again, keeping it there for more than the required minute: it registered 98.6°F ...!

'Jamie, you didn't bite the mercury at the bottom the first time I took your temperature, did you?'

Jamie shook his head violently. The notion that if he'd had his temperature taken away, wouldn't he be dead, still not erased from his mind.

The possibility that had occurred to her was that the source of his indisposition could have been that his brief encounter with the stream the other evening had brought Jamie in contact with some unpleasant bacteria or microbes which had gestated in his system. This solution disappeared immediately from Sarah's mind.

'Get your coat on and collect all the things you need for school. There's nothing the matter with you. Don't think you can twist me round your little finger: you can't; it's time you grew up.'

Stupid thing to say, thought Jamie, vainly endeavouring to envisage his mother wrapped round his index finger, let alone his smallest one. She says a lot of nutty things but I've never heard her saying anything quite so stupid for a long time.

'For heaven's sake; hurry up. Freya's waiting at the car already and getting cross. I'm dropping her off first today: Year 8 is only going in for a short while: the teachers are having a training session.'

It did not escape Sarah's eye that Jamie, with a quick look over his shoulder to see if she was looking, snatched up a glass half-filled with water which was on the draining board and tipped the contents down the sink. Daylight dawning, Sarah strode over to the wide-eyed boy and felt the glass; it was still quite warm.

'Jamie, did you put the thermometer in a glass of hot water?'

Well-nigh caught in the act, Sarah could tell by the startled look on his face that he had.

'Charlie said,' Jamie whimpered, 'if ever I wanted a day off school, get a glass of not-too-hot water, hide it from your parents – and your sister – dip the thermometer in it till it reaches the 102 mark and then carry on saying you don't feel well. He did say if he's got time he gets a sausagey cloth thingie with barley or something in it what his mum puts round her neck when she's got a pain in it and then puts this sausagey thing in the microwave when his mum isn't in the kitchen. He puts his head on it when the sausage is hot – he says about two minutes makes it hot enough – so that his forehead goes all red. He says that always makes his mum let him have the day off school.'

Sarah, who had only once attempted to fake illness as a child by putting her finger down her throat to make herself sick when her homework had not been completed, could not help herself admiring the ingenuity of this scam. Later, in her teaching years, knowledge of such ruses had primed her suspicions when any of her class suddenly feigned illness. Even super-innocent Freya had not been averse to quoting the time-honoured excuse that the cat had been sick, expecting her teacher to connect that statement with the appalling stains on her needlework. Unbelievably, she got away with it without censure, merely sympathy. Nonetheless, Sarah was irritated by her inability to spot the present artifice of Jamie's and, attempting to look stern, she indicated to Jamie that she was not letting him off the hook.

'Well, Mummy, you've caught me red-handed, just like Mr. Bolton caught my friend Wayne once last term when he was throwing someone's ball on the roof, which was when I learned that that meant he'd been spotted, so I shall have to confess. A bit like white lies, really, isn't it? Anyway, I looked in the fridge at breakfast time when you were making the beds but I could only find those cocked-tail sausages and I didn't think warming up one of those would be any good. And I looked on the label to see what the ingredients were and it didn't say barley so I'll ask Charlie what sausages he uses. Charlie says he gets better at lunchtime and his mum can't be bothered to take him back to his class – says it isn't worth it – so he says he needs some fresh air and she lets him out in the garden with his football to get some energy back.'

A now exasperated Sarah told him he was never, never to think about pretending to be ill ever again,' adding, 'You'll cry "Wolf" once too often.'

'I didn't say anything like a wolf does. I don't know how to make a wolf talk and I don't see how I should get a day off school by shouting Wolf, Wolf, Wolf. You'd think I'd gone mad.'

'If you don't stop winding me up,' Sarah responded tartly, 'there'll be no TV tonight and no ice cream after tea. Get in the car immediately and take all your things with you. Scram!'

That is not the first time I'd been told not to wind people up, Jamie mused as he walked quickly down the path, yet I don't know where the keys are you use to wind up people. Or where the slot could be on a person's body. Is it where the tummy button is? He vowed to get some spare keys out of the drawer one day when his mummy wasn't looking and try to open his tummy button when he undressed for bed. He would put the key in where that funny cross-thing was; he'd choose the key Daddy used which he called a cross-hatchet one if he could find it.

Whilst Sarah was locking the door and he had settled into the back, albeit with a grumble, he asked Freya if she could wind up her tummy button or – a lightning thought – did a key fit those funny knobs boys and girls have on the top of their chests and he'd seen on Daddy's? Did Mummy have those knobs on the end of her boobies? Do you need a special sort of key, like those ones Daddy can never find in his toolbox and the ones Mummy finds for him are no sodding good? Freya just stared at her brother in disbelief.

'You're nuts,' was her brutal reply as she returned to the book she'd been reading. 'Absolutely stark staring bonkers.' Sarah took her place in the driving seat. She had already had enough of the day.

'Mummy, it's not fair. It's my turn to sit in the front by you and Freya knows it is. She shouldn't be sitting in my seat. It's mine all day on Tuesday and it's Tuesday today.'

Convulsive throat-clearing came from Freya, head in *Pride and Prejudice* (a characterisation of Mr Darcy was required for Tuesday next week), as thoughts of the hero flew through the window. Oh my God, why do I have to suffer this unspeakable horror for a brother? How old is the bloody child … certainly old enough not to entertain such rubbishy demands which he actually, actually, can you believe, thinks are overriding rules to be kept sacrosanct.

'Oh, there's no need to worry, Jamie, we'll stop the car in the outside lane of the M40 for us to exchange seats – or would you like to climb over with that police car watching?' commented Freya sarcastically, going back to Darcy.

Sarah listened in disbelief. How on earth, with all that has transpired this morning, could Jamie ask for any favours. He had to be well aware how angry she was.

'Jamie, I gave you the last warning less than two minutes ago. You've now really tried my patience beyond all measure. There is no TV and no ice cream tonight.'

Freya turned from the front seat and transfixed him with one of her superior stares. Jamie thought how unfair the world was, sisters and parents in particular, but something inside him told him it was the time to keep his mouth tightly shut. Shame, really, 'cos he wanted to ask his mummy what she meant when she said she was letting him off the hook. It was very muddling to try to equate that remark with how his bait fell off his when he was fishing and, anyway, he didn't allow them to, they just did it.

★

Filing into the Class 5 classroom, the whisper went round: 'Mr. Bolton has lost his moustache'.

'Well, I'm not going to help him find it,' Jamie muttered emphatically to the girl beside him whose name he'd forgotten.

There was a mad scramble as they entered the room, in response to the order, 'Sit anywhere you like for this morning; I shall allocate permanent places after I have marked the test papers you are about to be given.'

After some pushing and shoving during which Jamie found himself nudged out of almost every seat he had attempted to sit in, he sat in the only place left, one in the front row next to a girl who, he noted last year – and told her he'd noticed – always had a runny nose. Mr. Bolton was standing by the whiteboard, arms folded. Noise subsided. Mr. Bolton remained perfectly still, erect and silent, every inch an officer, albeit non-commissioned. At least a minute ticked by. He raised his hand; pointed at the door; then at the line of desks to the right; finally, with a half-cupped hand, he pointed again to the door. All in slow motion. Awkwardly and without a word, that line of sheepish-looking children tiptoed out of the classroom, followed by Mr. Bolton. Wordlessly, he signalled them to face the other way, then returned to the silent classroom and repeated the routine with row 2 ... row 3 ... and finally, row 4. He then walked to the end of the immaculately formed queue, reminiscent of miniature soldiers, opened the double doors, pinning one back, and signalled the children through to the playground. Not a word was said; no oral instructions were given. Shamefaced, in perfect formation, the new Class 5 stood in the position chalk-marked 'Class 5' and, with heads slightly bent, remained for all of two minutes. Mr. Bolton stood ahead of the chastened children, some choking back nervous giggles, his arms folded once again, eyes looking straight through his charges, it seemed unblinkingly. The return to the classroom was also effected in near-military style, the only thing missing, Charlie, an avid watcher of army films said later, were the rifles, the caps with the shiny boots you could see your face in and the visors hiding your eyes.

'We will start,' spat Mr. Bolton, who never seemed to be able to say anything in a style which was not reminiscent of a drill sergeant, 'as we mean to go on. Or as *I* mean *you* to go on. You will soon understand that I stand no-nonsense in my classes. You will learn respect and in return, I will respect you. In that order. After I have called the register, I shall hand you your test paper. Put up your hand when your name is called so that I can put face to name.'

This completed, Mr. Bolton walked from desk to desk in the random order in which the pupils had placed themselves, placing a booklet on the desk of each child.

'You have an hour to complete these questions. The instructions are straightforward. If you need to ask me a question, put your hand up. I will answer all sensible ones but don't expect me to give any help with the answers. Write your name now in the box on the cover.'

The sharpened pencils in the channel at the top of the desks were picked up as one. Almost as one they were replaced. Every movement in silence.

Jamie's hand went up. Mr. Bolton walked to stand beside him.

'Mr. Bolton, I'm sorry you have lost your moustache. Sorry for *you*, I mean, but not for me because I was frightened of you when you had it on your face. Where did you lose it, or did you forget where you'd put it?'

All covert eyes were on Jamie, then Mr. Bolton who, white-faced, but uttering not a word, shifted Jamie's chair so that he could get out from his seat. Without any contact with Jamie's body, the message was conveyed that he was to move forward … and forward … and forward, until he was standing beside Mr. Bolton's table. Mr. Bolton handled his ruler, looked at it, replaced it.

'I do not expect any impudence nor insolence. Do you understand? Have I made myself perfectly clear?'

He handled the ruler again and passed it across to Jamie.

'Can you feel its sharp edge?'

'Yes, I can,' said Jamie, marvelling at the simplicity of the question. Fancy making him leave his seat to show him a ruler and to tell him that he didn't like insolence or impudence. Who does, thought Jamie, and why tell me on my own, not the whole class? His ruler is no different than any of the rulers we are given. It had been on the tip of his tongue to inform him of that in case Mr. Bolton was under the misapprehension that his was dissimilar but, somehow, he thought he would rather see what the test papers were like. He could always discuss the matter with him later. Meanwhile, it was rather nice that he had been singled out from all the others to be the privileged one to be shown Mr. Bolton's. Mr. Bolton didn't seem to speak very much: it was quite funny that instead of asking you to go up to his table, he moved you up in that strange way with his feet and did the same in reverse when he no longer wanted you to stand there. Maybe he was a nice teacher after all; he certainly had strange habits, though.

Once back in his seat to complete his test paper, those in Jamie's row cast him a sidelong glance of approval.

'Now turn the page. Begin,' came the order. The heads of his peers bowed over their work.

The first section of this paper was on maths. He whipped through the mechanical part but thought some of the word-questions irrelevant:

'If you drink ¾ of a can of coke, how much would you have left?' Jamie answered: 'I can't say because I am not allowed to drink coke.'

To *'If you have 4 friends and 36 marbles to share and give an equal number to each one how many would each one receive?'* he wrote, 'All the Eagles are my friends and there are 6 of us so I would give each one 6 and still have 6 for me.'

He did find one hard to answer which asked, *'How many metres would you run if you ran twice round a playground which had a perimeter of 150 metres?'* His response, 'Too hard. I'd get exhorsted,' would hardly endear him to Mr. Bolton.

At the end of this section were the words 'Look over your paper, then turn over.'

What a crazy thing to say, Jamie puzzled. He observed his neighbour who had also reached the end. He wasn't quite sure whether his neighbour understood either: he didn't raise himself up to look over his paper, neither did his body make any movement to turn itself around. Perhaps these were trick words. He realised then what the last bit meant – but why didn't it say 'turn *the page* over'. Should he tell Mr. Bolton he had missed two words out, to save the rest of the class being equally puzzled? Mr. Bolton didn't seem to like questions, although he said he'd answer them, so perhaps he'd leave it to someone else to tell him this time.

He noticed his neighbour in the next row coming to the end of page 3 where it had the big writing on the bottom and, leaning across the aisle, winked as he turned the page over for Millie. Surprisingly, Millie banged her hand down hard on his which immediately brought Mr. Bolton to their sides.

'Jamie nearly ripped my paper,' Millie scowled at Jamie.

'I'm getting to know you fast. Jamie Chilton, isn't it? I always pick up the names of troublemakers first, so be warned … for the second time.'

He strode back to his desk.

'Keep your nose down.'

Jamie wondered, horror seeping over him, whether Mr. Bolton would start licking him into a different shape very soon now. It was horrible having this feeling of uncertainty. Just in case, he held his nose down as close as he could to the page. Unfortunately, it was then difficult for him to see the print. He experimented, cautiously raising his head, trying to keep it in the same plane, and hoping fervently that the position he finally decided upon would not incur Mr. Bolton's displeasure. He certainly seemed a very fierce man.

The next section, which Jamie was glad to be able to see, told children to read a passage then answer the questions. You had to fill in the missing words. They were all easy.

The coat the woman was wearing was red.
The woman was going to the chemist.
A man tied his dog up to the post before entering the sandwich shop.

The next three were easy, too.

The woman wore a red coat because she had a red coat.
The woman went to the chemists because she wanted to; it said it was one on the front above the door.

Dogs were tied up outside the sandwich shop <u>because there</u> <u>was a notice telling you to.</u>

Jamie smirked as he noted Charlie, who was sitting next to him, had got his answers wrong. To the first he had written 'it was her favourite colour', to the second, 'she wanted medicine for her husband who was ill', and to the third, 'it was not high-geenic to have animals where food was'.

He knew Mr. Bolton would be cross if he spoke to Charlie although they needed to speak if he was to point out Charlie's mistakes for him. Poor Charlie. It said in the passage this woman had everything red in her house: carpets, cups, cushions, curtains but didn't say what her favourite colour was. It didn't say anything about her husband being ill: he was in bed, the clock beside him read 11.25 and there was a chart beside him with red lines going up and up – he'd probably put his child's drawings up by his pillow so he could see these when he woke up. Was it a son or a daughter? (It was impossible to tell who was probably drawing a mountain range). He remembered doing this in Year 1 so his child was probably aged 6. But why red? Oh, his wife had everything red so probably had told him or her to draw mountain-tops red (perhaps it was the sun setting behind them). How silly; they really should be green … or white if they were snow-covered. And what a stupid answer for number three: didn't Charlie see the notice? He felt really sorry for Charlie: he seemed to have forgotten so much during the summer holiday. Perhaps he was no longer a bright boy. He would not get a place in the top group, wherever that was. This was the first class where the desks had not been arranged in 'tables'.

Then the last page had questions on 'Social Studies'. These were very, very easy.

A <u>mainger</u> *was where Jesus was born.*
The pyramids were built as resting places for <u>dead camels</u>
<u>and stinxes.</u>
The ice age was <u>before it got warm.</u>

Jamie put down his pen. Dutifully, he followed the instructions at the end of the paper:

'Now check your paper and make sure you have answered every question correctly.'

Jamie started at the beginning and ticked each question. At the bottom of the test paper he wrote, '20/20'. He sat up straight, abandoning the instruction to keep his nose down, folded his arms and smiled in the direction of Mr. Bolton. He noted he was the third to finish. He watched the hands on the clock silently moving ten minutes forward.

'Pencils down and pass your papers to the front,' Mr. Bolton instructed.

The bell rang. The class was waved to the door. Mr. Bolton stood there, watching until the last child had passed through the swing doors into the junior playground. Hey, cool! Freya was there outside the gate, looking for him, together with her friends.

'How did you get on? Tummy-ache gone? What do you make of Mr. Bolton?'

'To your last question, I would like to make him into a big scarecrow 'cos that's what he does: he scares us'.

The girls scoffed into their crisp packets.

'Oh, he's all right when you get on the right side of him,' said one of Freya's friends.

'What's wrong with his left side?' enquired Jamie. A shiver ran down his spine as he tried to remember on which side of him he had stood when he was shown Mr. Bolton's ruler.

'And what about when you are looking at him from the back side – it will be different whether you are looking at his front or his back side,' he added informatively.

The lips of one of the friends curled as she linked arms with Freya.

'Your brother's off his trolley. Come on Freya. We'll miss the bus if we don't hurry up."

They ran off, not wanting to waste any more of their free afternoon, leaving Jamie wondering when they'd ever seen him on a trolley. Did they mean those ones in the supermarket? He had not been allowed to sit in one of those since he was about three. It also reminded him of that doctor in the hospital who'd fallen off one. He found Charlie,

'Charlie, I'm ever so sorry but you got a lot of questions wrong. I would have told you but I thought Mr. Bolton would be cross if I spoke to you in the classroom. He really is quite fierce, don't you think?'

'I bet I didn't,' responded Charlie indignantly, ignoring Jamie's question, secretly liking his new teacher who clearly would not stand any of the nonsense some of his earlier teachers had allowed, especially from Jamie; you would always know where you stood with a teacher like that. His older brother had told him to 'keep your head down', and he would do well. 'Any idiot could get every one of those stupid questions right.'

He walked away when Jamie corrected him by saying he knew Charlie was not an idiot because he'd been an Eagle for about two years when the groups had names but he couldn't have got 20/20 as he'd done as Charlie's answers weren't the same as his, so that proved it.

The whistle blew and the children lined up in class ranks to go in for lunch. Juniors had second sitting. Dinner ladies allocated them to tables of ten. Jamie found himself sitting next to Rajiv on one side, Francesca (an ex-Duck) on the other, with Alfie opposite. Their table was signalled to go up first to choose from the menu or by looking at the array of food, set so high that in previous years it had been hard to see what was in the metal containers. With his recent growth spurt, this was no longer a problem.

'Hurry along,' the cook admonished. 'Can't wait all day.'

Jamie chose from the menu: 'Chicken nuggets, beans and chips.'

'Please,' said Cook.

Jamie smiled. Did she want him to give her back the plate he'd taken?

'No manners these days,' muttered Cook. 'Neither parents nor teachers expect or get any respect.'

Once seated, Jamie confided to the nearest dinner lady, 'These chicken nuggets are gristly. They're not like Mummy makes.'

'Not much here will be,' sniffed the dinner lady whose confidence Jamie had invoked. 'None of those celebrity chefs work here, you know. But better not pass your views onto Cook: she'll be none too pleased and will probably bite your head off and we'll get it in the stew next week.'

Mrs. Jackson prided herself on her wit.

Jamie sat back in his chair aghast. This was supposed to be a church school where all people were kind to each other. Love your neighbour as yourself. What would God think about teachers who lick you into funny shapes and cooks who bit children's heads off? He looked at Mrs. Jackson's flabby arms wobbling as she reached across the table to collect the plates. Freya often looked at ladies' arms and said they'd got dinner ladies' arms. Now he knew what they looked like. He didn't think his mummy had them but he'd look next time she wore a short-sleeved top and reached across the table.

Mr. Bolton was the teacher on dinner-duty, probably the reason why the children ate in total silence. When he noticed Jamie had finished, he walked over and stood menacingly at the top of the table.

'Chilton,' (nobody had ever used just his surname before.

Did it mean he was grown up?) 'wait at the door when your table is dismissed.'

'Ooh, perhaps he's going to tell me how pleased he is I got every question in the test right. Maybe he'll apologise for saying unkind things to me, too'.

'Huh, doubt it,' interspersed Charlie who had been made table monitor at the top of the table. Being table monitor had mixed blessings. You could pass people 'seconds' after collecting any leftovers from the serving hatch – but, if dinner ladies were out of sight, you could take an enormous helping of something you liked first before passing the container on. Not all good news because you were the one to be told off if there was trouble on your table. That could be sorted out later in the playground, however, when no one was looking so, on balance, being a table monitor was a desirable office to hold.

Charlie continued, 'Didn't you see his face? And he used your surname! That's a bad omen.'

Well, everyone on the table could see Mr. Bolton's face. So what? And he felt important that Mr. Bolton knew his name already.

Back in the classroom, Jamie waited expectantly for some words of praise from Mr. Bolton. Mr. Bolton picked up his ruler, fingered it and looked long and hard at Jamie, his lips curling. Jamie grinned.

'Your face looks very funny when you put your mouth like that and you screw up your eyes at the same time. It makes me want to laugh. I think it looks much nicer without that moustache you had, though I expect you are very sorry you lost it. You didn't answer my question before but I would like to know what happened to it. Did it fall off?'

Jamie was unaware that there are times in teachers' lives when they feel it is safer for them to put a solid object between themselves and the child whose bottom they would like to whack, whose neck they'd like to ring or whose knuckles they would like to rap. This was one of those moments for Mr. Bolton, the second that day, and he slowly moved himself round to the other side of his desk. To save his blood pressure from soaring (he was already on beta-blockers), he decided to ignore this pestilent child's supreme rudeness, about which he had heard much in staffroom tittle-tattle, and deal with the matter for which he had called this horror in to explain himself. A man who prided himself on 'taming' even the worst offenders when these unfortunate miscreants came under his care, he was not to be outsmarted by this particular one.

'Chilton, the fact that you only have a miserable seven answers correct you properly cannot help. Not everyone can be clever – although from some of your answers and from the insolent remarks you have just made to me, I suspect you were trying to send me up – but to take it upon yourself to mark your own work and claim full marks is something I will not accept. What do you have to say for yourself?'

Wondering who else Mr. Bolton thought was around to speak for him, he toyed with the idea of getting Mr. Bolton to agree that if he didn't send Mr. Bolton up somewhere (where to, he hadn't got a clue), would Mr. Bolton promise not to lick him into something horrible … or even nice, as he was quite happy being Jamie, a boy. Without quite knowing why not, he thought it better to answer Mr. Bolton's question; perhaps his teacher had not read the question paper himself.

'Well, you know what it tells you to do at the bottom of the page? I did it just as it was printed. It told you to check your answers and I did and I was right. The ticks added up to twenty and there were only twenty questions so I got full marks.'

It is best that the remainder of the exchanges go unrecorded. Suffice it to say that the first page of Mr. Bolton's record book (black) had already been completed by the end of the first day, the only name recorded in the wide margin being Chilton. The class seating arrangements, based purely on test results, were announced with erstwhile Eagles, with one exception (no prizes for which member) filling the back two rows. Two Moorhens were demoted who, together with former Ducks, found the first rows allocated to them, Jamie being on the single desk immediately in front of Mr. Bolton.

★

The year slipped by and autumn turned into spring. Even the nightmares were a thing of the past. Confiding his fear to an amused Mrs. Ackroyd on playground duty one day that he was living in dreadful fear of Mr. Bolton's tongue, he was greatly relieved to hear her say that, sharp though his tongue was, he would not hurt a fly. Mary felt a surge of compassion, coupled with self-satisfied reassurance in her interpersonal skills, that this ingenuous child had unburdened himself of his very real anxiety. Little did Mrs. Ackroyd know that Jamie's fear was of her unwitting making.

On a beautiful April morning, daffodils dancing, primroses turning their faces to the sun, blackbirds singing to their mates, ewes suckling their lambs, spiders weaving webs amidst the dewy, fresh-green meadows, a solemn meeting took place nonetheless at St. Michael's C. of E. Matt and Sarah had been summoned to a conference held to discuss fresh concerns held by the school in relation to their son, James. Matt's first reaction was to delegate Sarah but a three-line whip, or what passed for one in educational terms, was merely to offer him alternative dates. Matt had no option but to attend alongside his wife.

Mr. Holmes, Mr. Bolton, Mrs. Ackroyd (SENCo), Mr. Danesfield (deputy head), and the Chiltons sat stiffly on formal chairs brought in to the headmaster's room to accommodate extra bodies. As gently as possible, Jamie's parents were told by the SENCo that it was her duty to tell them that their son's current behaviour in class and around the school varied from day to day from inappropriate superciliousness to absolute rudeness. The behavioural idiosyncrasies repelled his peers, who often shunned him in recreation periods and it was left to the kindness of duty teachers to amuse him, often to rescue him from the vitriol of others whom he had irritated.

Sarah and Matt were reminded of the comments written in end of year reports under 'Personal and Social' which seemed to have a familiar ring year after year, referring to the fact that 'he was learning to integrate'. Amusing at the age of five/six; inexcusable at nine, unacceptable at rising ten. His impudent answers to comprehension questions were based on text he could read faultlessly, 'and even on the most basic text he could read with his eyes shut' ('as he could when he was only four: he would read *The Sunday Times* headlines upside down, to our amazement', Sarah had interjected at that point), yet wrote ridiculous answers to comprehension questions as if it was beneath his intelligence to provide the intended answer. Not only did everyone shy away from him in the playground as he spoiled their games, he was the last to be chosen for team games and only that morning he had again shown flagrant disregard for instructions he, Mr. Holmes, had given out in assembly.

'Which were?' Matt had interrupted, recalling his own schooldays when he had spent more time sticking two fingers up at authority figures than paying attention in class, let alone assembly when those trite little homilies went straight over his head.

'I gave out that the grass was to be cut today.'

'So?' enquired Matt icily.

'The insinuation here,' Mr. Holmes responded curtly, 'which every pupil fully understands, is that the playing fields are out of bounds for the day, primarily because of the need to keep the field clear and the pupils out of danger from flying stones and finally, because the cleaners do not want to spend all evening sweeping up grass cuttings from corridors and classrooms.'

Fully prepared to take up battle, Matt threw down the gauntlet.

'I would say then, Headmaster, you were at fault for not adding, "so no one must go on the field today".'

'Just for the sake of your son?' queried Mr. Holmes in clipped tones. 'For the clarity of mind of the only child from Years 1 – 6 who required the statement to be interpreted? Mr. Chilton, please.'

Barbs continued to be thrust and parried for the next half an hour, Mr. Holmes trying his utmost to make his contributions in measured tones without categorically stating the united opinion of the staff that this pupil was suffering from an unacceptable conduct disorder. Eventually it behoved Mr. Bolton to ask permission to put his record book in front of Matt and Sarah.

Matt turned the pages quickly, merely skimming the entries.

'It seems rather one-sided, Mr. Bolton, Mr. Holmes, Mrs. Ackroyd, Mr. Danesfield. I do not see any explanatory mitigating comments written by my son and I need you to tell me why not. I believe the mission statement of your school includes the phrase, 'Every Child Matters'. Doesn't that suggest that every child also has a right of reply?' adding as the teaching staff conferred through eye contact with each other, 'I also think I am within my rights to demand a photocopy of all contents in the record book relating to my son.'

'Mr. and Mrs. Chilton,' Mr. Holmes' voice took on a more even, conciliatory tone as he was none too sure which side would be taken by Father Harrold in any altercation – the line of least resistance, he thought grimly – and felt the meeting was becoming rather too adversarial. 'As I said at the beginning, the Code of Practice which all parents have access to is available to study in my secretary's office. This statutory document requires us to flag up any child who causes us concern in any way and suggest the means whereby teachers need to exercise specific skills in an attempt, usually successful, to 'bring out the positive' and use this to reduce the identified weaknesses of a child. Mr. Bolton has used his own impressive techniques to guide your son to see the errors of his ways and this term, additionally, has sought the advice of our special educational needs coordinator. You will be aware from the Code of Practice guidelines, that we should now devise a programme with the consent and cooperation of parents, which will be formally recorded and monitored at regular intervals by us all present in this room today. As you know, we tried this successfully for a short period in Year 3, so the process will be familiar to you. This, as happened then, is often all that is required to change a recalcitrant child to order and turn him (it is, I'm afraid, often a "him") into a pupil of whom both parents and school can be proud. Sometimes, however,' he added darkly, 'this takes time and patience.'

As would be expected, this was not enough to placate Matt's fury; he wanted to know what the next stage was in this police state which employed such Stalinist measures to transform a defenceless, actually not-yet-ten-year-old, into a gibbering, mindless conformist. The intimation that 'this had been tried before', he glossed over, planning, for clarification, to take that remark up later with Sarah. He was none too pleased when further explanation of the outlined procedures took in a referral to a 'shrink', (actually Mr. Holmes had mentioned something about an educational one, whatever difference that made), who would 'assess him'.

'Assess him?' exploded Matt, 'Assess him for what?'

'A more formal positive behavioural programme,' Mr. Holmes had continued, 'would be written in conjunction with the advice of our educational psychologist and, if not successful despite a lengthy trial period, it would be seen what a spell for a year to eighteen months in a Pupil Referral Unit could do for Jamie.'

Matt had snorted that he assumed this would be a cross between a junior Belmarsh or mini Abu Ghraib-type institution. Mr. Holmes, a double whisky and dry ginger dangling just out of reach in his subtly fertile imagination, expressed the view that the discussion ('held in the best interests of Jamie') was getting a little heated and perhaps should be concluded.

'Adjourned,' said Matt, thumping the table, 'till my wife and I have spoken with the chair of governors.'

Briefcase in hand and without a glance behind his shoulder, he rapidly steered Sarah out of the room along the corridors almost kicking over the bucket of the cleaner mopping the floor and causing Sarah to dislodge the 'Wet Polish' warning sign, and out into the fresh air. Once inside the car, Sarah burst into tears.

★

'Well that's set the cat among the pigeons,' Mrs. Ackroyd said, collecting her wits as the retreating backs of the Chiltons signified the meeting to be at an end.

'Crows, you mean,' Gordon Bolton corrected her, in the sort of tone which indicated he'd enjoyed every minute of the encounter. 'Can see where that kid gets it from. Nasty piece of work, that man. Knows his rights – but undoubtedly had never heard of the Code of Practice.'

'Oh, will that be held against us?' Mrs. Ackroyd enquired hastily, recalling that only Mrs. Chilton had been present at that earlier meeting some two years ago when they had all been relieved that work commitments had prevented her husband from attending.

It was only then that they noted Mr. Holmes slumped in his

chair. In less than fifteen minutes the shocked members of this uncomfortable meeting had rapidly leapt into action, paramedics had checked pulse and heart rate, finding both much higher and more irregular than would enable them to do anything other than make a decision to transfer him for tests. Geoff Holmes was quickly placed on a stretcher and on his way into the care of the local hospital. Temporary relief of his responsibilities to the Chilton family would certainly form part of his recovery.

Recriminations followed thick and fast as each mentioned their concerns that Geoff Holmes' health had clearly not been up to the job of facing such a formidable opponent as Jamie Chilton's father. Corridors resumed an uncanny silence as all but the deputy, stunned with the tragic outcome of this frightful day, returned to their families, memories of the meeting wiped out almost entirely by the horrors of the past hour. It was left to Peter Danesfield to drive to Geoff's home, fortunately close by the school, to break the news as calmly as he could, to his wife and offer to escort her to the hospital.

★

Sarah did her best not to grip tightly to her seat as Matt broke practically every speed limit there was between the school and home, twice swerving to avoid oncoming cars as he overtook any drivers keeping safely within the law. Sarah did not make any comment, either about his driving or the shock of the meeting: any word from her and Matt could burst an artery. Screeching to a halt on the gravel drive, slamming shut the door, sweeping past the babysitter, taking the stairs two at a time, bursting open Jamie's door and yanking a sleeping child from his bed, he thundered,

'What have you got to say for yourself, you disgraceful child. What in God's name do you think you have been playing at at school? Come on, say something. Explain your appalling behaviour. Right now, do you hear me?'

Jamie, roused from his slumber and a pleasant dream in which a worm, wearing one of those short dresses a ballet dancer wears and with the face of Mr. Bolton, had wriggled along the window sill of his bedroom, turning somersaults as he progressed towards a stripey patterned curtain, blinked and did his best to wrest himself from the vice-like grip his father held him in.

'Dadd-eey, you are hurting me. I was having a nice dream,' he protested, his voice heavy with sleep. 'I was thinking of having a funny wormy thing to do acrobatics at my this year's birthday party.' Wide awake now, Jamie added accusingly, 'Oh please, take your hands off me; it's really painful what you are doing to me. In my dream all my friends in my row bought me the most amazing presents. Alfie bought me a helter-skelter like you have in fairs, Sam gave me a car just like the one James Bond had in that film we saw at the cinema, *Live and Let Die*, wasn't it? Do you remember I spilt all my popcorn? Daddy, are you listening? Oh, that's better: your hands have gone all limp.'

Matt wondered if he could cope with any more this evening. Was his son using well-practised avoidance techniques? Now fully awake, Jamie was fully determined to hold his father's attention for as long as he could. He would be able to tell him all the wonderful things about him he had learned from Mr. Holmes. 'He was there, wasn't he?'

'Oh, I remember: you were going to a special meeting all about me. Did Mr. Bolton tell you that he keeps writing about me in his very important book? He said there wasn't anyone else in it. Just a bit about Alfie. He really sounded excited this afternoon when he said how much he was looking forward to showing it to you and Mummy. I expect he told you he chose me to go and pick up litter from the playground this morning. I've done that for him quite a lot of times. He said today that in all his days of teaching he had not had a boy like me, but he does say funny things sometimes. There has only been one 'me', hasn't there? He's going to give me a new place in the cloakroom to hang my coat, you know. I heard him telling Miss Griffin he was going to take me down a peg or two. I think that is because I have to keep telling him that my coat is always falling off onto the floor, so often that people have to tread on it; they say they can't help it. No one else's, actually, falls off onto the floor so I think it must be a faulty peg, don't you? Anyway, if he gives me a low one, I can make sure my things hang on properly.'

In disbelief, Matt had a feeling that Jamie was in total denial. Had he got any idea whatsoever of reality? He didn't feel he could take any more. The opinions of the teachers and that supercilious head had hit home more than he would have liked to admit – indeed, many of those raining down on his ears he could have suggested himself.

'Daddy, don't go away. You don't usually come up to say goodnight. You always have to work late at work so there aren't many times I can talk to you. Will you read me a chapter of the book Mr Holmes has been reading to us? Mummy got it for me from the library. It's in her bag, I think. It's called *The Silver Sword* by Sir A. Lear*, Edward's brother, I expect. I wonder if the A stands for Alfred, Alfie for short. That would be a coincidence, wouldn't it, 'cos Alfie is in our class.'

The pent-up anger was fully spent. This incredible disregard by Jamie of his father's wrath was completely inexplicable to Matt. He knew he had to leave for fear of doing something drastic to vent his feelings which he would forever regret. He forced his legs to carry him to the door.

'Or I could talk to you all about the galaxies I have been learning about from watching those TV programmes on astronomy, Daddy. Oh, I haven't answered your question yet, have I? I've been playing charades at school with Millie and Flora and Ruby; that is what I have been playing at.

'Oh, oh, plea-ea-se come back.'

---

*   Serraillier

Sarah had been listening with horror at the bottom of the stairs. At Jamie's pleading that Matt should stay, she slipped quietly into the kitchen and put the kettle on. Matt could, and probably would tonight, lose himself in the whisky bottle, she thought, but what she had had to bear in Mr. Holmes' office that evening could not be assuaged by any liquor. She needed solitude to recall every aspect of the meeting so that she could put every accusation that had been made about her beloved son into proper perspective and understand what the teachers were trying to put across to them. Why did Matt take it as an affront to his manhood, to his parental capabilities or whatever-she-knew-not?

Sarah also needed the calming effect of a valium tablet which Dr. Allinson had prescribed for the tinge of depression he had diagnosed a few months ago when she felt her marriage was not in a very happy state. This tiny pill would be her saviour once more. She had found hotel bills in the pocket of his jacket on the occasion Matt was racing round the house, creating mayhem, because he had accused her of putting his car keys in a stupid place when she was tidying up one day. Of course, there they were in the jacket he had taken on a business conference weekend, but the dates on the hotel bill did not match and was in a different town miles away from the conference hotel brochure he had shown her and left lying around in a conspicuous place in the sitting room. Sarah, internally bruised, had felt too sick at heart to tackle him about it, preferring to think the errant hotel bill had been associated, for what reason she could not think, with another of his friends. Perhaps Matt had been given it from a friend as a reminder to book it for themselves one day? In her heart of hearts, however, she knew it was all adding up to something that would break her very spirit. She couldn't get it out of her mind, though, and when their wedding anniversary came and went unmarked, she spoke to Dr. Allinson, claiming her despair was related to the recession and having to make do and mend in such hard times when even Matt's job could be in jeopardy. Although she felt she no longer needed these tranquillisers on a regular basis, her doctor had advised her to take one whenever she felt herself being the proverbial cat that had to be mangled. His prediction proved all too correct.

The vitriol which subsequently poured down upon her head when Matt stormed into the kitchen behind her, Sarah later reflected, was probably the worst she had ever had to endure. Fighting back tears welling up in her eyes and the choking feeling in her throat, Sarah did her best to let the insults pass over her. Aspersions were cast upon her ability to see her children as young pre-adolescents, her ability to instil discipline, her preference for daughters being such that she was doing her best to turn Jamie into one, his disappointment in her as a wife and a mother to his son. The battle for her emotions lost, tears rained down, and down, and down. Down, down, down she felt herself falling, down into a bottomless pit. Sarah's knees collapsed beneath her and she crumpled to the kitchen floor.

'Sarah, oh Sarah, what are you doing to me?'

Matt's shoulders shook. The choking sobs were painful to the babysitter's ears, listening outside the kitchen door. Thankfully, both her charges were asleep upstairs. She tiptoed to the front door, smartly collecting a £10 note before passing through, quietly closed it, entered her little car and drove herself two avenues away to her home. Throwing her university scarf over the hall chair, she said nonchalantly to her mother,

'I think you should phone the Chiltons, Mum. They had a major row, Sarah's fainted and Matt seems to have lost it. If you startle them by ringing them up, I guess one of them will come to their senses. Just say you are sorry Hannah told you she'd left without saying goodbye. That should do it.'

Not for nothing was Hannah Green reading social sciences at University College, London.

Chapter Seventeen

The shuffle of senior staff was inevitable. Whilst news of Mr. Holmes was good and his condition not nearly as serious as it had seemed, 'the show must go on' principle had to be enacted. When discharged from hospital after five days, complete with pacemaker, he was advised to take things more easily until Easter, avoid stress in any form and then undertake only light duties during the summer term.

Meanwhile, Peter Danesfield became acting head, Gordon Bolton was catapulted into the position of acting deputy while Mary Ackroyd decided to remain in her role as SENCo, leaving Miss Griffin to be given power as acting senior mistress to ensure the politically correct presence of even representation of the sexes in senior roles. Not for nothing was Faith Griffin a stalwart member of the N.U.T.

During this changeover, Father Harrold huffed and puffed and put on hold any meeting with the Chiltons. He felt he needed to brush up on the legal side and read up on negotiating skills: rumour had gathered much moss as the likely reason for Mr. Holmes' sudden heart attack had spread. Without a doubt, Mr. Chilton was not a man to be reasoned with. Furthermore, as the chairman of governors, a position he was beginning to rue, necessitated him to support the staff as much as possible in their preparations for the forthcoming OFSTED inspection. Gordon in his capacity of acting deputy had hinted to him that Mr. Chilton could take his objections to the senior inspector if he was not tamed into submission, could even get more parents on his side and the resulting report could put the school in an unpleasant light, even spiralling downwards towards a 'Special Measures' grading. Gordon Bolton also intimated slyly that this would not go down well with the Diocese and, tongue in cheek, urged the chair of governors to pull out all the stops to enable the school to show itself in its best light in order to outweigh and countermand any parental complaints. The significance, in this respect, of any repercussions in lowering of reputation since he had become chair was not lost on Father Harrold. The last inspection some five years ago had graded St. Michael's C of E as 'excellent in all respects, with outstanding pastoral care for children with special needs'.

The first steps, Father Harrold determined, were to obtain a copy of Mr. Bolton's record book and of the entries in that of the headmaster. Oh dear, the responsibility of the chair of governors weighed heavily upon one's shoulders, he reflected gloomily. Events were turning out quite differently from what he had been led to believe by his doting parents, his mother having been a member of a church school governing body in a stockbroker belt for many years. She had regularly regaled him in his youth of being fêted at school galas, presenting prizes at speech days, sitting alongside the mayor on special occasions and being given front seats at concerts and services. Mrs. Harrold particularly enjoyed the lavish hospitality at private staff functions throughout the year which she was always telling him had to be seen to be believed. Although he telephoned her to ask her advice on how to manage these incensed parents, he found this conspicuously lacking. 'Oh surely, darling, you can charm them with your winsome smile'.

Father Harrold speculated whether it would help if he started the meeting with a prayer and a blessing. He could call upon Our Lord to grant moderation in our tones, in our thoughts, our intentions and our actions, remembering that any unkind word from one to another is an unkind word to his

'Holy Person'. That should do the trick. He had noticed Mrs. Chilton's spasmodic attendance at church on a Sunday, always leaving without queuing to shake his hand at the end of the service as most of his congregation did, although could only recall having seen the father once, sloping in late at Midnight Mass last Christmas.

★

Mr. Bolton relished his temporary role as acting deputy, one he had aspired to since relinquishing his rank as sergeant-major following two tours of duty in Iraq. The horrors he had witnessed in the Theatre of War, as it was called (some theatre, he had dryly boasted to his friends who would hang on his every word, worse, far worse, than any Chamber of Horrors or thriller film), had, despite his bravado, brutalised him in some way as well as imbuing him with what was later called post traumatic stress disorder. Thankfully, his wife, initially shattered by the change in her husband on his eventual discharge from the Marines, found Gordon Bolton was made of sterner stuff.

After succumbing to an immediate period of depression, the stalwart and compassionate care of Maggie, his wife of ten years, enabled him to manage to put that behind him, take a post-graduate degree in primary education and embark upon a second career. Most of those who knew him felt that his talents, love of discipline, order and routine would be more suited to adolescent students but Gordon felt that in his still-fragile state of mind, he would prefer to commence work with more formative minds than with those which, he thought, could already be too worldly wise. He could transfer to secondary education later. To his surprise he gained immense satisfaction from moulding the characters of youngsters who seemed to need some regimentation in their lives and he developed an ambition to manage a junior school of his own before his forties were out. He suddenly found himself, by good fortune, catapulted to the second rung of a ladder which, he hoped, would lead to rapid promotion. Indeed, he was aided in this by the decision of Peter Danesfield to make himself responsible for the admin side of the acting headship, delegating day-to-day management of school routines to Gordon. The ambitious Gordon, although appearing nonchalant about his new and unexpected role, was determined to milk this opportunity to the utmost.

Furthermore, luck had now favoured him in another manner. He was secretly delighted when Mrs. Ackroyd had to take eight weeks' sick leave for surgery for a 'women's complaint'. (Why did the female members of staff have to pussy-foot around with specious euphemisms: every man knew it meant a hysterectomy. Thank God, he thought, no more treading on eggshells in the staffroom during her 'time of the month', fortunately a short-lived period. You could always tell the date when nothing ever went right for her. Little did he know that he was the only member of staff who was the recipient of an unexpectedly sharp tone when Mrs. Ackroyd felt strong enough to criticise his disciplinary methods as rather extreme). He found it easier to work with Ms. Craddock, a newcomer to the position of SENCo, quite an ingenuous lady, he decided, and one he initially had no qualms in dominating. However, he found she soon became a match for him and put forward her own ideas as to how the position to which she had been temporarily appointed should be managed.

It was his turn to take assembly, Peter Danesfield having delegated this task to him with inner gratitude. A man to take the easier path if one presented itself, why not take advantage of Gordon's ambitious streak? My, how he'd managed to raise the stakes. His themes became more and more humanistic, with a mere touch of Christianity and all that being nice to your neighbour stuff but, as for not being the first to cast a stone, were the British to stand waiting for the hand grenade to land at their feet? He made sure he allocated the Jewish Passover to his deputy, excusing himself with some such subterfuge as having to speak collectively to the cleaning staff or meet new parents. His inventiveness in finding reasons to absent himself when it came to festivals or holy days knew no bounds.

On more than one occasion, however, Gordon Bolton's patience was sorely tried by the perpetual thorn in his side, Jamie Chilton, a child whose intentions were impossible to fathom. His insolence knew no bounds. In the classroom his work oscillated from extreme quirkiness to blatant impertinence. Project work indicated knowledge superior to any other pupil in the class (infuriatingly so), which contrasted abysmally with assignments submitted bearing no relation to the context set. To a great extent, despite his class management par excellence, albeit relying mainly on intimidation, Mr. Bolton found that very little he could do, say or demand, would instil respect in this unspeakably recalcitrant child or divert him from following his own agenda.

It was when he had finished giving out the Notices for the Day (usually a set of 'don'ts', rarely including any 'do's' and with any praise conspicuous by its absence, were the views held by his colleagues), that Jamie Chilton put up his hand. Without waiting for a sign of approval, he informed the assembled school that he had a most important announcement to make.

'This most precious object, the one I now hold up for all to inspect,' (necks craned to see the very small item Jamie held up between finger and thumb) 'was given to me by the finder who told me I was just the right person to display it in assembly. It is a real *gold* safety pin, which I understand, is very valuable because of its special carrots: apparently it has eighteen, but I'm not sure where these are at the moment. Most probably in the owner's kitchen. Mr. Bolton, as not everybody can see it from where they are sitting, may I have your permission to take it round to every class later so that it can be properly examined and the owner identified?'

Mr. Bolton looked as if he was about to burst a blood vessel. Teachers sitting at the side of their year groups, eyes as large as saucers, looked expectantly towards the acting deputy. Repressed snorts from the back line trickled down to the front row where the Reception children wondered what all the muffled gasps were all about.

Gordon Bolton said not a word. His face puce with controlled rage, he pointed one by one to the year group teacher. Each class tiptoed out through the double doors with only a sidelong glance through lowered eyes, first at Jamie Chilton, still standing erect, then at Mr. Bolton, until the only class remaining was that of Mr. Bolton's.

'Year 5, stand. Into the playground, quick march. Stand at attention and in silence in four straight lines when you get there.'

An expectant shiver went through the groups as Mr. Bolton joined them.

'At each whistle blast you hear, you run in the direction I call. Ready, now.'

A shrill blast sounded.

'To your right!' Another shrill blast. 'To your left.'

A full five minutes later the exhausted Year 5's were ordered back to the classroom for, as one pupil said later, the interrogation. Jamie had been ordered to the front of the room.

'Now, I want the finder of this pin to join Chilton. I am convinced Chilton was not in this prank alone.'

The class stared ahead. No one moved.

'Mr. Bolton, it was Freddie, Charlie and Brendan who found it and gave it to me.'

Glowering at Jamie the three named miscreants joined him. It was a most bewildered, tearful Jamie, who during the ensuing painfully long tirade learned his so-called friends had told him lies and had done so to get him into trouble.

★

Even Matt, after this episode, could not prevent the inevitable referral to the Educational Psychology Service on Action Plan Plus.

Chapter Eighteen

Father Harrold was not in the habit of evading issues which his calling in life compelled him to confront. He had brought comfort to the dying, sitting by their hospital bedside hearing the confessions of penitents (sometimes offensive to his unworldly ears), anxious to make their peace before departing this world of sin. Indeed, his words of absolution had been heartfelt. The burden of guilt of 'things left undone' by the bereaved whose loved one had met a tragic and untimely end, had been assuaged by Father Harrold's soothing words. With couples in the throes of separation or divorce he had prayed that the time he had spent with them in their hour of need would go some way towards salving their wounds, enable them to put aside their differences and move towards a renewal of the vows they had made in front of witnesses and the altar.

Percy Harrold (only Percival to his mother, his long-suffering father having pre-deceased her) reflected that the most difficult task he had had to do so far had been to attempt to help a couple consumed with grief at the loss of their teenaged daughter to a rare form of leukaemia. He had explained, rather gauchely, that the pain of losing a child was a sacrifice being made to God, as once was the intention of Isaac: it was a means of purifying their own souls. 'God moves in mysterious ways,' he had said, 'our lives on this Earth are as mere billionths of a second in relation to eternity and your beloved child is being called by our Heavenly Father to prepare a place for you in His sight.' A feeling of impotence still engulfed him when the memories of his approach seeped into his consciousness.

Indeed, in retrospect, Percy had been made aware from the parents' reaction that he had unintentionally expressed what he had planned to be soothing sentiments in what had appeared to them to be such a crassly pompous, inept manner, that he'd felt the need to seek his own absolution from the vicar in charge of his parish.

Now, at a time when he felt an all-consuming sense of foreboding that he was fast approaching another occasion when he would be completely out of his depth and be found wanting, it was to be his good fortune to be able to shelter under the canopy of extenuating circumstances in respect of his vocation which could enable him to take time to prepare for the trial ahead of him. Easter would be his salvation. Meanwhile, prayer was the answer to every problem: prayer to keep calm, prayer to think clearly, prayer to avoid controversy and sidestep adversarial comments from the opposition. Percy pulled himself up short as the mention of 'opposition' struck him forcefully as already getting himself in the wrong state of mind. But was it not wonderful that his Beloved Lord had straight away brought him to that realisation?

What was Percy's immediate salvation was that the meeting between the senior staff of the school and the Chiltons had taken place the day before St. Michael's C. of E. broke up for Holy Week and the solemn preparations for Easter. His duty to his congregation and his Blessed Lord took precedence over his duties as chairman of governors. His response, therefore, to Matthew Chilton to discuss 'matters of gravity in respect of my son, Jamie', was to defer a meeting until the second week following Easter Day. It was customary for all clergy to take a vacation in the seven days following the Glorious Day of Resurrection and he, Percival (as his mother insisted on calling him), would be returning to her bosom for that period.

He vowed to spend the week in contemplation of the serious matter which would test his diplomatic skills to the full on his return. Meanwhile, without any of his parishioners in the final stages of terminal illness, marital distress, or in such a state of penury that the bailiffs were beating a path to their front door, he would be able to offer up his Holy Week penances to his Blessed Lord to give him the strength to face the battle ahead: 'Oh, please my beloved Saviour and that of all mankind, remove these acrimonious predictions from my mind, and guide me to deal with this family with empathy, rigour and judgment. Give me Thy Grace, dearest Lord, to avoid unctuous platitudes and to keep You in my mind at all times.'

Thus did young Jamie Chilton have a profound effect not only on the SENCo of St. Michael's but also upon the Easter solemnities and celebrations of the incumbent of the parent Anglican church. Only Gordon Bolton was able to sleep smugly and soundly in his bed those nights, far away from school and the church who paid his salary.

Easter came, a festival looked forward to by the junior Chiltons not for its religious significance but for the joys of being allowed to eat their fill of chocolate in all its animate forms without restriction. Matt's mother, who always came for the Easter weekend, joined the family for church on Easter Day itself. Matt, however, conspicuous by his absence, was again choosing to 'brush up on his golf' instead. Sarah, for her part, had had her suspicious thoughts when she needed to chase after his car as it reversed out of the garage that morning in order to wave his golf-shoes at her near-departing husband. She also had just cause to reflect on this later.

St. Michael's was at its glorious best. The resonant sound as the choir processed from the east door to the altar, windowsills, pillars, the ends of pews bedecked with spring flowers in hues of yellow and violet, was a tonic for jaded spirits emerging from winter. The celebrant in magnificent cope of cream silk, the full choir thundering out their alleluias, with the congregation in full throttle, added to the jubilance of the ceremony. Even Father Harrold's sermon for his first Easter as priest-in-charge, was mercifully short and his sentiments captured the mood of the moment. Every parishioner exuded magnanimity towards their neighbour during the Kiss of Peace, normally a perfunctory, rather shifty, affair but for once a seemingly true expression of The World being at one with each other.

Jamie had held his grandmother's hand as they both walked up to the altar rail, she to take Communion, he to receive a blessing. On the way back to his seat, Jamie confided that Father Harrold's hand on his head had felt tickly and made him want to sneeze but he'd managed to stop it although he had to giggle because he thought that his sneeze would blow that ice cream wafer thing in Grandma's hand right off. He told her that he was very glad she had her eyes shut so she hadn't seen him pinching his nose hard to stop the sneeze coming. Grandma said he ought to know better; better than what, Jamie wondered, justifiably he thought. What could be better than stopping himself sneezing? He then received a nasty dig in his ribs from Grandma when a fit of giggling unfortunately bubbled up despite his desperate manoeuvres. Visions of the ice-cream wafer bit being blown up into the air and landing, perhaps in that silver cup or in Father Harrold's curly hair as he bent downward to administer the wine, had almost caused him to have hysterics. The more severe second nudge from Grandma coupled with her loudest whisper, 'Stop that nonsense, you naughty boy: you are in church, not on the recreation ground,' reduced him to a compulsive state of mirth. Oh dear, oh dear: Jamie's mind transported him to the local park, ice-cream wafers in abundance floating, ducking and diving at the behest of the wind, scooped up by pigeons, snaffled by nearby magpies, all released by a motley collection of children, sneezing for all they were worth.

Sarah pushed in front of Grandma, took hold of Jamie and marched him out into the fresh air. Her condemnation of his behaviour covered expectations for a nine-, let alone a near-ten-year-old, duty to God, disgrace to his family and more. Jamie had no option but to accept each statement as true but, in mitigation, made the point that the sneeze was probably because of all that smoke stuff that man kept blowing over everybody from that swinging ball thing: 'It was really stinky up at the altar and I could feel it at the back of my throat and up my nose. I tried to snort it out but it ended up as sneezes.'

More alleluias filled the air. Silence as the final blessing was given. The organ blasted out Bach's "Toccata and Fugue". The congregation poured from the west door. Father Harrold, scuttling around from the vestry almost fell into Sarah and Jamie in his haste to greet his parishioners each, personally, with an earnest wish for a Happy and Blessed Easter. Sarah, therefore, was the first to be greeted.

'Father Harrold,' enquired Jamie, 'do you wear ladies' clothes all the time or just on Sundays? You look very nice in them, I must say. Is the gold stuff real gold? Your coat-thing must have cost a lot.'

As Father Harrold's face turned a delicate shade of puce, Jamie added,

'I can see your trousers on underneath, though. Didn't you have time to take them off?'

Noticing the Hennessy-Shawcrosses immediately behind the Chilton family, Percy Harrold hastily told Jamie he would learn about priests' clothing in school next term … but this did not stop the inquisition.

'Father Harrold, I think I ought to point out to you that children like Alfie might think you are a perv if you wear your church clothes to school, so I wouldn't if I were you.'

On the way back home in the car, Sarah had to suffer the added humiliation of being cross-questioned by her mother-in-law as to whether Jamie should be brought up to show more manners and respect. Freya kept her peace; quite an impossible task for her brother, she reflected, although she knew he felt very wise now he knew that 'the right side' meant to know what pleased a person and he was going to make sure to do it. Aware that her mother was not in the happiest state of mind, Freya volunteered to set the table on arrival home. Scheming Freya was also aware that, should she do so, she would earn more 'Brownie points' from her grandmother than would her brother; it was certainly a good plan to keep on the right side of this rather pernickety old lady, she thought. She had several times heard her grandma say to Sarah, 'if ever you doubt my love for you, I will cut you out of my will', and she also knew how partisan Matt's mother could be. She fervently hoped that 'Brownie points' would transform into something more tangible and vowed to keep in her grandmother's good books throughout the duration of her stay.

Back in the kitchen, Sarah put the finishing touches to the shoulder of lamb, dispatched Jamie into the herb patch to pick some mint for Freya to chop finely before adding wine vinegar and sugar, and shelled the first of the broad beans picked from the greenhouse. Freya seized the chance to skin these: she knew the husk got between Grandma's teeth. With some irritation, Sarah noticed the time had jumped forward to 1.30 p.m., half an hour later than Matt had promised to be back by. Where was he? Having put the serving dishes onto the hostess trolley to keep hot (rarely used as it was such an awkward object to steer and was always in the way), Sarah forced herself to pour a Tio Pepe for her mother-in-law and a gin and tonic for herself.

'My dear Sarah, my favourite tipple; you really are a dear to remember. And I see you are still getting a lot of wear out of the hostess trolley Matthew's dear father and I bought for you one Christmas. They really are a godsend. I do miss my late husband so very much, my dear: a tower of strength. A strong marriage is so much a thing of beauty, one to be cherished, as you and Matthew know yourselves.'

'Particularly when the man-of-the-house is more entranced by a golf course on Easter Day than by his own family,' Sarah wished to have replied, but kept her counsel.

'Another, mother dear?' Sarah enquired, with a level of composure she didn't feel.

'I really shouldn't, dear, but you know, I don't drink at home so it's such a luxury, but I really would like just a top up. You don't feel like it when you live all on your own. It hasn't been the same, you know, since my Desmond passed away.'

A lace-edged voile handkerchief doused in lavender water was produced to dab each eye, gestures which were accompanied by indrawn breaths and sniffles. Fortunately, Jamie's complaint addressed to his grandmother that the terrible smell of old ladies ponging out the room was the one he hated when he spent any time in her bedroom, was drowned by the nose-blowing.

'I think I'll phone the golf club to see what's holding Matt up,' Sarah interrupted, refilling her mother-in-law's near-empty schooner as the grandfather clock in the hall chimed two o'clock.

'No, Mrs. Chilton, your husband hasn't signed in today. He may be in the bar, however, and failed to do so; he wouldn't be the first one. It's a new rule of the club. Please wait – or would you prefer to phone back?'

Heart beating wildly, Sarah confirmed she would hang on. Three minutes later, her feelings of foreboding were not assuaged.

'I'm very sorry, Mrs. Chilton. No member has seen him today. In fact I'm told he hasn't been seen for quite a few weeks. If he does appear, I'll tell him you called.'

Sarah returned to the sitting room, intending to serve

lunch without any further risk to the lamb and the vegetables being overheated and dry. In passing the sideboard, she noted the sherry bottle had even less in than when she had offered Eleanor her previous 'top up'. A sight she would have preferred not to see greeted her. Her mother-in-law, her head resting on Freya's shoulder, both sitting side-by-side on the sofa, with Jamie standing by her side, was convulsed with sobs.

'It's all about Grandma's teeth, Mummy,' explained Jamie, helpfully, he thought. 'She's upset because she has gaps in them. I told her that I'd heard on that Classic FM radio you have on in your car that you could have beautiful teeth any day for a tenner – that's £10, you know. I've heard a man say that he's felt so much better for going to this place that does it and he's sat in so many dentist's chairs over the years without any dentist being able to help him before. There's also a lady who says she's able to smile at her friends now she's had hers done. I just thought Grandma ought to know she could get help, too. I don't think she listens to Classic FM, so I thought it best to tell her what she could do to herself to make herself look better.'

Jamie realised that he had slipped up by not switching to 'white lie' mode. As for himself, he would listen to Classic FM all day if he could and particularly enjoyed the advertisements, most of which he knew off by heart even though he sometimes misheard them.

'You can see how upset she is that she's got such funny teeth, all odd and with spaces in between; she will not stop crying about it. I told her that she needn't give me her usual five pounds for my birthday and that it could be put towards the tenner. Maybe Freya could do the same and Grandma won't have to wait so long. Next time I hear the man talking about how he can smile at everybody now he's had his done, I'll write down the name of the dental surgeon. He is a very important man to be a surgeon.'

Eleanor sobbed, 'Telling me the gaps didn't look nice brought back that awful memory of when he asked me a few years ago why I was putting make-up on my face. I told him it was to make me look pretty.' Loud sniffs accompanied the lavender-soaked handkerchief dabbing her eyes. 'Do you remember what he said then? I shall never forget. "Why doesn't it then, Grandma?" was such a cruel thing to say. And by my own grandson, too.'

The telephone rang. Sarah, heart pounding at an even faster rate than before, left the scene of iniquity and, with trembling hands, picked up the phone.

'Darling, I'm so sorry. Steve and I are still slogging our way around the course. We were held up badly at the fifth by some new members who took their time at every hole but the way they messed their shots up should be reported. We're going to put in a complaint: quite unjustified behaviour. Steve wants to reduce his handicap so I can't let him down. Do carry on with lunch. I guess I'll be home around four. Keep the old girl amused for me, will you darling?'

Sarah did not respond. Tears choked her as she replaced the phone in its cradle and her legs sagged beneath her. 'Must just repair my make-up after cooking over the hob,' she managed to call out from the hall. Simultaneously, some twenty miles away, Matt, casting off a Holiday Inn dressing gown, eased the raven locks from his shoulder, sighed and smothered the languid body below him with a million kisses.

★

'Oh my God it was a hellish day for golf. April showers in March added to our delay. Did you get any here? Anyway, Steve is getting his handicap checked; thinks he's down to four now. I'm sorry you've never met Steve. Maybe you will one day but probably not, he's being transferred to a branch in the

Midlands. Banker, you know. What's up darling? You're not cross with me, are you?'

'Why on earth should you think that?' Sarah responded, with as much heavy sarcasm in her voice as she could muster. 'I just adore entertaining your mother.'

'My mistake, obviously; I am sorry. I thought you two women would be only too pleased to have a natter together – she really does miss my father such a lot. Must have her over more often. Should my ears have been burning while I toiled my way round the course?'

Matt's glib patter sickened Sarah to the core.

'I phoned the golf club, Matt, to get a message to you. The receptionist said he would not fail to catch you as you left.'

'Oh darling, darling, no wonder I detect a little frigidity in your tone. I forgot to tell you: we played at Steve's club.'

A glimmer of hope stirred in Sarah's breast. It was not to last long.

'Your mother is none too pleased with Jamie. I think she's recovered now but he really did upset her,' Sarah said with a tartness in her voice which did not go unnoticed by her husband. Under the prevailing circumstances, he determined to keep his counsel.

'You know how embarrassed she has been all her life about her badly spaced teeth? Well, Jamie knocked her for six by telling her about some advertisement he'd heard on Classic FM which offered teeth restructuring. Volunteered his birthday money for her to pay towards it. Didn't help that she'd polished off at least three schooners of Tio Pepe: not sure whether it was the shock of her grandson pointing out he'd noticed her misshapen teeth, or the unaccustomed alcohol,' adding dourly, 'a combination of both, probably'.

Matt, the memory of his infidelity still advising caution, somewhat distractedly assured Sarah that Eleanor had been very tetchy since losing Desmond and she shouldn't take it to heart that she would rise to the slightest bait. The old girl should have more of a sense of humour, certainly needed in Jamie's company otherwise you would go mad.

'Freya was the only one of us who could comfort her: she was marvellous and said all the right things to relieve the situation. Your mother seemed to think I'd put Jamie up to it.' Sarah rose to her theme. 'She said a child wouldn't notice such a thing and he must have overheard me commenting to you about it. To add insult to injury, she said she wasn't surprised you preferred the golf club to being at home with your family. All I can say, Matt, is I'm hurt and more than a little shattered. Now please go up and sort your mother out. She's resting on her bed.'

Sarah turned on her heel and went into the kitchen where Freya was filling the dishwasher, first having tucked up her sleeve the £5 note her grandmother had insisted on giving her, despite her mock resistance. Sarah kissed the back of her neck and turned to the hostess trolley, still switched on. She had the presence of mind to wrap the lamb in cling-film, resisting the temptation to hurl it into the waste bin, and to label the plastic bags she filled with the vegetables; these would form the basis of a mulligatawny soup for a lunch next week. Noting that Matt had left his golf clubs by the kitchen door, his golf shoes on the mat, Sarah picked the latter up and turned them over to inspect the soles. Not a speck of grass; not a trace of mud. Tears prickled at the back of her throat.

Matt's footsteps were behind her.

'Wonderful club, Steve's. Do you know, the caddie cleaned every bit of our equipment before we left. Even washed and blow-dried our shoes. I think the annual sub is a little higher than ours at The Heights but it's worth looking into. I wouldn't mind transferring myself there. I'll give the secretary a ring next week and enquire. Oh, by the way, Mum's asleep. Didn't want to wake her in view of what you'd said had happened.'

He paused, and looked quizzically at Sarah.

'What's up with you, darling? Has the day been too much for you?'

★

From that fateful Easter Day onwards Sarah was on high alert. Every phone call where the caller rang off without leaving a number, every late night covered by the same flimsy excuse of working to finish a deal, new Calvin Klein briefs appearing in his drawer, made her wince especially as he usually asked her to buy him some from M&S. Her mind was in torment. All she had to go on at the moment was her suspicions: she must not sacrifice her marriage and family stability to 'the green-eyed god' just for putting two and two together without ensuring these actually did make four.

'Too good an offer to miss: saw them in that Savile Row gentleman's outfitters I used to go to. You know what they say? Never miss a sales bargain if you see one,' Matt had explained away his seemingly rash purchase.

'Unless it's your wife who sees it,' Sarah had retorted. How she regretted the meagre lunches she had made for herself to ensure the money she paid for the 75% discount bargain was fully compensated. How cruel under the circumstances that Matt had gone through the roof at the very thought of her 'extravagance'. Why did she spend time calculating the piffling savings made if she bought a 400g box of blueberries for £4.50 rather than those on sale for two of 150g at £4? Now she guessed why.

'My darling, did you really take that rebuff seriously? I've always liked to pull your leg from time to time, you know that. Where's your sense of humour gone? Do you remember the April Fools we used to catch each other out with? Yours were always the cleverest. I know how sensible you are – if you want something for yourself, buy it. When the money's gone, it's gone.'

Chapter Nineteen

Unexpectedly, Mr. Holmes was declared fit for full duties when St. Michael's resumed for the summer term. Senior staff relinquished their temporarily upgraded posts, all but Gordon Bolton being relieved to do so.

Gordon had particularly relished the prestige Geoff Holmes' absence had afforded him, especially as the staff tended to refer to him rather than to Peter Danesfield, who preferred to spend his days filling in forms, checking the accounts, sending for quotations for window cleaners, mowing services, and other administrative duties, his aim being to demonstrate to his boss that savings could be made in every direction. Conversely, Gordon had spent his time patrolling corridors, overseeing cloakroom tidiness, ensuring litter-free playgrounds and, his favourite task of all, checking teacher lesson forecasts and reviews. He found it particularly galling that Geoff's return, with no restrictions being based upon his workload, deprived him of the reflected glory of a potentially extremely favourable OFSTED report: he knew he ran an extremely tight ship (despite his Service life being spent in the Army and not the Navy), and was looking forward to quoting the undoubtedly excellent sentiments which would be expressed by the inspectors. Gordon could envisage his CV now; my, how it would impress any interviewing panel for the positions of responsibility he intended to seek. Indeed, entirely responsible for the academic and behavioural management of a sizeable school, he could even be so bold as to put himself forward directly for a headship and omit the usual preparatory stage of deputising. Nothing ventured, nothing gained, would henceforth be his motto. Now such an illustrious opportunity to have the credentials to embark upon an early career in management was unlikely to be denied to him.

Widespread relief was felt by every staff member that the school would now return to normality. It had been a rather frenetic half-term with Gordon throwing his weight about, unnecessarily prying into their schemes of work. The rigour with which they covered every facet of the curriculum was carefully examined, the frequency with which miscreant members of their classes had been delegated to be on litter duty, were all excesses felt to be beyond the call of their duties. In contrast, quite a number of 'litter pickers' were extremely well disposed towards this means of delaying the start of their next session. Lucy Shadbolt's class, for example, were more than pleased to be chosen, quickly hitting on the idea to scatter litter strategically, but surreptitiously, in out-of-the-way corners in order to spin the task out even longer.

Even Charlie had come unstuck: Gordon had got wise to his pranks and was priding himself on reading between the lines. Jamie had at long last acquired the ability to question the wisdom of following Charlie's recommendations: the latter was no longer leader of the pack in the wily manner in which he knew how to place himself in the good books of the teachers. Certainly Jamie had not been informed that his name featured more frequently than that of any other pupil on the written records of children's behaviour. He had been immensely proud to think he held a prominent position in what he assumed to be an illustrious journal of good conduct, but somehow a number of Charlie's suggestions had not turned out to provide him, Jamie, with the promised accolades.

The first occasion Mr. Bolton had spotted a rat was when Charlie had brought in an advertisement for Virgin holidays, depicting a line of planes bearing the Branson logo queueing on the runway ready for takeoff. Mr. Bolton, Charlie had confided conspiratorially to Jamie, was going on a Virgin holiday this year and it would be a friendly act to show the picture to Mr. Bolton and warn him that he'd heard that four and twenty Virgins had set off from Inverness. 'That's in Scotland, you know,' Jamie interrupted, thinking it appropriate to inform his friend. 'But,' Charlie had continued, 'Mr. Bolton needs to know that at the end of the journey there were twenty-four Virgins less. That's a lot of planes crashing all at once. It could happen to one he was on, too, and that would be awful.'

The fact that he was about to quote a rowdy rugger song was unbeknown to him. Jamie had asked Charlie if he had any idea why these planes had crashed. He could not help agreeing that he thought it important that his teacher should find out before paying his money to the company.

It so happened that Charlie, not Jamie, was the one to incur the wrath of Mr. Bolton. Perhaps for the first time in his life Jamie remained unscathed; the prank misfired and, unusually, brought opprobrium on its perpetrator. Mr. Bolton was suspicious when Jamie, having found him alone in the classroom, had enquired if he could warn him of something he ought to know before parting with money for his holiday. With the mention of twenty-four Virgins based at Inverness – 'you know, Mr. Bolton, the aeroplanes' – he had stopped Jamie in mid-flight to enquire whether Charlie had been telling him that he was taking his family on a Virgin holiday. At the reply in the affirmative, Gordon strode out of the room to find a sheepish Charlie endeavouring to make a getaway. Charlie's presence in the classroom that afternoon was conspicuous by its absence. Not a piece of litter was in sight that day ... or for a number of days to come, much to the chagrin of Miss Shadbolt's class.

The impending OFSTED inspection filled all with foreboding, all members of staff that is, with the exception of Gordon. Class teachers grudgingly gave thanks to Gordon for his scrupulous reviews of their lesson material and implemented his suggestions. A full staff meeting debated the wisdom of sending Jamie home sick on the morning of the inspectors' arrival: the prospect of Jamie letting the cat out of the bag that the lessons they observed had already had several trial runs did not bear thinking about. Such an innocent confession would clearly wipe out any positive effect of Jamie being noted by them as a pupil unsuitable for mainstream education and an opening for him thus rapidly found in a special school for emotionally and disturbed children.

Mary Ackroyd resolved the dilemma in a most satisfactory manner by recommending that the Schools Psychological Service be asked to assess Jamie on day one of the visit. That would keep him out of the way and under the supervision of the educational psychologist, an action which would, in any case, show St. Michael's made full use of ancillary services. With any degree of luck he could be sent off the very next day for any other assessment the psychologist could suggest: optometric, speech and language, etc., perhaps? In any residual time in school he could be parcelled off to a class which had already been inspected. Things were looking up! Mr. Holmes relaxed: he had his school in good order and had cause to be grateful to his senior staff.

Matters were also rosier for Father Harrold. The proposed planned meeting with the Chiltons had, inexorably, been cancelled as Mr. Chilton was required to spend more time overnight attending various executive meetings and writing reports so that he was hardly ever at home, even at weekends. A jaunty spring was seen in Percy's step: surprisingly to the teachers, but not to Sarah, Mr. Chilton had accepted that matters should take their course. Popping more of Dr. Allinson's pills than Dr. Allinson had recommended, Sarah felt she had a little more room to manoeuvre.

Of great surprise to her, Lucy Shadbolt had been put forward, all expenses paid, by the St. Michael's Contingency Fund, for a three-day course, 'First Aid in Schools', for which purpose she was unable to fathom as Faith Griffin's responsibility was health and safety. Nonetheless, she was very pleased to have been selected, quite a feather in her cap, especially as Mr. Holmes was loathe to spend money rashly on continuing professional development. Little did she know that this was the only course running at the local Teachers' Centre that week; she could have been 'a suitable candidate' for almost any topic. St. Michael's would even have found a solid reason for signing her up for a football course had that been the only one on offer: after all, should both the male members of staff be indisposed at the same time, who would be able to act as substitute for coaching and arranging the fixtures in their absence? Miss Amelia Craddock, the most able relief-teacher during Mr. Holmes' absence, was re-engaged to cover for Lucy.

Preparations reached fever pitch. Classroom walls and corridors were awash with specially commissioned artwork, essays, reports of experiments, all triple-mounted. Children noticing the names of pupils who had long since transferred to senior schools were told that displaying such work reflected St. Michael's over the past four years and it was perfectly legitimate for their contributions to grace the walls. Children were drilled in manners, suitable questions practised and classroom debates rehearsed. Subtle threats were made of dire consequences if any pupil deviated from the set-pieces or, horror of horrors, gave any indication whatsoever that the lesson being inspected had been presented on previous occasions.

★

The dreaded day dawned. The three inspectors purred their way through a show assembly, taken by Year 5. A rendering by the school orchestra of "Food, Glorious Food" preceded a short excerpt from the Oliver Twist musical in which Oliver asks for more. Prayers were offered, all written by the pupils, exhorting Our Lord and Father to provide food for all the world's children, to give us strength to use our talents and available resources to cultivate the land and that others who have plenty, should freely give to those who have little. A resounding success, thought Mr. Holmes.

As the headmaster made his way to the improvised stage to pay his compliments to the performers, Mrs. Lawson came in with a message for him which he relayed in front of the assembled children:

'Jamie Chilton, your mother and a visitor to see you, are waiting in the medical room.'

"Amazing Grace" was then sung lustily, Jamie's treble enhancing the somewhat unmelodious voices around him. Grace Brooks from Class 3 looked stonily ahead in embarrassment as she knew full well what to expect at playtime: horrible teasing from those nasty boys in Class 5. She wished she had known in advance *that* embarrassing hymn was to be sung; she would have simulated a contagious illness to the extent that her mother would have kept her at home and the derision she knew was going to come at her from all sides when the children were released from class would be avoided.

Mr. Bolton moved along the line and prodded Jamie in the back, hissing, 'Why haven't you done as you're told?' A baffled Jamie remained in position, and an equally puzzled Mr. Bolton withdrew, the inspector's gaze being upon him. Row by row, class by class, the children filed out to the strains of "Oliver, Oliver". Mrs. Lawson, waiting by the door, grabbed Jamie as he passed through. Just behind her was a stranger, smiling down at him.

'Ah, Jamie. I have been looking forward to spending the morning with you. I thought you'd never come!'

Jamie assured Dr. Holroyd, for that was the educational psychologist's name, that he could not leave the Hall until his class was signalled but thought it was nice of Mr. Holmes to tell the school that his mother and a visitor were there; he had not been aware he was expected to join them at that point as Mr. Holmes hadn't asked him to.

Dr. Holroyd explained that it was obviously a poor message he'd been given but that didn't matter: there was plenty of time still for all the puzzles they were going to work through together. He explained that Mr. Bolton knew that he would be absent from lessons that morning, he'd already had a chat with his mother while waiting for him and he and Jamie would now spend some time together talking and doing special things.

'We shall play some games together which I've brought for you. You will have great fun, I'm sure, and I expect you'll enjoy these better than what you would have been doing in class.'

'Ooh, cool!', said Jamie, 'I'm very good at chess. I'm better at that than I am at playing draughts but I don't mind playing either. How long are you staying?' adding doubtfully, 'We might not have time to finish a game of chess, though.'

'The games I've brought are a little different from what you have at home and are used to but I'm sure you will enjoy them,' replied Dr. Holroyd. 'I shall teach you how to play them.'

Feeling reassured by Dr. Holroyd's remarks that he, alone, had been specially chosen from all the children in the school to take part in the activities that this nice man had brought with him, Jamie confirmed that he would be delighted to take part in any game whatever.

The session proceeded without a hitch, Jamie cooperating with all he was asked to do. 'I'm really enjoying this; it would be really cool if you'd come every day with special things for me.' Jamie had recently learned that you said 'cool' when you were pleased about something; it did not have anything to do with what temperature your body or the room was and it now featured prominently in any of his conversations.

Dr. Holroyd gave Jamie lots of puzzles to work through, fun questions to answer, Mastermind-type questions to think about and checked how well he could remember things. There were pictures to look at and comment upon and illustrations where he had to match the sentence to the picture. It was lunchtime when Dr. Holroyd began to pack up his case of special games and make his farewells.

'Well, Jamie, I'm so pleased Mr. Holmes chose you to spend the morning with me. I have enjoyed it tremendously. You are quite a mine of information and you have such terrific ideas. You're going to go far, young man, and I am looking forward to telling your parents what a great morning we've had together.'

'I'd better practise my running then 'cos I'm not all that good at that,' Jamie interjected, honesty shining out of his eyes. 'I will be able to go a long way then.'

Jamie glowed with pride. He hadn't spent such a satisfying morning ever, he thought. Mr. Holmes then came into the room and told him he was to spend the rest of the day with Class 2: they needed him to help them with their work. The inspectors were with his class during the afternoon as well as the morning and Jamie's desk was needed for them to use to make their notes. School was really improving, Jamie reflected happily: being especially selected for a private lesson and now promoted to some sort of teacher-assistant for the afternoon was awesome. 'Awesome' was a word Freya always used when things were perfect and it seemed just the right word for how his day was going.

As he made his way to Class 2 after lunch, Jamie passed the

inspectors going into his proper classroom. Jamie hurried to open the door for them.

'This is my classroom normally. I do hope you like my desk. That's mine you're going to sit at to write your notes and, to make room for you, I am going to help Year 2 children. I'm looking forward to doing that.' Then, to the discomfiture of two of the team, he exclaimed in some consternation, 'Ooh, I hope you can get your legs under it,' a remark addressed to a gentleman of a rather generous stature and, to the only woman, he expressed the wish that there would be enough room for her tummy.

'It will be a bit of a squash, I think. Perhaps you could swap mine for Mr. Bolton's chair. If you ask him nicely, he'll probably let you but do be careful: he can use quite a cross voice.'

★

Dr. Holroyd made an appointment to meet with the Chiltons at his office on the Friday afternoon following his assessment of Jamie three days earlier. Matt had given Sarah his assurance that whatever his company had planned for him that day would be jettisoned and the two duly presented themselves at the Child and Young Persons' Office in Greysbury as requested. Sarah was sure she felt more nervous than she had ever done in her life before. Matt was in a belligerent mood.

'So this quack thinks he can tell us all about our son, having only met him for three hours, and feels he knows him better than we do after spending more than nine troublesome years with him. In all likelihood he is straight out of his university and trying out his skills on others. Well, I shall be more than a match for him.'

Sarah kept her counsel. What was the point in engaging in argument with a closed mind?

Dr. Holroyd was a little older than Matt had anticipated, probably mid / late forties. Coffee and biscuits were already there on a side table and not even Matt, who abhorred slovenliness in any shape or form, could find fault with the orderly stacks of files, serried ranks of uncracked coffee mugs and a clutter-free desk. He was all smiles as he drew three armchairs around his coffee table, placed a pile of papers in front of him and opened the discussion with pleasantries about the 'great morning' he had spent with their son and what a delightfully intriguing child he was. 'You must be very proud: he is a credit to you!' Sarah noticed Matt's jaw tightened a little and put in a contribution before her husband could sour the discussion.

'Jamie is great fun at home. We never cease to be surprised by his quite insightful remarks sometimes. Sadly, these do not always go down so well in other situations, school especially, and I, for one, feel a dreadful sense of disappointment that he is hardly ever invited to parties or other children's houses. He sometimes asks why he can't go as his friends will be there. Jamie calls the children sitting near him "his friends" but mostly they ignore him or make jokes about him which he doesn't realise ...'

At this point, Matt interjected, glowering at his wife and cutting Sarah off in mid-sentence.

'Well shall we cut the crap and get to the point? My time is limited. In my mind, there are two ways of bringing up children,' Matt interrupted – contemptuously, Nigel Holroyd thought. 'One is more authoritarian, the other more laissez-faire. Without being too much of a disciplinarian, I have no doubt in my mind whatsoever that a newborn child is, quite simply, a formative creature, merely a piece of plain paper at birth and it is the parental role to write the guidelines for the child to follow. To allow the child to dictate the path he is to follow is to damage the child irrevocably, what I call a recipe for disaster.'

Listening very carefully, an encouraging smile spread across Dr. Holroyd's lips. Sarah's heart sank. Was there to be collusion between these two males. A brother-bonding? Matt continued.

'Now, I feel this meeting is a vehicle for me to express my feelings about the rather wayward behaviour of my son. In reality, there has been just one parent responsible for Jamie's upbringing. As the only breadwinner in the family since his birth, and the recession hitting all salary-earners so hard, I have rarely been at home during the hours in which I could have had contact with my son. I believe I now have no option but to say, between these four walls – and I understand this discussion is completely confidential (correct me if I have been misinformed) – that I am convinced Jamie's behaviour which, to people other than my wife, is weird, insolent and sometimes downright rude, is due to her lack of guidance, even to the point of collusion with the boy's misdemeanours.'

Dr. Holroyd purposefully took a long draught from his coffee mug, enabling Matt to continue unabated. Sarah was well aware that any form of counsellor, marriage therapist, psychologist, psychiatrist, was trained to listen to the client most carefully. Well she remembered in the early days of exploring how her professional life was to evolve, she had spent a day in a child guidance clinic and had found the experience quite uncomfortable: the psychotherapists asked open-ended questions and left her to expand, so much so that she had found herself explaining herself in the most confessional ways, filling silences out of sheer inability to prevent such one-sided scrutiny.

Matt expanded on his crucifixion of Sarah who was listening to the cruel outpourings in stunned silence. Let Matt reveal his vindictive feelings to a professional: if his opinion was condoned by this experienced man, then she would not be able to withstand future criticisms of her child-management style. With a sinking heart, Matt's words ringing harshly in her ears, she knew she would never be able to discipline their son in the severely strict manner Matt advocated.

'She has allowed Jamie's behaviour to become out-of-hand, disrespectful and quite egocentric. I'm sorry, Sarah, but this has to stop … and maybe Dr. Holroyd will be able to recommend some parenting classes you could attend, unless he feels it is now too late.'

'Mr. Chilton, I have every respect for your views. Every respect. But I do hope sincerely that as a result of my analysis of the findings of the morning spent with Jamie, which I feel is now the appropriate time to explain to you, both of you will more easily understand Jamie and the very real person he is. May I give you a refill?'

Sarah moved her mug forward. Matt covered his with his hand.

'As with all individuals, he has undoubted qualities and it is my very pleasant task to help all three of you, and Jamie's sister as well, to understand him and how he can be enabled to use the most creditable skills he has to help him overcome the differences which, in this society, tend to set him apart from others. I would like you to listen most carefully to what I'm about to explain to you about Jamie. Do stop me any time, but it would be best if questions are kept to the end. Most especially, I sincerely hope to be able to allay any suspicion that either of you holds of each other in respect of poor parental management.

'Indeed,' he added, after a pause to give Matt time to settle back in his chair after his impassioned condemnation of his wife and looking warmly at Sarah, 'It is possible that Mrs. Chilton could well say that she has felt she could have received more support from a male authority figure over the years.'

Dr. Holroyd's length of experience had given him the

determination to 'even things up' between married couples as far as possible, thus deflecting any danger of the session deteriorating into a slanging match. An already shattered Sarah, shaken by her husband's poisonous tirade, did her utmost not to show the wave of relief and gratitude flooding over her and withheld any response.

Sarah and Matt were then shown a graph plotting Jamie's 'intellectual profile', Dr. Holroyd stating that it was important to demonstrate firstly what 'thinking tools' Jamie had been endowed with. He explained the nature of each of the points on a graph which he displayed in front of them.

'It's a little like looking at the Alps, isn't it? Few people are evenly developed in every skill that is measured but the differences between Jamie's "highs" and "lows" are far greater than expected, and I will now explain why this is occurring. Firstly,' Dr. Holroyd's finger pointed to three scores plotted near the topmost points of the vertical axis, 'I want you to note how extremely high his personal strengths are.'

Matt interrupted. 'We are perfectly aware that our son has a high intellect. It is his behaviour everyone is concerned about. That is what you have been engaged to address.'

Choosing not to respond to this further example of the testiness of the father whilst at the same time being determined not to let this client dominate the meeting, Dr. Holroyd expanded on the feedback he was giving to enable the parents to have a clearer understanding of the nature of their son's problems which had a cause beyond Jamie's control.

'All in good time. It is essential first to establish quite how highly intelligent Jamie is as that gives us a yardstick by which we can expect him to perform in social situations. Next, because I have had the benefit of working very closely with Jamie for three hours and have the additional input of the school's concerns over the years and the information you kindly provided me with, not to mention the additional input of my experience over the years working with children with similar "behaviours" to those of Jamie, I'm able to make a judgment. Thus, I can give my opinion that Jamie experiences a great deal of difficulty in understanding that many words and phrases have several – indeed, sometimes many – different meanings according to the situation to which they refer. Individuals like Jamie tend to take language literally: the words they hear mean precisely what they first learned them to mean. Such children are not aware there could be a different interpretation.'

Matt shifted in his seat. Just because this child expert had a string of initials after his name, what right had he got to lecture him on how his son learned? How did more than nine years of living with him compare with three hours and a bag of information which was probably skewed anyway?

'Let me remind you how we all learn to communicate by making sounds which other people understand. Every human, indeed, every animal I believe, does this. You see, a newborn baby has to learn precisely what every sound means: you will remember how your baby would jump (this reaction is called a "startle reflex"), at everyday household sounds such as the telephone, the vacuum cleaner, a banging door. Steadily the baby learns what these noises relate to and no longer shows fear when these sounds occur.'

Matt looked at his watch obtrusively. With indrawn breath, fidgeting in the violence of his irritation, he had every intention of confirming his frustration with the way the meeting was going and how he utterly disliked being 'lectured' to. What the fuck had the habits of newborn babies got to do with what they had come to hear? Sarah noticed his epiglottis constricting, something of which she was conscious of happening when his blood pressure was rising.

'It is the same with voices: each parent, sibling, familiar adult has distinctive features and vocal tones but unfamiliar voices might cause concern until the baby builds up a steadily increasing awareness of the different meanings of tonal quality, to the extent that sooner or later they recognise nuances in speech, what represents anger, joyfulness, sadness, etc.'

Matt's rising irritation was beginning to come to boiling point. What did this idiot think? That he needed a Dr. Spock baby-class lesson? He gripped the arms of the chair as if to bring the meeting to an end.

'Bear with me, Mr. Chilton,' (Dr. Holroyd usually encouraged parents to be on Christian name terms with each other from the start but had wisely summed up the situation as being one in which such familiarity would get the meeting off on even poorer terms than the downhill direction they were now taking), 'it is so important to set the scene, just as you did earlier yourself in describing the different parental management styles which affect a child right from birth.'

Looking daggers at Dr. Holroyd, Matt resisted the urge to leave the room, simultaneously throwing a look across at Sarah which said, 'You've set me up in this, haven't you?'

Dr. Holroyd continued his theme.

'Now the greater majority of babies and infants acquire this discriminatory ability quite naturally; there is a span, or interval if you like, of time in which this is expected to happen. But some individual babies take considerably longer to do so: their anxieties continue to show when noises or sounds that their peers accept happily still seem to be intrusive to them. These children do not recognise the more subtle sounds, either, even long after they have learned not to be disturbed by noises now taken for granted by children even younger than themselves. Neural connections are not formed as is naturally expected.

'Is this making sense to you?'

Matt stared out of the window, tapping his fingers on his knees in frustration. Sarah nodded slowly.

'Take this notion a stage further; in fact, let's leap ahead.'

'Not before time!' interjected Matt, tersely.

'Language itself has patterns. We have to learn when, how and where to say certain things. As examples, telling your mummy you think she looks funny in that hat and it doesn't suit her can be helpful. Telling the next-door neighbour or your grandmother the same thing is considered cheeky. At four or five years of age, this is not so outrageous as it would be at eight or nine, when it is downright rude. Children usually pick up these subtleties quite quickly; a few do not.'

'Now I am strongly of the opinion that Jamie is one of the children who have this kind of difficulty with the multiple meanings of language and, like the examples I have just given you, is unaware that statements made in one setting are acceptable, whereas in another can be regarded as pure insolence.' He paused, looking from one to another. 'Do you feel this is anything like how your son appreciates the world around him?'

'Perfectly possible,' Matt retorted angrily, almost choking on his words. 'If you were to analyse why there are certain children who make outspoken remarks, I fully expect you to have evidence that parental management is 100% at fault. Perhaps you could do another doctorate on that question. In our case, I hold the view that he has been allowed to go his own way and his mother has even encouraged it.'

Sarah looked askance. Dr. Holroyd let the slight on his professionalism pass. He saw no point in letting him know that his specialism, in fact, and the subject of his doctoral thesis, was an aspect of autistic spectrum disorder. He poured more coffee from the thermos into Sarah's and his own mug. Matt's was untouched and he shook his head violently when invited to have his 'freshened up.'

'And what occurs, in your mind,' Matt cuttingly enquired, 'as my theories are clearly disparaged by you, to cause such children to have this problem?'

'In most individuals whose intellectual profiles are so erratic, changes like this occur because of something like birth trauma, pre-or post-natal injury or illness, particularly if there has been a very high temperature, or, indeed, any other "insult" to the brain which science has not yet identified.' He paused. 'Or maybe genetic influence, making the newborn predisposed to a particular condition encountered by his ancestors.'

Dr. Holroyd gave time for an intervention; none came and he continued:

'Now you're also aware from the discussions you have had with Jamie's teachers over the years that he tends to be what can be called the "fall guy" in schools. Sometimes he gains kudos from his class by being, as they believe him to be, the class jester, the one who will happily risk censure by sticking up two fingers against authority figures. I have noted the school records, which I know you are acquainted with, of singing rather vulgar words to familiar songs (not, I hasten to add, that Jamie had any understanding that these words would create mayhem), and has implemented the roguish suggestions of his friends. He has believed his pseudo-friends' advice that he will incur favour by so doing.'

'Do you mean the safety pin incident?' meekly enquired Sarah, bottom lip quivering. Dr. Holroyd nodded in acquiescence. Matt was staring fixedly out of the window, giving Dr. Holroyd the opportunity to edge the Kleenex box in Sarah's direction.

'So now,' concluded Dr. Holroyd, 'the million-dollar question is: how do we help Jamie to cram six or seven years' worth of acquiring what he sees as "peculiarities of language" into the shortest time possible. The starting point, the most important stage of all, is for all who have the pleasure of living and working alongside your delightful and charming son, to understand that in no way whatsoever is Jamie intending to be rude, insolent, eccentric or anything other than the child, Mrs. Chilton, you see him as: extremely clever, a little naïve, one desperate for friends but, as are all other children like Jamie, one lacking in the social and speech skills to make and maintain friendships.'

'And the billion-dollar question for me, Dr. Holroyd, if it is not, "in your opinion", maternal pussy-footing around her dear little boy whose daddy is so hard on him, is what *is* the underlying cause in our son's case? You quoted birth injury – none; you can look through his health records if you wish. Childhood accident? He fell off a swing long after he had shown up as a scaredy-pants in school and a cheeky one at that. Well, there's only one cause left. Genetic, huh! My father was a scientist, I am an advertising executive, Sarah has been a deputy head. That's Jamie's pedigree. I could go deeper into the ancestral line if you so wish.'

Dr. Holroyd realised that he still had to tread very delicately, in fact, even more so.

'There are a number of other cogent reasons, Mr. Chilton. As I implied earlier, neuroscientists are making great strides with P.E.T.* scans, gene research and in steadily unravelling the mysteries of DNA. Genetically, such "communication difficulties", as they are often called, are passed down the generations in quite an erratic manner. If you have no relatives with similar problems, such as aunts, uncles, cousins, grandparents, either of you, then a genetic cause can be excluded. But I always advise parents that the cause of any difficulties or weaknesses is not relevant; what the most important factor is, is moving from the here and now of a "diagnosis", for want of a better word, to what can be done to use their child's strengths to outweigh weaknesses. And that is what we are about to consider right now.'

---

*   P.E.T. = Positron Emission Tomography.

During this last exposition the colour drained from Matt's face. He slumped back in his chair, his eyes closed. Images came thick and fast, tumbling into each other as if he was hallucinating. Visions of Max, his nephew whose vapid mother fawned all over him. Visions of his aunt, his father's sister, whom Sarah visited but without the support of Matt's companionship. The spectre of his crazy-inventor great uncle, his grandfather's brother, who had been unable to obtain work as he was so unpredictable and erratic, had never married, lived for many years with increasingly aged parents until their death. His sole means of a livelihood was by inventing incredulous Heath Robinson-type machinery which never lived up to the impressive predictions he had of their powers of transforming people's lives and came to nothing. When his parents eventually passed on to the life hereafter, he had depended entirely on the charity of siblings as if it was his right, even writing to the one who voluntarily took most responsibility for his impecunious younger brother's welfare that payment was rather later than he had expected and insufficient for the purpose he had intended.

The office clock thundered out the minutes, the second hand crashing through the pregnant silence.

In scarcely a minute, Matt's hands dropped from sheltering his eyes. He stumbled up towards the door and through it, casting a muttered comment as he passed the psychologist,

'I will demand to see your professional credentials before I accept a word of this slanderous inference you are making.'

Sarah, appalled, sat frozen to her seat. Dr. Holroyd, despite his experience, misreading the force of the vengeful reaction which he should have predicted from Matt's demeanour throughout, cursed himself for extending the possibility of a wider family influence. In an instant he also realised the professional crime he had just committed: not de-steaming a painful situation before a meeting's closure; never letting a client leave a session in a distressed state. An experienced counsellor, he felt extreme irritation with himself that he had allowed his compassion for this downtrodden wife to distract him from keeping away from any attribution of what a client could call 'blame'. Why had he fed the notion into her husband's head which, from his immediate demeanour, indicated that perhaps he, the father, was the genetic carrier? His heart felt heavy. Dr. Holroyd pressed the buzzer for his secretary who, alarmed by the excessively loud voice and the banging of the door by her boss's client, was already hovering in the wings. He slipped a hastily scribbled note into her hand.

'I'm calling a taxi for you. The taxi rank is just outside this office, Mrs. Chilton, and our secretary will accompany you to ensure you are not too shaken up when you arrive home. She will make a cup of tea for you first, or would you prefer another coffee? There is still so much to discuss but you will not be able to take this in after the negative effect our meeting has had on your husband. I will be writing to you to reconvene.'

Handing Sarah another couple of tissues, 'Here, take the box,' he escorted the two women from his office and towards the taxi rank, Sarah having refused a further coffee. A taxi was already pulling out.

'I can't thank you enough, Dr. Holroyd,' Sarah choked, doing her utmost to quell another bout of weeping. 'It is so much of a relief to know Jamie is not bad, not disobedient. I knew in my bones he wasn't and I can even cope with Matt criticising me all the time now I know Jamie has been born with a horrid condition he can't help. I will do all I can to follow your advice. Can we meet again soon?'

'The taxi fare has been settled. Look after your husband. I think he has had a terrible shock – maybe you're aware what has hit him so hard. If I can be of any more professional help to either or both of you, do please ring my secretary.'

Dr. Holroyd pressed his card into Sarah's hand. He turned and walked humbly back to his office, his professional pride temporarily in tatters. An awful ending to what should have been, to this highly experienced and sought-after psychologist, a normal day.

If there had been one in Jamie's garden, the effects of Jamie's idiosyncratic behaviour would have made yet another notch on the totem pole.

★

Matt's cracked voice on the phone.

'Sarah, I'm sorry. I can't get my head around this. I need to think, to be on my own. I've checked in at the Marriott. I'll call you tomorrow.'

'Matt, is it about Max?'

The phone was already dead.

Grotesque scalps on a totem pole.

More ripples spreading far and wide in a pond.

★

The next day, the call came in the early evening. Hating herself for her suspicions, Sarah let it ring. As the trilling died down, she dialled 1471.

'You were called at 1831 hours. Telephone number 01496 064414.'

With trembling hands, so much so that she needed to redial, Sarah felt so faint, she hardly heard the reply, 'Chandersfoot Hotel, Andrew speaking. May I help you?'

'I'm so sorry. Wrong number. Silly of me.'

Freya burst through the front door, flinging her coat on the chair.

339

'Mummy, guess what? I got a credit in my 'cello exam.'

She paused in mid-track.

'Mummy, you look awful. Are you all right? Oh, you're not all right. Oh my God, whatever is the matter?'

With her hand to her mouth, Sarah rushed into the downstairs loo, locked the door and sank onto the closed lid, her head in her hands.

'Mummy, can I help? A glass of water? Are you being sick? Answer me. Please!'

Not getting any answer, Freya made her own decision.

'Don't worry, I'll get the supper. Jamie, Jamie, come and help me with some beans on toast. Mummy's being sick.'

★

9:30 p.m: With the children in bed, kissed by a subdued Sarah who said they were not to worry, she was fine. Something she'd evidently eaten which had made her quite nauseous. She would be back to normal in the morning and what terrific news about the music exam.

'All that practice paid off. Clever girl!'

A plaintive, sleepy voice from Jamie's bedroom: 'Mummy, when Daddy comes in, please ask him to give me his usual kiss. He does it on my forehead. Please, Mummy; don't forget.'

9:40 p.m: Telephone. A very weary voice.

'Darling, I'm so dreadfully sorry but I find this whole thing extremely difficult to take. Incredibly difficult to understand, in fact, and I can't get my mind around it. Work is just piling up at the moment and it's hard to focus with this fresh millstone round my neck.'

Sarah, with all the feigned sympathy she could muster when her heart felt like lead, assured her husband that she would never bear any grudge that Matt had put the blame on her shoulders.

'Matt, my darling, we'll get through this together, I promise. It is so plain to me now where Jamie is coming from. It's like a blind has been pulled from my eyes. Poor, poor Jamie, that he has been struggling all this time without anyone understanding. Oh, Matt, I just want to hold you to me. We mean so much to each other, and always will.'

A pregnant pause on the end of the line. With dawning realisation that the very worst of her suspicions were coming to fruition, Sarah clutched the phone to her breast, swaying as she awaited the response.

'Oh, Sarah, I clean forgot to tell you, with that ridiculous meeting going as it did, that I had to go to Leicester tonight. Phoned you earlier but you didn't pick up. Will be here 'til Friday. You can get me on my mobile any time but not, please, during working hours: it's too distracting when I'm in the middle of a meeting. See you at the weekend and we can discuss plans. Sorry I left that maniac's office so quickly but I couldn't take any more of his ramblings and knew I had to get on the road before the motorway got jammed with rush-hour traffic. Are you all right?'

No answer.

'Good night, then; kisses to the kids.'

Matt's voice had sounded strangulated. Why hadn't he used his mobile earlier instead of giving the game away by phoning from the hotel he was in? She also knew, because he had told her this trick a long time ago, that he could have put in a code before dialling the number so that his call could not be traced back. Why didn't he cover his tracks?

Little did Sarah know, although the hideous suspicions were growing in her mind as to the nature of Matt's 'pressure of work', that the earlier phone call which she had purposefully allowed to go unanswered, had been made in high dudgeon by a raven-tressed young woman who had shrilly announced to her half-clothed companion,

'If you won't tell her, I will.' With that she popped a pill in her mouth, reaching over to the bedside table to replace the packet in the side-drawer.

'Honey, what do you need those for, you silly woman. You know I've had a vasectomy so there's absolutely no danger of you getting pregnant.'

'Better be safe than sorry is a maxim I live under. Never can be too careful. I'll keep them up, anyway, until I know you're going to marry me because if you're not, then I can claim freedom immediately, without any risk.'

Tossing her hair she deftly resumed the sensuous undressing of her lover.

★

Upstairs in the Chilton house, itself as shiveringly dismal as a morgue, a nightdress-clad child moved from the banisters and crept silently back into still-warm bed. With a wisdom borne of dawning adolescence, Freya was only too aware of the implication of that phone call. Heavy-hearted, her head sank into the welcoming pillow, soon to become sodden with the tears that welled from eyes which had witnessed the sadness of friends whose families had already been torn apart by marital disharmony. Was she now to join their ranks?

Chapter Twenty

The inspection had gone as well as could be expected. Staff had nothing but inward praise for Gordon's prior appraisals of their record-keeping which had been examined so scrupulously by the OFSTED team. One by one, a number of his detractors grudgingly told him so. It was not long, however, before the few words of thanks for his zealous preparations stuck in their throats when, on overhearing their unguarded praise of his tactics, Mr. Holmes made this a permanent routine.

Mr. Holmes took Gordon into his confidence and assured him that he would look most favourably upon him as a replacement for Peter Danesfield who was expected to retire to his bolt-hole in Cornwall in a year or two's time.

'It would be with reluctance that I would provide you with an excellent reference should you choose to apply elsewhere in the immediate future,' he had added, 'but of course, it would be good for you to get interview practice.' A shrewd warning that he should be prepared for rejection at his first attempts.

Lucy Shadbolt lost no time on her return in inadvertently getting up Faith Griffin's nose by giving her details of the latest methods of dealing with insect bites and stings, burns, sudden collapse, etc. When she added insult to injury by catching her one lunchtime and asking whether Faith knew the difference between hypo- or hyper-diabetic collapse, she was smartly told that she, Lucy, could have her job if she wanted it and perhaps she would like to suggest this to Mr. Holmes? Sensitive Lucy realised all too well she had been treading on eggshells and had over-stepped the mark, but the apology for her temerity in passing on the contents of her three-day course fell on deaf ears: the damage had been done. Even thick-skinned Faith herself privately questioned whether the real reason for the ruse in getting Lucy out of school while the OFSTED inspection was being conducted was not to avoid exposing a weak teacher to scrutiny but to gradually depose her from her position as health and safety officer.

Prior knowledge of the inspection had enabled Mary Ackroyd to benefit from attending weekend courses on a variety of special needs subjects during the previous three months (all-expenses-paid-from-the-school's-S.E.N.*-budget), and she had been an avid purchaser and subsequent reader of textbooks recommended by the lecturers. This had paid off handsomely. Her insightful reports on children on Action Plan had received commendation: two inspectors had watched a group lesson of hers where she was teaching spelling patterns to children diagnosed with dyslexia. She was extremely gratified that they were most interested to hear her views of the behavioural problems of the boy who was being assessed by the educational psychologist that morning. Mary very cleverly explained that his remark to them about repetition of lessons was due to the fact that this pupil was always given a personally tailored preview of the lesson content in the humanities; much would otherwise go over his head, despite his high intelligence. Later the class lesson would be followed up by reinforcement given to him and two other differently learning-challenged children who were considered to be slower or easily distracted learners. The explanation seemed to satisfy the inspector who had raised the point to a somewhat startled meeting with senior management during a post-inspection discussion. Although Mary felt her defence was no less than shameful, she had felt it her sacrificial duty to protect the staff from Jamie Chilton's unwitting faux

---

*   S.E.N. = Special Educational Needs

pas. After all, it was not her intention that the inspectors should generalise her remarks from the particular to which they actually referred, was it?

Faith Griffin had been delighted that the only epileptic child in the school (and by pure good fortune, a pupil in her class) had obliged her by having a mild attack in the presence of the senior inspector. She had been escorting the class around the school field on a pre-prepared nature walk that early-summer morning and the dappled sunshine filtering through the unfolding leaves of the line of ash trees brought on a photophobic seizure. Faith ministered to the stricken child, then hastened to assure the inspector she was always prepared for any eventuality. 'The swift and deft attention to the pupil by the Year 1 teacher and her teacher assistant who calmed the class, continuing to draw the children's attention to snail trails, lacy, dew-covered spider webs and evidence of nesting birds, was most laudable', and a highlight of the section of the report on pastoral care.

One inspector, however, was rather sceptical about whether children's mounted work displayed on the corridors and in the Hall was entirely representative of present pupils. She had overheard a Year 6 pupil pointing out pictures to another boy, claiming them to be drawn and painted by his brother and his friend. 'Luke's getting A's in art at Hemingway Boys' Grammar' (to which around 20% of St. Michael's' boys transferred following 11+ examinations) 'and is going to go to art college.' Sucking in her cheeks and raising her eyebrows, she had passed by the unwitting and innocent tale-tellers without comment – at that moment at least; Mr. Holmes had a little explaining to do some time later. A general overview on the critical side implied that the staff in general exuded an air of complacency which should be addressed in the next year. Was this a dig provoked by the lady inspector's inference that displays on walls had a rather 'tired' look?

The state of cleanliness of the school was highly graded, for which the caretaker also had to swallow his pride and offer grateful thanks to Gordon Bolton. His previously notoriously slack care of the premises, despite the all-pervasive smell of disinfectant, soon attracted the eagle eyes of the acting deputy, only to be too glad of the much yearned for opportunity to direct him to areas which had not been approached by a duster or a broom for many moons.

Peter Danesfield did not receive a personal mention but believed honours to be due to him when the financial state and budgetary management was graded as 'good'.

All in all, St. Michael's was able to sit back fairly comfortably, resume their more perfunctory attention to specified routines and hope that their next turn to be inspected would not be the horrendous event that all teachers now predicted: the minister of education, horror of horrors, had announced that schools would no longer be given the date in advance, leaving no time for 'spring-cleaning' and other frills of presentation. 'That'll be a recipe for disaster,' Faith predicted, 'with not a few staff absences from stress.' She had always wondered why inspections had been given so much forewarning for so many years, leaving it rife for sabotage and fabrication. Were OFSTED inspectors quite so gullible? She knew one school which you wouldn't send a dead cat to which was given a favourable review. Faith had long since ascribed this anomalous grading to the essential nature of governmental ministers to present education in the best light. Spin, it was called. Really, matters had sunk to such a despicable level that it was good that a change of government was tightening up procedures. Faith was also highly suspicious of the swift 'turnarounds' made by schools who had been put on 'special measures'. Silk purses cannot be made out of sows' ears overnight.

The inquest on the OFSTED report eventually became a topic of the past and matters turned to Jamie. Mary Ackroyd,

Gordon Bolton and Mr. Holmes met together after school shortly before the summer half-term to discuss with Dr. Holroyd the conclusions drawn from his assessment of Jamie. At the commencement Dr. Holroyd praised their later handling of Jamie but explained that they were treating the symptoms, not the underlying cause. They listened in growing understanding of the dilemmas which had faced Jamie from day to day and which they had blindly condemned so harshly. He assured them that they need have no real recriminations: many children of a similar make-up are erroneously channeled into a conduct disorder category, he told the mortified teachers. Many, he said, are never properly diagnosed and end up in prisons or joining suspect religious cults, the latter often following incarceration in the former, as they are so susceptible to persuasion. Dr. Holroyd then explained that, with parental agreement, an onward referral to a language therapist would be appropriate as speech and language was the true domain in which his problems arose and this service should spearhead Jamie's special programme. For his own part, he would write a set of recommendations for each teacher, suggesting that he would be only too pleased to mastermind an in-service training day on the type of communication disorder which was the root of Jamie's wrongly attributed 'behavioural problems'.

Teachers were given to understand that there would be a long path ahead which they would all have to travel to help Jamie to become more aware of the multiple meanings of language, how to recognise emotions felt by others and displayed through bodily movements and facial expressions, and how to behave in order to make and keep friends. Dr. Holroyd said he would discuss Jamie's case with the language therapist who, he hoped, would be able to work with Jamie on what he called 'social skills training'.

'Above all,' he said, 'all adults involved with Jamie should speak to him in as literal a manner as possible, as he accepts any figurative language at "face value". If the action required is phrased, "Open the window, please, Jamie" (a clear instruction), he will comply. However, if the request is phrased, "Can you open the window, Jamie?" he will merely agree that he is capable of doing so but the window will remain resolutely shut! In the latter case, he presumes someone is enquiring about his capability.'

To the incredulity and wry amusement of the humbled staff, Dr. Holroyd also used the example of the message relayed by Mr. Holmes in the assembly. This had been intended as an instruction for Jamie to go to meet the E.P. but Jamie 'merely took it as a piece of information given to the assembled children, a general announcement, not a personal message for him to act upon.'

Finally the teachers were told that whenever Jamie looked perplexed, or did not comply with any order, the adults should reflect back to the language they had used, re-phrase their instruction or explain in simple language. 'I am sure you will be surprised how many confusing "multiple messages" there are in the English language. Confusing, that is, to a boy like Jamie.'

The senior staff listened in fascination, more than one reflecting not on what they had just said, but on the rather strange children they had had in their care over the years who had behaved in similarly inexplicable ways. Although not quite as profoundly affected as Jamie, they had passed from St. Michael's to the senior school labelled as 'troublemakers', 'oddballs', 'behavioural problems'. They knew from feedback received, that these pupils had, more often than not, ended up in schools for emotionally disturbed adolescents and were therefore unfairly lost without trace in the jungle of maladjustment. How many so-called criminals, floundering in what could be described as a University of Crime, are as undiagnosed as was Jamie until the present time, was the animated subject of a later staffroom discussion.

The problem to be considered in confidence was how Jamie would manage in Year 6. Privately Mary Ackroyd had a word in Mr. Holmes' ear: she would dearly love to be responsible for Jamie's well-being and was there any possibility he could reshuffle staff in such a manner that she could replace Peter Danesfield as the Year 6 teacher?

Mr. Holmes, a new man since the insertion of his pacemaker and a lengthy sick-leave, said he would 'work on it'.

★

Mr. Holmes was not the only person to feel in a completely rejuvenated frame of mind. A tremendous load had lifted from Sarah's shoulders to the extent that she felt strangely euphoric. For a number of years the idiosyncratic behaviour of her son, in so many ways her brilliant son, had perplexed her, frightened her and on far too numerous occasions reduced her to a phantom of her former confident self, seduced into this state not only by Jamie, but also by her husband who taunted her over her 'feminisation' of his son. She knew deep in her heart that had she been of a suicidal nature, she would have succumbed to this urge on any number of occasions but had the good sense to seek other means of solace in the knowledge that her own removal from the scene would damage the children far more than if she kept her head above water … but below the parapet. In more ways than one, standing on the latter had its risks for her own mortality: demise by her own hand or from the barbed arrows aimed by Matt.

Now two uncertainties had been resolved. Jamie's strange reactions were through no intentional fault of his own: they were of genetic inheritance and thus Max, equally afflicted, as to a mild extent was Aunt Edith, was as misunderstood not through malice-aforethought, but by an accident of birth.

How she longed to talk with Julie ... But all in good time. Neither was she responsible for Jamie's lack of manners by not being as authoritarian as Matt and his mother had wanted her to be.

A further uncertainty had been her husband's possible unfaithfulness. Now that she was being discarded, the doubts in recent months as to the nature of his work, the weekend conferences in far off venues, the mysterious hotel brochures, the immaculate golf apparel on a day of torrential rain, rapidly transformed into a high probability that this treachery was a reality. Why, despite a heart as heavy as lead, should she simultaneously feel so liberated? Was the pain of *knowing* better than the pain of suspicion, the pain of mistrust? It took some days for Sarah to realise that her strange elation came from the sure knowledge that Matt was, undeniably, in the throes of an affair. Until this time she had always had nagging doubts as to his apparent deviousness: why could she not accept his word instead of working herself up into such a state of confusion? Now she knew her suspicions were confirmed, she could focus on the future, rebuild the family as a threesome and not perpetuate any charade that Daddy 'was working so very, very hard to keep us all happy'. She was not the only single mother she knew and now she was likely to become one she could re-frame her life and plan accordingly. Matt had been so mercilessly unkind to her, to the point of verbal abuse even in Dr. Holroyd's hearing, and she would be the better, and stronger, not to have to submit to it. The worst part for her to consider in the immediate future was to tell her children Daddy wouldn't be coming back – he hadn't said so but she knew within her bones that evening after he'd swept out of Dr. Holroyd's room that he was, essentially, intending also to sweep out of her life.

Dr. Holroyd told his secretary to put Sarah on the urgent list of clients who needed to see him. The appointment was carefully arranged for 1:30 p.m. one afternoon, giving Sarah time to compose herself before school ended and children needed collection.

'Dr. Holroyd, before we discuss Jamie, I need to tell you that since our meeting last week, my husband hasn't returned to our family. I also have reason to believe he is seeing someone else.' Sarah's lip trembled. For so many days now she had hidden her true feelings; now, in this understanding man's company, she could maintain this mask no longer.

'He hasn't been in contact with you or the children? You have evidence that he is with this woman?' the psychologist enquired.

Slowly, trying to withhold her tears, Sarah continued, her voice barely above a whisper and at the point of breaking.

'I have reasons to think this, and also that at some stage he will come clean and tell me he wants to be free.' Pausing momentarily to collect her erratically straying emotions, she continued, 'I have thought this through and think it will be best if I agree to a divorce. I have to tell you, Dr. Holroyd, that I have managed to keep myself bright and alert during the day for the sake of the children, especially for Freya who is at secondary school and not too far away from choosing her GCSE subjects.' Using the tissue Dr. Holroyd had passed her, she took her time before referring to Jamie. 'Jamie will take his selection exams this autumn and, although his scores will be weighted for age and also for being male, I want to keep all worries away from him.

Sarah twisted her sodden handkerchief in her hands as she continued: 'You see, Matt has not been happy at home now for a number of years, something which I have tried to live with, but my heart has been heavy and at night I have not slept.'

With a wry smile and again dabbing her eyes, she added, 'That is to say, not without the help of a little Valium.'

Without any inflexion in his voice which could be interpreted as criticism, Dr. Holroyd commented that if the present absence from home was his first, then nonetheless, despite her lengthy period of misgivings relating to Matt's disillusionment with his marriage, she should not act too precipitously.

'Matt has had a shock, Mrs. Chilton, an extremely painful one. He would not be the first to seek solace in the arms of another woman, one entirely dissociated with his family circumstances, often even an entirely different character from anyone in his family or of his acquaintances. Given a little time to come to terms with the reality that there may well be a congenital factor in his son's social, interpersonal communication, he may well realise the injustice he has inflicted upon you over the years by blaming you as principal carer for mismanagement of inappropriate behaviour.'

Sarah smiled weakly. Perhaps, her listener thought, it was her turn now to deny what should be glaringly obvious. Perhaps it was also giving this long-suffering wife the permission to start afresh with a new life herself. Nigel Holroyd toyed with the two hypotheses as Sarah continued.

'My own doctor has been so kind but has warned me that he is only giving me a short supply of tranquillisers just in case I felt so low that I took more than the stated dose. He rings me every other day to see how I am,' her voice tapering off.

Dr. Holroyd intervened at this point, to give Sarah time to compose herself. 'Do you have any close friends with whom you can go to a cinema or concert, perhaps? Anything to take your mind off. Fresh air and exercise can help, too.'

Quickly dismissing from her mind contacting either Jane or Julie, her sister-in-law, Sarah's voice increased in strength as she firmly assured the kindly psychologist that, indeed, she had looked up a few references on the internet and her bedside reading included one on how to separate without scarring your children. 'I will learn to make a new life for our family and return to teaching when Jamie is also at senior school. Freya, our daughter, will be devastated not to see her father at home but I am determined they will see him as often as possible and will keep counsel as to why the separation has occurred.'

Adding that she would take Dr. Holroyd's professional advice and bide her time before seeing a solicitor, she finished by saying that, as Dr. Holroyd had intimated, 'Jamie will probably accept whatever he is told as a statement of fact, without realising the full implications. Freya is already asking questions and doing her best to trip me up.'

Without the forbidding presence of Matt, Dr. Holroyd resumed his usual interview informality.

'I'm Nigel. May I call you Sarah? It is so much more personable to be on first name terms.'

Sarah nodded her acquiescence. Nigel Holroyd, pausing as if searching for words, began:

'Sarah, for many years your husband, Matt, has held cherished hopes for his son. So many men have a need to fulfil their own thwarted aspirations through their male offspring. Sporty chaps who never quite made the first XI or XV, coach their sons to be talented sportsmen, middle managers encourage examination successes in order to advance their sons' prospects of university life under the dreaming spires of Oxbridge. You are not the first wife to be belittled by their disappointed husbands.'

It was so reassuring for Sarah to realise how much she needed the advice, not of a doctor or even a marriage guidance counsellor, but of a professional who was in touch with the emotional side of life. She felt the weight of carrying her troubled state of mind for so long was gradually being lifted, not entirely onto another person's shoulders, but lightened to a more bearable burden.

'I know it can't be Matt's fault entirely that his personal dreams are shattered. You see, Jamie was so clearly what is called an infant prodigy that at first his remarks were assumed to be the precocious interpretations of a child dabbling in ideas well beyond expectations of his chronological age. And Matt just didn't think that outsiders and teachers did anything other than take these out of such a context and attribute them to a wilful, naughty child. Matt has never entertained any other than the view that a stern disciplined approach was what was needed and without the time himself to implement this, expected me to do so.'

Nigel felt it time to throw a compliment or two Sarah's way.

'At our meeting last week I observed Matt's outburst: he condemned you as the perpetrator of your son's unconventional behaviour and I noted the stoicism with which you accepted this abuse – for abuse, you must accept, it was – in such a subdued manner. It was, I must say to you, every bit as if his intention was to goad you into reaction, a bitter row, in order to throw his hands up and say to me, "Now you know what I have to put up with". I really admired you for keeping your emotions under wraps and not reacting to what could be called his character assassination of you.'

Sarah meekly kept her head low, almost as if receiving a benediction. Nigel's intuition told him it was important to drive his points home.

'And then came the information he did not want to hear. He didn't want to hear it so badly that something inside him, perhaps some fear that he had already suspected the truth, made him demand to know the answer to his "million-dollar question": the origin of his son's malaise.'

He paused before resuming. Sarah said nothing to break the continuity.

'And when he had understood the genetic implication, he could not take the horror, to him, that he was in all probability the carrier of the genetic make-up which resulted in Jamie's disordered communication skills. In some ways he feels as if he has fallen into a yawning void. No, Sarah, he did not specify the relationships but I guessed from his demeanour and his abrupt departure, that Jamie's misunderstood quirkiness came from his side of the family, not yours.' He paused, looking her unflinchingly in the eye, 'Am I right, Sarah?'

Dully, Sarah responded, 'We both knew; we both knew. After my first meeting with you, I spoke at length with my sister-in-law, perturbed that her incredibly intelligent son has been unable to keep down a job because of his strange interpretations of the nature of his responsibilities. I have now learned that this young man, Matt's nephew of twenty-nine, has been diagnosed as being on the autistic spectrum. He has Asperger's Syndrome. Matt's aunt is eccentric, as is a great uncle. Matt's mother also has some mild traits which I believe could be of a similar nature to how you have explained Jamie to us.'

The emotion evoked by the discussion once again reduced Sarah to near-breaking point. Her roller-coaster feelings ebbed and flowed with every reminder of the savage shock her husband had received. Overwhelmingly she yearned to be able to draw him closely to her to comfort him, to tell him she understood. She would never hold any grudge against him that his anger and disappointment had been vented on her.

'Sarah, it is important, so important, for you to understand where Matt is coming from. The pain of producing a son which, in his troubled mind, is imperfect, is real, and powerful. He may well be, and you believe he is, seeking solace in the companionship of associates who do not see him, Matt, as an imperfect "creator". You have known him, I imagine before Jamie's infancy, as an attentive lover, a supportive husband and father to your daughter and proud father of a newborn son.' Again he sought confirmation. 'Am I right??'

Dr. Holroyd reiterated the last phrase in such a forceful manner that it passed through Sarah's mind that he could be

speaking, heaven forbid, from personal experience. The tears
fell. The Kleenex box did double duty.

'I am going to ask you to think of yourself in the coming
weeks, Sarah: what you want as a wife, as a lover to your
husband, with your husband as a faithful partner and a loving as
well as a beloved father to both his children. Take time. You will
have plenty. Matt will need time: he, too, will need an enormous
amount as he faces this crisis in his life without the support of
a compassionate family, a choice he has made himself. Pride is
a hideous burden for the sufferer. Then, when the time comes
for serious decisions to be made about your and Matt's future,
you will be resolute in the action you take.'

'Dr. Holroyd, Nigel, you're too kind. You have encouraged
me to feel that my grieving time will be short-lived, helped me
to believe that Matt's reaction to Jamie's diagnosis will only
be temporary. I shouldn't expect you to show me so much
empathy when it is Jamie, not me, who is your client.'

Nigel silently repressed an overwhelming surge of
admiration for the calmness and humility of this wronged
woman. His professionalism could not allow him to show
sympathy but it was almost too hard not to do more than
merely soothe her unconscionably bruised feelings.

'Jamie is a member of a quartet, Sarah, maybe a trio,
temporarily or permanently. It is impossible to help Jamie
without helping you and Matt and Freya as well. If ever you
have the opportunity to say so to Matt, do let him know that
I'll be more than happy to talk with him, too, on his own and
then, perhaps, if you both wish, with both of you.'

Nigel handed Sarah a small book, a pair of happy children
on the cover, arms around each other. 'You can read this with
Freya. It is a lovely little story about how an elder sister guides
her little brother through the difficult maze of interpersonal
relationships and the deepening love between them as they
explore the intricacies of language together.'

'Now let me explain in greater depth, the nature of what we call a communication disorder.'

Sarah listened with growing understanding to Dr. Holroyd's thorough explanation of what 'evidence' he had been presented with during the assessment. 'And an assessment begins the minute I read the referral information and begin to postulate hypotheses. It continues the second I meet with a child and gathers momentum as I work through a range of materials which compare the child with other children of his own age group, not just, in Jamie's case, St. Michael's, but in the whole of the western world and, in particular, the British Isles.'

She learned of Jamie's quite idiosyncratic responses to some of the questions, this characteristic being that this only happened because he had misconstrued the precise language used. Sarah was told how brilliantly he had revealed his factual knowledge (very direct questions, Dr. Holroyd had stated), and how he had shown, through his own comments, that language confused him. Dr. Holroyd said he had thrown in some trick questions like 'Can you turn the page over?' to which Jamie had firmly given his assurance that he could (but didn't act accordingly).

The psychologist then explained that through the materials he had used, his original hypothesis had been proved. 'Statement-matching' pictures were regarded by Jamie as 'easy-peasy' but the majority were incorrect. Jamie had been unable to see the humour in some simple jokes he was told; in others with slapstick humour he had 'almost fallen off his chair with laughter'. He had given inappropriate suggestions as to how he would join a group of peers already involved in a game of their own, was unable to take the perspective of another person and could not accurately attribute emotions to people by looking at their faces and noting their bodily mannerisms.

Finally, Dr. Holroyd explained that he was intending to run a session at St. Michael's to help all teachers become aware of how they could help Jamie. He said he would be writing a number of recommendations down and these would assist teachers in their better understanding of Jamie and improve his use of language and his awareness of appropriate social interaction. He asked if Sarah would allow him to ask the Speech Therapy Service if they would offer Jamie some sessions, these to include how to make and keep friends, and suggested she and Matt also wrote a letter to the Service, giving their permission for this to happen. Sarah was handed some leaflets to read. The session ended with Sarah's assurances she would keep Matt informed every inch of the way and obtain his counter-signature for permission for therapy.

And so began a new phase in the life of Jamie Chilton, his companions and teachers, his sister and his mother.

Chapter Twenty-One

Jamie was surprised, as were his classmates, to find Mrs. Ackroyd to be their teacher when they rejoined St. Michael's in September after a long, lazy summer. Mrs. Ackroyd had taken Jamie aside to answer his concerned question that he had learned everything she could teach him; he had spent a year, 'as have the others', in her class in Year 3. They didn't all need to hear everything all over again. He understood the situation a little better when it was explained to him that every teacher was trained to take any class in their school, dependent upon the department they were in. She, Mrs. Ackroyd, was a middle school trained teacher and could teach Years 3, 4, 5, 6; Miss Griffin was trained for early and first-year children so would have special expertise in what was called the Early Years: Nursery, Reception, Years 1 and 2.

The first assembly of the year proved exciting for Jamie. Firstly, he was chosen as one of the children to give out the hymn books. What a tremendous thrill it gave him to prepare his allocation of books before the bell signalled classes to entry. He piled them in heaps of twenty, the back bindings pointing to the east and the unbound edges open facing to the west, all perfectly aligned. He observed the girl who managed the CD player putting The Dambusters tune on for the children to march in to the hall. That would be a job he would aspire to. Maybe if he performed with a punctiliousness which overshadowed his fellow hymn book monitor on the other side of the room, he would receive quick promotion. He wondered what the next important job would be. Perhaps the school could have four book monitors and he could be the team captain. Something to aim for, Jamie thought happily. Churchwardens did the job in St. Michael's so he'd suggest to Mrs. Ackroyd that they should be called assemblywardens; this sounded more important and official than just being called a monitor which always reminded him of the monitor lizards he had seen at the zoo, lolling in the sun. The word 'monitor' gave the wrong impression; we are not lazy, like those animals he'd seen were.

The children filed in. To Mary Ackroyd's chagrin, any child taking a hymn book from the pile, rather than one proffered by Jamie, received a sharp rebuke and, horror of horrors, if a pile became dislodged in any shape or form as a result, Jamie was not averse to patting them on the head with the book he was holding. It was not long before a substitution book monitor replaced Jamie, to his consternation. 'Too far, too soon,' Mary admonished herself. In her preparations of the new book monitor's responsibilities, she had not predicted the perversity of Jamie's enthusiastic approach to his coveted role. As an alternative, she intended to sit him in the front row of the school to watch how the replacement monitor fulfilled the task but realising the Reception class position in the Hall might appear to his contemporaries as a serious demotion, sat him by her own side so that she could whisper instructions as to how he could improve his 'distribution skills' and be re-appointed at some time in the future. There was a steep learning curve involved in managing the idiosyncrasies of Jamie, she told herself.

At the first lunchbreak, Charlie, Freddie, Sam and Millie, together with Jamie, were to accompany Mrs. Ackroyd to the medical room, a room which performed a dual purpose. It was, in addition, the room where small groups were given special teaching unless a sick child was lying on the camp bed awaiting the arrival of the parent to take them home. If this was the case, a corner of the dining room was then used, much to the annoyance of the cook who felt this to be part of her personal empire, making no bones about it by clattering metal chafing dishes, cutlery or anything she could think of, to make it known in no uncertain terms that the intrusion was unwelcome. Teachers, however, always disregarded Cook's possessive sniffiness, feeling that such a large area being otherwise underused for a large proportion of the school day was a waste of taxpayers' money.

Mercifully, as the first lunch sitting was already underway, the medical room was free. Mary Ackroyd began by saying how much she was going to trust this very special group of children to be her associates, her helpers. Would they be willing to be her confederates? Vigorous head-nodding signified assent. Jamie announced that if no one else would say they would, then he most certainly would be happy to be Mrs. Ackroyd's assistant. 'Like I was in assembly, for instance, but the others messed it up for me.' Mrs. Ackroyd was learning by the minute what close contact with a child with disordered communication would be teaching her: how these poor sufferers unwittingly 'set themselves up' without provocation. It was going to be the steep learning curve she had predicted for herself and, perhaps, mental preparation for daily pitfalls would be helpful. At the moment she was beginning to feel clad in Wellington boots when maybe ballerina pumps would be more appropriate. But she believed herself to be up to the challenge with all the background information she had gleaned from the courses she had attended in the past four months. What a triumph this would be for her if she managed to turn things round for this poor innocent child. And how pleased she had been that Mr. Holmes had taken up her 'hint' with alacrity and, sheltering under the OFSTED 'room for improvement' issue, had shuffled all staff as a measure against 'complacency'.

Mary began by talking about 'a band of brothers' and five, not three, musketeers. When she felt she had done sufficient ground work, thus paving the way for the real motivation for this 'set piece', she carefully mentioned that Freddie's glasses were really smart and made him look a bit like Harry Potter. Freddie smirked.

'Wasn't always like this, though. When I first had to wear them, people used to call me Four Eyes. Some asked if I wanted a white stick. They were laughing at me, and because I was an Eagle, that didn't help: they thought I looked like some boffin or other. I broke two pairs on purpose so I didn't have to wear them … but then I couldn't see the writing on the whiteboard again so I got really worried I'd be demoted. Then there was the first Harry Potter film and, do you know, Mrs. Ackroyd, everyone wanted to borrow my glasses! They made them feel sick though because their eyes didn't need them. Now I sometimes pull them down to the bottom of my nose and stare over the top at anyone who dares say anything nasty. I did that to Jamie once when he said I looked like the battered old owl his sister kept on her bed. He just said he'd try to do that on Freya's owl, so I gave up.'

Mary Ackroyd took each of the five through slight differences she had noted in each of them, bar Jamie. Sam was very clever, but his handwriting was 'all over the place, isn't it, Sam? A bit like that of Prince Charles, all spidery, so you are in good company'. He told her his friends said he must have got a pocket full of ants to crawl all over the pages he was writing on. They also got cross when he accidentally knocked their things on the floor and said he'd done it on purpose to annoy them. He wasn't very good at football, either, so he said that his mum had told him to say that you can't be good at everything and would they like to recite their 14 times tables like he could or spell 'catastrophe.' At this point, Jamie chanted in a sing-song voice, 'Once 14 is 14, two 14s are 28,' before Mrs.

Ackroyd laughingly intervened to move the discussion on. Charlie hated being called 'Teacher's Pet' but did not seem to be able to resist the urge to tell tales when rules were infringed – unless he was the one to break one. 'Too self-righteous,' Mrs. Ackroyd had described him. Charlie's copper hair (carroty nob, or worse, the boys mocked) had also been a source of embarrassment to him. 'No, I've noticed you don't like being called a ginger nut, do you?' interrupted Jamie, helpfully he thought and would have continued had not Mrs. Ackroyd smilingly put her finger up towards him, shaking her head to signal him to desist: the time for the second sitting lunch bell to sound was fast approaching. Freddie was too short for his age and didn't like the teasing he received for being taken for a year younger than he actually was. He was 'awful' at long or high jump on Sports Days, let the relay-race team down and, to increase his height, had rigged up a stretching frame at home from two door handles, getting his older brother to open one slowly whilst he lay on the floor with his legs and hands tied to the rope, this extremely risky exercise only being stopped by his father's intervention. Millie said how awful it was to be the only girl in her group in the earlier years until Ruby had been promoted to the Eagles.

'Well,' said Mary, 'so we all have something which makes us a little different from our friends. Now Jamie what about you? Are you in any way different from your friends?'

Jamie furrowed his brow and took a minute for reflection.

'No, I'm not different. I don't wear glasses, my hair is not copper, I don't tell tales but I am very good at telling stories. I'm not a girl. I'm not short and I'm not tall, just average height like most people. So, really, I'm not different, just the same as any other boy.'

Just as she had asked the others to agree to the 'confessions' of others, Mary posed the question to the group.

'Do you agree with Jamie, that he is just like anyone else?'

The four looked at each other, then shook their heads slowly. 'Well?' Mary probed.

Charlie was the first to break the silence.

'Whatever Jamie might think, Mrs. Ackroyd, he *is* different. He says nutty things. He interrupts our games and expects us to do what he wants us to do. He doesn't have the savvy to know when we are asking him to do stupid things; he does them and wonders why he gets into trouble.'

Jamie looked puzzled. He was aware from experience what 'nutty things' meant but he couldn't recall any instances when he had made those sorts of remarks that he was being accused of.

'I always say what I know to be true. I know other people who don't say the right answer and am extremely surprised when the teacher says something like, "Good effort". They should be told they are wrong. After all,' Jamie added brightly, 'black is black and white is white.'

The group exchanged knowing looks. Jamie continued his self-justification.

'And of course if they choose me to do things, I'll do my best to do them. Everyone knows I am a person to be trusted. A man of integrity, I am told by Father Harrold, and I know it is good to be that.'

The group, eyes downwards, swallowed sniggers. From that point onwards, the 'differences' came thick and fast.

'I think that is quite enough,' Mrs. Ackroyd intervened. 'Jamie, the others have all told everyone about how they are different; they know it and we don't have to tell them. So that is the difference which is most important of all: you do not know when your behaviour or your reactions are not the way most others would behave or react.'

'Well, to be honest with you,' said Jamie, 'there was some Scottish poet who wrote a lot of things which no one could understand unless you could speak that kind of English, but when you understood things like "giftie gie us" what it meant was that it would be nice to know how to see ourselves as others see us.' He paused, 'Am I like him?'

'A little,' Mary Ackroyd acknowledged, then went on to explain what she meant by telling them they were to be the 'Band of Brothers'. Brothers 'look out for each other'. Immediately realising Jamie would interpret this as meaning you should be sure to notice them when in their company or at a distance, she explained this as a phrase which meant we would look out and warn or protect each other if we noticed them to be in a difficult situation.

'Now, here's a piece of paper for each of you with everyone's name in a separate column. I want you to write in each column the *good* things you notice about each person in this special group.'

The positive points were then listed on the white board, name by name and the teacher said how wonderful it was that nice things could be said about each one of them. Mrs. Ackroyd then emphasised what she meant by 'looking out for each other'. She explained how important it was then to step in whenever any of them was aware that one of the Band was being taunted. She said she'd meet them again in the following morning to enquire progress.

'How very interesting,' Mary had said the next day when each of the group had informed her that no one had been taunted, no one had needed help. Jamie was the only one who had anything sinister to report. He announced he had checked with several of the class whether they needed Freddie's glasses, thought Charlie's writing looked like ants on a page, Sam was too short or Millie behaved too much like a girl.

'But they weren't very nice to me when I asked them questions. I was told by some to "buzz off", "get a life", or "go and drown yourself", and I didn't know what to do. Why did they think I was not alive and, if I wasn't, why did they tell me to kill myself? It made me very unhappy.' His mouth took a downturn as he added in a choking voice, 'Really, Mrs. Ackroyd, I don't think I want to be in your Band of Brothers. Perhaps you could choose someone else.'

Apart from Jamie's unexpected reaction, Mary's intervention, for that was what she planned, had got off to an extra good start and, otherwise, had seamlessly reached exactly where she wanted it to be. She explained that each of the children except one had to work through their problems for themselves. The one who hadn't, was Jamie. This was his difference. And a very important one, too. Part of the learning curve for me, she reflected, recalling how Dr. Holroyd had complimented her for managing this child's behaviour so well last year but explained that the problem remained that it had been the symptoms which she was endeavouring to extinguish whereas it was the causes which must be addressed at the same time. This, clearly, was a good example of the misunderstanding of the entire staff.

'Now, in confidence: will you shake hands on this as a Band of Brothers should. I want you all, now, not to look out for each other, but only for Jamie. And when you explain to Jamie, this must be done privately. You will be his buddies and we will meet here every week on Tuesday lunchtime to see how we are getting on. Okay? Agreed?'

Mary apologised that she hoped a shortened lunch hour once a week wouldn't matter too much to them. The reward was for them to know that they were helping another child like themselves but one who couldn't recognise what was real and what was nonsense or untrue. However, in addition to the nice feeling they would have inside themselves that they were helping Jamie to do what they were each able to do without the help of others, a reward in itself, she would have a special treat lined up for them all at the end of the term.

'Mm. Wonder what that would be. Might be really nice because it would be near Christmas.'

The group shook hands, slapped each other on the back and left Mrs. Ackroyd feeling an inner glow she had not felt for some time.

★

Jamie felt quite a different person as the autumn term progressed. How wonderful it was for Charlie to explain to him something when he got the 'wrong end of the stick' when the teacher had given an instruction or a friend had made a certain remark. Charlie told him it could be the sharp end of a stick or a smooth end, or one dipped in something nasty which would sting you and the other perfectly clean. 'You see, one way is right, one not. You've taken the instruction the wrong way, so think what the other way would be.' Furthermore, Sarah knew, and had confidentially alluded to this to give him confidence, Mr. Holmes had placed him highly on the list of children felt to be academically suitable for a grammar school education and an extra time allowance had been granted to give him a fair chance of thinking what questions were actually asking of him.

There was no doubt that sometimes the desire to place Jamie in a vulnerable situation was exceedingly hard to resist but the quartet satisfied themselves by chortling over what they could have suggested to him and what the overall reaction certainly would have been. The flip side of the coin was that Jamie was now so alert to the possibilities that recommended actions of his friends were actually 'setting him up', a term he now understood, that he questioned the most mundane, everyday requests to the extent that at least one member of the Band would lose patience.

'For goodness sake, Jamie, think for yourself. We're not always going to be around to protect you.'

The language classes went well. The mysteries of 'keeping a blind eye', 'striking while the iron is hot' as well as simple metaphors as 'like two peas in a pod', 'mad as a hatter', became easier for him to interpret in ways other than literal, but it still did not come easily to Jamie when one of these phrases came up in real life.

But it was the social skills lessons he particularly enjoyed. He was not only shown videos illustrating how other people interacted with each other but the speech therapist also engaged some children from the local secondary school to come and act out scenarios she had planned. The main character then dropped out, to be replaced by Jamie. The therapist had a 'big thing' herself about what she called 'Changing the Environment for the Troubled Child': if sensitive awareness by the peers of children such as Jamie could be made more acute, then secondary life would not be the hell it had been for some sufferers in the past. Through these videos Jamie was shown, by being talked through what was happening, how easy it is to bore listeners when going on for too long on a subject of which the listener was familiar or cared little about. When explaining things to others, he was asked to think out what the person already knew of the topic he was about to tell them: did they know a lot (in which case, build on that), or a little (in which case, start from the very beginning by setting the scene).

Life was good for Jamie. The icy cold ripples in the pond were also dying away for almost all who had been affected by his behaviour.

But something else was happening. The effect of everyone's enlightened understanding of Jamie's difficulties was generating another, warmer set of ripples to cascade, first from the knowledge Dr. Holroyd had passed on to all the adults in Jamie's orbit, then to Jamie himself and to his peers. Even Father Harrold had a spring in his step: he had appreciated the heartfelt thanks given to him by Sarah following the fulfilment of her request for a discussion on the Church's view of infidelity.

Chapter Twenty-Two

'This can't go on for much longer, Matt. I feel I'm in limbo. It's been four months now since you moved in and six since you told me you are going to file for divorce. For all I know, that was merely a sop to keep me interested in you. I've now got another card to throw into the ring and jolt you into action.'

Matt, already familiar with the line the conversation was taking yet again, was startled by this sinister-sounding proclamation. Karen was unlike Sarah who, even after the starry-eyed days of their courtship and marriage, had never been so brittle and forthright as Steve's secretary, to whom he had been introduced some eighteen months ago at the Group Marketing Conference weekend in the Channel Islands. More seductive than Sarah, more blatantly the sex-kitten, but with a hardness about her that he could not quite fathom, at first these facets of her personality were part of the attraction as being in complete contrast to Sarah. Now they were beginning to grate. Karen, Marlboro smouldering between her index and middle fingers, strolled to the mantelpiece, nonchalantly leant one elbow on it and stared through hooded mascaraed eyes at Matt's reflected image in the mirror. For his part, and with a constricted throat, Matt could only fixate from his seated position upon the flowing coal-black tresses.

'I kept an appointment at the fertility clinic this afternoon. Steve was kind enough to drive me there; he said he was owed some free time and he'd have great pleasure in taking it.'

'And?' Matt managed through clenched teeth and with

a mouth as dry as sawdust, rising from his chair unsteadily, a feeling of nausea preceding the imparting of what he had already anticipated would be *the* crisis of his life to date. So Steve should know before him. Unbelievably, Steve, who had provided all the alibis while he was living at home and before the ghastly shock of the derivation of Jamie's diagnosis, Steve, who had supported him whilst he was ostensibly working in the Midlands and staying either in 'his place' or hotels, was probably at this moment signing a snappy congratulations card before ordering a bottle of Moet to be placed on the table at the restaurant they were all going to tonight.

'The obstetrician examined me and confirmed the results of the pregnancy test I'd taken myself last week, following which I had made the appointment to see him.'

Matt's colour drained; never before had he felt poleaxed but he did now: the ground beneath his feet seemed to him to have developed a yawning chasm. Clasping Karen, his hands running through those ebony locks, he was not sure whether this was because of his need to restore his balance or the awareness that she was expecting a giant embrace accompanied by roars of delight was the reason. How the fucking hell could this happen? His vasectomy of eight years ago, why did that not protect him from such a catastrophic disaster. Had he got any redress against the clinic? Oh yes, he thought, more bitterly than he had ever thought in his life, they would blandly refer him back to the small print of the indemnity form he had to sign which meant he had acknowledged the 99.9 success rate. Now he was the one in a thousand who would still be capable of impregnating a woman. His mind was in a whirl, of the like he believed he had never encountered before. Not one word could he utter. When they came, all he managed was:

'Babe, Babe, you told me you'd never miss a pill, for the reasons you gave me some weeks ago. And you hated the thought of me wearing those hideous passion-killers so, for me, it was a safety valve against my vasectomy ever letting me down. That was why I didn't encourage you any further to throw them away.'

The contemptuous retort was spat back immediately. 'Well, you thought you were infallible, didn't you? Not quite as perfect as you thought you were, are you? I've not been taking those for weeks. Read about the dangers of getting heart problems or having a DVT. And I thought a baby would be sweet, cuddly and smell gorgeously of Johnson's talcum powder. So I was happy to take Steve's advice.'

Rising to her theme of character assassination, she added, 'And I believe you promised another woman to honour and obey? Until death us do part? Shucks, isn't this something to do with kettles being called black?'

Karen gave a vixen-like shrug and pulled away from the half-hearted embrace.

'So, no two dozen red roses, no diamond ring, no bridal bouquet?' Her lip curled. 'I had to bring you to your senses. It was Steve's idea and, certainly, it didn't take long for me to get pregnant.'

'Well,' she spat, with all the venom she could muster. 'Now you have no option but to call home and inform your wife that you are leaving her permanently. Or would you prefer me to have that pleasure? And as I have no intention of being a single mother or of living in sin, as my grandmother would call it, we'd better set the date for the wedding. How about Freya as a bridesmaid, Jamie a pageboy? Steve will be delighted to be the best man, he said as much.'

'I shall determine who is my best man,' muttered Matt, feeling sick to the core.

'And I shall choose my bridesmaids and pages,' shot back Karen. 'Meanwhile, I have ordered a celebration dinner for us tonight; Steve's pulled out. Says he doesn't want to play gooseberry. The executive chef of The River Front has prepared it today to my specifications.' Her tone changed as, moving sensuously towards her shattered lover, she purred, 'I thought it would be great to be alone, just the three of us.'

Karen smirked. 'Actually, there's been three of us for the past eight weeks.'

'Then put that cigarette out. The warnings on the packet can't be plainer.'

But after the initial shock of the worst eventuality actually coming to fruition, another thought struck Matt forcibly. Could the baby be someone else's? Had she been two-timing him? Should he ask for a DNA paternity test? He had to face it, instead of playing along with her idea of marriage – which was most certainly not his intention, she was merely his temporary antidote to the situation he had found himself in at home – he had made an enormous pile of shit for himself to wade through. Whilst still not completely averse to a permanent break-up of his marriage – he needed time to think it through – Karen was most unlike the woman he would want to replace Sarah. Should the DNA result show him to be the one in a thousand 'failures', there was no doubting his mind: he would have to give in to the schemer and do the honourable thing. Which would obviously mean accepting the risk that the new child could also inherit his blasted genes. His heart sank irretrievably.

'Karen, there is something that has to be ironed out first before we think of any kind of celebration. Are-you-having-it-off-with-anyone-else-who-could-be-the-father? I need to know. I MUST know.'

But what was the point of accepting or rejecting her fervent, 'Darling, how could you even think of such a thing. You know you are the Man of my Dreams.' If she could trick him into pregnancy, she would be capable of any deceit.

Or she could be telling the truth.

The celebration dinner was muted to say the least. The

card from Steve was in very poor taste, the Moet turned out to be Prosecco and the bonhomie was probably jollier in an OAP home.

★

Communication between Matt and his family had been scant since that fateful outburst at the Child and Parent Office. That man, Dr. something-or-other, had looked so smug and the sympathetic looks he had cast at Sarah had made him want to heave up. In reality, the misunderstood and misinterpreted, rather quizzical, looks cast in Sarah's direction had been to give her permission to defend herself from the character assassination to which the psychologist had been forced to bear witness. Matt had written a curt letter to her after the first fortnight, saying it was all over between them and that all communication should be addressed to Steve's home, where he was an indefinite guest. When each of the children's birthdays had come along he had requested that Sarah should either drop them both off at his office or send them there by taxi. He informed her that, until she chose otherwise, they should keep up the charade of their father working away from home on a lengthy assignment. He would provide her with the usual housekeeping money that had been made available to her to look after four – but in the long run, when both children were at secondary school, he would expect her to resume her own career and remove him from the burden of supporting two households.

Double confirmation of his unfaithfulness and his lying.

Sarah had reflected long and hard before she sent her response. She pondered upon the innate need for men to father a child in their own likeness but, far more importantly, in order to satisfy their own aspirations. The relief she felt, and the freedom from the burden of guilt she had experienced because of Matt and his mother's accusation that her parenting skills were at fault, was palpable. She would use her new-found strength of purpose to make up her own mind what response she would give. Then, only then, would she seek more professional advice as to her rights in any divorce. But, if she was to believe Nigel Holroyd, and in her heart of hearts she desired this from its very depths, she would open the door a chink in the sincere hope Matt's absence was merely to give himself time to come to terms with the knowledge that a genetic cause was the root of Jamie's eccentricities and these were not of her making. Surely, oh surely, their commitment to each other could never be eroded in so abrupt a manner. Surely he will know himself that he needs her, and only her, to help him understand that there is no such thing as 'fault' where genetic inheritance is concerned and that she would never, never blame him for the unwitting 'card' Jamie had been dealt at birth because of a blip in his bloodline. No more was it the fault of George that Max should be afflicted, or their ancestors knowingly responsible for his aunt's or great uncle's idiosyncrasies.

Deep down, Sarah felt a strong intuition that as time passed, Matt would return to the solace of his family. She would hold on to this hope until the very last. She would not waver. At last, she committed her conclusions to paper: with a firmness of mind and hand, she wrote:

Matt, who will, always, be 'dear Matt' to me,

I have considered your letter and wish you to know that despite my continued deep love for the husband and lover with whom I shared so many beautiful experiences for at least nine of the seventeen years of our marriage, I'm willing for both our sakes, to make my own life from this moment onwards without you.

I cherish and thank you for those times which will remain in my mind as cameos to take out, dust down, polish and be warmed by in any dark days ahead. I am strong enough to keep these unsullied by events which have followed, in order that the children's respect and love for you will remain unblemished.

Our dear Jamie's behaviour has affected all our lives. You made me believe that the so-called rude, impertinent, oppositional and near-delinquent behaviour was due to my negligent guidance. I now have that burden of imposed guilt removed from me and the sense of purpose I now feel is such that, with or without you by my side, I shall do everything in my power to help Jamie to live as society demands and to understand correctly all the messages that bombard us every day of our lives.

In closing this valediction, I want you to know the door will always be open for you as the caring, affectionate, passionate husband and father to our children I had dreamed of in my childhood, the man I married and who I will always love.

Adieu and farewell,
Your once-darling,
Sarah

P.S. I want you to know that Dr. Holroyd said how sorry he was you had to leave as he was about to explain to us how we can help our son. I have seen him again and he has given me much to help me understand. If you could plan sometime to book in an appointment, he would be happy to suggest how you, too, can help Jamie. This is very important as, wherever you are living, we should all pull together to help him make better sense of the world he lives in.'

Enclosed between the folded page was a faded, dried rose petal from her wedding bouquet.

★

To his own surprise, Matt put both the letter and the rose petal into the zip pocket of the leather wallet which had been the first present Sarah had ever given him.

Sarah had honoured his wishes and duly accompanied the children to their birthday visits. She always made excuses to Freya and Jamie that she had a meeting to go to and, as Daddy was away so much, how nice it was for them to have him all to themselves: their birthday treat with her would come at the weekend. It was Freya who 'read between the lines', remembered the bleakness of that phone call she had overheard and questioned Matt incessantly. Jamie, delighted to be with his father, took their meetings, now extended to weekends, at face value. No one in the family tried to disabuse him of his lack of awareness of what really was going on between his parents.

'Daddy, how is it that you work in Leicester mid-week and then have to work in your office at weekends? Why don't you bring the work home like you used to?'

Matt explained with almost monotonous regularity that his work was now so much more complex that he needed solitude to write his reports and reviews and also, it was so important to have access to all the data his office held. Not all he needed was stored electronically. He couldn't transport his office to his home, now, could he? Freya would then pester him as to how long these assignments were to go on for. Were they to do with the government? Ooh! Top secret? Was he really a member of MI5?

'Oh,' interjected Jamie at such points, eyes as wide as saucers. 'Are you a spy, Daddy? That's so cool. I'll tell Charlie and Freddie and Millie and Sam – they're my best buddies; we are in the Brotherhood even though we have a girl as well – and they will be proud to know the son of a spy. I'll tell Mr. Holmes … and Dr. Holroyd. He's my special Eepee* you know.'

---

* Eepee is Jamie's perception of an Educational Psychologist's title. (In his own mind he feels Dr. Holroyd has something to do with a Red Indian teepee).

Matt did his best to nip Jamie's ardour in the bud for owning a father who was a special agent. Realising how easy it was to pull the wool over Jamie's eyes (what would his son make of those two idioms hardly crossed his mind), he warned him how serious it would be if he passed this secret information on. Matt also learned the importance of always referring the questions back to Freya.

'Now, Freya, you answer your own questions. Nothing has changed.'

★

But one day came, shortly before Christmas, when after the usual prologue, Jamie added his own contribution to this well-practised dialogue.

'Mummy,' confided Jamie, 'has lots of my friends round to our house and we all play games together. She shows me how to take my turn and wait till it comes round to mine again before I roll the dice the second or third time. She tells me about watching their faces to see if I'm saying things that make them bored. You know I used to think that people were turned into cardboard when someone made them bored but I have lots of practice with my language therapist who makes me think of how words mean different things in different places, or settings, as she calls it. Freya, you help me, too, don't you?'

'Yes, I love to help him.' Freya moved across the room to put her arm round her brother's shoulders before continuing, 'He is a great learner too, aren't you Jamie? We have fun looking at the films the therapist sends him home with and my friends at school join me to act out scenes with him.' Jamie, looking up to her, although the height gap was rapidly closing, nodded his head in approval so fiercely that it seemed possible that his head would fall off. Freya laid her hands on the top of his head to stop the violence of the shaking, grinning at her father. As she did so, Jamie continued his description of home life without his father, using far less of a monotone than he used to.

'Mummy sings a lot, too, round the house and sits with us while we watch the CDs my language teacher makes. It's great: really cool. I'm the star in them. Just think of me, Daddy: I might be in a real film one day, maybe even go to Hollywood where all the big stars live. I'll be able to buy a big house for us all to live in then and earn so much money you won't need to do all that special work you have to do.'

Even Matt became caught up in his son's fervour for the reconstitution of his family. He squeezed Jamie's hand. What was that choking feeling in his throat? Why was Jamie making him feel so wistful?

'Then we all talk about what was in the CD,' Jamie continued enthusiastically. 'She's always smiling and laughing and I now know when to ask for things like when she can play with me or drive me to my friends' houses and I don't ask any more if she has a sad look on her face. I know what a sad look looks like now.' Jamie glanced upwards at his father and held his gaze. 'Daddy, Daddy, that is a sad expression on your face right now. Are you sad? Do you wish you could come home with us?'

Freya was unwilling to stop this inquisition; she dearly wanted to hear her father's reply. But already Jamie had returned to his descriptions of the lessons he was having at school.

'I practise recognising how people feel with Mrs. Ackroyd; she shows me pictures and different faces of herself so I can see how she's feeling. She makes Charlie or Freddy or Sam or Millie pull faces at me – we are all in the Brotherhood, you know; all except Dominic. Did I tell you that? I can explain, if you like. I then say whether I think they are miserable or happy or puzzled or cross when they look like that.'

'So is Mummy sad often?' Troubled Matt could not stop the question escaping from his mind. Freya, wise beyond her years, caught her breath. Why was Daddy returning to quiz Jamie on the state of their mother's emotional state? Was this an actual glimmer of hope that all yet would be well?

'No, not really, but she was on her wedding anniversary. It's yours, too, you know. Did you feel unhappy you couldn't be together because of your spy work? She brought the picture of you and her downstairs again, just like it used to be. She looked sad then, I could tell: her lips went down like this. She normally has this picture by her bed and sometimes in the morning when I creep into her bed, I find it under her pillow. Do you know, I've seen her kissing it. Actually, I think she spills the water she takes up to bed with her 'cos the picture is often wet and I tell her she really shouldn't drink the water when she is looking at your photograph. She said it's nice to love somebody and she loves us all. I love everyone too, and you, Daddy.'

'Daddy, the look on your face at the moment is still a bit sad, too. When will your spy work be finished?'

Matt, pangs of joy in his children's happiness and mutual admiration, did not want to spoil the atmosphere, charged as it was with family unity. He had never felt more of an outsider in his family's welfare and he did not find this to be a pleasant feeling. What was he doing to himself; to the lives of the family he and Sarah had created together? He heard himself saying that he hoped it would be soon coming to an end.

★

Matt had been hit hard by the news that he was to be the father of a third child. Karen, of course, had no reason to be aware of Jamie's idiosyncratic and unconventional behaviour, a condition that he now believed he himself was responsible for, and he felt sick at heart that he was putting another foetus at risk. Freya had been born unscathed, Jamie not: a strong chance, then, that a third baby of his would be similarly afflicted. He knew little about the statistical probability, nor whether Freya would be a 'carrier'. Knowing what he did about his own gene pool and how this characteristic had wormed its way through the extended family over the generations, he believed there to be a serious possibility that the baby Karen was carrying could be similarly disadvantaged. How could he join in Karen's exuberance? How could you leave a family who has been blighted by him, merely to recreate the problem afresh? The anguish Matt felt knew no bounds; he felt himself to be unclean, a leper, precipitator of human misery, at first unwilling, now culpable through his own intransigence by ignoring the 99.9% factor. He had known that Karen did not leave 'protection' to her partner, for reasons plainly stated those weeks ago but now knew she had not just thrown caution to the winds but actively pursued her goal of tricking him into marriage. He still toyed with the idea of having a paternity test but, although he had been suspicious, he had not been able to work out how she could have had an affair, even a 'one-night' stand, when she came straight home after work and they were always together at weekends … except, of course, when he had 'access' to the children. Then she was usually involved back at the home they shared, cooking or gardening. She wasn't that much of a good-time girl, was she, to squeeze a sexual encounter in on those days? No, he could not seriously entertain that idea; he was clutching at straws. But still he avoided the commitment.

As the days ticked by into weeks, Karen had become more sharp-tongued and caustic about his lily-livered approach to filing for divorce and breaking forever with his former family. Karen presented him with books of names. How about Delilah for a girl, Lothario for a boy? Catalogues of nursery items were displayed around the home, the most outlandish and expensive being marked with double asterisks. Then came the post-maternity brochures, private lying-in nursing homes. *The Lady* magazine was marked where night-nurses were registered. The torture she was inflicting on his mind knew no bounds.

'Aren't I keeping my figure beautifully?' she had enquired time and time again, pulling up her bottom-skimming skirt and pressing Matt's hand across her flat abdomen. 'And I'm twelve weeks now. I'll look really good at the Divisional Ball next Saturday. You are a lucky man: I won't need a new dress. I can still wear my spangled midnight-blue strapless gown. You like me in that. I was wearing that, you remember, when we met.'

Matt had more pressing things on his mind. He had not yet cancelled the children's visit for that Saturday: they were expecting to be taken to the circus that evening. He cursed himself not only for forgetting: work had been taking up too much of his attention, but also for allowing Karen to amuse herself every night, seeing her friends. He needed now to choose between disappointing his children or annoying his mistress … or 'future wife' as she preferred to be called. Before he could perfect the embryonic plan formulating in his mind, Karen made up his mind for him.

'Steve phoned this afternoon to say he'd booked a room for us at the Grand. 'Knowing my condition,' he had said, 'he thought it best if we all stayed the night there after the Ball. He is driving us, you remember.'

Matt put his plan into action. Circus tickets, three, were placed in an envelope with a 'with compliments' slip: 'Desperately sorry can't make it. You three go: the seats are good ones. Will be thinking of you. Take a taxi. Love you.' He enclosed £25 for the taxi, another £20 for the programmes and ice-creams.

★

Late on the afternoon of the Ball, Matt couldn't get out of his mind wistful visions of his still-precious children. Jamie would be beside himself with excitement, ever-prosaic Freya taking the prospect more sedately, probably wondering whether at rising-fourteen and on the cusp of moving into the adult stage of life she should more properly be viewing a visit to the circus as childish entertainment. As quickly as he could he dismissed these notions from his mind at the point when he found himself watching his family from afar, the absolute personification of Ebenezer Scrooge being taken through all his Christmases, and envying his former wife for having this undiluted pleasure of witnessing first-hand this phase of their children's development. As a further interruption to his thoughts, Karen was more skittish than ever. She danced around their sitting-room, already attired in her striking ball gown, ignoring the sharpness of Matt's pleas to remember her unborn child.

Then came the bombshell, his third to poleaxe him.

Waltzing around the seated Matt, Karen playfully tousling his hair or twitching his bow-tie as she swirled past, the following words of confession crashed relentlessly through his consciousness one by one. No tasering could have been more vicious in the hideous impact shattering his already bruised ego.

'Mattie, Mattie, Mattie,' (this endearment itself, each accompanied by a fresh tug at his hair, grated to the very core of his being) 'you, the man who two-timed his wife. Now you're about to learn the same is happening to you.' Pausing to wag a ruby-red manicured finger under her lover's very nose, she continued her appalling disclosure.

'You, my hero, my Apollo, my lover-boy, who takes me at the dawn of the day, in the woods, in the moonlight, in the kitchen, are being two-timed by your mistress. Isn't that fun?'

Karen whirled towards the drinks cabinet and downed a large slug from the whisky bottle. Her voice changed. Each word was explosively spat from between curled lips. Her hands, triumphantly raised in the air, appeared to the dumbfounded Matt to have taken on the form of witch's claws.

'You break promises as if they are hen's eggs to crush. How many times have I heard you are about to speak to your lawyer to sort out the finances preparatory to a divorce? No, I'm not pregnant. Never have been. It's a ruse dreamed up in Steve's flat. I told him you were back-pedalling on your offer of marriage so he said you'd soon tie the knot if I was pregnant. So ... I said I was. And – you – fell – for – it.

'But, oh, how you changed when you knew you were going to be a father again! What do you think your attitude did to me? Well, I'll tell you. Steve's bed was much more comfortable than yours so I went back to him. And I think I'd like a child of my own one day. So what's the point in shacking up with someone who's had the chop?'

A stunned Matt, the colour from his face and the energy from his body deserting him, weakly questioned her use of the term 'back to him'.

'Oh! Yes. Steve and I had been secretly dating for years. But he's not the marrying kind, he likes his fun and "swinging around" as he calls it. And I think I like that best, too: what a bore to be stuck with the same lover for years. So, if you're up to it, there is a bedroom booked for tonight and three of us to sleep in it, so if you're not going to marry me, how about it? A little bit of swinging does no harm. Try it!'

An unaccustomed wave of nausea swept over the shattered Matt. He staggered from the room to the bathroom, locked the door and sat quivering on the edge of the bath.

So the boot was on the other foot. At the sound of the doorbell, Karen waltzed out with Steve, with barely a glance behind her.

★

A listless Matt spent the evening making phone calls to landladies, packing up his possessions and transferring himself to a bedsit which then became his second home since walking away from his family. The immense relief of neither fathering a third child nor having a faulty vasectomy had not yet raised his spirits: he felt far too damaged by the whole episode involving this woman. Why did he have to make such a poor choice of companion as relief from frustration with his family, a companion he would have been fearful of introducing to his mother and had dreaded the thought, even entertaining the idea that, of course, she could go the same way as his father and no introductions at all would need to be made?

★

Living alone in his sparsely furnished lodgings, albeit in a pleasant area of town and with an affable middle-aged couple as his landlords, he still arranged to see his children at his office. He could hardly afford the rent now he was no longer sharing Karen's flat but without a needy, nymphomaniac mistress to satisfy, in monetary terms as well as physical, he was just about able to manage. Matt's relationship with Karen had ended on an extremely sour note and one that he preferred to extinguish from his mind at that. But, as with all horrific experiences, these tend to return to haunt their recipient, even only if in repugnant flashbacks.

Chapter Twenty-Three

The week before Christmas, Matt kept the appointment he had made with Dr. Holroyd. An intrigued Dr. Holroyd walked into the waiting room to call Matt in.

'I'm Nigel; may I call you Matt?'

★

The following week Matt browsed through the pamphlets Dr. Holroyd had given him. He read two of the four books he had been lent. He had much time to reflect upon all of the data he'd been given about genetic influences and the emotional effects on a parent learning that a child you had produced was damaged or flawed in some way.

'In a sense,' Dr. Holroyd had said, 'this is not entirely true. It may be that our society itself is damaged. Each individual is unique but in order for people to live together in harmony, rules have to be established, honed, refined and replicated over the generations. If individuals such as Jamie were the norm and not outnumbered, their rules would be the ones to be abided by.'

He had gone on to say that there were many Pacific or Indian Ocean Islands where the customs and rules were entirely at variance with our own. He recalled a particular one in the Pacific Islands where the barefooted tribes had been given leather sandals by a seemingly philanthropic shoe manufacturer, only to be shocked when the islanders demanded replacements but were told they must pay for them.

Anthropologists had studied some of these and the ethical problem for the world was, should we change these societies, bring them electricity, television, transport, new fabrics, etc., or should we leave them to live their lives untrammelled by modern civilisation. 'In fact,' Dr. Holroyd had philosophised, 'what is civilisation?'

Dr. Holroyd had told him how well Jamie was progressing and how pleased everyone was with him. 'Jamie has taught his school and his mother and sister a fantastic amount. The teachers at St. Michael's no longer see him as impudent, rude, insolent and badly behaved but as a child nonplussed by everyday communication we all take for granted, and seriously in need of guidance and understanding. I saw his termly report when I visited last week. Mr. Holmes had written – well, Matt, I should ask Jamie to show his report to you. Will you be seeing them on Christmas Day?'

Matt had not replied. He had, however, had a last question before warmly thanking Dr. Holroyd for his time and understanding.

'Dr. Holroyd, I have to call you that as well as Nigel. I have a feeling you bring so much more insight to your profession than, perhaps, is generally the case. It isn't, is it, because you have personal experience of what you refer to as "flawed" children?'

Dr. Holroyd had responded that whilst he had used that description he doesn't like to use it.

'No child is flawed. It is our perception of what standardised, "portion-controlled" individuals should be which is at fault. It may be that our standards should be adjusted.'

He had continued, 'But, to answer your question: Yes.'

Nigel's eyes had misted over.

'I had a younger brother who was profoundly damaged during the birth process. He was born with multiple paraplegia and even had to have his head secured in a frame because his neck could not support it. He had no speech, little sight, scant hearing. But the light in his face when we wheeled him into the sunshine, when we stroked his misshapen limbs, when we held his hands, was the most beautiful present we ever had.'

A lengthy pause came during which Dr. Holroyd had seemed to have had difficulty in composing himself.

'He died when he was twelve.'

'Your parents?' Matt had scarcely dared to ask.

'My mother – you see that was so long ago, before there were counsellors and school psychologists – she never forgave herself. She believed herself to be a failure as a mother; it was her body, her reproductive organs, which had failed.'

'My father?' answering Matt's unspoken question, 'He left us when Maurice was six and I was nine. He couldn't take it anymore and he blamed my mother.'

Matt rose in silence. His eyes met those of Dr. Holroyd.

'A Band of Brothers', whispered Dr. Holroyd from behind closed eyes.

★

It was Christmas Eve. Freya and Sarah, being the tallest of the three, garlanded the room at cornice level while Jamie unscrambled the tree lights and, jumping up and down, asked if he could please, please be the one to switch them on. Freya gave him a big squeeze.

'Of course you can; you are still the baby of the family.'

Dressed in their pyjamas, the mince pie for Father Christmas, the carrot for Rudolph and the glass of wine were all placed on the hearth in front of the wood-effect fire. Jamie giggled.

'Father Christmas will have a job getting down our blocked-up chimney, won't he? But we all – know – Father Christmas – is – Daddy, don't we?'

And he burst into tears.

'It's Monday. Daddy will be in Leicester.'

'That's perfectly all right, Jamie,' Freya comforted him, 'Mummy is Mummy Christmas, so we still put up our stockings. Daddy will see us on Boxing Day, anyway.'

Jamie choked back his tears.

'Enjoy your glass of wine then, Mummy. We thought that would be better than cocoa because the cocoa would get cold and have that horrid skin on top. Now, if you are being Mummy Christmas, who is Rudolph? Is that going to be next-door's cat?'

'Jamie, you are such a fun brother. I love you lots and lots and lots.'

'And I love you, my big sister. And Mummy Christmas.'

★

For at least an hour, Sarah listened to the two children calling to each other from their separate bedrooms.

'I can't get to sleep. I'm too excited.'

'Are you asleep yet?'

'Well I was but you've woken me up.'

'Has she been yet?'

'It's so funny thinking of Mummy as Father Christmas.'

At long last: silence.

Sarah tiptoed up the stairs, quietly substituting the long red knitted stockings at the foot of the bed for two bulging red and green pillowcases with 'Happy Christmas' stamped all over them. She tiptoed back down to the sitting room, unwrapped two silver-plated frames and removed two A4 pieces of card from separate envelopes. Each card was carefully inserted into the frame and set at each end of the sideboard. The first said:

> **Freya Chilton**
> **Awarded a Credit for**
> **Grade III**
> **Violincello Examination**
> **7 – 10 – 2012**

The second said:

> **Jamie Chilton**
> **Gold Star**
> **Awarded by**
> **the Headmaster**
> **for being**
> **Making the Most Progress In Our School**
> **19 – 12 – 2012**

Sarah picked up her glass of wine, then after her first sip, went upstairs. She brought down her wedding photograph and placed it in the centre of the sideboard. She downed the remainder of her glass.

Should I have another, she wondered?

The phone rang.

'Sarah, your letter meant so much to me. More than I can ever say but I am going to do my damnedest to show you. I've parked the car in the drive. Is the front door still open for me?'

★

As the grandfather clock in the hall chimed midnight, Matt climbed the stairs to place two small packages on the top of the red and green sacks. Attached to each was a silver star emblazoned with the inscription,

'With all my love, Father Christmas, whose work in Leicester is finished for ever and ever and ever.'

On the sideboard a dusty, faded rose petal embellished the wedding photograph. On its reverse was pasted the letter from Sarah.

Balanced against a scarlet poinsettia was an official-looking brown envelope, the unmistakeable crest of the County Council emblazoned on the top left-hand corner. Carefully opened and then re-sealed, only Sarah had knowledge of its very special contents.

★

As the newly reconstituted family sat down for their Christmas lunch at a table bedecked with crackers made by Jamie, napkins transformed into flowers by Freya, humble, home-made decorations brightening the walls, Sarah presented Jamie with the brown envelope to open.

'Mummy, it is addressed to you both. Can I really open it?'

Ripping off and discarding the manila envelope, Jamie scanned the first paragraph, then let out an ear-splitting roar. His excited voice could have been heard on the moon as, throwing the contents in the air, he rushed to fling himself first on his father, then onto the lap of his mother, tears streaming down her cheeks with the pent-up emotion of the family's reunion and the relief of Jamie's achievement.

'Daddy, Mummy, this is the very best day of my life; the fabulous, grabulous, coolest day I've ever, ever had. Daddy's spy work is finished and I've passed, I've passed, I've passed! Daddy, Mummy, Freya, I'm going to the same school as you, Freya. Oh, I'm so, so excited! When can we buy my school blazer? And my tie?'

Reaching for Sarah's hand, Matt whispered to her softly, his eyes twinkling. 'Now is not the time to remonstrate about success, failure and the substitution of "the right school for you", my darling. We can't spoil his special moment. Let's all just celebrate his amazing achievement against the appalling odds which have been stacked against him.' Raising his voice, he looked across the table to Freya. 'Pass me the champagne from the side-table, will you please, my beautiful child.'

A magnum of Dom Perignon, now chilled to perfection, had been presented to Matt by one of his clients as a Christmas gift.

Eyes like saucers, and vowing she had never seen such a magnificent bottle, Freya carefully carried the bottle in its ice-bucket to place in front of her father then raced to open a window through which Matt could aim the cork. Jamie shot to the sideboard and retrieved the liqueur glasses the children had been allowed in previous years for their 'finger-full' of wine.

'Not quite like the old days, darling Sarah – and I intended this just for us – but this has to be a moment which all of us should share.'

★

That night, with the crispness of the sheets around them, limbs entwined, Sarah, eyes tightly squeezed shut and hardly daring to breathe, posed the question she had to ask if the horrors of the past months were to be permanently assuaged. It came baldly from her lips, stark, undisguised.

'Matt, was she like me?'

Not in all his married life, not in all his college days, never since reaching double figures, had Matt broken down in the presence of another, not even his mother, never ever his beloved wife. He clung to Sarah's welcoming body, his tears dampening her cheeks, her arms enfolding him with all the passion she could muster. Not until the shuddering sobs had subsided, the memories of the past infidelities with the woman so many light-years in contrast with his beautiful, forgiving wife, been exorcised from his memory for all time, could they both be completely at peace. Sarah now had the confirmation she so desperately sought, that Nigel Holroyd's prophesy that her husband would seek solace in a woman so far removed from his own wife, had been fulfilled.

★

A day or so later, when the Christmas holidays had finished, the New Year had established itself and the children had returned to school, Matt and Sarah slipped into St. Michael's church, prayer books in hand and knelt in front of the altar. Hands linked and eyes firmly on each other, in the quiet stillness of that wintry day, shafts of sunlight piercing the sapphire and emerald brilliance of the rose window above the altar, the familiar vows of the wedding service were quietly repeated. That afternoon, the fireside rug in the sitting room added a further page to Sarah's book of precious memories.

Peace, tranquillity and joy pervaded the arenas in which Jamie's presence manifested itself from that Christmas moment onward. Matt, following Sarah's example, joined in the 'What Did You Say; What Did You Mean?' sessions with gusto, Jamie revelling in his father's support. 'It is so cool, Daddy, having a real spy to play games with.' No member in the family had the courage, or whatever was needed, to disabuse him from his entrenched view that his daddy was involved in espionage: the time for that would come but meanwhile, Freya and Sarah impressed upon him that this was a tightly held secret to be kept amongst their family alone.

After Easter, when all children had been informed of the specific school they were to attend in September, Mrs. Ackroyd arranged for Matt and Sarah to visit the grammar school with her to meet with the member of the special needs staff so that the level and nature of the guidance he would need on transfer would be assured. It was agreed that he could spend an extra two days during the summer term, map in hand, to familiarise himself with the specialist rooms and the daily routines he would be expected to follow in the autumn term. Mrs. Ackroyd had been invited to accompany him; Mrs. Craddock had been recruited to replace her during her absence. Two of his Band of Brothers had also been awarded a place at the same grammar school, so all augured well for Jamie in Year 7. Dr. Holroyd was to hold an In-service day on communication disorders for the staff at the beginning of the new school year, also to include ancillary members and teachers who were part-time only.

St. Michael's learned it had been given the top grading by the OFSTED Inspectors, the special needs support being given particular commendation. A feather in Mary Ackroyd's cap, she was invited by the adviser in special needs to represent the county at a national conference, Geoff Holmes gave her the day off to attend the annual exhibition at Earls Court, relevant to her specialist post, with a sizeable budget to order any resources the school and teachers themselves would find helpful in the classroom to cover any specific learning difficulties which children in their care experienced. Faith Griffin was asked to be the child protection officer and, with due regard to her new responsibilities, mellowed in her approach to the differences each child brought to learning. Lucy Shadbolt took over the post of health and safety, a post Faith was secretly pleased to relinquish: the sight of blood always brought on a feeling of nausea, and Gordon Bolton enrolled for a part-time MA in Business Administration with a view to applying for headships in three years' time. Father Harrold, aware that he would benefit from sharpening up his counselling skills, made tentative enquiries as to how to go about obtaining training in this respect.

Max became a valued member of the staff of a museum and his translation of a Latin manuscript was published in a learned journal.

No more Scalps on Totem Poles.
No more Ripples on Ponds.

Epilogue

Drop a pebble in the water:
just a splash, and it is gone;
But there's half-a-hundred ripples
Circling on and on and on,
Spreading, spreading from the center,
flowing on out to the sea.
And there is no way of telling
where the end is going to be.

Drop a pebble in the water:
in a minute you forget,
But there's little waves a-flowing,
and there's ripples circling yet,
And those little waves a-flowing
to a great big wave have grown;
You've disturbed a mighty river
just by dropping in a stone.

Drop an unkind word, or careless:
in a minute it is gone;
But there's half-a-hundred ripples
circling on and on and on.
They keep spreading, spreading, spreading
from the center as they go,
And there is no way to stop them,
once you've started them to flow.

Drop an unkind word, or careless:
in a minute you forget;
But there's little waves a-flowing,
and there's ripples circling yet,
And perhaps in some sad heart
a mighty wave of tears you've stirred,
And disturbed a life was happy
ere you dropped that unkind word.

Drop a word of cheer and kindness:
just a flash and it is gone;
But there's half-a-hundred ripples
circling on and on and on,
Bearing hope and joy and comfort
on each splashing, dashing wave
Till you wouldn't believe the volume
of the one kind word you gave.

Drop a word of cheer and kindness:
in a minute you forget;
But there's gladness still a-swelling,
and there's joy circling yet,
And you've rolled a wave of comfort
whose sweet music can be heard
Over miles and miles of water
just by dropping one kind word.

James W. Foley
1874-1939

The Ripple Effect

– author unknown

The Master was walking through the fields one day when a young man, a troubled look upon his face, approached him. "On such a beautiful day, it must be difficult to stay so serious," the Master said. "Is it? I hadn't noticed," the young man said, turning to look around and notice his surroundings. His eyes scanned the landscape, but nothing seemed to register; his mind elsewhere.

Watching intently, the Master continued to walk. "Join me if you like." The Master walked to the edge of a still pond, framed by sycamore trees, their leaves golden orange and about to fall. "Please sit down," the Master invited, patting the ground next to him. Looking carefully before sitting, the young man brushed the ground to clear a space for himself. "Now, find a small stone, please," the Master instructed. "What?" "A stone. Please find a small stone and throw it in the pond."

Searching around him, the young man grabbed a pebble and threw it as far as he could. "Tell me what you see," the Master instructed. Straining his eyes to not miss a single detail, the man looked at the water's surface. "I see ripples." "Where did the ripples come from?" "From the pebble I threw in the pond, Master." "Please reach your hand into the water and stop the ripples," the Master asked. Not understanding, the young man stuck his hand in the water as a ripple neared, only to cause more ripples.

The young man was now completely baffled. Where was

this going? Had he made a mistake in seeking out the Master? After all he was not a student, perhaps he could not be helped? Puzzled, the young man waited. "Were you able to stop the ripples with your hands?" the Master asked. "No, of course not." "Could you have stopped the ripples, then?" "No, Master. I told you I only caused more ripples."

"What if you had stopped the pebble from entering the water to begin with?" The Master smiled such a beautiful smile; the young man could not be upset. "Next time you are unhappy with your life, catch the stone before it hits the water. Do not spend time trying to undo what you have done. Rather, change what you are going to do before you do it." The Master looked kindly upon the young man. "But Master, how will I know what I am going to do before I do it?" "Take the responsibility for living your own life.

If you're working with a doctor to treat an illness, then ask the doctor to help you understand what caused the illness. Do not just treat the ripples. Keep asking questions." The young man stopped, his mind reeling. "But I came to you to ask you for answers. Are you saying that I know the answers?" "You may not know the answers right now, but if you ask the right questions, then you shall discover the answers." "But what are the right questions, Master?" "There are no wrong questions, only unasked ones. We must ask, for without asking, we cannot receive answers. But it is your responsibility to ask. No one else can do that for you."